DISCARD

BACK
FROM THE
BRINK

ALSO AVAILABLE BY EMERY HAYES

Nicole Cobain Mysteries
Cold to the Bone

(writing as Suzanne Phillips)
Chloe Doe
Burn
Lindsey Lost

BACK
FROM THE
BRINK

A NICOLE COBAIN MYSTERY

Emery Hayes

CROOKED
LANE

NEW YORK

Published in the United States by Crooked Lane Books, an imprint of The Quick Brown Fox & Company LLC.

Crooked Lane Books and its logo are trademarks of The Quick Brown Fox & Company LLC.

Library of Congress Catalog-in-Publication data available upon request.

ISBN (hardcover): 978-1-64385-598-1
ISBN (ebook): 978-1-64385-599-8

Cover design by Nicole Lecht

Printed in the United States.

www.crookedlanebooks.com

Crooked Lane Books
34 West 27th St., 10th Floor
New York, NY 10001

First Edition: July 2021

10 9 8 7 6 5 4 3 2 1

Giselle

Strength, courage, dignity—you possess each of these

1

The baby was quiet. For days, he had moved. Kicking his feet, his tiny hands fluttering and then pushing against the womb. Sensing her anxiety? Sure. She believed it. Feeling the increase in cortisol as she teetered between fight or flight? Definitely. But now, as she pushed through thick vegetation, running but clumsily, picking up speed in the open spaces, sidling through dense cover, her arms wrapped around her middle as she fought the cloying branches, the baby was quiet.

Miles from the house now, she still felt them with her. No closer than when she had slipped out the second-story window, slid down the rough shingles, hung from the gutter, falling as the tubing peeled away from the eaves and set her on her feet at the back of the house. They were still inside then, thundering up the stairs, slamming doors—bedroom, bathroom, closet.

"Keep moving," Matthew had said. It was not enough to just hide. She smiled at the thought of him, and then, as the memory of the men in her house and what that meant about the man she loved crowded her vision, she stifled a sob. But she wouldn't let tears slow her down.

She stumbled and broke free of the tree line, lost her footing and balance as the earth tilted. She hit her knees, and because her arms were wrapped around her baby belly, she could not break her fall. She turned enough that her shoulder took most of it. She bounced and the wind left her lungs in a thick whoosh that stunned her. She turned and got to her hands and knees. Then she heard herself crying. Heard her tears knot in her throat and the wet snot as she drew a deep breath and prayed, prayed that their baby was all right.

She was tired, but she stood. Her arms hung heavily at her sides and in the pitch darkness she turned in a slow circle, looking for life. She found it in a small, white light, so far away. It blinked on and off, but then she realized that it was she who moved as she wavered on her feet. If she stood absolutely still, the light remained steadfast. A promise. And she moved toward it while behind her she heard the sharp rustle of leaves as branches were pushed aside, as first one pursuer and then another cleared the trees and burned her heels.

And she took off. Not in a straight line. She knew better than that. She knew about cross hairs and zigzag patterns and the possibility of surviving even the most ardent hunters. Matthew had prepared her for that while at the same time promising she would never need to use the knowledge. And she couldn't, absolutely could not, tear her eyes away from the hope in that white light.

The land sloped, and when she found herself in the gullies, she fired her engines until she came to the crest and saw light. She stood still long enough to open her lungs, then trudged forward. It was impossible to tell how far away salvation was, with the moon and the stars tucked behind clouds and the landscape draped in darkness—the trees darker than the earth but lighter than the night sky.

Her chances were slim to none. Matthew had told her that. Those pursuing her were trained for this kind of thing and she was not. Evasion of any kind was not her forte. But she was bold. She was even foolishly optimistic. She had to believe.

She picked up steam. Her legs burned with the effort. She knew from the way the earth slanted, the soft rise and fall of the hills, that she was on track, heading toward the lake. That the light was on the other side, that she would have to skirt the edge of the water, another mile or more, before she had a door to knock on, help at hand.

She felt another ripple of pain across her abdomen. A cramping below that, sudden, breathtaking, the kind that seemed to pull her insides out. The baby was coming.

She remembered Matthew's words on mental toughness. It was the difference between failure and success.

One mile. She could do that. With more than that already behind her, she had come farther than Matthew had thought possible. And a

2

bubble of pride swelled inside her. It made her feel light on her toes. Eased the pinch in her lungs. She would do anything for Matthew. Anything for their son.

* * *

Nicole was up, her legs over the side of the bed, before she realized it was the phone that had woken her. She rubbed sleep from her eyes as she reached for her cell on the nightstand. It rang again, a sharp trilling that pierced her ears. The display read DISPATCH. She opened the call.

"Cobain," she said.

"Hi, Sheriff." Her night shift operator, Lodi. "I have Border Patrol on the line. Patching through."

Nicole waited. Calls this late into the night—it was 2:37 AM—were rare from BP. Blue Mesa was the seat of multiple agencies. The sheriff's department, Border Patrol, and Highway Patrol all kept offices in the small town, and while the late hour was unusual, working together was not.

"Sheriff? It's Kyle Monte." A senior agent at BP North. Nicole had worked with him many times. Since the shift in 2016 of presidents and policies, immigration in particular—the border with Canada was fourteen miles from the town proper—their paths had crossed far more frequently. Monte was an easy man to work with. He listened more than he spoke, understood that nothing was superficial, and Nicole had never heard a bullshit party line from him.

"What's up, Monte?"

"Have a DOA here. Can't get to ID. Probably a UDA." Undocumented alien. Nicole could hear the disappointment in his voice. New policies on immigration had led to riskier border attempts. Since January, seven bodies had been recovered. All women and children. All succumbed to the weather. But Nicole and her office hadn't dealt with those. Her team was brought in only when foul play was suspected and the sheriff's office had jurisdiction. "And there was nothing natural or circumstantial about his death," Monte continued.

Nicole stood and turned on the bedroom light. She pulled a uniform off a hanger in the closet and laid it over the bed.

"Location?"

"Middle of Lake Maria."

That gave her pause. The lake was thawing, its edges completely fluid now, but a quarter mile in it was slushy, with floes that drifted on the currents. At its center were solid patches of ice that reached all the way to the bottom. "What?"

"I came out on a tip. You know we've been getting more of those than ever and most of them are good, so I didn't hesitate." Nicole listened to his story unfold. Monte had arrived at the lake more than an hour before. Their caller was waiting at the water's edge. The man had reported seeing a group of young men—four or five—board a boat and head north. They wore dark clothing and each had a day pack with them.

From the northern edge of Lake Maria, it was a seven-mile hike through dense forest and steep passes to the Canadian border. But it was a cool night, twenty-seven degrees with a heavy mist in the air and cloud cover. All of which complicated the passage.

"You catch up with them?" she asked.

"Nah. We have officers at the border, of course. Spread so thin a herd of trumpeting elephants could charge through unnoticed." And so there was little hope of rounding them up before they crossed the border into terrain both steeper and colder than stateside, where life and death and the line between them blended into the landscape.

"What makes you think your DOA is my business?"

"His hands and feet are tied. We can see that much. You're going to have a job here, cutting him out of the ice."

That surprised her. "He's frozen?"

"Yeah. Damn ice cube. And you know how that goes, right? His face tells it all."

Nicole had seen it before. Ice preserved its victims, including casting facial expressions.

Monte gave her his coordinates, and then she hung up and called dispatch. She arranged for a deputy to meet her at the south side of the lake with the department skiff. She had Lodi rouse MacAulay as well—they couldn't move the body without the ME first working the scene. Next, Nicole called Mrs. Neal, grateful for the woman's flexibility.

Nicole walked through the house, toward the kitchen and the coffeemaker. She looked in on Jordan but didn't wake him. It was enough to watch the comforter rise and fall in sync with his light snoring, to feel his warmth from across the room. She stood in the doorway and thought about the young man he was becoming. Four months ago Benjamin Kris, his father, had arrived in town and done his best to destroy Nicole. His weapon of choice had been their son. Nicole had stopped him, but only with the help of a young man, Joaquin Esparza, to whom she would always be indebted.

She let out a breath thick with gratitude and closed the door.

She took the time to brew coffee and to shower. She couldn't go anywhere without a boat and the ME, and it would take a half hour or more to get that set up. After she was in uniform, she pulled her hair back in a ponytail and filled a thermos, topping her coffee with vanilla creamer. Twenty minutes after her call to Mrs. Neal, the woman was working her key into the front door. Nicole met her there.

"Thanks for coming so quickly."

Mrs. Neal smiled, though Nicole saw shadows pass through her eyes. It would be a long time, if ever, before either of them forgot about Benjamin and the havoc he'd wreaked on their lives. He'd taken Jordan from this house and left Mrs. Neal to die.

"Not another child, I hope," she said.

"No." It wasn't often she was called out in the middle of the night, and she thought of Beatrice Esparza and all she'd lost here four months ago. "A young man, as far as I know."

"I hate hearing it."

Nicole agreed. "Go to bed. I'll lock up on my way out."

Nicole's home, a single-story ranch remodeled over the years, had three bedrooms. She had fixed up the spare as a guest room and kept several of the niceties Mrs. Neal favored there. Nicole had hired the woman for afternoon and weekend help. She picked Jordan up from school, ran him to friends' houses and sometimes Scout meetings, and prepared their dinner before leaving for home. Their arrangement included some late-night calls as needed. But Mrs. Neal had become more to them. Nicole's parents had died in a car crash when she was twenty-two years old. She missed them, her mother in particular, and Mrs. Neal softened that ache. She was good with Jordan too. A fierce grandmother figure.

Nicole watched the woman walk toward the back of the house, then grabbed her thermos and headed out the door.

* * *

People could not fly. Not unless they were inside an airplane. Or a helicopter. Wouldn't that be amazing? she thought. For a helicopter to buzz by, with searchlights and the right people inside, looking for her. For them to find her, here, right now, standing up to her ankles in frigid water with mud oozing around her shoes, pulling at her feet, making it hard, almost impossible, to go any farther. Wouldn't that be God, to pluck her out of this situation and into the night sky? Saved. She would like that. But she had just enough grit left on the inside to know dream from reality, hallucination from dire circumstances.

She would die, by man or by her own foolishness, but she would see the sunrise first. She would birth her child and swaddle him in whatever she could find and leave him on a doorstep, under that white light that blazed across the water and offered her hope.

It had to be that way. The men chasing her wanted only her and what she could give them.

It was always farther than first thought. With anything. The words kept playing through her mind. It had taken a long time for her father to die. Even longer for her mother to leave him. It had taken too long to come of age, so she had cut corners there. Terrified of the marriage her father had arranged for her in Syria, of being placed on an airplane at the age of sixteen and sold for a *mahr* of ten thousand American dollars and interest in a smoke shop in Aleppo, she had slipped through her bedroom window at fifteen, with just babysitting money in her pocket and a change of clothes in her backpack. That first breath of independence had more fear in it than freedom, and given her circumstances, that had surprised her. But she had made it. She had purchased a bus ticket with some of her money, showing her aunt Aya's driver's license when the cashier doubted her age. Thirty-seven dollars got her out of Wyoming and all the way to Billings. She'd gotten by that first year waiting tables at a diner and more babysitting when she could find it. She'd rented a room in the back of someone's house. And later, she'd met Matthew Franks.

She pressed her fist to her mouth to push back the cry. Loss. Her life had been full of it. But she would not lose this baby.

She looked across the water. A string of lights, triangular and bobbing on the tide, caught her attention. A boat was out there. If she called, would they hear her? Possibly, but so would the men who followed her. They had killed once and would again.

She turned away and sought her compass. The white light was steady and no closer, but it had to be. She had not stopped moving. She had not changed direction. And yet the distance seemed to have doubled. Or maybe her optimism had sunk.

Behind her they scrabbled over the hillsides like crabs. They had guns and needles filled with propofol. Matthew had said there would be at least five of them and probably more. And they would stop at nothing to have what she had. And she understood that. She understood that freedom was everything.

The pain came again, sharp and deep. She stopped and bent at the waist. The pressure was building. The baby wanted out.

"Not now," she whispered, her voice thick with tears, gasping for breath. "Please not now."

She'd read about it. She'd asked the midwife many questions. She liked to gather wisdom and face the unknown with facts. In that way, she was ready.

She wished for something better. Safer. For Matthew's arms around her, his deep voice coaching her, like they'd practiced. And she thought again about flying. How beautiful that would be. Altitude. Matthew had told her about climbers on Everest, those who were not prepared. When the Os were thin and the body not acclimated, people dreamed. Hallucinated. Died.

She was breathless but bound to the earth. She was desperate and quickly running out of options.

* * *

They were still deeply into night when Nicole arrived at the southern edge of Lake Maria. She glanced at the clock on the Yukon's dash: 3:15. Cloud cover minimized the natural light from the moon and stars, and once she extinguished her headlights, the trees loomed large and menacing.

7

Nicole pulled her Colt Commando from its console holster, grabbed her thermos, and shouldered out of the SUV.

Ty Watts waited for her at the bottom of the concrete ramp. The skiff was already lowered into the water. It was a fast, simple vehicle with a Sailfish center console covered by a small canvas roof and powered by a Yamaha four-stroke outboard. It was fully equipped with sirens, emergency lighting, a radio, and rescue/first-aid equipment. The hull was manufactured with a special blade at its pitch to cut through the ice.

"Hey, Sheriff." Ty hailed her when she was still several yards distant. She had recently promoted him from a strictly patrol position to case duties. It was a fifty-fifty split, because their department was small and their jurisdiction vast at nearly two thousand square miles, but he was happy and he had earned it.

"Hi, Ty." Nicole felt her breath bloom in the air between them. It seemed a bit cooler than the twenty-seven degrees Monte had reported. "You bring the chainsaw?"

His smile gleamed in the shadows. "Yeah. And the ME too."

MacAulay. Their family doctor turned ME. That was how it was done in small towns.

Nicole pivoted on a bootheel. She didn't see another man standing nor a crouching figure in the shadowed boat.

"Where is he?"

Ty nodded toward his cruiser, a Yukon similar to hers but currently hooked to a boat trailer. The lights were off, but the engine was running.

"Had to pull over twice to let him hurl," Ty said.

"He's sick?"

"Flu or food poisoning, he said."

But Nicole was already heading for the cruiser, trying in vain to push the heavy hand of guilt off her shoulder.

She had seen MacAulay the day before. Early. Jordan had Scout camp and she had spent the weekend with the man. Two solid days. Just the two of them, laughing, cooking, a long hike, some fly-fishing and plenty of time in bed or somewhere close to it. It had been . . . sublime. Altering. Scary. She'd left his side before sunrise and returned home for a shower, a clean uniform, and a few moments to steady her nerves. She considered herself a smart woman. Careful and self-aware.

But yesterday she had woken in that man's arms with the absolute certainty that she had fallen in love with him. And that was followed by the clear gonging of a bell that, she feared, was heralding the end of a good thing.

Nicole did not do romantic relationships well.

She pulled open the passenger door and the cabin light snapped on, startling MacAulay. Nicole's hand fell naturally to his shoulder to steady him.

"You okay?"

He nodded. "I'm a little worried about the boat ride," he said. His cheeks were flushed, but his skin was otherwise pale.

"Ty says you're sick."

"He's got that right." MacAulay shifted in the seat, turned toward her, and his eyes grew thoughtful. "You okay?"

She held his gaze, felt awareness rip through her body, then lowered her eyes. "I'm good."

"I called," MacAulay said, and Nicole felt a wince surface from deep within her. She had avoided calling him back. And he had needed her, if only to bring him soup and NyQuil.

"Sorry," she said. She didn't try to skate free of the accusation, didn't try to bury it under job duties, though she could have gotten away with it after two days completely disconnected. She owed MacAulay more than that.

She lifted her hand and brushed her fingers over his forehead and into his hair. He felt hot, feverish.

He caught her wrist, held it gently in the palm of his hand. "Forgiven," he said.

She sought his gaze and nodded. His eyes were warm, always welcoming. But she needed distance. Work should have been enough to make the separation easy. She was big on keeping the personal out of the professional, and MacAulay respected that.

She took a step back. "I'll help you to the boat."

"I'll need a window seat," he said.

"No problem with that."

He turned and planted his feet on the ground. Nicole took hold of his arm as he stood.

He was taller than her by a good six inches, and broad shouldered. She loved the fit of her head beneath his chin, the steady beat of his heart in her ear, the warmth of his skin against her cheek. But that was not for now. She tried to shake the memory loose and focus on the moment.

"We need to work on getting you a backup."

"I have one. It's Calabasas over in Polk County, but he's in the Keys. Marlin fishing is good this time of year."

They started for the boat ramp.

"My bag is in the back seat."

"Ty will get it."

Ty took the bulk of MacAulay's weight as they helped him transition from land to water. The boat rocked beneath their feet, and Doc groaned and clutched the rails.

"He gonna make it?" Ty asked.

"He's going to have to," MacAulay answered for himself.

"We'll stand upwind," Nicole advised, and jerked her chin toward the cruiser. "Get his bag. Back seat."

She settled MacAulay starboard, at midpoint so he'd receive less thumping from the bow once they started over the water. She handed him a life jacket and shrugged into one herself. When Ty boarded, she tossed him another, and then she stowed her gear and made her way to the front of the boat.

"Ready," she called over her shoulder. She spared MacAulay another glance. He was snug in his vest and clutching the rail, his ME bag on the floor between his feet.

Ty took the wheel and began edging the craft away from the ramp. They had all lights running, but Nicole knew how treacherous the lake could be during the thaw. As they got under way, she stood in the bow of the boat, making sweeping motions with a handheld strobe to light a greater expanse of the lake in front of them. There were a lot of trees in the water, sheared by subzero temperatures and cutting winds over the winter, and slow and careful was the only way to proceed. They tried to keep to the path of the BP skiff, which had broken up the ice, but they weren't a quarter mile in when they hit their first floe. It brought the skiff to a near stop, the motor whining. Ty turned starboard and motored around it. A third of a mile ahead she saw the BP skiff, the lights bobbing gently as the current moved beneath the vessel. It was quiet, the wind no thicker than a sigh. And with no natural light, the boat seemed adrift. They were not close enough to hail across the water. Nicole pulled off a glove and retrieved her cell from the deep pocket of her parka. She dialed Monte's number and waited.

"How are we going to get a body frozen into the lake back to my morgue?" MacAulay asked. His voice was softer than usual, and Nicole realized she didn't like that. She liked MacAulay strong, even when they argued. She worried about dragging him out into this weather when his body was raging with flu. But there was nothing to be done about that.

"Chainsaw, Doc," Ty answered.

Nicole turned in time to see MacAulay nod.

"I thought so," he said. "That conference in Toronto—" The department made it a practice to send MacAulay to two or three trainings a year. He was, by trade and by heart, a family physician and had stepped into the role of ME when the county became desperate for the services of one. He'd had a steep learning curve but had handled it well, sometimes exceeding expectations. "One case study was a body found bobbing in the Saint Charles River. It was cast in a solid block of ice. 'The Human Ice Cube,' it was called."

His words stuttered to a stop, and Nicole turned and found him leaning over the side of the boat, vomiting. She didn't say anything. She hesitated, the strobe in her hands still, her knees bent to absorb the bounce of the hull against the water.

MacAulay straightened and caught her gaze.

"If there was another way," she began.

"But there isn't," he said.

She turned back to her cell. The call had gone to voice mail and she disconnected. No sense leaving a message when she would make physical contact in five minutes.

The water was thick slush and slapped against the hull. The weight of it dragged against the boat. They slowed as the port side bumped against solid ice. The clouds parted, revealing a half-moon and a handful of scattered stars. She was grateful for the sudden clarity. Even in April, the lake was just as often covered with dense fog. The sky misted and sometimes hailed.

Per protocol, Ty gave the skiff's horn a two-one blast to announce their approach. Nicole lifted the strobe and let the high-intensity beam fall on the BP skiff. It was shouldered against solid ice on its port side. They were still thirty yards out but close enough to hear the engine idling. Close enough that they should have seen Monte and his partner standing in the bow or stern. She adjusted the strobe in her hands, chasing the shadows from the fore of the skiff, and found nothing.

2

Ty realized the grim truth the same time she did.

"Shit." He pushed the throttle into reverse and brought the skiff around so that they stopped a good twenty yards from the BP vessel. Then he shifted into neutral and let the current pull them slowly closer. "Ghost boat."

He murmured the words but she heard them, carried on the breeze. Doc heard them too. The boat shifted under their feet as he stood and moved port side.

"Where are they?" he asked.

She ignored the question and caught Ty's gaze. He shook his head—they were all at a loss.

"Bring her up close," she said. "Keep five or ten yards between vessels." She was going to look but not touch. She didn't know if they had a crime scene on their hands or if the disappearance of the agents was accidental. "Ty, radio dispatch. Have them put a call in to BP. Tell them we've made contact with the vessel but no souls aboard."

She inched forward on the bow, port side, and braced her feet. She used the strobe, shifting it slowly over every inch of the skiff visible from the starboard side of the vessel, which was a lot. A small pocket of shadow on the port side, behind the Sailfish console, was too small to conceal an adult male. Monte was gone. And his partner too. Monte hadn't mentioned another agent on board, but she knew they seldom scouted alone. So, for the time being, they were looking for two missing agents in the middle of Lake Maria.

Nothing seemed disturbed on the skiff. There was no sign of blood. She recognized heavy boot prints on the gunwale, but they could have been made by the agents when boarding. The prints were starboard side, closer to Nicole and away from the ice floe. It was possible someone had boarded the boat out here in the middle of the lake. Perhaps Monte had been taken by surprise when an approaching vessel turned out not to be from the sheriff's department. But it was more likely that an accident had occurred. Perhaps a man had fallen overboard and in an attempt to execute a rescue, he had been pulled in as well. In waters this cold— thirty-eight degrees Fahrenheit when she checked yesterday—the body would quickly become numb and slow to follow commands from the brain.

She heard Ty connect with dispatch. He read the registration number off the boat's bow and reported its current state—adrift, no souls. She felt MacAulay ease his weight aft, where he picked up a Maglite and began a search of the ice. The floe was fractured and butted up against another of similar shape and breadth. Their lights reached no further. The second floe could measure a football field or stop abruptly after only a hundred feet. Was the ice solid enough for a man to transverse? Probably. She had seen it done. But it was a risk not worth taking, especially when the ice ended too many meters short of land. She knew for a fact that the entire shoreline of Lake Maria was fluid.

Monte would have known better than to chance it. Always best to stay with the vessel. The man was seasoned, reasonable. Had intellect and instinct.

Ambush? Or accident?

She lifted the strobe and searched the BP skiff for its ring buoy. It was in place, attached to the transom. No attempt to rescue had been made. No man overboard.

She became aware of the reassuring weight of her side arm, holstered at her hip, beneath her parka. And the Colt Commando strung over her shoulder. She knew Ty was armed. And that sometimes the deputy carried a Sig P365 in an ankle holster.

She hit her shoulder radio and requested backup from dispatch. Lars, her second-in-command, and two additional deputies. There was one big problem with that—the department had only one skiff. "Lodi, tell Lars to borrow Gunnar's boat." Gunnar was a local fisherman, one of the earliest each year to navigate Lake Maria following the winter freeze. His vessel was prepared to deal with the elements.

After receiving an affirmative, she signed off. Silence descended. She listened for any anomaly in their surroundings. A splash of water too loud or forceful to belong to the natural current of the lake. Or a creak of ice indicating a shift in weight. The distant drone of a motor.

Nothing.

The wind skittered over the ice and added chop to the water. Nicole loosened her knees so that she rode the stronger current beneath her. She counted her breaths as she waited for the wind to calm.

"MacAulay, hand me the bullhorn," she called, and stepped back from the rail as the boat shifted with his weight. "It's in the compartment under the transom."

Her cell phone rang, and she reached into her pocket for it. She checked the display—BP North.

"Cobain." She heard the sharpness in her tone, the result of mounting tension.

"It's Green." Division commander. Nicole knew him to say hello. "You've made contact with Monte?"

"Negative," she said. "We are one-point-zero-seven kilometers east off the southern shore of Lake Maria. We have your BP skiff here. No souls."

"No souls?"

"How many agents are we looking for?"

"Two. Kyle Monte and Melody Baker. Both experienced."

Both missing.

"There's been no apparent attempt at rescue." The skiffs were similar in design and cargo. She explained that the life buoy was still intact and that there was one life jacket strapped to the console. One was gone.

"And no bodies?"

"Not on board," Nicole confirmed. "Not on adjacent ice floes. We haven't searched the water."

"What the hell?"

She knew only the pieces Monte had given her—a tip, a group of refugees braving the elements in the hopes of making it to the Canadian border and asylum. What didn't she know?

"Start at the top," she told Green. "Tell me everything I need to know."

He took a moment—to gather his thoughts or to pick through them, choosing what to share and what to keep to himself? That whole marking of territory for which Nicole had no patience.

"We're sitting ducks out here, Green," Nicole emphasized. "Start talking."

"We've had some activity on the lake recently. Politics are making this all dicey. Desperation is at an all-time high. UDAs putting in sooner, risking more."

To have more.

"The drownings last week?" she asked. BP had claimed jurisdiction, had recovered the bodies after a failed rescue attempt.

"Identity was confirmed yesterday. They were Syrian refugees trying to walk across," he disclosed. "The woman fell through, clutching her baby." He paused as that sank in. "We also learned that more attempts were planned. We think there's somewhat of an underground railroad leading up this way. Monte's been out on the lake every night this week."

That explained the presence of the boat but not its missing crew.

"Has he had any trouble out here?"

"Nothing reported. Not since the drowning last week. His last check-in tonight was at one hundred hours. All good. Then the body. We'd been looking for it for a few weeks now, but that's like a needle in a haystack. That tip came in to us by phone, a woman's voice, accented, and we assumed a UDA passing over the ice discovered him. No coordinates given, one of those 'about a half mile from the southern edge of Lake Maria' descriptions. Monte called in the find. I talked to him myself. That was at two twenty."

Nicole sifted through the facts and came up empty. There were no clues, no fingers pointing to what had happened.

"I have backup moving in," she said.

"And I have two teams on the way. My ETA is twenty-five minutes."

She ended the call. "We need to get over there." She nodded toward the BP skiff and the ice beyond. "We need to see the other side. Clear it." And then they needed to do a surface search of the water. And if that wasn't enough, they would have to use fishhooks on long poles to get under the ice. Sometimes bodies were pushed upward by the life vests and jammed under the floes.

"You looking for a volunteer?" Ty asked.

"I'll go. We have any plastic booties on this boat?"

"I'll get you some," MacAulay offered. He stood close to the console, the bullhorn in hand. Nicole reached for it, and he relinquished it but not without a little hesitation. When she looked into his face, she saw his concern. It gave him a pondering expression, but he stopped short of expressing his feelings, and she appreciated that.

Nicole turned back to the BP skiff. It rocked gently. Beyond, the sheets of ice swayed with the current. And beyond that, a sprinkling of white lights broke the darkness. Too low and too close to be stars. Homes nestled along the shore, less than a half mile as the crow flies.

She raised the bullhorn and announced, "This is the Toole County Sheriff's Department." Her words echoed over the lake, hit the mountains beyond, and came back to her. "Is anyone in need of help?" She waited, but the quiet wasn't broken. She repeated her words, finishing with, "We're here to help you," hoping that any refugees who heard her appeal would trust it.

Wishful thinking. They would risk it all, this close to freedom. To safety.

Nicole rummaged through an equipment bin and pulled out the X-370. It was a relic but had never failed them. Not even in the dead of winter, not in negative degrees or in wind chill that ripped through a person like knives. She brought the camera with her to port and stepped up on the gunwale, bracing herself against the railing. She began to take photos, of everything she could see in the BP skiff and of the shadows that concealed who knew what, if anything, from several different angles, stretching over the transom to get closer. She would have to board to get the pockets hidden in shadow. To film the floe and the surrounding water, and to do it in three hundred sixty degrees.

She stepped down and pushed the strap of the camera over her shoulder.

"Bring it close," she told Ty. "Five feet if you can."

Soon the BP vessel would run out of fuel and sputter to a stop. She didn't know how long Monte and Baker had been afloat, idling, or how many miles they had trolled the edges of the lake, searching, before that. But she knew the gas tank held eighteen gallons and possibly four hours of forward pull.

"They dropped anchor," Nicole called over to Ty. Its rope trailed from the bow of the BP skiff. They had stayed with the body. And they'd do that only if there was no reason to pursue life. They had lost sight of the refugees, if they'd ever had it.

"So the body's here, somewhere, but what else?" Ty returned.

Nicole slipped on the booties and traded the strobe for a flashlight. A yard or so of slushy water separated the boats, and Ty was pulling back on the throttle to maintain the distance.

"Going," she called over her shoulder, and timed the jump to work with the current, toeing off as soon as the skiff rose on the swell.

"Shit."

"What?" from both Ty and MacAulay.

"It's taking water," she said. Not quite ankle-deep, which was fine in terms of gear—her boots reached midcalf—but when she landed, the spray had hit her face and rolled down her neck under the gaiter tube. "Not a lot. Two inches maybe."

The spray had frozen on her face, and she peeled it off in thin layers resembling Scotch tape. She rubbed the skin with her gloved hands, creating heat through friction. Frostbite prevention 101.

"You see the damage?"

"Looking."

The beam from the flashlight chased the shadows from the boat. There were no boot prints because the entire hull was covered in lake. She moved around the console, prying the darkness from the cubbies under the gunwale with the Maglite.

"No bodies," she reported. "No bullet holes." She pulled on the weapons locker. The padlock was engaged and rocked against the steel sheeting. She knocked against the door. There was no hollow timbre. Intact. Monte and his partner hadn't felt the need to arm up.

She moved deeper into the bow and followed the seam under the gunwale looking for damage, first along port side, which was solid against the ice floe and rubbing with every lift and dip of the current, then turning at the bow and running down starboard. She didn't get two feet before she found it. A stretch of molding puckered and straining against the steel pins. Water flowed from three spouts formed in the tubing. It was more than a trickle, but just barely. She ran her hand along the outer fiberglass and felt the buckle that surrounded the leak. She knew these things worsened quickly.

Had they hit something? Or had someone hit them?

She rose to her feet and turned back toward the department skiff. "There's damage here," she said, and took hold of a steel ring. She bent over the side of the boat and snapped several pictures from different angles.

"Contact," Ty said.

"Another vessel," Nicole agreed. "Heavier than the skiff but bearing closer to the water's surface. What kind of boat is that?"

The damage, what she could see of it, was a pair of scrapings. Deep gouges running parallel to and about nine inches below the gunwale.

"Get a picture of that, MacAulay." Nicole tossed him the camera.

She stood and peered through the darkness and the distance and the leaping shadows created by strobe and current. Ty was good with boats. With engineering and tracing the contours left by collisions, both on land and on water.

"Blamer Howard's boat," Ty said. "That's an example. His isn't the only party barge but the one I see most on the lake. Late spring through fall, Ski Heights rents them to anyone old enough to drive. Hitch included."

Nicole filed that piece of information in a mental folder. "You think it could be a run-in with a party boat?"

"Did Monte say what kind of boat the UAs boarded?"

"No." And she hadn't asked.

"You ready for me?" MacAulay had moved to the gunwale, strobe still in hand, ME bag in the other.

"Not yet. I need to get the pump going." But she stood a moment longer and turned toward open water. She listened to the slap of the current against the boats and beyond that the absolute silence. "Something not right about that."

"About what?" Ty asked.

"What do you hear?" Nicole asked.

They all stood silently, feet braced against the current, listening.

"Makes me edgy," Ty said.

"Me too."

"What does?" MacAulay asked.

"Do you hear anything, Doc?" Ty asked.

He thought about it, and though Nicole couldn't see his face so deep in shadow, she knew his eyebrows were now drawn tightly over the bridge of his nose.

"The water."

"Yes," she agreed. "And nothing else."

"We have a great population of snowy and horned owls. They carry on out here like a Guns N' Roses concert. Usually. Fish jump at night. Crickets complain about the cold. Foxes chatter and wolves howl."

"Why are they quiet?"

"Trespassers. Something's riled them. Something bigger than themselves," Ty said.

"Survival quiets them." She began searching the cubbies, opening the doors at the transom first as she searched for the pump. "Keep the strobe pointed toward open water, MacAulay. And turn in a slow half circle." She was feeling penned in. Open to the same fate as the BP agents. "Sweep the surface of the lake and about five feet above."

They had no defense, hemmed in as they were. Evasive moves, yes, but in water thick with slush and the danger of trees felled by the winter cold and ice floes set adrift by the spring thaw, there wasn't much they could do, if they needed to do anything at all.

BP was still twenty minutes out, and that was just to make shore. Another twenty to navigate the waters. Her own team was slightly closer.

"You think someone's out there?"

"It's possible." Probable. Monte and his agent were somewhere. Perhaps aboard the boat that had sideswiped theirs. And whether it was friend or foe, that was best-case scenario.

"Call in," she told Ty. "Full report and request a car in constant motion on the Lake Road."

Ty followed orders, and Nicole set up the pump.

"Best thing to do is get our vic back to shore," Ty said.

If they could find him. Monte had stayed with the body. He'd told her that, and she hoped to find it in the ice, where the BP skiff was anchored at the floe. But that had to wait.

"Agreed. But we need to work the scene first."

"It's a bad idea to just sit here."

"Better if we had reinforcements," she agreed. "But you know the deal with crime scenes. The longer we wait, the more we lose."

"One of us needs to move with the boat," Ty said. "Maybe you leave me and MacAulay here and motor out. You wouldn't have to go more than thirty or forty yards."

"It'd put me in a good position." She'd be able to play offense or defense out there but was capable of very little here. "But you and Doc? Not so much."

An inescapable truth.

"Why don't you just let me in and let me get the job done?" MacAulay suggested.

Nicole considered their positions, their strengths and weaknesses, the possibility of danger lurking beyond the reach of their lights. And the swift deterioration of evidence exposed to the elements and time.

"You'll stay," she told Ty. "I've never cut a corpse out of the ice before."

"My specialty," Ty agreed.

He had worked rescue in Prince William Sound for two years prior to joining the sheriff's department three years ago. Winter weather there was brutal, with ice floes and temperatures that rarely rose above freezing.

She reached for MacAulay's bag and set it aft, on the bench seat, then stood clear as Doc prepared to jump boat to boat. His long legs reduced the stretch to merely a hop, which he carried out with grace. It was impossible to tell if his fever had worsened, bundled up and exposed to the chafing wind as he was.

"Quick," she told him.

"Without compromising the evidence," he said.

She looked into his eyes. Steady. That had bothered her in the beginning, but now she relied on it. Personally, professionally. MacAulay had an inner strength that ran deep and a stubborn patience that got things done right. Turned out, steady was what she was looking for.

"Right," she said. Her hand fell briefly to his arm. "I don't know what's out there. Definitely something. I don't know if we're in danger. If it's immediate."

"But time is of the essence."

Nicole nodded, then stepped on the stair at starboard and up onto the gunwale.

"Boarding," she called to Ty. She leapt. The toe of her boot caught on the lip of the department skiff. She landed and stumbled into a crouch. Her joints and reflexes were beginning to respond to the cold, even swaddled in layers of winter gear. She looked toward Ty and he nodded.

"Same here," he said. "I'm starting to feel spongy."

There was a big difference between the cold on the water and that on land. One far more often led in a dance to your death.

Nicole checked her watch. "Twenty-eight minutes." Since leaving shore.

"Right on time," Ty agreed.

"If he starts shivering"—she nodded toward MacAulay—"if you notice slurred speech, anything like that, hail me."

"I know what to look for."

She nodded. "Reinforcements are coming. If we can't get the body now, later will do."

He locked the throttle, and Nicole handed him the strobe. After he had made the leap, she handed across the chainsaw.

"And here," she said, lifting her thermos from the console. She tossed it in a wide arc, which he easily picked out of the air. "Two to one." And, on the ice, they would need the warm brew more than she did.

"Always good odds," Ty said.

Behind him, she watched MacAulay as he leaned over aft, already at work.

"Life first, if it comes to that."

"Always."

Nicole pulled back on the throttle and maneuvered away from the BP skiff. When she had a good ten yards between the boats, she made a loping turn using the strobe mounted at the bow for guidance. It wasn't much. Visibility was cone shaped and eight yards deep. And so she

22

motored slowly, peering over her shoulder at the bobbing BP skiff. Ty held the strobe over MacAulay as he chiseled away at the ice, collecting what could amount to evidence, and the thought came to Nicole again, teasing her nerve endings, tickling that primitive part of her brain at the base of her skull, that they were exposed. Defenseless. Sitting ducks.

3

MacAulay pried loose a fragment of what looked like flannel. It had appeared to him as a shadow. A dimple in the ice, perhaps, but training had taught him it could be much more than that. He had used an Eskimo eight-inch stainless-steel bit to drill around it so he could pull the piece out still encased in its bed of ice. And it had reminded him of his rotations through both surgery and emergency medicine, the need for precision, for just enough and a little bit more.

He held the piece under the light—bigger than an ice cube, smaller than the palm of his hand. He turned it over and made note of the pattern. Yes, flannel, and not a match in color or fabric to the shirt worn by their vic. The body was pressed close to the surface of the ice and wore a lined denim jacket and a shirt MacAulay recognized as linen, in a solid color that could be burgundy or brown.

"Doc?" The deputy caught his attention, and MacAulay dropped the cube into a plastic evidence sleeve and sealed it.

"I know, the sooner the better," he said.

"I don't want to rush you."

MacAulay heard recrimination in the man's voice.

"No good ever comes of it," MacAulay agreed. He was growing into the ME position, beginning to feel comfortable with his skill base. And the results were gratifying—putting away criminals before they could strike again. But that required patience, care, methodical procedure. "Do you think we're in danger?"

"I don't like the feel of this, and neither does the sheriff," Ty said.

"She's very good at her job."

"The best."

MacAulay again used the steel brush to cut through the surface of the ice, then a whisk broom to gather the shavings. He placed these in another bag, sealed it, and dropped both into the cooler. He'd done this with every square inch of ice in a twelve-foot circumference around and over the encased body while Nicole idled in the department skiff half a football field away and police and Border Patrol cruisers began to line up along the shore.

He had been on the ice more than twenty minutes, less than twenty-five—Ty called out the time in five-minute intervals. The deputy stood on the boat, feet spread and knees bent. A few minutes ago, the current's steady push had picked up tempo. It was a stronger, pulsing beat now, and MacAulay's stomach, currently a good meter for measure, protested. If he'd had anything left in it, he would have hurled.

His eyes swept over the sheet of ice, prying into the darkened edges. He had done what he could here. A surface sweep and collect. And now it was time to cut the man out. To attach the winch through steel hooks drilled into the ice and lift him aboard. Possibly three or four hundred pounds, including the ice coffin that embraced him. They had decided on a six-by-six-foot cut, as the man's hands, legs, and feet were visible. Tied into a fetal position, hands behind his knees, he had surfaced in profile. MacAulay tried not to stare too frequently at the man's face. It was stretched into horrors unspeakable, and unforgettable.

Six by six was enough to guarantee a clean cut with no involvement of limbs.

MacAulay pushed back on his heels and was about to rise when he heard a metallic shriek tangled in the sleeves of the wind. Close and deafening, like the engines of an airplane as it gathered torque for takeoff. The floe shifted, swelled as though a wave had risen beneath it. Behind him the boat rocked madly and the strobe light wavered in the deputy's hands before it fell, shattering into sharp fragments over the encased body of the vic. MacAulay reached out and swept the pieces into a pile for collection—they needed to be gathered for exclusionary purposes.

He looked up.

The cruising lights on the BP skiff flickered. The deputy stood aft, feet braced, his head turned as he scanned the surrounding water.

"Something wonky." Ty spoke, his words followed by the crackling of the radio pinned to his shoulder.

"What happened?" Nicole's voice, distant and drowning under the pulse of the department's skiff as it gathered speed.

MacAulay turned, watched as she changed bearing, skirted ice, and met with the swifter current as she trundled toward them. He heard the rustling of the water, churned by the blades of the motor. And something else, something buried under sound and urgency, something he couldn't grasp.

"Ty? Report." The wind buffered her radio and seemed to steal her breath.

"The pump is failing," the deputy said, speaking into his mike. "But there's something more. Something heavy. Rocked the boat, the ice Doc is standing on."

"Not wash?" From a passing boat. If they'd heard the engine, seen lights on the water, possible.

"The only time I've ever felt anything like this was rapid ice melt," he said. "Big pieces breaking away from something as solid as a glacier."

Or the sudden collapse of ice patties once rooted to the lake bottom. It wasn't always visible above the surface but arose from a natural disturbance, often with catastrophic results. It could change the level of the water, the geography of a shoreline. He'd read about it but had never experienced it.

"Stand ready," she said. "And get MacAulay back in the boat."

He didn't need to be told twice. He stood and the ice creaked, fissures running beneath his feet. He stilled, breathless, yet wavered as the ice heaved on the current. He was four feet from the gunwale. He could scale that easily. He bent and picked up the cooler chest. The latch was secured, so he tossed it into the boat. He swept up his tools and dumped them into his bag, zipped it up, and tossed that also. Ty was crouched behind the console, the rifle he'd carried strapped across his back, tucked now into his shoulder and aimed into the darkness. Not trusting their circumstances to nature.

The suction on the pump, a steady piston surge and purge, sputtered, coughed, and began gurgling. It was drowning under increased demand. The boat was sinking.

Ice melt. The sudden shift had rocked him on his feet. The current had changed, become more forceful, and the BP skiff, already floundering, couldn't hold up. It wobbled, stirring the water.

He was torn. It was a physical sensation, straight down the middle. Go down with the boat or plunge into the icy waters of the lake when the floe completed its fracture? The odds seemed better where he stood.

"Abandon ship," MacAulay called to the deputy. "It's going down."

Even as he said the words, the gunwale tilted and rose, away from MacAulay and toward a sure capsizing. Aboard, he heard the deputy scrambling. Ty tossed a Maglite and then the skiff's rescue bag. Both hit the ice with a solid thump. The flashlight skittered several feet. The bag settled. The ice held. Then the deputy leapt, rifle in hand.

MacAulay felt every cell in his body brace for disaster.

"Get down, Doc," Ty called. The deputy scooped up the Maglite and shoved it into a pocket. He was fluid motion. The leap, the crouching crawl over the ice, the pocketing of the flashlight. "Grab the rescue bag. We need to get to thicker ice."

Yes, that made sense. Move toward center. But in the dark, every step was one of faith.

MacAulay fumbled with the handle of the bag. It was fear; he felt it in the shallow basin of every breath. It was the elements, exposure to freezing temperatures for going on an hour now, making his movements slow and clumsy. It was the flu racking his body.

It was a terrible night for murder.

"This way." The deputy's voice was a harsh whisper. Sound carried over water. Even the scraping of their feet on the ice. "And in the name of salvation, get down. Crawl or scuttle. Slide on your ass if you have to."

MacAulay chose the crouch. He pulled the rescue bag along beside him, thumping on the ice, his long legs folded like paper clips and just about as useful. He kept close to the deputy by following the sound of his feet and the sharp puffs of his breath. Away from the skiff's lights, his eyes began to differentiate between the darkness of the sky and the inky blackness of the water and take in the startling lightness of the ice compared to the two. He thought about that and about the senses and how they grew acute in times of need. A very primitive reaction and suitable to the circumstances—MacAulay felt like the hunted.

27

"You think someone's out there," he said. It made sense.

The silence. The changing current. Possibly the wash that had overwhelmed the pump.

"We know it. But we have other things to worry about," Ty said. "Ice has a feel to it, Doc."

The deputy had stopped, and MacAulay almost barreled into him. "What do you mean?"

"It was solid back there. Not a whole lot of give. It wavered a little when I jumped ship, but nothing more."

"Yeah, I felt that."

"It's turning spongy now," Ty said. "Our feet are sinking a little more into the ice. Means it's beginning to turn to slush. Nothing major yet, but a few more yards and it could turn into Swiss cheese."

"So we don't move forward," MacAulay said.

"Or in any other direction. Ice doesn't always melt around the edges first. It doesn't decompensate at the same speed throughout."

"So now you're making me nervous."

"Nervous? Nah," Ty said. "Not yet. Just means the only way out is the way we came in."

"And if they come?" *They* meaning predators. Whoever was out there and closing in. Whoever had taken the BP crew and left a sinking ship.

The deputy tapped the butt of his rifle on the ice. "Then we stand and deliver."

*   *   *

Nicole hit her radio mike. "Update on backup, dispatch?"

Static. She looked toward shore, where bar lights rolled. Two distinctive patterns. Her officers had arrived along with the BP teams Green had promised. Close but stopped. Which meant Gunnar's boat was not yet in the water.

"Several units, ours and BP, already on-site. Gunnar's boat en route. Trying to get an ETA on that."

They were on their own.

She listened to the shrill whine of the engine as she leaned on the throttle. The Commando hung from its shoulder strap, bumping against her side. The wind cut over the bow and plowed into her. It was like falling face first into a snowdrift. At thirty yards out, the BP skiff tilted aft. It was a slow wallowing as the gunwale lifted and the cruising lights wavered, flickered, and then pulled it together to flare brightly. She watched Ty. Weapon drawn, he tossed the rescue bag to the ice, leapt. MacAulay stood tall, squared against a backdrop of night. The skiff turned a graceful somersault, slow but smooth. The running lights shimmered under the water. Nicole could see it even from that far out. And then the hull was bottoms up, a cradle upended, and the men she had left adrift faded into the darkness.

"Still ten minutes out, Sheriff." It was Lars's voice. Strident. Her second-in-command was a steady, reliable presence. He'd heard the exchange over the radio. "What's going on out there?"

"We're not alone," she said. Ice melt be damned. She agreed with Ty: there was something else out there.

Ty wouldn't use the flashlight until it was an absolute need. He would not betray their position. Life and death were equal motivators. A stray thought streamed across her consciousness: MacAulay, not especially suited to this work and sick on top of that. She snipped the thread and let it flutter away. Worry did absolutely nothing to help a situation. A clear mind, sharp and buoyant, was the only way.

"What and where?" Lars asked.

"No confirmation on either."

And then it loomed aft, a dark, flat-bottomed barge. At the mercy of the current, it rocked forward and back. The vessel was empty and adrift.

"Sheriff." Ty's voice was distant, scratched out by increasing static. He gave his coordinates, and Nicole glanced at the GPS on the console. As the crow flies, thirty yards west from where they had abandoned ship.

"Would be good if you could grab us now." His breath came thickly between his words.

"On it, Ty. Can you see my lights?" The strobe and running lights were on, but she flipped a switch and added the red and blue bar that turned and flashed above the console.

"Affirmative—" His voice stopped abruptly, and the radio snapped with static. Then, "Prob . . . here, Sheriff. Our . . . way out is . . ."

"You're breaking up," she said. Radio and cell phone service, nestled as they were between mountain ranges, had its moments of interruption, no matter how many towers they planted. "What's the problem with pickup?"

"Ice is unstable," Ty reported. His voice cut through her radio with sudden clarity. "Our way in is our only way out."

Which posed a problem. Nicole had to keep her distance from the BP skiff. Too close and it would drag her with it when the air escaped the hull and it plunged toward the bottom of the lake. She decided to approach the floe by port. To await a visual before edging closer. She hit her mike and hailed Ty.

"In position." *Come now.*

Starboard side, she could still see the lights on the BP skiff, wavering under the surface of the lake.

She waited, her hand on the throttle. Inside her glove, her palm and the skin between her fingers were slick with sweat. She watched the point where darkness rose from the ice. Her back was to shore, but from the corner of her eye she saw rays of red and blue cast over the lake from the units that had arrived and took comfort in that.

Then two figures emerged from the gloom. Ty leading the way, rifle at his shoulder, and MacAulay bringing up the rear, the rescue bag in hand. They loped, not in the crouch they'd used when seeking shelter but boldly facing come what may. They kept a straight line, returning the way they had left, and Nicole pulled on the throttle, backing the skiff several feet so that she was closer to where they would end up. They lengthened their strides—less contact with the ice, less danger of breaking through. The floe rocked beneath their feet. The last ten yards they slipped and slid over the slick surface and Nicole realized it was awash with lake water.

The floe was breaking up, and as she watched, the fractures chased their footsteps. *Faster, faster!* she silently urged them.

They threw themselves against the gunwale, and Nicole left the throttle to pull them in. They had trouble getting to their feet and keeping their balance as she moved back to the console and went through the motions of pulling away from the floe, away from the downed BP skiff and the dangers beneath the water.

"There are some life blankets in the forward compartment," she called over her shoulder. "Get into them."

4

"What is it, MacAulay?"

Nicole kept her distance, rocking back on her heels, but her gaze never wavered. The ME was on his knees in a dense patch of forest beside a congealed pool of blood and . . . something else. Something pulpy. Something contained within a thin, saclike membrane. Something that was possibly human but so foreign it could have come from another planet. If she had to guess, without further information, she would say organ. The heart of a big animal?

She lifted her gaze, looked beyond MacAulay's crouching figure and through the trees. The lake washed up not twenty yards west from where she stood. So much activity condensed in a small area and within a limited amount of time.

After reaching shore in the early-morning hours, she had sent MacAulay home for NyQuil and sleep. He hadn't protested. Ty had changed his clothes, downed some hot coffee, and then gone back out on the water and cut the DOA out of the ice with the help of Arthur Sleeping Bear, her chief forensics officer. The victim was in deep freeze waiting for MacAulay. Nicole had hoped to give him until that evening, but the dogs had turned up this and been reduced to a frenzied barking. She'd had to call him in.

"Animal, vegetable, mineral?"

"Animal." He poked at the mass with the end of a thermometer. It was malleable. He inserted the instrument, and Nicole heard the tissue give with a wet sucking sound. "Human, in fact."

"Human what?"

He turned so that he was looking over his shoulder at her. "Placenta," he said. "It looks like a woman gave birth here, and not too long ago."

"That's a placenta?" It turned her stomach. She hadn't seen hers. It had passed through her shortly after Jordan was birthed, and she hadn't given it another thought. But it had given Jordan the gift of life, and because of that it was a beautiful thing.

"Not what you expected?"

"Not at all."

"Women rarely have the opportunity to see the placenta. The baby is the star of the show, naturally, and once he's born, we're all about that." He turned back to the pulpy mass and pulled the thermometer out. Fluid oozed around the puncture, and that did nothing to improve Nicole's weakening stomach. "Seventy-two degrees," he said. "A baby was born here, seven or eight hours ago."

Nicole checked her watch. It was 10:23. "The middle of the night," she said. Possibly right around the time she and MacAulay and Ty Watts had boarded the skiff for a rendezvous with BP agents that had never happened. BP agents who were still missing and presumed dead. BP agents and officers from Nicole's department were still out on the water, combing the shore, searching for evidence.

MacAulay nodded. He sat back on his haunches, and she watched as his gaze roamed the area surrounding their scene—crime scene? Not yet.

"The umbilical cord is underneath," he said. "I already took a peek. It's intact but tied off."

"Is that unusual?"

"If the baby was born in a hospital, the cord would have been cut an inch from the navel." He shrugged. "Out here, without the right tools, good thing she knew something about emergency aid."

"Tying it off was an act of desperation?"

"An act of necessity, for sure," MacAulay returned. "No scissors, no knife when you're on the run."

"You think that's what happened here?"

"That's for you to figure out," he said, "but if what Tandy reported is truth, then maybe this is a crime scene. Maybe we'll find a woman and child nearby, but I hope not."

Nicole turned and let her gaze fall on Tandy Longhorn. She was short, thick, quiet in both words and manner. She waited at the top of a hill. When Tandy had walked into the station that morning, she had spoken her concerns—an old woman's story of wild thrashing in the woods, of a young woman's desperate run through the shallow waters of the lake and the whimper of a newborn baby—and then she had taken a seat. Nothing more. Not until Nicole had approached her, had asked questions about time and place and descriptions.

There were none. It was dark, the moon and stars swaddled in cloud. Tandy claimed to have arrived at the young woman's home, but too late. She had followed a broken trail, heard the splashing of water and the thick breath of a woman as she ran, the heavy footsteps of men, many of them, the weak cry of a baby just born.

Nicole left MacAulay examining his find and climbed the rise, the thick grass beneath her feet still wet with dew.

"Tandy?"

"A placenta, yes?"

"You knew?"

Tandy nodded. "I am a midwife," she said. "And a nurse."

"On the reservation?"

The woman nodded. "That is nothing new to my eyes."

"The baby was born hours ago," Nicole said. "In the middle of the night."

"Two thirty or three," Tandy confirmed. Which fell within the time frame MacAulay had provided.

"Why were you out here?" Nicole asked. "In the middle of the night? In the middle of nowhere?"

There was no easy access to this part of the lake. It was a hike through trees, full now with spring, and over the soft mulch of an earth reviving.

"I knew she was coming due," Tandy said. "I came because she needed me."

"You came here?"

"To her home first," the old woman corrected, and it seemed to Nicole that a small amount of censure had entered her tone. She was annoyed, perhaps, that Nicole had asked her to repeat her story. "And I followed her footsteps here."

"You're a tracker?"

"I am a midwife," she repeated. "And I am a woman of some intelligence."

"Her home—"

"She was chased out of it."

"And you followed her here?"

The woman held Nicole's gaze but didn't bother to respond.

"Why didn't you report this earlier?"

"It was three-thirty by the time I arrived here and too dark to pick my way out of the woods without turning back the way I had come, which was too far. I waited for first light."

The town of Blue Mesa proper was a main street with a single traffic light and a cross street that divided modern conveniences from necessities, such as the police station and courthouse.

"Did you deliver the baby?"

She shook her head. "As I told you, that had already happened."

"And when you got here, the woman and child were gone?"

"And the men."

"What did the men want?"

"The baby," she guessed. "Or the woman. But not both."

"Why not both?"

"If both, why run?" Tandy posed. "We are miles from her home. If the men were to take the woman and toss the baby or take the baby and leave the woman behind, she would have to run and keep on running. But if there was some reassurance of keeping her baby, she would have faltered. Nine months pregnant, a three-mile run at this point, she would have stopped. She would have hoped for another way."

"And you don't know her name?"

"I know he called her Georgia and she called him Matthew. I know they wanted an at-home delivery. They were young. Maybe she was eighteen. Maybe not yet. They loved each other. That is what I know."

Nicole's radio gave off a blast of static, and then Lars's voice came through. She had sent him ahead to the home of the young woman Tandy was concerned about.

Nicole turned away and took several steps toward MacAulay. "You have something, Lars?"

34

"Affirmative," he said. "DOA, circumstances unusual."

Meaning Nicole would not hear the details until she had a place of privacy. She scanned the woods, the lake, and turned back toward the old woman. Tandy stood her ground atop the hill, her long white hair thick and silky, the ends lifted by the wind. Beyond her, a quarter of a mile, Nicole's Yukon was parked at the side of the road.

"I have MacAulay here," she said. "Also unusual."

"I'll secure and wait."

"Shouldn't be too long." They would bag and tag, and after MacAulay delivered their evidence to his lab, he would be en route to Lars. "An hour tops."

"DOA's not going anywhere."

"I'm sending you a deputy." And she'd call in a crew here. They would start at ground zero, at the evidence, and fan out. Somewhere out there were a woman and child. If they had survived. "Gender and age on your DOA?"

"Male, approximately twenty-three years old."

She signed off and called in to dispatch, moving deputies and forensics around on the map. Then she turned and walked back to Tandy.

"You remained here last night?"

"Until first light," she confirmed.

"There was a disturbance on the lake last night about the same time you arrived here," Nicole began.

"Earlier," Tandy said. "And miles from here."

"Yes." Two plus miles. "But the young woman who gave birth, perhaps she ran by at the right time to see or hear something," Nicole said. "And you too."

"I was concerned with the mother and child," Tandy said. "And the men who had come for them."

The group of men Monte's tipster had seen boarding a boat? Possible. The timing was right.

"What did you see?"

"They wore dark clothing. Still, I noticed one standing on the roof, outside a bedroom window. I saw others run from the front door and into the brush." She spoke thoughtfully and paused to consider her next words. "They were good. One or two of them anyway. They read the signs of her passing easily enough and dove into the trees."

"And you followed them?"

"I couldn't leave her alone." She shook her head, a shadow passing over her face as she perhaps revisited a brief moment of indecision as she'd stood above the sloping earth while a young woman, an expectant mother, ran for her life. "There's only so much a woman like me can do. I followed, but that was all." She turned toward the east and raised a hand to point out a dense copse of trees and brambles a quarter mile back and snuggled against the lip of the lake. "She lost them in there. It was like her feet caught wind. Even I had difficulty following after that."

"Where did the men go?"

Tandy's expression changed, her gaze floating out over the lake. "They saw the same as I did. Two boats tangled on the water. They were that close. The wind brought the sound of engines. I think that scattered them."

"What else did you see out on the lake?"

"Trouble. A struggle of some kind. Sound travels over water, of course, but even then I heard only voices raised in anger. Male voices, but the words were not clear or I was not attentive to them. I had other concerns."

"Male voices only?"

"Yes, of that I am sure."

"And then what?"

"Nothing."

"No gunshots?"

"No. That is a distinctive sound, isn't it, and one I would not forget."

"Eventually the boats separated," Nicole said, leading the woman into her next observation.

"Yes, but I didn't see that. When I looked over again, the bigger boat was on its way toward shore. Slow and moving northeast, away from me. Even so, I noticed it wasn't a straight line. More like swooping." And Tandy lifted her arm and gave a waving motion that seemed to gather armfuls of air. "Back and forth and the passing each way big enough that I paused and considered it."

A pattern search, looking for someone or something in the water. "And what did you think?" Nicole asked.

"Seemed a strange thought at the time, but not so much now," Tandy began. "I thought maybe a person had gone overboard, that the boat was searching the water to attempt a rescue. After that I didn't look again, not until you arrived. You or someone from your department. I saw the lights across the water, flashes of blue and red."

"Why didn't you call nine-one-one?" Nicole asked. "When you realized the woman was in trouble?" When there had seemed to be trouble on the water?

"I'd left my cell phone in the truck—I'd packed it into my medical bag so I wouldn't forget it. Sometimes there are emergencies during birthing. Rare," she conceded, "but more than I can handle with my limited resources for a home delivery." She paused, and when she spoke again, her voice was full of gloom. "And then I was too far into the woods and couldn't give up on her. She is strong and one for courage," Tandy explained. "And I wanted to help if I could."

"But you never caught up with the young lady or the men pursuing her?"

Tandy shook her head, and a solemn regret fanned out from her eyes. She sought and held Nicole's gaze. "The girl was gone, and in the early light I saw no sign of her or the baby."

Just the placenta, Nicole thought.

"Do you think the men have her?"

"I hope not," she said. "With the commotion on the lake, I think they spooked and left. But then, where is Georgia and the baby?"

Nicole left Tandy waiting on the hill and walked back to MacAulay. He had thrown together the basics of a ME bag, his now being on the bottom of Lake Maria. He pulled out a metal scoop. He already had an evidence bag open and waiting.

"I'd like to get this whole," he said, sensing her approach. "I don't want to puncture the sac." Again. "We'd have a real mess then and it'd be about impossible to collect it all."

"That scoop isn't big enough." Nicole stated the obvious.

"It's what I've got." She heard his frustration and watched his frown deepen as he considered his situation. "Actually, I have a better idea."

He stripped the latex gloves from his hands and fished a new, sterile pair from a package in his box. "Grab a pair of these," he instructed, "and hold the bag open for me."

Nicole did as instructed, stepping into what he called the halo—the area of importance around a victim or evidence he didn't want contaminated, the fewer bodies inside it the better. She crouched beside him, holding the mouth of the bag open, and watched him slide his hands under the placenta. The organ shifted and conformed to the cradle he formed.

"Lars has a body," she said.

"What do we know?" he asked as he slipped the placenta into the bag, sealed it, and stored it for travel.

"Male, twenties." Nicole stood while MacAulay gathered his tools and spoke a final note into his digital recorder. "I told him you'd be there inside an hour."

MacAulay nodded. "And so I will be."

5

Tandy Longhorn rode to the crime scene with MacAulay. She'd left her truck there, but Nicole had told him she wanted the midwife to ride along for different reasons. She wasn't ready yet to let Tandy loose. Depending on what they found at the home of the missing woman and baby, Nicole could have more questions for Tandy, and she hoped MacAulay might ease the way to getting some answers.

The two of them rode in a county vehicle, a van fitted with skate brakes and a variety of hooks and compartments for tools MacAulay was just getting comfortable with. When it became clear that their vast county needed an ME, he had stepped up as a matter of duty. It had taken a while, three years in fact, for him to see his role as an important part of speaking for the victim. The science he practiced produced some of the strongest evidence that made it into the courtroom, and he liked that.

"I appreciate the ride."

"You walked a long way."

"For an old woman?"

"For an old woman through some dense tree cover and up and down some pretty steep slopes."

She nodded, and MacAulay turned his attention back to the road.

"Do you always make house calls? I mean, before delivery?"

"Almost never," she said. "I prefer they come to me. I have a pretty good setup."

"You were a nurse," he said.

"Does that give me more credibility with you?"

He thought about that. It was true. The more training a medical professional received, the better the outcomes. "Yes."

"Well, I still am. A nurse," she clarified. "I keep up my state certs."

"I've been out to the reservation. I've seen your place."

"Surprised you?" There was challenge in her voice.

"Yes," he admitted. "New equipment. Some of it top-shelf." Some of it better than what he had in his own office.

"Grant money. It built us a new clinic, got us an X-ray machine, ultrasound, a mini lab even."

"You were never around when I was there."

"Oh, I was around," she told him.

He nodded. "I thought as much."

"Your sheriff comes around too," she said. "Part of that community justice agreement."

"She keeps her word," MacAulay said. Nicole believed in restorative justice and atonement. She believed the victim benefited as much as the perpetrator. And she believed tribal issues should be hashed out, as much as possible, on tribal grounds utilizing cultural norms. At this point, only capital cases committed on the reservation were moved to the courtroom.

"So far."

He understood that Tandy's caution was steeped in a history of betrayal, so he didn't push further.

"Who are we looking for?" he asked.

"A woman not much older than a girl. Not from around here."

"You really don't have a name?"

"They paid cash," she said.

"But for your records," he pressed.

"Last name Peach."

"Let me guess, first name Georgia?"

"I had a choice to make. Not the first time. Keep the girl healthy or cut her loose."

"So you gave her some prenatal vitamins and her next appointment," he said, and nodded. He'd have done the same, if it came down to that.

"You respect that," she said.

"I do."

The GPS spoke up then and suggested he take the next left turn, leaving the Lake Road behind. He followed the direction and then returned to their conversation.

"But Georgia Peach? That's not even trying."

"And I appreciate that. Bite my tongue every time I get a Smith or Jones."

"Is she healthy?"

Tandy nodded. "She worked at it. She wrote things down, what she ate, any questions she had, and she sat in my office and opened that little book and asked every one of them every which way until she got the answers she needed, even if it meant she had to change up a few things."

"What things?"

"Exercise," Tandy offered. "She said she wasn't much for it but started walking every day as soon as she knew there was a baby on the way. She was good on fruits but not veggies. She changed that too. A lot of people won't do either."

"So she's responsible," he said.

"More than most."

She turned and gazed out her window, and MacAulay caught her profile. The tension had eased from her mouth and forehead, but not the worry. Her lips trembled on what he suspected was a whispered prayer.

"You like her."

"I like most of them," she said, but then nodded. "Yes. She was determined to get things done right, up against odds that made that difficult."

They were still on pavement, but there was more gravel here, rising from the asphalt and pinging against the undercarriage. The tree line thickened the farther they drove, and the homes were fewer and the distance between them greater. Eventually, just glimpses of the lake were visible.

"What odds?"

She shrugged. "I know nothing for sure, other than she was eating and exercising and they loved each other. That I saw with my own eyes. The rest is . . . a guess."

"It could help save her life," MacAulay said. "And the life of her baby."

She sat with that a good two minutes before she turned toward him and said, "There's been a lot of talk lately about the passage of friendlies seeking the border."

Friendlies. MacAulay liked the word. It fit better than *UDAs* and worse, the terms bandied about in the newspapers. Refugees from unstable countries seeking asylum.

"Yes," he agreed. "I've heard it."

"I've seen some pictures, in the papers and on the news," she said. "It's possible the young lady is one of them."

"A friendly?"

"Yes. She has the same coloring. An accent. She's careful about that. I heard it only once, in her excitement, when we determined the baby's gender. But it was like she fell back into her comfort zone, spoke several sentences, and they had a musical lilt to them that was real natural."

"The friendlies are from a lot of countries," MacAulay said. He remembered that Tandy had first reported the woman as Caucasian, so that narrowed the possibilities.

"Middle Eastern," she said. "Beyond that—" She shrugged. "Geography was not my favorite study in school."

"And the baby's father?"

"American," she said. "He served."

"You know that for sure?"

"*Semper fi,*" she said. "It was tattooed on his bicep."

"I'll pass that along," he said.

"I figured you would." She lapsed into silence, but it was heavy with consideration and MacAulay waited for her. "Those are just a few things that stood out about them."

"What else?"

"At first they arrived on foot. It was like that for months. When she was far enough along a ride became necessary, they switched it up a bit. A different car each time. I noticed a rental tag on more than one of those. The one time she came without the father, she got a ride from a friend. An older woman I thought might be a grandmother to the baby. The woman came back for the exam, which I thought was pushy." Tandy shrugged. "She was respectful of privacy and didn't speak much, but she had a commanding presence and Georgia wasn't entirely comfortable with her."

"Did she give her name?"

"Georgia called her Lois."

"How did you know her address?" MacAulay asked. "I mean, since they gave you fake names."

"Prenatal vitamins," Tandy said. "I was worried about her age. If she was under eighteen and still growing . . ."

"Prescription," MacAulay said, and nodded with approval. "And they always require a verifiable address." An address that checked out in the computer system. Proven existence and no PO boxes.

"Did you tell the sheriff any of this?"

"Not much," Tandy admitted.

"You know I have to."

"I'm hoping you will."

"So he was military with health benefits they didn't use," he said. "So maybe they weren't married."

"No rings," Tandy said. "But maybe he left the service."

Maybe they were both running. He steered the van through a series of turns as the road curved.

"It was right about here I noticed some cars parked last night."

He felt his eyebrows lift. "You tell the sheriff about that?"

"She didn't ask."

"You remember color, make, or model of the cars?"

"I remember some of that. The only reason I don't have a plate number is because there were no plates."

They rounded the last curve, and the house came into view. Nicole had already arrived and was standing at the foot of the porch steps, talking to her second-in-command. Crime-scene tape was stretched across the porch posts and the front door. Forensics techs were crouched in the driveway and garden beds casting plaster prints.

Tandy sat forward and pointed west, to a break between a bramble of huckleberry brushes. "She went through there," she said. "And the men followed."

6

Lars stood on the porch, a shoulder propped against a support beam, and rolled the cuffs of his shirt back. Eleven fifteen and the sun was turning it up. The body inside would begin to bake, and if MacAulay didn't arrive soon, the evidence would decompose at an accelerated rate. He'd opened an upstairs window, the only one with a screen intact. Wouldn't do much to help the situation, but it would stir the air a little without letting in the bugs.

He began a mental review of everything he knew.

Another dead immigrant, this one murdered. Trussed and dropped into the lake to drown—a guess at this point, but he was fairly certain MacAulay would find water in the vic's lungs.

Missing BP agents with no sign of struggle.

They would pay more attention to the agents, because they were life and the possibility of rescue. They were also the emotional pull. The dead bodies would stir more interest, because they were the biggest clues. They had connections that could speak, a network of complicated wiring that, fused together, could light up the entire investigation.

A party barge adrift. They weren't made to withstand conditions of ice and slush and didn't even put in until the weather was warmer. This was perhaps the biggest anomaly. The barge was weird, so far out of the box and easily assigned a place low on the list of priorities, but following it could blow the case wide open. He'd seen it happen before, a small detail spring the lock.

The guy upstairs. One shot between the eyes, point-blank. There were powder burns, and the skin at entry was seared and puckered. It had been an abrupt killing. Angle suggested the young man had been on his knees, the shooter standing. Hands and feet free, no indication of bondage. At least one accomplice to hold the victim in place. Nothing about the killing here similar to the murder on the lake.

Sweat rolled from Lars's hairline, and he loosened his tie. He watched the place where the road curved and the dense tree cover parted, and a few minutes later he heard wheels turning on the gravel road.

* * *

Nicole parked the Yukon behind Lars's, well back from the house. There was a forensics van off to the side and two techs involved in a grid search through the gravel driveway, carrying casting kits—if they found prints, foot or tire, they would begin evidence collection. That was all the personnel Nicole could apply to this crime scene. Her deputies were spread thin over the lake and surrounding areas, and even with help from Border Patrol and Highway Patrol, there were wide-open spaces that needed plugging. Two missing agents and a woman and baby on the run, and somehow the jumbled pieces fit together.

She climbed from the vehicle and nodded at Lars. Then she looked at the house, small and narrow but well maintained. The paint wasn't more than a year or two old and the porch was sturdy. She scanned the small yard—square, the grass trimmed, a slatted fence at the back serving as a barrier between the cultivated yard and nature. An upstairs window would provide an unobstructed view of the lake, at least a mile southwest from where they stood. The earth between the house and the shore sloped sharply and was thick with bushes and fruited brambles, evergreen and aspen. It was a rough hike to the lake, and while she observed a few trailheads, she didn't see an established path. Probably access to berry picking and what looked like an abandoned chicken coop, she thought.

"MacAulay?" Lars asked. He left his jacket hanging over the porch railing and climbed down the stairs.

"Right behind me."

The ME was a cautious driver. He never let urgency direct his moves. They both knew it could be five minutes, maybe ten, before he rolled on-site.

Nicole nodded toward the house.

"One between the eyes," Lars said.

"An execution?"

"My guess," he confirmed. "In an upstairs bedroom, occupied. Clothes hanging in the closet, toiletries on the dresser. Across from that bedroom is a nursery. Crib and a changing table. Nothing fancy, but clean. There's a box of diapers and wipes, but the closet is empty and no dresser. Not yet."

"No baby clothes?"

"A few sleepers and onesies. Not enough."

Nicole told him about Tandy, the placenta, the young woman on the run.

"She was expecting a boy," he said. "All blues and tans."

"That fits. Recent ultrasound confirmed it."

"Looks like entry was through a downstairs window," Lars said, and nodded toward the porch, where a screen had been removed from the window and set against the siding. "Three windows upstairs. Two of those screens are out, and the piping for the rain gutter is hanging from the eaves. I think the occupant escaped through there."

"They trash the place?"

"No. A table overturned in the living area. Pillows thrown to the floor in the bedroom. But no evidence of a search."

"They knew what they wanted."

"The girl," he said.

"Or the baby," Nicole said, remembering Tandy's words. *But not both.*

"So she got out of the house, and then what?" She looked at the trees pressing on the fence, crowding the perimeter of the yard, framing the gravel driveway. "Took cover in the trees?"

"I can show you where she entered." He turned, and Nicole followed. Apparently the young woman had run across the driveway and pushed through a thicket of huckleberry bushes. Limbs were broken and dangling, marking her path of escape as well as the passing of the men who had chased her. Lars already had an evidence marker at the site.

"We have a tracker on staff," Nicole said. "In forensics."

"Yeah. Dan Carly."

"I'm going to pull him from the lake," Nicole decided. "Have him start where she did."

"Good idea."

Nicole called it in.

"He works alone, you know," Lars said. "No dogs. No partner."

No distraction. She knew where Lars was going with his comments. The woods were far from secured, and whoever had done this—chased a pregnant woman from her home, stayed on her heels through miles of thick vegetation—was still at large.

"He'll be armed." Even forensics were required to train and pass a marksmanship test.

She heard the approach of a vehicle, gravel churned by tires, and turned to watch the ME's new van thunder around the curve in the road. New to them, anyway. Nicole had overseen the purchase, tracking down a suitable vehicle that was low on miles and didn't break the budget. She'd found it in an online auction as the sheriff's department in Seattle, Washington, was downsizing, and had it delivered. It had all the bells and whistles. More specialized equipment at MacAulay's fingertips and no more using the county ambulance for the transport of bodies. Next, he needed an assistant, but there was no money for that in the budget. Not this year. MacAulay was talking about taking on a partner, or maybe an intern looking for rotation through family medicine. That would lighten the load in his family practice but not supply him with an extra set of hands in the ME's office. That would make her proposed budget for the next year.

She and Lars left the perimeter and walked toward the house. MacAulay stopped the van behind Nicole's Yukon and stepped out of the vehicle. Through the windshield, Nicole could see the white hair of the midwife gathered around her face and connected for a moment with the woman's level stare. Tandy Longhorn was holding back. Nicole was sure of it. The woman spoke in measured pieces. Nicole had watched it in tribal meetings. She imparted few words and preferred to spend as little time as necessary in conversation.

"I've seen her before," Lars said.

"She runs the clinic on the reservation."

Lars nodded. "Tribal justice."

"Yes." They had monthly meetings. On rare occasions, when there was a conflict in Nicole's schedule, Lars filled in for her.

The woman climbed easily from the truck. She wore a pair of Asics in a vibrant mix of sunset colors and had taken off her jacket and kept it folded over an arm. Behind her, MacAulay opened the back doors of the van and removed the gurney. He began loading it with the tools of his trade.

"You take MacAulay up," she said to Lars. "I have a few more questions for Tandy Longhorn."

Nicole approached her. The woman crossed her arms over her middle and waited.

"How did you know the young lady was in trouble?"

"She missed her appointment," Tandy said. "And she never did that. Not even once. She never even rescheduled."

"And her appointment was yesterday?"

"At four o'clock," Tandy confirmed.

"But you waited until two o'clock in the morning to check on her?"

"Before that," Tandy said. "Yesterday, clinic hours started at two and ended at nine thirty. I called twice during the evening. I left messages. When she called me back, it was almost midnight and she was certain she was in labor. We stayed on the phone, measuring the minutes between contractions. Nine minutes and her water hadn't yet broken. So maybe she was in labor, maybe not. I knew there was time. I hadn't eaten dinner because we were busy and there was much paperwork to be done after closing. After hanging up with Georgia, I prepared two sandwiches, ate one and packed the other. I collected my medical bags and called one of my nurses. That's the arrangement. When I'm on a delivery, the nurses cover any emergencies. And then I came."

"What time did you get here?"

"I got lost," Tandy said. "It's very dark up here, and once the pavement ends, so do the streetlights. It took me longer than I expected."

"Did you look at the time when you arrived?"

"Two AM."

"Exactly?" Nicole challenged, knowing she wasn't making a friend in the woman.

"Two-oh-two on the dash clock," Tandy replied.

"And the first thing you noticed?"

"The quiet. It was not natural." She walked toward the perimeter. "You found it, then," she said, and indicated the trailhead, marked with a yellow cone. "I followed, but not nearly as fast and starting much behind her and the others."

"How far behind?"

"I did not see her but knew I had missed her by minutes. The men were running from the house, scrambling over the hill. They were dressed in black and had guns and packs."

"Anything else?"

"Like I told the doctor, the cars. There were two, and neither had a license plate. They were dark. SUVs. But I can't tell you make—all of that was removed, and I've never been good about those things."

"They were in the driveway?"

"Of course not. They were a half mile back, parked at the side of the road, already turned around. There was no one in them."

"You checked?"

"As I passed by, the moon peered from behind the clouds and I could see through the windows. The vehicles were empty."

Nicole considered that and nodded. "So you followed on foot?"

"It was the only way."

Nicole looked over the woman's head to the silver Toyota Tundra parked in the turnout at the side of the road. "Driving would have gotten you to help faster," she said.

"But the trail would be lost. Her fate hopeless."

Nicole wanted to point out that following had done little to change that, but there was nothing to be gained from it other than an expression of her own frustration.

"Is she strong?" Nicole wanted to know.

"To think in a moment of panic?" Tandy asked. "Or to outrun a den of wolves?"

"Either. Both," she hoped.

49

"I think she could push past panic. She was nine months pregnant though. At some point her body would tire, and you can't push past that."

Not even if her life, and the life of her baby, depended on it? Nicole wondered.

"I asked you this before, and I'd appreciate a straight answer—do you track?"

"I know what to look for," Tandy said. "The signs of someone's passing are as clear to me as words written on a page are to others."

And still Tandy Longhorn had lost the woman's trail.

"There's a young man upstairs, dead," Nicole said. "Did you know about that?"

"If I had known, I would have told you."

Nicole pulled her cell phone out of her pocket and brought up the picture of the victim who still lay in the upstairs bedroom. "It's not pretty," she said. "But not as bad as some."

"I have seen worse," Tandy said. "I'm sure of it."

Nicole turned her cell phone for Tandy's viewing. "Is this man Matthew?"

Tandy looked in silence. She stepped closer and took hold of Nicole's hand to tilt the cell for better lighting. She squinted, taking her time.

"There are similarities," she said. "The hair color and cut. The shape of his face. But the father's eyes are blue, and this man had hazel. And Matthew has a scar above his left ear, in his hairline but peeking out at the temple. It's red and thick, not to be missed." She stood tall and shook her head. "No, this man is not the baby's father."

She stepped back, and Nicole pocketed her phone.

"As I told the doctor, the baby's father has a tattoo over his left bicep. *Semper fi*. You could look for that on this man," Tandy suggested.

"The baby's father is a Marine?"

"That's what I saw."

"What else did you tell the doctor?"

Tandy shrugged. "Ask him. I think I've told you about everything, but he is younger and a man for details. He might remember things differently."

Nicole planned to compare notes with MacAulay later.

"I can go now?" Tandy asked.

"I'm sending a sketch artist out, Tandy. For a picture of the girl." And maybe Matthew too.

"I'll be waiting," Tandy said. She climbed into the cab of her truck and shut the door. The powerful engine turned over, and the midwife made a wide U-turn and headed out.

7

Nicole covered her nose and mouth with the tail of her shirt. The window in this upstairs bedroom was closed, the screen kicked out from inside and lying on the peaked roof. The door was narrow and propped open with a rachiotome from MacAulay's bag. Still, there was little movement in the air. The stink of rotting flesh was thick, though Nicole could see little outward evidence of decomposition. MacAulay was talking into his recorder.

"GSW to the head . . . entry at the glabella . . . skin around the wound burned and puckered . . . left pupil blown, indicating a downward trajectory through the frontal cortex, penetrating the skull and severing the optical nerve . . ."

An execution at close range. Likely the muzzle of the gun had been pressed against the man's head.

"How long, Doc?" Lars asked.

"Hours," he said. "Not yet half a day."

So after midnight. A lot of activity in a small window of time. The discovery of the man in ice, the missing BP agents, the running girl, the birth of a baby, and the dead man here.

MacAulay pulled a thermometer from his bag and pushed the dead man's shirt up to expose an area of skin close to his waist. The corpse had fallen forward after the gunshot, head turned toward the window, arms at his side, fingers loosely curled. The body did that as a last physical act, involuntary muscle relaxation. Before that, forced to his knees and kept there, hands clenched in fear and possibly rage, had he looked his killer in the eye? Or had he looked out the window, at the black night, hoping his sacrifice had saved a young, pregnant woman?

MacAulay slid the thermometer into the man's liver for a reading. That, and taking into consideration the current temperature in the room, the degree of gradient as outdoor temperatures dropped during the night and heated up from sunrise on, would give them the best estimate of time of death.

She and Lars heard the pop at the same time and stumbled backward. There wasn't a lot of space in the room—about a hundred square feet filled with a bed and dresser and nightstand. MacAulay grabbed a beaker and held it under the thermometer. He shook his head.

"I've read about this, of course," he said. "Seen it in film."

The liver was a dicey organ. It just as often filled with bile during the end-of-life process as it shuddered to a stop. Sticking it was sometimes like popping a balloon.

Outside she heard the closing of vehicle doors, and from where she stood in the small upstairs bedroom, she watched her forensics techs as they changed out gear and headed toward the house. A few minutes later one of them arrived at the top of the stairs, sidled past the gurney MacAulay had left in the hall, and stopped at the threshold to the bedroom, a tool kit in each hand.

Nicole greeted the tech, Jenner Lee. "Thanks for staying," she said. He was one of the first who had arrived on scene at the lake, and in fact he had been waiting onshore as Nicole pulled the skiff into dock.

"I always appreciate a little overtime," he said. The smile was genuine, if somewhat worn. The night shift in forensics was a skeleton crew consisting of two techs. With a start time of ten PM, Jenner was running at fourteen hours.

"Standing room only," MacAulay said.

Nicole didn't need further invitation. "I have some calls to make." She brushed past Lars but on her way out said to MacAulay, "I understand you and Tandy had a good conversation on your way up."

"We did," he agreed.

"So let's talk before you leave the scene."

"I'll find you," he promised.

Nicole took the stairs quickly, grateful for increased ventilation. In the living room she found the second tech, Molly Sounder, crouched at the window where the screen had been removed. She'd already dusted for prints—the powder was visible from several feet away—and was peeling something from the windowsill with a pair of long tweezers. Nicole stopped and watched.

"What is that?"

"Tread from a boot is my guess," she said. "Seen plenty of it. Thinking military style. There's pattern on this piece." She held it under the light from the window. "So it's a good find. We can get make and model from this, even size."

"All that in something the size of a splinter?"

"That's at least three centimeters in width and a half an inch long." She sealed it in an evidence bag. "So far the most valuable trinket we've recovered here." She smiled at Nicole. "I already casted several prints in the garden bed outside the window. Similar treads, different sizes, and all of them had to plant in order to lift themselves up and into the house. I don't think I've casted better."

"How many men were there?"

"Five. Some of the prints are partials—there was a lot of trampling—but five distinct size and weight combinations in the mix."

"That's good work, Molly," Nicole said. She was never short of impressed when it came to forensics. The more science they had behind an arrest, the better the outcomes. Always.

"Thanks, Sheriff."

Nicole walked into the sunshine and the cool air. Noon and the temperature was a balmy sixty-two degrees. So far north, April often brought them unpredictable weather. She pulled a bottle of water from her Yukon, then closed the door and leaned against it as she typed a few notes into her phone. She'd been up and running eleven hours with only a few hours of sleep before Monte's phone call. Ten hours of high-adrenaline pulls and lows in between. She was tired but doubted she'd see her bed before nine or ten o'clock that night.

The evidence was beginning to accumulate in the county morgue. The original vic was stowed in a freezer compartment, awaiting MacAulay's attention. He had stopped long enough to place the placenta in cold storage, and the body here would soon follow.

MacAulay had mentioned needing blood type and a DNA sample from both inside and outside the placental sac. Both were easy tasks.

The GSW here could be processed with perhaps an hour or two of time. The vic on ice was more complicated. He would need to thaw at room temperature with tissue and fluids collected along the way. She did a quick Google search. Up to twenty-four hours for a corpse to defrost. And the process included a caving in of flesh and other grue-some breakdown.

Lars came out the front door. He had his cell out and stylus in hand. Digital note-taking was the rage. It cut down on paperwork and improved their ability to read case notes when all they needed to do was push print from their cell phones.

"TOD between midnight and three AM," he said.

"Wow, that's good."

"Numbers don't lie," Lars said. "Doc was up there taking temperature readings inside and outside the body, looked up temps through the night and the rate of rise and fall and barometric this or that."

"You're impressed."

"Yeah. You can teach an old horse new tricks."

MacAulay wasn't that old. In fact, he was younger than Nicole by eleven months.

"So right around the time of Monte's call and inside the window for the birth of the child."

"We need to find the young woman," Lars said. "If nothing else, the timing could be helpful."

"She saw or heard something," Nicole said. "Whoever happened to Monte and Baker could have happened to her."

Lars nodded. "MacAulay said Tandy told him she was Middle East-ern, coloring and accent. Possibly Syrian."

"And the vic upstairs looks a lot like the baby's father."

"Both soldier types." Lars made a note in his phone. "I'll put calls through to the closest bases, see if they have any missing persons."

The vic upstairs wore combat boots and a buzz cut. He was fair-haired and pale skinned. Georgia Peach's boyfriend had similar coloring. *Sem-per fi.* There were no Marine bases in Montana, but the state had an Air Force base, an army reserve, and a secreted regiment that was all about missiles and wing captains. But all of it was far away from Blue Mesa. They were hardly a hub of military action. Militia, that was another story.

She was aware of a few factions, calling themselves by various names, who gathered in the name of patriotism.

"Yeah, do that. And contact USMC, see if they will provide a list of servicemen with connections to Blue Mesa."

"Now you're asking for gold from a silver mine."

True. The military was tight with information, classified or not. They might help with an ID if they had a body, but not if a soldier was in the wind. "Ask MacAulay to examine the body for tattoos first thing."

Lars nodded and made a note of it. "We checked for dog tags when we rolled him. Nothing."

"There's been talk of an organized movement," Nicole began. "All under the radar. Supporters of refugees who provide them with a place to stay, a meal, clothing, even medical attention."

"That 'underground railroad,' " Lars agreed. "I've heard whispers of it."

It had been strictly a BP concern up until that moment, and Nicole and her department hadn't received a briefing on any of it. It was a question for Green, their division chief, when she saw him next.

"I can see Tandy doing that. Providing medical care," Nicole continued. "I mean, it's not like she let something as small as a name bother her."

And there was no telling how many she was helping, not that Nicole was particularly concerned about the numbers. But if the young woman they were seeking was Syrian and Tandy had information that led to family connections, finding her would not be nearly as impossible as it seemed. Nicole would have to take another pass at the woman.

"You get a look at the DOA on ice?" Nicole asked.

Lars nodded. "That was something."

Terror, stark and thick enough to slice.

"Nationality?"

"Could be Syrian," Lars said.

"I thought so too. It fits the activity we've seen around the lake."

"Shadows against the backdrop of night," Lars said. "There are homes in our jurisdiction providing help."

"Yeah, but which?" Last Nicole had heard, BP hadn't gotten close to identifying known sympathizers. "We'll circulate his likeness," she said. Not a picture but a police sketch. Anything else would be frightening.

"No missing-person reports that come close to matching the guy."

Of course not. UDAs couldn't take the risk of reporting a missing loved one. "MacAulay says he couldn't have been killed before Thanksgiving week, when we had that three-day stretch of temps in the teens. The human body needs that long and that cold to deep freeze."

"Five months."

Or less, but missing for how long on top of that?

"Female is possibly underage," she said. "Tandy didn't say for sure, but that's the feel."

"An illegal crossing," Lars began, "draws BP out on the lake. They make no mention of contact with the UDAs in their base reports, so they lost that thread but stumble on the dead guy in the ice. That's a weird one. It's not like they were following a treasure map. What drew them to that particular spot?"

"They've been looking for the ice man for weeks," Nicole said. "Maybe last night Monte was lucky."

"Before you arrive—what was it, thirty-five, forty minutes from the time you hang up with Monte until Ty is loading the boat down the slip?"

He scrolled through his notes, but Nicole knew the answer.

"Thirty-eight minutes from call to scene," she said.

"Another twenty minutes before contact is made with the BP skiff. It's not such a small window of time," Lars said. "But add the party barge, a pregnant girl, and the guy upstairs, and the night is standing room only."

"Tandy said she saw the party boat sweeping the lake."

Lars raised an eyebrow. "Really?"

"She was still uphill then and had good visual. She heard the voices of men raised in argument and then saw the bigger boat searching the water."

"Man overboard," Lars said.

"At least one," Nicole agreed. "And there was time for that. Time for whoever was aboard to search, to make shore, and for the current to pull the party boat back toward the center of the lake."

"The lake is the common denominator," Lars said.

Nicole looked past the house, past the marker indicating where the woman had entered the foliage. The earth sloped sharply and beyond it lay the lake, a clear and glistening blue. The woman had run for cover and kept on running. She had run to the lake, where the homes were grouped more closely together. The way was rough, some parts impassable. But she had deemed the road an impossibility. Within a mile either way were homes and help. Why not duck into cover alongside the road and maintain a parallel passage? For a young woman, nine months pregnant and on the edge of delivery, certainly that would have been the best option.

Unless she was running scared, unable to think through her actions.

Or if she was an undocumented alien and couldn't risk exposure.

Or . . . maybe the escape was planned, a strategy worked out in advance.

Because she'd known she would be hunted.

Yes, that made sense. The lake drew her, because help was waiting somewhere along its shores.

"She's a UDA," Nicole said. "She couldn't just run to any neighbor for help."

"Explains the phony name, the medical care off the grid," Lars agreed.

Nicole walked around the hood of her Yukon and closer to the perimeter. She took sight of the window where, inside, a young man lay dead. The woman had come from that bedroom. She had slid down the roof until she made the eaves and then hung from the piping. The rain gutter peeled away from the trim and the woman landed at the side of the house, in a soft bed of newly turned soil. A tech had cast her prints—a pair of sneakers, size six. Then the woman ran to the trees. Not in a straight line, which would be expected for someone whose mind was filled with terror and clicked into survival mode. The entry was twenty yards southwest, and Nicole wouldn't be surprised to find that it offered the best accessibility.

"She knew she would have to run," Nicole said. "She had an escape route already mapped out."

Nicole moved closer, off the gravel and into the grass. She skirted the woman's trajectory, stayed well beyond her path. But she could see her—medium build, Tandy had said, strong—arms pumping as she closed the distance and then ducked into the dense foliage.

"Why do you think so?" Lars followed, his gaze measuring the woman's progress from eave to trailhead, and he got it. "Not a straight line. Not a frantic pattern of flight." He nodded. "She knew."

"And she had a plan." Nicole wondered what else the woman had set up in advance to save her life. "Why the lake?"

"Someone was waiting there for her," Lars said.

"Yes, or if not waiting, willing," Nicole agreed.

"We assume she knew what she was doing, where she was going," Lars said.

"Agreed. And that she was well on her way to her place of safety when she gave birth."

"We assume she made it, and we start knocking on doors."

"We're stretched thin. I have every available man looking for Monte and Baker." Nicole thought for a moment, mentally moving deputies across the board. "We'll go separately. You and me and a third—I'll pull one deputy."

"Three of us for seven miles of waterfront property." Lars didn't like the progress notes likely to come of that. She could see it as his eyebrows pulled together over his nose. "And that's the first wave. If she crossed the Lake Road and moved into the developments there, we've doubled our field."

"They're connected," Nicole said, because while coincidences certainly existed, they didn't apply to crime. "The proximity and time overlap . . . Monte, the pregnant girl, the murder here. Something went very wrong last night, and she's the only live thread to grasp and follow at the moment."

"If she's still alive," Lars said.

8

"He's a beautiful baby."

"Yes."

He had her dark hair but Matthew's chin, strong and dimpled, and a mouth ready to smile. She lifted the flannel blanket so that it covered his neck and kept the draft from his ears. Then she turned away from the woman, but not before she noticed the way age weighed heavily on her shoulders. Her face was sharp, from her hooked nose to her narrow eyes.

Some women were like that, Adelai reminded herself. She had lived with a mother hewn by her father's hands into a wooden idol.

"Come put the baby down," the woman said, and indicated a cushion she had taken from the sofa and placed on the floor. "He will be safe here."

But Adelai shook her head. "He is happiest when I'm holding him."

She had learned so much about him in so few hours. Not just the shape of his toes and the quiet, watchful way he had, but his preferences. When she offered her finger, tucking it into his palm, he held it tightly. When she spoke his name, he turned to her, his eyes open and inquiring. He woke up the same way. He'd had three naps since his birthing that morning, and each time he had shaken sleep from his body quickly and regarded her with a *let's go* expectancy.

"You have to put him down sometime," the woman chided. And Adelai knew it was true. Her mind and body craved sleep. But not here. Not now. Not today.

She knew that, to this woman, she was the door prize. Adelai had learned that expression from Matthew when he'd described those in the area who were friendly to immigrants. Lois and Eli Embry in particular. They were powerful, retired attorneys. They could make things happen for Adelai. They were big on advocating and on drawing all the attention they could to their altruistic handouts.

But the woman was always close. And she had a way of making a request bear down on a person like a demand. There was a struggle of power here, and it was making Adelai weary.

She wished Matthew would come. Knew it wasn't possible. That would never happen again. He had saved her twice now. It was her turn. She would save their baby and she would do whatever that took.

Don't look over your shoulder, Adelai . . . Matthew had warned her about regret, about remorse. One was self-indulgent and the other a luxury. There was no time for either.

Little Matthew cried, his voice already strong. He batted his hand against the blanket. It was time for a feeding.

"I will get him some air," Adelai said.

"You can't go outside."

"Of course we can. Just in the backyard. No one will see us there." There were trees and blueberry brambles just beginning to bud. There were new leaves, as wide as her hands, and the dock and the lake were down a long and rugged path. It would not be easy to find them.

"Adelai, you need rest. Put the baby down. Sleep."

She was moving toward the back door. The day had warmed and the windows were open. "We're going outside, Lois. Just on the back porch." She opened the door and slipped through it. "Just to sit in this chair," she called over her shoulder. "Surely that's okay."

And Adelai did exactly that.

She had found help and she wasn't necessarily caught, but trembled just the same in that outstretched hand.

*   *   *

Nicole returned to the lake, not to join the search for the missing BP agents but for an update on its progress and to let Larry Green know firsthand about the pregnant girl, the birth, and the man executed in the young woman's home. It was one thirty in the afternoon and they were ten hours into an all-hands.

"And you think this is connected to my missing agents?" Green's voice was rough from the cold and the long hours on or near the water. From lack of sleep, from the encroaching thought of loss. Two agents missing, possibly perished. A nightmare for the division chief. For any leader.

She had spoken briefly to MacAulay on her way over and had narrowed their timeline. She gave it to Green, then said, "It's tight. That's a lot going on at the same time within a few miles of each other."

Green nodded. "Yeah. It's not like this is New York or LA." Where crime populated the streets and was crammed into every minute.

"What are you going to do now?"

"I'm going to take a deputy—" No CO wanted to hear that, a thinning of the forces at ground level. "He'll join me and Lars for a door-to-door along the Lake Road."

He was nodding. "I understand that. Really, I do," Green said. "But that's a lot of houses. And the girl, how could she even be involved?"

"Just the northern rim," Nicole said. "We think it's worth the time and manpower. Finding the young woman could be key to opening this case."

"I don't see it," Green said. "What could she do for us?"

"If she saw something," Nicole said. "The timing—"

"Could be off," Green insisted.

"I don't think so. We have a witness who observed two boats on the lake. And she was just a little behind in time from the young woman."

"What do you mean, a witness?" he demanded. "Who? And where is this person now?"

Nicole ignored Green's demands. Truth was, the sheriff's department would be taking over the lead in this case and probably should have done so already. She was treading a slippery slope, respecting the feelings of an outside agency, needing their skills and efforts, but protocol and good policing would soon demand that she relieve Green. And he knew it.

"We're doing this," she said. "Any information we gain from it, we'll let you know."

"Yeah?" he challenged. His voice was loud and belligerent, and it raised the hairs on her neck. "Like you're letting me know about this witness?"

Nicole took a step closer to Green. "Rein it in," she told him, keeping her voice deliberately calm. "You're running low on sleep and high on adrenaline." Not to mention mounting desperation. "Get a grip and loan me one of your agents," she decided. That would make it four officers canvassing the lakefront.

Green held her gaze, and Nicole watched the fight drain from his eyes. He inhaled deeply, and the tension in his shoulders loosened. "Okay," he said. "Fine. One agent."

He lifted his head and scanned the crew assembled along the edge of the lake. Nicole did the same. Some were searching the shore for possible evidence washed up by the current. Others were photographing with long lenses and video equipment. A team was mapping out the terrain that spread from shore to woods and beyond, and agents were being given grids to search in an organized pattern that would leave no stone unturned. But there was a lot more land than officers and little time to fill the gaps.

His attention turned to the water, where seven small craft—several rented from local shops—were attending to drags and sweeps and trolling the shoreline while officers used high-powered binoculars to peel between the layers of foliage. It was a big operation focused on three areas of pursuit: water, shoreline, and a quarter mile of inland.

"Take one from the Highway Patrol too. Make it a united front," he said.

Nicole nodded. "We're working on a sketch." She looked at her watch. She had called in the request only an hour before. "For now, we're going with a physical description."

"I know. Coloring, weight, and height. I heard it come across the wires. Didn't know it would become a part of our investigation." His lips peeled back with disapproval, but he pushed through it. "Of course, she has a baby with her. Nothing like a newborn's cry. People will remember her."

"You're right about that." Whether drawn by the cute factor or repelled by the noise level, people remembered babies better than they did humans of any other size.

"There's something I should tell you," Green said. "I'm not wanting it public knowledge yet. Maybe not ever, because maybe there's nothing to this," he cautioned.

Nicole's radar went on alert.

"Monte and Melody," he began. "Agent Baker. They're good agents, both of them. I've known Monte going on sixteen years. Melody was assigned to the Canadian border eleven months ago. I have no reason to wonder about Monte's integrity. Very little reason to question Baker's."

"But . . . ?"

"There's talk in-house. Whisperings, you know how it is," he began.

"Gossip?"

He shrugged. "Suggesting a closeness that went beyond a partnership. More times than not it's bullshit. And there are a lot of years between them, so I thought maybe it was a mentoring thing. Still, I took a look. Nothing official. Just went out of my way to observe them, in and out of the office." He shrugged. "There seemed to be an intimacy there."

"You think they may have been romantically involved?"

"I'm saying it's possible." He was quiet a moment, a heaviness building in the air as he considered the matter. "You know Monte lost his wife a few years ago. A terrible car crash involving a semi. His kids are grown, out of college already and living across the country. I'm saying if it's true, we can trace it back to loss, loneliness, that kind of thing, on Monte's part. Melody's a big girl. Thirty-three years old, divorced, no familial attachments."

"So if it's true, and it's possible, loneliness could have brought them together?"

"Yeah."

"And then what would have happened?"

"Reassignment," Green said. "And that's no easy thing. It's not a matter of separating them by shifts. It would be moving one to another office. Current possibilities would mean transferring Melody to our Arizona station or keeping her on the Canadian border but placing her in Baileyville, Maine."

Both more than a thousand miles from Blue Mesa.

"And how do you see this impacting our current investigation?"

"I don't. I'm mentioning it because it could be a factor."

"Because they're missing together?" It didn't add up. Not yet. "What else?" she asked. "If they wanted out, all they had to do was leave their badges on their desks and walk." That made sense. "What aren't you tell-ing me?"

He hesitated, and Nicole waited. "In the essence of full disclosure," he began, and paused to trouble over his next words.

"Just spit it out, Green." She could hear the clock ticking over her shoulder, and it made her voice impatient.

"About a year ago some evidence went missing. Nothing big, but enough to reduce a case to a misdemeanor. There was no break in the chain of evidence, but it had been transported from our office to Bill-ings and from Billings to the crime lab in San Diego. We needed the SEM—scanning electron microscope—and we have only a few of those per region. There was a lot of finger-pointing between departments but no real suspicion cast our way."

"But it happened again?"

He nodded. "Twice. The evidence lost"—he shook his head and whis-tled thinly between his teeth—"millions in both money and drugs."

"And the missing evidence changed the direction in court?"

He nodded. "One case was thrown out. Another was dropped from attempted murder to possession. A difference in twenty years to life."

Nicole found it hard to swallow and knew Green must have choked on it.

"But I want to make sure you know there's no reason to suspect Baker. No reason at all. Melody worked only one of those cases and wasn't even assigned to Blue Mesa for the first loss." He paused. "And Monte—" He shook his head. "I just don't see it in him."

But betrayals were the bee's stinger. They welted. Spread. Caused an entire department to itch. And they hurt.

"That they've both vanished, from the same boat, at the same time . . . two trained agents? No exchange of gunfire? It must have been a hell of an ambush." His words rang with doubt.

"Could be one turned against the other," Nicole offered. Love gone wrong. It wouldn't be the first time. "We've been on the lake going on eleven hours. Soon we'll have to change the direction of the investigation."

From rescue to recovery. From victims to perpetrators.

A tow truck, king-sized and usually reserved for pulling semis from off-road mishaps, pulled in ahead of the slip and stopped. Its diesel engine idled, huffing and puffing, and on its bed was the salvage boat that would pull the BP skiff from the bottom of Lake Maria.

Green followed Nicole's gaze and said, "I'm hoping there's something you missed and as soon as we raise our crime scene from the deep we'll see it."

Before he could turn away and start organizing the salvage, Nicole stopped him. "How do you want me to proceed?" she asked. "Given the possibilities you revealed."

"Quietly."

"That's a given," Nicole assured him. "But you told me for a reason. Do you want me to look into it?"

"I want you to keep it in mind."

"I'll have to do more than that," she said. "Soon."

"You're talking about taking over the investigation?"

"You know it's going to come to that, especially in light of the information you just shared."

"It wasn't information, it was conjecture."

"Not the missing evidence," Nicole said. "That's fact. There's something amiss in your department."

He nodded, and his mouth drew into a thin, flat line. "You think we aren't already crawling with Internal Affairs? They've had us under the microscope for months. I haven't taken a piss by myself since December."

"Fair enough." For now. "What about the party barge?" Nicole had ordered it towed back to the lab. Forensics needed to comb through it for any possibility of DNA. Nowadays the samples could be microscopic and still draw a hit.

"We used a department trailer," he said. "It left about twenty minutes ago."

"My lab or yours?"

"Mine, of course," he said. "Your guys processed it, afloat and after we had it on dry land. The rest is ours."

That didn't sit well with Nicole. Someone in BP had something to hide. And she was coming to believe that whoever it was, they were willing to kill in order to remain in the shadows.

"You don't like that," he said, and his lip curled with derision.

"You wouldn't either."

"Given similar circumstances," he agreed reluctantly.

"Make the call," she said. "Redirect that party boat to my forensics lab."

She thought he would refuse. It was written all over his face, a stubbornness that went inches deep. And if he did, Nicole would have to exercise her command. She would have to take over the investigation, here and now, call in the FBI or the Department of Homeland Security to assist—she wasn't sure which agency kept BP on the burner but would now make it her business to find out.

"So be it," he said. "I'll redirect." He called in the order while Nicole waited. "The tags on the party barge were stripped, but we have the serial number."

"And ownership?"

"Still waiting on that. Going through DMV and the manufacturer. Seeing who can get back to us first. Definitely not a rental, though."

Even with their instant connect, without a tag number it could take the DMV hours to sift through the digital paperwork on recreational vehicles.

Green called over an agent, a woman younger than Nicole and dressed in jeans, tennis shoes, and a hoodie. Her badge was on a chain she wore around her neck. The casual look, even her gender, would put people at ease. Green explained her reassignment to the canvassing of the lake homes, and she stepped forward, offering Nicole her hand.

"Agent Leigh Calder," she said.

Nicole shook her hand. "We're going solo, more ground covered that way."

The agent nodded, and Nicole allowed her to gather her things before meeting at the Yukon.

"When they raise your skiff," she told Green, "it's mine. It goes directly to our forensics impound."

"Bullsh—"

But Nicole shook her head. "One way or another, a crime has occurred out here. That's my jurisdiction."

"We could argue that."

"Not successfully. As we stand, here and now, it's me and you—" But it wouldn't stay that way. There was protocol to follow, and she hoped someone within BP, bigger than Green, had already made the necessary calls. "You want me to change that, say the word."

Her words were as good as drawing a line in the sand. They both knew that. Green's eyes flared at the challenge, but she stood her ground no problem. She could probably bend steel with her gaze. "You know as well as I do," she said, "when rescue turns to recovery, the sheriff's department becomes the leader of the pack."

They faced off like that for a good twenty seconds before Green conceded. "I know regulations."

"Then abide by them."

Nicole walked away. She needed a word with Ty before they left to canvass the lake homes. With Lars accompanying her, Ty and Arthur Sleeping Bear would have to hold things down on this end. Ty was a natural choice, already steeped as he was in the investigation. But he also had specific water and land skills that placed him above others. He knew the look of currents and what they meant, the feel and shape of land formations and what it took to scale them. She found Ty working his way through a grid search just inside the wooded copse. She explained the circumstances, the canvass, and made sure he knew their department was top dog.

"You comfortable getting into it with BP?"

"I'll go rabid if I need to."

Nicole smiled. "Arthur knows to keep chain of evidence on our side. You may need to help him with that."

"No problem," he assured her.

She nodded. "How you holding up?"

Ty's gaze was unwavering and the circles under his eyes minimal, and for a moment Nicole allowed herself a flare of envy for the resilience of youth. She was beginning to fray around the edges from lack of sleep.

"You know I'm good," he said.

"I know you've been up around the clock," she returned. "And I need you at your best." She glanced at her watch. "I should be back by five. I want you to go home then and sleep. Plan to be back here at seven AM tomorrow."

"I'm on patrol shift tomorrow."

But Nicole shook her head. "Not anymore. Not for the duration of this investigation."

He smiled big. He was exactly where he wanted to be, and if they had the budget for it, it was where he would stay.

"You've got a friend in me." His voice lifted with the tune, and Nicole smiled.

"Keep me happy, friend," she said, and walked off to pull a deputy who would join them for the door-to-door canvass.

9

There were more than two hundred houses, including cabins and vacation rentals, along the Lake Road. Nicole had arrived with Agent Calder five minutes before. Lars was already there and they were waiting on her deputy, who had stopped at Montana Highway Patrol to pick up an extra hand. The strength of the afternoon sun was waning as it moved ever westward. They had less than six hours of daylight left. Enough to finish the job.

She had called MacAulay to check on him. "You get anymore sleep?"

"I'm going to take a nap right now," he'd promised.

"Try to get a little more than that," she suggested.

"No can do," he said. "I have fluids to collect from the ice man at five thirty."

"After that," she said. "It's back to bed." She needed a ME who was well, who could tackle the bodies collecting in his morgue.

"Meet you at midnight?" he said, and she could tell the NyQuil was already kicking in—MacAulay was a lightweight when it came to antihistamines and was a little loopy. "A romantic rendezvous, bedside of DOA number one."

Nicole chuckled. "I like you like this, MacAulay."

"Will you ever call me by my first name?" he asked.

"Do you have one?"

Of course he did. It was unforgettable. Morrison. Named after the front man of the Doors. Nicole had a hard time reconciling the two. MacAulay was responsible, steady, even predictable, and Jim Morrison had been anything but.

"You know," MacAulay continued, "they never did an autopsy on him. Shame, really. His COD forever a mystery."

"I thought it was a drug overdose," Nicole said.

"Yes, maybe. But we'll never really know. Not for certain. And did he die in his bathtub, or was he moved there? Was it heroin? Was the drug tainted? Who was with him? He was a man who did not like to be alone . . ." His voice drifted. "So many stories told about his last day, the characters and plot changing . . ." He yawned and exhaled heavily. "I was born on the twelfth anniversary of his death, did you know that?"

"You mentioned it," she said.

"Hard to live up to a reputation like that."

And Nicole burst out laughing. "You're good for me, MacAulay."

"Well, in that regard, at least, I am succeeding. My namesake was known to please the ladies."

Nicole heard herself laugh with the memory, and that pulled Lars's attention toward her.

He raised an eyebrow. "You sharing?" he asked.

Nicole felt her face warm and hated the reaction. She wanted to lower her chin and hide behind—*anything*—but wouldn't allow herself. She met Lars's gaze and said, "You probably wouldn't find the humor in it."

"One of those relationship funnies," Calder said.

Lars didn't know about Nicole's romance with the ME. No one did at this point, except Jordan. While there was no code against such a relationship, she was an elected official and constantly aware of her vulnerability in that position. She was wrestling with the how and when to come out with the news, which was progress. Until a week ago, she'd refused to believe that it would ever come to that kind of permanency.

"Let's talk bodies," Nicole suggested. "Because that's the best of what we have." That and the party barge, which didn't fit the rest of the tangle. *One of these things just doesn't belong . . .* and yet it was there, a piece of the puzzle.

"How's Doc going to do the autopsies?" Lars asked.

"Divide and conquer," Nicole said. "He already removed samples from the placenta and sent them to the lab in Billings. He won't go back to that until the autopsies are completed. First up is the GSW."

"Straightforward. That'll take a couple of hours."

"He completed prelim on the vic already"—and the body had been free of tattoos and other deliberate blemishes—"but he wants to compare tissue from the body to the DNA in the placenta."

"Establishing a connection, if there is one."

"Tandy's was a slow no," Nicole said. The midwife had taken her time about it. "She pointed out similarities, and I think it's worth a closer look." Perhaps a familial connection between the baby's father and the DOA. "The man from the lake requires special handling," she continued. "A slow melt while evidence is collected through the process."

"Does he have the equipment here to do it?"

"He says yes. What he needs is an assistant."

"Agreed."

"He's reaching out to universities, hoping to get an intern or two."

"Good thinking," Calder said. "Cheap labor in return for experience."

"But it will take time," Lars said.

Nicole placed another look at the budget on her mental to-do list. Living quarters and a stipend; how much could that run? And the county would be lucky to get such an arrangement.

Her deputy drove up then, the MHP officer riding shotgun. Nicole had already divided up territory, and they stood in a circle around the map. She and Lars would take the older neighborhood, the houses with lake access. She was sending the others into the McMansions set farther back in the hills.

"Three hours," Nicole said. They couldn't afford any more time than that. "If you get a hit, alert the rest of us."

*   *   *

Nicole rolled her shirt sleeves up, but that gave her little comfort. She'd shed her jacket and changed from her boots to sneakers earlier, pulling from a store of clothing she kept in a box in the back of the Yukon. Still, sweat gathered at her hairline and curled around her ears. She was approaching her thirty-seventh house and spoke the address into her smartphone as she kept the list going. She had made anecdotal notes along the way as well, indicating the homes where there had been no answer and homes that had sheds and barns where a woman on the run could have taken refuge. For each of those, she had accompanied the owner to take a look inside. So far, nothing. Twenty minutes before, Ty had called. The BP skiff was on the trailer and on its way to forensics. They had gotten lucky there. The boat had settled on a sandbar some twenty feet below the surface of the lake. Divers had used inflatable scaffolding to lift the skiff and tow it to shore. Green had crowed about wanting possession but caved fairly quickly. Ty had been prepared to climb aboard and stake a physical claim and had seemed a little disappointed that it hadn't been necessary.

Nicole pocketed her phone and walked up the gravel driveway. There was a truck parked in front of the garage and a small compact beside that. The garage was detached, with a bank of dusty windows that reflected rather than allowed a peek inside. She walked past it and up the paved sidewalk to the front door.

There was no answer to her knock. She waited a long moment, gazing at the front of the house. It was well kept, with new paint on the siding, a pale gray, and black shutters at the windows. Someone had begun spring gardening, turning over the soil in the beds and clearing them of weeds. The windows were open and the breeze stirred the curtains. The mail hadn't been collected. A grocery ad and several white envelopes stuck out the top of the box. They'd used block letters on gold stickers to place their name, EMBRY, on the lid. It wasn't yet four o'clock, and possible the owner was at work. She tried again, rapping hard on the solid wood door. When there was no answer, Nicole turned and walked over the pavers, stopping at the driveway. She opened her phone to make a note—someone would have to come back later—when she heard a soft female voice tangled in the breeze. Singing. Crooning almost, and in a language she didn't recognize. She heard wind chimes too, a soft clattering of shells maybe, and beyond that, perhaps the mewing of a kitten. Only that wasn't quite right. It wasn't the cry of a baby, although Nicole's mind played with the possibility. A newborn's cry was distinctive but not feral.

She followed the noise to the back of the house.

A long expanse of yard, a wide porch with deck chairs, blueberry brambles framing a worn path to the lake. This was prime real estate, with pocket views of the water, and beyond that, some ninety miles distant, the Glaciers, still heavily dusted with snow.

A rack with several kayaks was set up under the shade of a lodgepole pine. Beside it, an older man stood with his back to Nicole. He had a manual tree trimmer in hand and was leaning against the five-foot pole. Several cut limbs littered the grass. She noticed a phone's docking station and speakers on the patio table. The song that had caught her attention emanated from it and was winding to a close.

"Hello," she called.

There were twenty yards between them, but he heard her fine and turned, startled. The trimmer fell from his hand. He bent to pick it up as Nicole walked toward him.

"Sheriff Cobain, Mr. Embry," she said. "We're going house-to-house."

He was upwards of sixty, with silver hair trimmed close and a compact stature that moved fluidly. He met her about halfway. "What for?"

"Looking for a young woman and a newborn baby."

He took out a handkerchief and wiped his brow. "What's wrong with them?"

"Mostly, this is a wellness check," Nicole said.

"Sometimes you hear of a stolen baby."

"Not the case here," Nicole assured him. "But needing medical attention." And protection. But from what? Were the intruders after her traffickers? Or something else entirely? "And we'd like to ask her a few questions."

"Is this about the missing agents?"

"There could be a connection." She nodded toward the path. "That lead to a dock?"

"Yes. We don't put in as often. More when the grandkids come."

"Do you own a party barge, Mr. Embry?"

He shook his head. "Been a long time since we had one of those."

"Have you noticed any unusual activity on the lake? Anything amiss?"

"Nothing yet," he said. "I've heard they're coming. Immigrants. Mostly from Syria and Sudan. Can't say I blame them."

Nicole nodded. "It's a long walk from here to the border. And dangerous."

"About seven miles, if you can make the climb, get through the brush."

"I suspect a lot of them can't," she said.

He held her gaze and nodded.

"The missing agents," he said. "You're thinking illegals are involved?"

"I think several passed through during the night and the agents were following."

Passing over Lake Maria cut down on time and visibility. Walking the road around the lake, even in the shadows of the trees, added two or more hours, exposure to the elements, and greater chance of discovery.

"Even after last week's drowning?"

"Even then." Freedom was worth the risk. Behind them, many undocumented aliens left death and sometimes worse.

"The woman you're looking for, is she an illegal?"

"We don't know." She gave him the description, the dark hair and build, and told him the baby was a boy named Matthew.

But he shook his head. "Haven't seen them, but I haven't been out of my yard yet today."

"You've been busy," she said, nodding toward the garden beds. The ones back here had been tended to as well. "You do the yard work yourself?"

"Most of it. Hire out twice a year to have the trees and bushes around the perimeter and lake path trimmed." He planted his hands on his hips and looked up at the house. "Just finished up the painting last week. I hired someone to do the sanding; that's the hardest part. Didn't care for the reach"—he nodded toward the peaked roof—"but I got a fresh coat on. Figure it'll be the last time I have to do it."

"Mrs. Embry inside?"

"No. She's on a run into town. Grocery shopping and the like."

"Mind if I go down to the dock?"

"Help yourself," he said. "Okay if I stay up here? I was just about to take a break."

"No problem."

"You come back up, I'll have iced tea on the table."

"Thank you, Mr. Embry, but I've got to move on. A lot of houses along the lake."

She moved toward the path but stopped and asked, "You have any animals, Mr. Embry?"

"No. Our retriever passed a few years ago, and we haven't had the heart for another just yet."

"Thought I heard some kittens," she said.

"There are a few of those around," he said. "Hear them myself sometimes, out in the woods. Feral cats, they come into the yard, rumble around down by the lake too."

She nodded. Another song was playing, a throaty torch piece accompanied by piano and guitar.

"What language is that, Mr. Embry?"

"Arabic," he said. "That's Verdi's *Aida*. Goes all the way back to 1871."

"Doesn't sound like opera." Which Nicole thought was more booming than crooning.

"This is a modern version of Verdi," he said. "I like it better than the classical."

"You have an interest in the culture?"

"I lived in Cairo as a young man," he said.

The voice rose dramatically but was deep rather than soprano. "It's beautiful," she said.

"Yes," he agreed. "Calming, and powerful, and many things."

She turned and headed toward the dock.

The path was hard-packed dirt, pale from use and the recent freeze. It was wide enough to fit two shoulder to shoulder, and dense foliage grew beside it. The leaves were full and vibrant shades of green with silver underbellies. Deciduous mixed with evergreen, the sudden, golden-tipped tamarack among the saskatoon, their white blooms just emerging. Spring was new. By summer, passersby would feel crowded by the growth, and Nicole could see why Embry had the way cut back. There was no fence line.

The path sloped and curved, gradually so that it could go unnoticed. The way back would be easy. At an eighth of a mile the trees parted to a swath of brambles, and Nicole could see the black teardrops that were forming into berries. And just beyond that the lake. There was very little shore here, and what was exposed was strewn with rock and detritus. A tree closest to the water had broken at the knees and fallen into the lake, its branches perpendicular to the sky. The dock was sturdy, weathered to a shiny gray. Two brilliant orange cones topped the pylons—not unusual, if you expected company.

Nicole walked to the end of it. The lake moved beneath her and slapped the boards. The water was dark, and the closest floe was a football field away—enough free flow a boat could have idled up and dropped off or picked up passengers, legal or otherwise. A maneuver that could have been quickly executed, given the position of the dock and the clear water.

Problem was, most of the private docks along the lake offered the same opportunity. She turned and looked toward shore. In this older section, the houses were situated on acre plots, sometimes densely wooded. She saw roof peaks and boat houses. Next door, a Quest was moored and bobbing on the current. A little early for sailboats to put in, but not outside reason. There were few craft active on the water now, and the scene of investigation was too far southeast of where she stood to glimpse any of it. As far as she could tell, nothing here was amiss.

She turned and left the dock. The path was an easy climb, as expected. She was almost back to the house when she heard it again. The mewling of a cat. It was soft, as far as complaints went, and distant. Feral cats were not uncommon, and spring was a birthing season. Still, the sound struck a chord with her. Not quite the cry of a baby, was it? But there was none of the predatory curl at the end of the cry, the way it scratched at the air, sharp and insistent with wild cats. She quickened her steps, rounded the curve, and the house with the new gray paint came into view. Mr. Embry sat on the back porch, iced tea in hand. Not at all moved, as she was, by the cries.

Nicole approached him and asked, "Did you hear that, Mr. Embry?"

"The cats?" he asked.

"A newborn has a particular cry," Nicole told him.

"I know it," he said. "I have three sons. All grown, of course. But I walked each of them through the darkest hours of night."

"That's the cry of a newborn," she asserted.

"In the woods?" he said.

"Are you hiding a woman and child, Mr. Embry?"

The cry grew louder, changed so that it sounded like a shriek. Embry nodded toward the woods, and Nicole turned. Kittens, mottled in color, tumbled out of the tree line and onto the plush grass. There were three of them, but only one was raising its voice in a yowl.

"They sound like a baby, don't they?" he said. He lifted a hand toward the pitcher of tea and an empty glass he had placed on the table. "If you can sit for a while, Sheriff."

Her gaze returned to the kittens wrestling in the grass, pouncing on each other and nipping at a neck or a tail. It did not feel right. And yet, beyond the kittens, the air was silent. She turned back to the house. The music continued to play, but he had turned it down, and behind him the curtains shifted with the breeze. There was a hushed quiet. She shook her head. "Not today, Mr. Embry. But I'll be back."

She turned then to leave, but thought better of it.

"The cones you have on the dock—are you expecting company?"

"This weekend," he said. "The reason we've been sprucing up. My youngest and his crew will be coming. I expect we'll be using the kayaks plenty, and maybe we'll get lucky."

"Oh?"

"Yeah. Weather's supposed to be almost tropical."

Plenty of melt, and Nicole wondered what else might float to the surface.

10

The house was small, with a screened porch out back and a path that led downhill toward the lake. Lars had looked in the garage windows as he passed them. A blue pickup truck with a custom back-windshield decal of Old Glory, her stripes waving, was parked inside. There were tools hanging on the walls, a sit-on lawn mower, and several bikes, two of which belonged to kids. But the house was quiet. There hadn't been an answer to his knocking and the windows there were covered in curtains. The screened porch contained a mud area for shoes, and he'd noticed two pairs of men's boots on the mat. There was a long picnic table covered in a plastic cloth with a snowflake motif, but no dishes. He thought about following the path to the lake. They were short on time, but if he located the owner at the dock, then a return visit could probably be eliminated.

The hinges on the back door were oiled but still gave a soft squeak. Lars turned toward the sound. A man had emerged from the house. He wore a Border Patrol uniform and firearm, was tall and about his own age.

Lars walked toward him, meeting the man at half point, some twenty feet from the patio door. "You're on the job," he said.

"I am. What are you doing here?"

"Door-to-door," Lars said. "What's your name?"

"Luke Franks, field agent, BP."

Lars had never heard the name, but he recognized the face. They had never met formally but perhaps come across each other as a matter of overlapping jurisdiction somewhere in the past. Frank's face was stern, his lips pressed tightly over any words that managed to escape.

The man radiated a lot of tension.

"You've been in touch with command?" Lars asked. "You know why we're out looking?"

"A woman and child," the agent said.

"A baby," Lars said. "Newborn. The woman is young, eighteen, if that."

"And you think they might be here?"

"We think they might be somewhere along the lake."

"So, alive?" Franks said, and Lars noticed a subtle shift in the man's shoulders, a loosening of his facial features. Relief or something close to it. "You wouldn't be looking at houses; you'd be looking at wash-up otherwise."

"We hope so."

"And you didn't come here special?" The man pushed his cap back on his head. "You weren't sent to roust me?"

"Sent by whom?"

"My boss, maybe."

"I don't work for BP."

He considered that. "No, you don't. Where's Cobain?"

But Lars ignored the question. "You leaving for shift or just coming back?"

"Leaving."

"You work yesterday?"

"I've been out sick."

"Yeah? How long?"

"I've seen you before," the agent said. "You and Cobain."

"That's not unusual."

"I'm wondering where she is now."

"Why?"

"There's been nothing on the news about a change in lead."

"You worried she's going to take over?"

"I'm hoping she will."

Franks had a problem with Green, that much was clear.

"Why's that?"

From inside came a low thud, not footsteps but maybe an object fallen to the floor. Lars turned his head and surveyed the windows, but neither curtain fluttered; there was no movement behind the sliding door. The screened patio was empty.

"You home alone?"

"Never. That's our retired German shepherd, Roxy."

Retired as in a former working member of the BP.

"Our?"

"My wife teaches at the elementary school."

"The same one your kids attend?"

"That's right. How do you know that?"

"Two bikes in the garage—purple and pink, baskets and bells."

He nodded. "My daughters. Third and fifth grades."

"They're not home from school yet?"

"School's out," he returned. "But there's dance and gymnastics, stopping at the grocery store. My wife schedules it all so she doesn't have to go back out."

So why wasn't Roxy's nose pressed against the slider? There had been no barking upon his arrival, not so much as a whimper.

Lars shook his head and met the man's gaze. "There's no dog inside," he said.

"I'm not lying." He raised an arm and pointed out the doghouse under a shade tree.

"That proves nothing. I haven't heard a single bark. Not a whimper to join his master's side."

"The dog is trained to listen to commands," the agent pointed out.

Lars met that with silence. He was content to wait, but Franks wasn't.

"You think I have the woman and baby inside? I don't," Franks assured him.

"Then let me take a look for myself."

But the agent shook his head. "That would take a search warrant, for which you have no cause."

"Sounds like you have something to hide," Lars returned.

"You would let BP trample through your house?" Franks raised his chin in challenge, but Lars ignored it.

"It wouldn't take much to convince a judge. Missing agents, a dead man or two, evidence of a break-in, and chase of a pregnant woman."

Lars watched Franks's face grow grim. "Starting to sound pretty good, isn't it?"

"It is." His eyes grew thoughtful as he considered Lars. "I've heard good things about you and Cobain. The kind of things I'm hoping I can trust." He turned and walked toward the house but said over his shoulder, "I'll call her out."

Lars followed his progress across the yard. Birds sang and squawked in the trees, frogs carried on closer to the lake. Nothing seemed off, but Lars felt the tension mount in his body and brought his hand up. The metal of his gun grip was cool and reassuring.

Franks opened the slider and called into the house, "Roxy, come!" He whistled, short and sharp. And the dog came barreling out the door, skidded to a stop before she came to the end of the patio, looped back, and sat at Franks's heels. She was still young, strong, with a shiny coat and alert eyes.

"She's retired?"

"She pulled a kid out of a meth lab fire. You know what that does to a dog's sense of smell? Wipes it out. Burns right through those mucus cells and they're never the same."

Franks closed the slider and walked back to Lars. Roxy accompanied him.

"You're not going to let me inside?" Lars asked.

"You know by now something's not right inside BP?"

"That's what we've heard. Haven't seen much yet to confirm."

"Heard from whom?" Franks wanted to know. "Green?" He shook his head. "You've got to go deeper. Sift through the ashes. Open some files. Take out the trash."

"You think Green is dirty?"

"I've heard he's warming up Monte, getting ready to serve him as the main dish," Franks said. The man's voice twisted with disdain.

"And you don't think he's the way to go?"

"Check out the man's service record," Franks suggested. "And look deeper into Green's personal life. Beyond the surface, there are many layers."

"Why don't you tell me what you know?" Lars suggested.

"Earlier you said there was a break-in at the girl's home. You said there was a dead man or two," Franks said. "Are those connected?"

"What do you know about it?" Lars returned.

"I know about the ice man. We've been looking for him for weeks."

"Based on an anonymous tip," Lars said.

"Yes. But about the break-in," Franks began again. "Was there a dead man at the house?"

"You seem to think so."

"Was it a BP agent?"

"You'll know all about it as soon as you clock in."

That was met with silence, and it took Franks a moment to digest it. His nose flared as he drew an agitated breath and his shoulders tightened, but so did his lips. And Lars wondered what he knew, or suspected, and how heavy it must be to keep his mouth shut.

"We'll wait till then, I guess," Franks said.

"Because you have nothing more to say," Lars pressed.

Franks shook his head. "We'll talk again," he said. "Soon."

He walked back to the house, opened the slider, and let Roxy in. Then he cut through the yard, to the garage, opened the door, and climbed into his Silverado. He pulled out and idled in the driveway, waiting as Lars made his way to the street. Franks pulled up and stopped, rolled down his window. "Stay off my property, Solberg. Don't come back around."

"You're going to come find me, then?" Lars asked. "For that talk you mentioned."

Franks nodded. "It's inevitable."

11

Nicole arrived back at the Yukons just minutes before Lars. His face was a mix of sweat and possibility. She could tell he was still working through some thoughts and left him to it as she brought him up to date.

"The others are finished and on their way back to the crime scene. The most interesting thing to come up was a few hijabs drying on a back-yard clothesline. Calder questioned it. The occupants claimed they were left behind after a recent visit with friends and they were preparing to mail them."

"Calder was okay with that?"

"She pursued it," Nicole said. "They invited her to come back with a search warrant."

That raised an eyebrow. "Sounds like she hit a nerve."

"They had a cut-to-the-chase attitude, but she was fifty-fifty it went beyond that. Recently moved in from New York, thick East Coast accents and an eye on the clock."

Not unusual. Many of the residents of Blue Mesa were from anywhere but Montana. They were a popular community, tucked into the mesas just a rambling toss from the foothills of Glacier National Park. The beauty here was boundless, the air so clean and clear it left you breathless. It took transplants a year or two to release the grip of the outside world, relax into the rhythms of small-town living, establish relationships with their neighbors.

"How 'bout you?"

"No woman and baby," he said. "But I did run into Luke Franks, BP agent."

"No kidding?"

Lars nodded. "And he asked if we'd found a dead man at the house."

"He didn't know?"

"He's been out sick," Lars said. "Seemed to know only what the news was reporting."

"He say anything else?"

"He wondered if the dead man was a BP agent."

That made Nicole's pulse kick up a notch. "He thought it was possible," she said, "that a BP agent was in the house."

"Puts a slant on things, doesn't it?" Lars said.

"That, and he seems cut off from the crew," Nicole said. "Something this big going down—two fellow agents missing—you'd think he'd at least call in, get the details."

"Or show up at the scene to pitch in," Lars agreed.

Solidarity. Brotherhood. "He's outside the loop."

"Maybe not a bad thing," Lars pointed out. "He said we should take a close look at Green."

"Yeah? I'd like to hear more about that."

"Me too."

"We'll go back. Put a little pressure on him."

"That's going to need to wait," Lars said. "He was on his way to work when I left."

"Tomorrow, then," she said. If she didn't bump into the man when they returned to the lake.

Nicole switched gears.

"Kittens ever sound like a crying baby to you?"

"Always," Lars assured her.

She nodded. "I heard it a few times. I was almost convinced there was a baby in the woods, but then a tangle of kittens tumbled out of the tree line. I was looking right at one when it lifted its head and yowled."

"And it sounded like a baby?"

She nodded.

"But you're not sure?"

"No."

"So we go back."

"Probably. But we have two missing agents and a murder victim. Two. No time for a wild-goose chase."

It was probably no more than what she'd seen—a litter of wrestling kittens.

"Green called for a briefing at five thirty," Nicole told him. The call had come just as she was finishing up her sweep. "He figures they'll be ready to clear the scene then."

"Any new information?"

"Seems so." They hadn't had the chance to talk before diving into the canvass, so Nicole began by telling Lars about the missing evidence at BP and the suspicion that the two agents were romantically involved. "Green seems to think it's possible."

"Monte?" Lars shook his head. "Never got that feel off of him."

The kind of guy who would corrupt justice, sleep with an underagent, and steal away into the night? No, Nicole agreed. Monte hadn't built up those kinds of calluses.

"His wife died four years ago. Green said it's grasping at wind, but if there's a reason, that would be as good as any."

"Monte was vulnerable," Lars said. "So we keep it in mind."

"I'd like to see Monte's notes, going back the last month or two at least," Nicole said. All agents kept a notebook, whether digital or paper, of quickly jotted hunches and leads, of trails they had followed that presumably led nowhere, of questions, suspicions, and possible avenues of investigation.

"You ask Green?"

"I'm going to."

"He's been open to help."

"Marginally," she said. "And not sure who he can trust in his own office."

They moved toward their Yukons. "I'm stopping at Blondie's," Lars said. "Want something?"

Lunch should have been hours ago, and she hadn't stopped for breakfast. Someone had handed her a cup of coffee and a bear claw soon after light, while the body in ice was being cut out and brought ashore and the search boats were trolling.

It seemed days ago rather than hours that Lake Maria had become a crime scene. From 2:37, when Monte called and reported the ice man, till now—it was nearing five o'clock—fourteen hours had elapsed, and so far what they'd learned could fit inside a thimble. Two dead, a pregnant woman, some rotting flesh in the BP field office. Those were the sure things. A romantic relationship that defied regulations and Syrian refugees were promising threads to follow.

"Can't decide?" Lars prompted.

"I really want the burger and curly fries," she said. "But I'll take a chicken Caesar salad and a side of raw veggies."

Lars almost stumbled and pulled up short. "Even now?" Because in the clutch, they were used to eating whatever they could choke down, and if it was hot they had really scored.

"Especially now," she said. If she could keep it good even under pressure, then old habits were broken. "I'm running again," she revealed. "Well, a slow jog with a lot of walking in between."

"How many miles?"

"Five and a quarter."

He whistled through his teeth. "How long have you been back at it?"

"Two months."

He nodded. "So, you are seeing someone," he said.

"Because I'm eating right and exercising?"

"Yes, and because you were all but stuttering earlier, when Calder brought up the relationship funnies. And right now you're about to blush."

"I don't blush."

"That's what I thought."

She considered drawing her weapon but decided it would be overkill.

"So what?" she said instead.

His eyebrows shot skyward. "Yeah? Anyone I know?"

"I don't kiss and tell."

"So it's gotten that far?"

She speared him with a glance. "Not even my girlfriends ask so many questions."

"You don't have any," he returned. "Casualty of the job—not a lot of time to build relationships. Which is why I'm happy to see it. Took a hell of a long time for you to mate up."

"Mate up?"

"Well, you don't hook up. That's not you."

She stopped mincing words. "Small town. People would talk," she said.

"True that," he agreed, and changed his tone, resigned to her fate. "So, salad and veggies."

"Yeah, makes me like me less too."

Nicole walked around the Yukon and climbed into the driver's seat. In front of her, Lars started his engine and pulled out. She had a few calls to make. She wanted to see the composite the department's sketch artist had drawn according to Tandy's memory. By now, four hours since starting the process, he had to have something viable. Something they could get onto the evening news, show around town. And she needed to touch base with her desk sergeant. Blue Mesa was pretty quiet between ski season and the summer sun and fun, but she had two thousand miles of jurisdiction to keep tabs on.

But first, she pressed speed dial for Jordan. He answered on the second ring.

"Hey, Mom."

"Hey, son. What's up?"

"Playing a little cribbage," he returned, and Nicole hooted. She couldn't help it; that was definitely laugh-out-loud material. Jordan loved Mrs. Neal. She was the grandmother he'd never had. And he was a trooper when it came to sampling the woman's seasonal desserts and playing games most children Jordan's age had never heard of. "Who's winning?"

"I am, of course." And she could hear the good cheer in his voice. "But only because she's letting me. That's her strategy. She's easy on me when she's teaching the game, but then she turns into a shark."

"You wouldn't like it any other way." Jordan lived for challenge.

"True," he said. "You coming home tonight?"

"Definitely."

"Because I heard about the two agents."

"I've been working it for fourteen hours now," she told him. "I'll need sleep."

"Are they dead?"

"I don't know," she said. "It's like they disappeared into thin air." Evaporated.

"Like Mayakl."

"Who?"

"He's from Thailand, I think. Or a country close to it—you know all about my impressive geography skills. Anyway, he slips in and out of buildings. Climbs them, sometimes thirty or forty stories with no gear. He's gotten past the security system at the Louvre and later posted a selfie with the *Mona Lisa*. And no one can catch him. They call him *xakas bea-bang*, meaning thin air."

"You watch too much YouTube," she said.

"Where else would you get up-to-the-moment fascinating facts?"

"Why does he do stuff that could get him killed?"

"Some guys are like that, Mom. They 'dance on the serrated blade of fear.'"

"You get that from his bio?"

"As a matter of fact, yes," he admitted.

"How did we get into this conversation?"

"Because the agents are gone and they left no trace behind."

No trace. Had the agents been captured, or had this been some grand design to flee prosecution?

Green and his higher-ups wouldn't like her picking through their trash, but as far as motive went, if Monte or Baker was behind the missing evidence, it was a direct connection to their case. Nicole needed bank statements, for a start, and that would be her next call. A warrant.

"Okay, buddy," Nicole said. "Tell Mrs. Neal I won't make it for dinner but definitely in time for the ten o'clock news."

The department had one officer who specialized in white-collar crime. Cases like identity theft and embezzlement, Ponzi schemes and fraud. She was also a deputy and at that moment was on patrol outside Jax Town. Nicole had looked at the duty roster that morning when she was moving players off the board and onto the scene at Lake Maria. She had the numbers of every one of her officers stored on her phone and began scrolling through her contacts. She hoped she had only one Jane, because she couldn't remember the deputy's last name. She was young, blonde, and freckled. Had a degree in computer forensics and lived only a few doors away from Nicole with a boyfriend and a bloodhound.

Jane Casper. Yes, that was the one. Like Wyoming and like the ghost. She answered on the first ring.

"Sheriff Cobain?"

"Hi, Jane. Can you clock a little overtime?"

"Absolutely."

Nicole couldn't pull Jane from patrol—she was the only deputy covering a hundred plus square miles.

"We need a warrant." Nicole explained the circumstances, which were circumstantial at best. They had very little to present before the judge, except that the agents lives were currently considered in peril. "I want you to get that ready when you get off shift tonight so that you're at the courthouse as soon as it opens tomorrow. And then I want you to spend the day following the money. Every little bit of it, beginning with the obvious—big deposits or transferring of large sums."

"I can do that."

"Are you assigned to patrol tomorrow?" Because Nicole would have to call in an off-duty officer to fill the spot.

"It's my day off."

"So more overtime," Nicole offered.

"That trip to Hawaii is getting closer."

She ended the call and started the Yukon. Green's briefing was scheduled to start in fifteen minutes. Nicole pulled onto the Lake Road and followed its curving ribbon through mountain and mesa. She spoke to her sergeant while she drove.

"A few domestic calls," he reported. "A fire out on Colfax Road. Fire department got to it before it leapt from the house to the fields."

"Injuries?" she asked.

"None. Grease fire, making breakfast as far as we know. The family got out quickly."

"That's it?"

"Two vehicular accidents, both on the interstate outside Adams. One fatality. One airlifted to Glacier Community, but he'll make it. Otherwise, quiet as a convent."

The next call she made was purely because instinct was a grueling taskmaster.

"Hi, Janice. Can I speak to Dr. Rose?"

Jordan had a husky–Saint Bernard mix, Cooper, who was constantly on the prowl, rousting skunks and porcupines whenever he could find them, and so was a regular at the vet clinic.

"Hi, Nicole. All okay with Cooper?"

"If leaping tall fences and chewing on chair legs is okay."

The doctor laughed. "Yep, sounds perfectly normal. So what can I do for you, then?"

"I heard a baby but saw a kitten."

That was met with a moment of silence.

"Well, that's disturbing," the doctor said, but Nicole clearly heard the amusement in her voice.

"You're not worried," Nicole said.

"Not even a little."

"Because it's common for kittens to sound like newborn babies?"

"For the adult females, yes. They're called queens, and their dramatics increase during the time of heat."

"When is that?"

"Right about now," Dr. Rose said. "You saw kittens today because the breeding season runs year-round, but it's most intense during spring and fall. And while the cat calls are sharpest at night, I've heard them carrying on during the day too."

Nicole thanked the doctor and hung up. She was close to the command scene, and emergency vehicles were parked along the side of the road in both directions. In front of them were the news vans and a small milling of concerned citizens. Nicole managed to squeeze between an empty boat trailer and Lars's cruiser. From where she sat, she could see officers and agents moving toward a central area. Forensics remained in the field.

She climbed from the Yukon and made her way down the grassy slope to the center of activity. Officers parted and let her through. Agents shuffled aside reluctantly. That whole marked territory between agencies, it never grew old. She allowed a mental rolling of her eyes and stepped beside Lars.

"Something come up?"

"An itch I can't scratch." And she couldn't pull men to sweep the woods behind the Embry place, not when they were so thin. But no harm in returning herself for another look around.

Green started the briefing with a list of knowns and unknowns. There were no new details. He went through his expectations for closing the scene, then moved on to logistics.

"We're closing in on six o'clock. Sunset is at eight twenty-two tonight. Unless you are specifically approached by me, Sheriff Cobain, or Captain Oakley, everyone is off duty at eight thirty. Go home. Eat. Sleep. And we start up again in the morning. So let's get to it."

Personnel from the three agencies spread out, and Green approached Nicole.

"A word, Sheriff?" Green stopped in front of Nicole and anchored his hands on his hips. The wind off the water had chapped his pale skin.

"What's up?"

"Where should I start?"

"The party boat?" she suggested. She gave him no leeway. "We have a registered owner on it?"

"There is none," he said. "No private owner. Took so long figuring that out because the vessel was stolen from a showroom in Pantucket, Michigan."

"They have any leads on who?"

Green shook his head. "Four guys, hooded and gloved. In and out in under two minutes. There's video. Police in Pantucket said they looked like synchronized dancers, had it all figured out, in sweet harmony."

"I'd like to see that."

"Me too. Video's on its way. Might already be in my email."

"So what else?" she asked.

"We've recovered a department parka. It belongs to Monte, has his name stitched across the left shoulder."

That made her blood tick a little faster. "Where was it found?"

He nodded over her head, due north. "It washed up on shore. Thing is, the coat is intact. Not a tear on it. Not a button missing. No gunshot residue at first pass, but a small spatter of blood under luminol. And I'm talking very small. Doesn't mean it got there last night." He shook his head, stumped. "Seems like he just unzipped it and dropped it into the lake, but that doesn't make sense." He caught her gaze. "I sent it with your forensic guys."

"Good." So he was following her orders but wasn't happy about it.

"In fact, I want your department to take possession of all evidence. It's really your show now, isn't it?"

"It's looking that way," she agreed. "Unless there was no crime committed here on the lake." The ice man and the GSW at the house would remain her business, but if the missing agents were alive and well and on the run with a cache of stolen money or drugs and fleeing charges, then the sheriff's department was involved by invitation only. "If your problem is strictly internal."

He gazed over her head, turned on his heels to broaden his horizon, then lowered his voice. "I had my computer geeks break through Monte's password protections and bring up his files. There's one in there titled exactly that: 'It's Internal.' I want you to take a look at it. He's got some kind of code writing going on. It's consistent throughout but still a difficult read."

"What does it say?"

"I'm hoping you'll know. Your name's in it."

12

Green had sent her a copy of Monte's digital files. Nicole sat in the Yukon and skimmed through the pages on her phone. Yes, her name appeared, and beneath it a listing of numbers, each one six digits in length. Possibly crime codes, but that she would have to confirm with Green. Agencies had different codes with no overlap, and she had no more than a passing exposure to the interior machinations of the Border Patrol. She understood little else in the file, but the numbers were a good starting point. One, she hoped, would unlock the rest of the cryptic writing, which for the most part was a series of bulleted notes or single words followed by an asterisk.

"This could as easily document his own criminal plans as implicate other agents," she said.

Lars was scrolling through his own copy of Monte's files.

"You're right about that," he said. "Why do you think your name is in here?"

She shrugged. "And that list of what looks like penal codes."

"Your name isn't hidden. And it's the first thing, top of page one," Lars said. "Makes me think he was getting ready to send it to you."

"You think?"

"He trusted you—asked for you by name."

Nicole put the Yukon in gear and joined the light traffic on the Lake Road.

"Franks said something to that regard as well," Lars revealed. "He told me he'd heard we could be trusted."

And that the sooner Nicole took over the lead in the investigation, the better. She thought over all Lars had told her from his interview with Luke Franks. "He said look deeper into Green. We're doing that."

"And he said Green was serving Monte up as our prime suspect," Lars said.

"Let's not forget that."

"Where are we going?" Lars asked.

Their dinners, even in their plastic bags and back seat location, made Nicole's hunger flare. Lars had unapologetically ordered a cheeseburger and fries.

"I want to stop by the Embry place," she told him. "You eat while I drive, then we'll switch off on the way back."

"Are we going to search the woods?"

"I hope it doesn't come to that."

She glanced east, past Lars and out his window. It was the golden hour, when the sun lost its heat, turned a deceiving, buttery yellow. It was during this hour that it blinded when looked at directly, that its incredible glare made it impossible to see what stood hidden within it. It was on its descent west and cast the ice floes on Lake Maria in a softer hue. Even the water, a vibrant blue from the glacier melt, held its rays and glistened.

She turned her attention back to the road. An MHP cruiser, bar lights rolling, blocked her way. Nicole stopped while an officer hustled back to his car and moved it enough that she could pass by. The scene would remain inaccessible well into the next day, but that wouldn't stop some of the curious, who would take to the water from private docks. They had stopped all public lake activity within a mile of the sunken skiff while law enforcement motored in ever-tighter circles, scanning the shore, the currents, the open alleyways between ice floes, searching for agents and evidence, hoping for rescue. At some point Green would have to make the call official, turning from a rescue to recovery. Nicole wanted to give him that time, to let it settle inside him. At the twenty-four-hour mark, she would officially assume the lead in the investigation and Green would be shuttled to the background, with limited access to evidence and few avenues available to him. Interagency efforts were always tenuous territory to navigate.

"So we're going to have another talk with Mr. Embry?"

She listened to the rustling of the bag as Lars searched for his food and braced herself for the steamy aroma of freshly fried potatoes. She was an addict. Jordan was right about that. Nicole didn't mind a salad here and there. She could walk past a veggie platter faster than zero to sixty, but fries and a quarter pounder, those were an anchor, her albatross, they sunk her.

She must have made a noise, or perhaps she'd made a grab for Lars's bag, because he leaned into his door, clutching his dinner, and asked, "You okay?"

She spared him a glance. Burger in hand, gooey cheese melted over the side of the bun and dripping ketchup, Lars stared at her with worry.

"Why does being good feel so bad?" She sang the words in an awful, warbling country twang.

Lars laughed, then took a third of the burger in his first bite. He chewed, swallowed, then offered, "Want the fries?"

"I want *one*," she said. He handed her two.

"A generous man."

He shrugged. "There's a thin line between friend and codependent."

She ate them both. "A friend would leave it at that."

"What if you ask for more?"

"The answer's no."

But when he pulled the entire sleeve from the bag and further released the hot, salty scent of fried potatoes, Nicole caved.

"Okay," she said, "one more."

"Don't you mean two?"

"I was hoping you would say that."

"Nope."

"What?"

"I believe the answer is no," he said, quoting her.

"Oh, that's low."

"Lower to supply an addict."

"You're exaggerating."

"Let's do this," he suggested. "You've been running for two months now? How long does it take for you to get it done?"

"Fifty-seven minutes." She was pretty proud she'd gotten it under an hour and so was Lars. He whistled his appreciation between his teeth.

"That's almost a ten-minute mile."

"My last mile is always the fastest. Nine minutes thirty-three seconds yesterday. Go figure, you'd think I'd be dragging my butt at that point."

He nodded. "What kind of time were you making your first week?"

Nicole snorted. "The first week all I could squeeze out of this body were two miles a run, and it took me thirty minutes."

"You see that," he said. "You're stronger, faster by far in comparison." He popped several french fries into his mouth and spoke around them. "You don't want to mess that up."

She spared him a glance as she pulled to the shoulder of the road. She parked the Yukon at the entrance of the Embrys' driveway. "You're a good friend, Lars."

"It was nothing," he said.

"You talked me down. Those hostage negotiation classes are doing both of us some good."

He chuckled, pushed the last few fries into his mouth, took a sip of his iced tea over that, and climbed from the Yukon. Nicole met him passenger side and they stood there, in the loose gravel at the side of the road, considering the house. It was down a gentle slope, maybe two hundred feet from the road. All the windows on the main floor were lit and three cars were in the driveway now, a blue Camry joining the truck and the compact.

"How do you want to do this?"

"Follow my lead, unless you have a better one," she said.

Their feet crunched in the gravel.

"Elias Embry was the only one home when I came by this morning, and he was in the backyard, gardening. Mid to late sixties, retired. His wife was grocery shopping."

She knocked and they waited. They heard movement, soft footfalls that didn't arrive at the door but shuffled somewhere toward the back of the house. Nicole knocked again.

"Mr. Embry," Nicole called through the door. "It's Sheriff Cobain."

He opened the door, pulling it back so that Nicole could see past him into the living room. The lamps were lit: polished wood flooring, a gray sofa and two floral chairs, a painting on the wall, a book, opened, face-down on the coffee table. The room was empty.

"You're back," Embry said.

"We have some questions," Lars told him. "Mind if we come in?"

Lars delivered it as a question but pulled open the storm door, and Embry stepped back.

"We're just starting dinner."

"We won't be long," Nicole promised.

"Sure, come in. I could get some of that tea you missed earlier," he offered as he turned into the living room.

"Thank you, Mr. Embry, but we won't be staying."

They followed him to the center of the room, but no one made a move to sit down. There were two hallways off the living area, one that led to the kitchen and the other to the bedrooms, Nicole assumed.

As Nicole watched, a girl stepped out of the shadowed hall and into the room, but no farther. Young, brunette, hazel eyes. She could pass for Caucasian but Nicole knew better. The girl met Tandy's description and closely resembled the department sketch. She had the baby cradled in her arms.

Nicole sought and maintained eye contact with the young woman. Her gaze was steady, her chin lifted. Not challenging but determined. If not brave, bold, and probably a good helping of both.

"You weren't honest with me this morning, Mr. Embry," Nicole said.

There was movement behind the girl. An older woman, hair the color of steel and facial features just as strong, stepped into the room. She held a bottle in one hand and a burping cloth in the other.

"This is my wife, Lois, and our guest, Adelai," Embry said.

The girl wavered on her feet. She was exhausted. Her skin was pale and bruised, with scrapes across her cheek, an arm, and both hands, such as one would receive from a terrifying run through dense foliage.

Nicole took a step toward her. Lois moved at the same time, crowding the girl and the baby.

"We were about to feed him," Lois said. "If you'll excuse us."

Nicole ignored her and held the girl's gaze. "I'm Sheriff Cobain. We're here to help you," she assured her.

"We're helping her," Lois said. Her voice was commanding, sharp when there was no need.

The girl stepped forward and spoke directly to Nicole, "Take me with you, please."

"Is that your baby?"

"Yes," she said. "His name is Matthew."

The scrapes on her hands and arms were new. They had begun to scab but were still red. And at the back of her mind, Nicole began an inventory of what must be done. Photos of the girl's injuries, the doctor would need to establish time of birth, a DNA sample taken to match to the placenta . . .

"He's tiny," Lars said. "Born today?" He had been cleaned and bundled but still had the scrunched facial features of an hours-old baby.

The girl didn't answer.

"How old are you, Adelai?" Nicole asked.

"Eighteen," she said, but Lois contradicted her. "Sixteen. Babies having babies." Her voice leveled censure at Adelai and the world in general.

The girl shook her head. "That's not true. I'll be nineteen in June. The twenty-fourth."

Mrs. Embry moved then, turned so that she pulled the young woman's attention her way. "You're complicating things," she said. "Let me do the talking. It's what we agreed on, and for good reason."

"I never agreed to it."

"But the baby's father," Mrs. Embry continued, "he wanted it this way."

And Nicole saw the wavering of Adelai's determination as her eyes misted and her teeth pulled at the corner of her lips. "He didn't," she said. "We hoped it would never come to this."

"They need medical attention," Nicole said.

"A nurse tended to them this morning," Lois Embry said.

"What nurse?" Lars pressed. "Can you give us a name?"

"When and if you need it," Lois returned. And Nicole wondered if Tandy had found her way here or if the nurse Mrs. Embry spoke of was another sympathizer. It was clear to her they had found one stop on the modern-day railroad north, a place where Adelai had known she could find help.

Nicole stepped around Lois and closer to the young woman and her baby.

"Do you have a purse?" she asked. "Anything you want to bring with you?"

Lois placed a hand on the girl's arm. "She's staying with us."

Lars moved then. He came to stand in front of the older woman, invading her space, the toes of his boots nearly touching her loafered feet. "Unlawful detainment?" he asked.

"That's your specialty," Mrs. Embry returned, but she removed her hand. She kept her place beside the woman and baby and held Lars's gaze with a defiant tilt of her chin.

"Move aside, Mrs. Embry. Any further interference from you will be considered obstruction." His voice was low but firm, about as impenetrable as concrete.

Nicole didn't wait for her to comply but nodded at Adelai and said, "Let's go now," and moved toward the door. The young woman followed. And when Elias Embry approached, Nicole held out her hand to stop him.

"Do you have personal belongings?" Nicole asked Adelai, while maintaining eye contact with Elias.

"No. Nothing," she said. "It's just us." She held her baby closer to her chest, and the baby sighed and his hand opened, his tiny fingers tangling in the girl's hair.

"Where are you taking her?" Lois asked, but Nicole ignored her.

In addition to emergency equipment, backup arms, a change of clothes, and a collection of bottled water and energy bars, Nicole kept a child's car seat stored in the back of the Yukon. It was a requirement that forty percent of the department vehicles have them. Most often they were used to transport children to child welfare following well-checks that went bad or domestic violence calls that required the removal of the child from the home. The closest social welfare office and its workers were nearly a hundred miles away.

They settled the baby in the seat and the girl beside him. When Nicole had the Yukon running, she asked, "Where to?"

"The hospital," she said. "I should have gone there first but was afraid."

Nicole hit the lights but kept the siren quiet.

Lars used his shoulder radio to call in their location. "Transporting a woman and her baby to Glacier Community Hospital. ETA ten minutes."

"Do you require EMT assistance?" dispatch asked.

"Negative. New birth, conditions stable."

Dispatch promised to alert the hospital, and Lars signed off.

"The baby was born today, wasn't he?" Nicole asked.

The girl nodded.

"Beside the lake?" she continued, pulling the Yukon onto the lake road.

"We didn't want it that way," she said. "We prepared for everything, including this."

"Men came to your house last night," Lars said. "They chased you into the woods."

"I ran into the woods knowing they would follow, but there was nowhere else to go."

"Why are they after you?"

"I'm not safe here, and neither is my baby." The girl's voice faded, and Nicole looked at her through the rearview mirror. Her eyelids were heavy.

"You're safe now," Nicole told her.

"No," she said. "There is no safe place. There never has been."

Nicole pulled into emergency and climbed out of the Yukon. She pulled open the girl's door as a nurse came out with a gurney.

"Mom and her baby," she said. "Born this morning." She assisted Adelai with her seat belt. "We're at the hospital," she said. The girl's eyelashes fluttered but did not open. "We're moving you to a stretcher."

She woke then, grasping for her son beside her. Nicole watched the frantic pulse in the girl's throat calm as soon as her hands made contact with her baby. She looked so young, so desperate, so alone.

"Are you really eighteen?" Nicole whispered.

"Yes. I promise."

The nurse held the gurney, and Nicole and Lars helped Adelai and her child onto it. A doctor came out the sliding doors and immediately turned back the blanket swaddling the baby. He placed a stethoscope to his chest, under his chubby neck.

"Color and heartbeat are good."

They started walking toward the double doors.

"Mom might be the worse for wear," Nicole said.

"Exhausted," Lars said. "Been up all night, ran three miles, chased through the woods, gave birth sometime during all that."

Nicole stayed with the girl. She had another, singularly important question. They walked through the double doors into a receiving bay loaded with emergency equipment, all of which they passed unneeded.

She looked ahead. The doctor would cut her off soon, when the staff pushed through the interior doors and took Adelai back to an exam room.

"Adelai," she called softly, but when the girl didn't stir, Nicole leaned in and repeated more firmly, "Adelai, this is very important." The girl's eyes opened. "Do you know the men who chased you? Their names? Where they're from?"

"Matthew said they would come quietly, and they did." She paused and sipped at the air.

"Who were they?"

"People who don't like people like me," she said.

They were fast approaching the doors. Nicole grabbed the girl's hand and gave it a squeeze. With her other hand, she slowed the progress of the gurney.

"Adelai," she called, and waited until the young woman's eyelids flickered open once more. "Did you notice a problem on the lake last night?" she pressed. "There was some commotion not far from where you had run."

"On the lake?" Adelai asked, and her eyes shifted, darting left of Nicole's gaze. It could have been nerves, but it was more likely evasion. "I didn't notice."

The gurney slid through the double doors to exam and Nicole stopped, watching the young woman and her baby move out of reach. Temporarily.

"People like her," Lars repeated. He stood beside her, his phone in hand. He had taken notes as Nicole questioned.

"And who could that be?" Nicole posed.

"Tandy was right," Lars said. "Adelai is Syrian. I've heard the accent before."

"Where?"

"The evening news, at least once a week, ever since immigration laws changed but refugee need hasn't."

Nicole nodded, following that thread as far as it would take her. "Who doesn't like refugees? Undocumented aliens?"

"Some of our finest citizens," Lars said, referring to the fringe of their community, masked men who called themselves militia. But they were no match to the almost military precision that had stormed the house, executed a man, and chased a girl into the woods without leaving much of themselves behind.

"The assault on that house was organized, efficient."

"Expert training," he agreed.

"Border Patrol," she said.

"Are there that many bad agents?"

"At least a handful," she said. "But I like the fit."

Another piece sliding into place. It made sense, kept all the players in a tight knot in the middle of Blue Mesa. Something had happened out on Lake Maria, and it wasn't the ice man. Murder always became the center of a homicide investigation, but perhaps in this case the body in slow melt in MacAulay's morgue and the GSW were but small pieces of the puzzle. And the missing agents and the mess inside BP were the centerpiece.

"Who is Matthew that BP wants him so badly they would kill a woman and child to get to him?"

"They already have him, dead or alive," Nicole said.

Lars looked at her over his smartphone. "You know something I don't?"

"Where were you when your children were born?"

"Exactly where I was supposed to be. I caught every one of them straight out of the chute. But not all men rise to the occasion."

"But Matthew would have. Adelai is sure of it."

She turned and headed back to the Yukon. Lars fell into step beside her.

"We need to put a deputy outside Adelai's room," she said. "Stay with her, Lars, until relief comes. Casper should be back at the station by now. I want her to look at the digital files Green gave me. If Monte was at work on something within the department, it will give us direction." If it was reliable. She was beginning to worry that anything Green gave her was tainted.

"Will do," he said. "Casper has that degree in cyber sleuthing or whatever. Encryption is part of it."

"She'll be a great help," Nicole agreed.

She glanced at her watch. Six thirty.

"Head home when relief gets here," she said. "You've been up almost as long as I have."

She planned to do the same, after she had filled out the warrant and delivered it herself to the judge, then gotten Casper up and running. The banks were closed, but BP ran around the clock. She wanted access to personnel files, including anecdotal notes and official reprimands, for both Monte and Baker. And anything the judge would allow on Green.

13

Nicole was up before dawn. She started the coffee, cut herself a wedge of pie she'd missed the night before, and sat down at the kitchen table, still bundled in her flannel pajamas and robe. Her conversation with Jane Casper had gone better than she'd hoped. The young officer had skimmed the file marked INTERNAL and revealed a few things right off—the numbers listed under Nicole's name were indeed criminal codes particular to the BP, and so both Nicole and Jane felt that Monte had been getting ready to contact Nicole about corruption in his agency. Embezzlement, stolen evidence, money laundering, and murder were among the offenses Monte had noted. The who part was harder. Monte had masked names under pseudonyms and pseudonyms under scratch. But there was a pattern. It was alphabetical, some kind of deletion and replacement, the deputy was sure. Casper would spend most of today trying to crack it and going over bank statements.

Nicole called in to her office for an update on the night's events, something she usually received when she arrived at the station. There had been no rescue or recovery on Monte or Baker. They'd had an otherwise quiet evening with a few domestic calls, an overturned truck on one of the state routes in the southwestern part of the county that had set more than four hundred chickens loose, and shots fired outside a home on Chatham Avenue. Next, she called Green.

He answered with a gruff alertness.

"No news on this end," Nicole told him. "Do you have an update?"

"Nothing's changed," he said. "I heard you found the woman you were looking for."

"Yes, we transported her to the hospital last night."

"What's her connection to all this?"

"Is there a connection?" Nicole returned. "We haven't established that yet."

"But there's a dead man in her bedroom and evidence of a chase."

The tracker Nicole had sent to follow the trail from Adelai's house had found nothing unusual. The girl's footsteps had been easy to follow, often in a zigzag pattern, so she had known some evasive tactics. But she had left the brush trampled, branches broken, making it easy for those in pursuit to follow. At nine months pregnant and in labor, Nicole couldn't fault her for that. It was a miracle she had gotten away. The men following had done better. Their footsteps had been heavy, the tread in their boots matching the castings taken at the house, but they had passed through the brush without snagging and leaving behind pieces of themselves.

"That's right," Nicole said. She had released the tracker's findings the night before. And she had let the team leaders know that the girl was in a safe place. "We'll show a photo of the dead man to the young lady today."

"What's her name?" Green asked.

"We have only her first." And Nicole found herself reluctant to share it. "She's my first stop today. If I see a connection, I'll let you know what I find out."

"Could you let me know either way?"

She felt her lips curl with indecision. Everyone at BP was a suspect. The thought was a whisper in her head. And that included Green.

"I'll call you," she said, and moved on to other details. "I have a deputy working on Monte's files. 'Internal' in particular. So far, we're pretty sure he was following up on suspicious activity inside your agency."

"I figured as much, but I didn't see any names."

"No, he masked them."

"Is there any way to uncover them?"

"We're working on it." And she felt reasonably good about a breakthrough there. "How many bad agents are we talking about, Green?"

"Not many," he hedged. "Two or three is my guess."

"What is Internal Affairs saying?"

"You know how they work, Sheriff," Green said, frustration rising in his voice. "They're saying nothing."

"Well, then, what are your suspicions, Green?"

He thought about that, and Nicole let the silence buzz in her ear without interruption. Through the window, the sky was just beginning to lighten. Clouds were parting, drifting in a cool wind. Stars were receding. The forecast had promised sun and a high temperature of sixty-eight degrees. Balmy for April in the North Country.

"Monte," he said. "All my training in personnel indicates he's most likely behind our troubles."

"Because you think he and Baker are involved?" she pressed.

"And because he has presence here. Men look up to him, follow his lead."

"And you can see him recruiting agents into wrongdoing?"

"Yeah, I guess that's what I'm saying."

"And Monte and Baker never worked together before Blue Mesa?"

"No. Monte was in Wisconsin for a few years before transferring here. Baker has a string of stations behind her beginning with Miami, then Texas, San Diego, and Arizona. Possible they could have met at conferences or trainings, but not probable."

"Is it common for agents to move borders?"

"Yes. We follow the promotional line. Blue Mesa was a big step up for Baker, but her first on the northern border."

"And Monte was teaching her the ropes."

"He has eighteen years on her, is a senior agent and a supervisor. Also a real nice guy who didn't complain about investing in an agent with a learning curve. Baker saw that and latched on."

"And that was eleven months ago?"

"That's right."

"And the trouble at BP started just before she arrived?"

"I told you that," he said. "Two months before Baker even got here."

"Get used to the questions, Green," Nicole advised. "We're just beginning."

She hung up and set her phone beside her plate of pie. She had yet to take a bite. And though the coffee had stopped percolating some time ago, she had yet to pour herself a cup. She sat back and stared out the window. The house was nestled into a knoll and faced east, so that through the large picture window the sunrise was just beginning to blaze across the sky.

She was in a good place, but it hadn't always been that way. She had made mistakes, big ones, and she had made reparations. She thought about Baker and her career path without the distractions of family. Those had been lonely days for Nicole. She could see the agent moving closer to Monte. A relationship developing. She was moving in that direction herself, but before coming to Blue Mesa she had been a mess.

Nicole had made detective at twenty-four, been promoted to homicide at twenty-five, fallen apart at twenty-six. A year of hitting rock bottom where she fell for the charm of a man she later learned was a common drug dealer. She'd been clutching at the wind, nose-diving with only herself to stop the fall. And stop it she did. At twenty-nine, she moved west with a toddler son and the promise of a job in Blue Mesa. It was a demotion but a saving grace. Three years after that, she had been elected sheriff. She was just into her second term and making a difference, even if it was coming about slowly.

And she was involved, and more, with a good man. She wasn't very good at waiting once she'd decided on a plan of action and figured if MacAulay didn't open a conversation about permanence soon, she would.

She sat up and worked her fork into the pie. Razzleberry, one of Mrs. Neal's best. Nicole figured the berries—and there were a lot of them—counted as fruit and not a sweet. The flaky pastry around it was a carb. Maybe not top-shelf, but there wasn't a lot of it. She could work that off before lunch.

"Hey, no fair," Jordan said. Her toddler son, now eleven years old, had come into the kitchen, wrapped in a Star Wars comforter. "Pie for breakfast?"

"No better time," Nicole said. She smiled and felt the sticky syrup at the corners of her mouth. "Want some?"

He shuffled into the room and sat down beside her at the table.

"I had two pieces last night."

"Two?"

"I'm a growing boy."

"Yes, you are." She heard her voice thicken and pushed back the memory of nearly losing Jordan four months before—the utter chaos and destruction, the violent cacophony of wind and the earth thundering beneath her feet, the bullets flying and a brave young man, Joaquin

Esparza, who had stepped up when Nicole couldn't. She would not forget him. To him she owed the best part of her life.

"Don't get all mushy on me," Jordan said.

"Trying." She passed a hand over his tousled hair. "You're up early."

"It's the only time I'll see you today."

Probably true.

"A lot has happened in a short amount of time," she said.

"I know." He folded his arms on the table and rested his head on them. He had a better understanding of her job now, having been caught in the swales of a criminal's intentions.

"So what's up?" she asked.

"Remember that Scout trip?"

She peeled through layers of memory to a conversation they'd had last week. "Hiking up Sunburst?"

He nodded, reached toward her plate, and swiped a finger-full of berry.

The Astum River Trail began north of Lake Maria, curved up over Eagles Peak, and ran parallel to the border with Canada. It was a popular hike, but more dangerous with the increased flow of undocumented aliens in that direction. It made Nicole uneasy, even though Jordan would be going with the Boy Scouts. It was sixteen miles round trip, with an overnight camp. Jordan loved the trips. Most were day adventures. Only a handful so far had been overnight. They were working toward a week of rafting on the Kootenai River this summer. Jordan would be twelve by then.

"It's tomorrow," he said, "and I need supplies."

"Will a trip to Outdoor Adventure do it?"

That perked him up. "Absolutely."

"If I can't fit it in today, I'll ask Mrs. Neal to take you."

"Okay. Or MacAulay," Jordan offered. When Nicole's brows raised in question, Jordan smiled and shrugged. "He's into outdoor stuff, understands the trail and what I'll need on it. He might even think of a few things I don't and that aren't on the list. It's a win-win."

MacAulay had accompanied Jordan on a day trip to the Bighorn tributary the month before. They'd talked about it for days afterward. MacAulay had come back from that and bought a new pair of hiking boots, socks, a hat, shorts, and a guidebook on the trails of the north and was talking about lightweight fishing equipment.

But MacAulay had two autopsies to complete and was just coming off the flu. Nicole didn't know if a trip to the outdoor store was likely, but she couldn't bring herself to disappoint Jordan. "You want me to ask him?"

Jordan shook his head. "I'll do it."

He stood and walked around the table to the refrigerator. He pulled out a bottle of vanilla creamer, carried that and a coffee mug to the counter, and mixed her drink. She smiled. Equal parts creamer and coffee, her brew had been the target of disdain far and wide.

He brought it over and placed it beside her now-empty pie plate. Together, the pie and heavily cream-laced coffee told a story.

"A definite sugar rush," he said. "You'd do better to eat a half dozen doughnuts."

"A girl's gotta live a little," she said.

"Not long on a diet like that."

"Hey, I've cleaned up pretty good lately."

He nodded and smiled, and Nicole's heart brightened. "Yes, you have."

"Lars had a cheeseburger and fries yesterday." She felt five years old, tattling on a friend. "And I ordered a chicken Caesar."

"Yeah, but did you eat it?"

She had to think about that. Yes, at her desk while she waited for Deputy Casper to arrive. The lettuce had wilted by then and the chicken was lukewarm, but for a dinner in the midst of a double-homicide-and-missing-agents investigation, it was nothing to complain about. "You betcha. Along with a side of raw snap peas and carrots. They might even have been organic."

Jordan pretended to fall over in his chair, clutching his heart. "A shock like that," he protested, "needs to come with some kind of warning."

She swatted his arm. "Go back to bed," she said. "You can get another hour of z's before you need to get up for school."

"You driving me?"

She shook her head. "Mrs. Neal. I'll make your breakfast, though."

Jordan shuffled out of the room, wrapped in the comforter, and Nicole stood. She pulled a frying pan from a cabinet, eggs and milk from the refrigerator, and went about making herself scrambled eggs rancheros, adding a double portion of bell pepper and onion and going light on the cheese. She had to compensate somewhere. She put half into Tupperware for Jordan to have when he got up for the day. She brought her half to the table and dug in. The pink and gold had faded from the sky, leaving it a stone-cold blue. She checked the time on her phone: 6:23. Still too early to call MacAulay. It'd been too late to call last night when she'd finished with Casper. She hoped he had slept around the clock, dosed with NyQuil.

Instead she called her deputy on duty outside Adelai's hospital room.

"She's been sleeping and feeding," he told her. "Seems to be on a three- to four-hour schedule."

Which sounded about right to Nicole. She did the math and figured the young lady would be awake again at nine thirty. She ended the call, then rinsed her dishes and placed them in the dishwasher. She had enough time to shower, dress, and drive over to the superstore for a quick shopping trip.

14

Nicole hadn't shopped for a baby in nearly ten years. For most shower gifts, she had handed over her share of the cost and been happy to let others do the shopping. Sometimes she had resorted to ordering online with direct shipment to the receiver. So perusing the baby section was a nearly foreign experience. For a moment it seemed like the air rippled and smelled sweeter. She wondered if they had a diffuser going or if they'd gone down the aisles sprinkling baby powder. She didn't see any evidence of it, but she responded to that heady scent of baby just the same and felt a little breathless.

Nicole grabbed a hand basket and followed a BABY ESSENTIALS sign to an aisle loaded with gentle shampoos and lotions and creams. She chose a boxed set that promised to cover every bathing need. Next she tackled clothing. She knew better than to purchase newborn outfits and instead grabbed sleepers size three to six months, because sleeves could be folded. She added two packages of onesies, socks, a hoodie, and a package of receiving blankets. As she passed an endcap, she picked up and tossed in a package of wipes. The basket wasn't big enough; she carried a box of diapers under her arm.

She might have gotten carried away. She remembered being a single mom, alone and scared, and that had propelled her through the aisles.

Her purchases filled two big bags. She placed them and the diapers in the back seat of the Yukon and drove to the hospital. The sun had sharpened and she drove into its radiant glare, squinting behind her sunglasses. Glacier Community Hospital was located just outside the town's center and close to the freeway. The big draw was, of course, orthopedics. With skiing injuries and hiking and boating mishaps, the hospital served a patient group of athletes, both amateur and hard-core. There was a wing for obstetrics and pediatrics, another for surgical recovery, and they had an emergency room that stayed busy.

Nicole parked, grabbed her purchases, and realized she felt a little self-conscious carrying them into the hospital. Her cheeks heated, which was out of character for her, and she did her best to ignore it.

Adelai was in room 108. Her deputy stood outside her door, sipping from a Styrofoam cup of sludge. Nicole sent him to get a real breakfast across the street at the Harmony Café.

"You're awake," Nicole said as she entered the room. Adelai was sitting up, propped against two pillows. Her son was sleeping in a plastic bassinet beside her bed. The TV was on but the sound was muted, and the young woman was reading the captions on the screen. It was tuned to a local morning news program. Nicole placed the bags and box of diapers in the big chair that doubled as a bed when unfolded. No visitors had come during the night, though Nicole wondered if Lois Embry might be by sometime that day. "And looking a lot better today."

"Thank you." Adelai held Nicole's gaze for a moment, and then her eyes skittered across the room, glanced off the TV, and settled on her son. "Am I in trouble?"

"I hope not," Nicole said. "But a lot has happened in the past thirty hours, hasn't it?"

"Longer."

"We have questions," Nicole began. "Some things must be answered, so why don't we start at the beginning?"

Adelai sat quietly while she gathered her thoughts, and Nicole waited her out, allowing tension to build. The only other sounds in the room were the slight buzz of the TV and the gentle breathing of Adelai's son. There was something extraordinary in that, the rhythmic breathing of a newborn. It seemed a silly thought, and oddly moving, so much so that Nicole began to feel uncomfortable with the emotions the young woman and her baby inspired in her. Of course, she had felt that with Jordan. She remembered gazing at him, his beauty new and breathtaking.

She gave herself a mental shake and prompted Adelai. "Maybe start with the baby's father."

"He's a good man," she said. "He loves me and our son."

"Where is he?"

"He didn't come home. He always comes home, and I had an appointment at the clinic that afternoon. He would not miss it."

"But he did?"

"Yes."

"Did he call you? Or you him?"

"I tried, but every time it went to voice mail." Her lips trembled. "And then the last few times not even that."

"You said the people after you don't like you—why, Adelai?"

The woman shrugged and looked away.

"Because you're Syrian?"

Adelai nodded. "Yes," she whispered.

"What happened? You said Matthew prepared you for this."

"You know, in case Immigration or Border Patrol came looking for me," she explained. "I would run so they couldn't take me away."

Adelai's hands curled into the sheets. Shadows passed through her eyes.

"There's more," Nicole insisted.

"Matthew got phone calls, from someone who did care. He told Matthew to leave and do it quickly. But we had just gotten here. We had a home and there's a clinic close by, to help with the baby. I felt safe here, for the first time in . . . forever." She looked at Nicole with unshed tears in her eyes. "I didn't want to leave. And Matthew said his family would come around. Once we were married, they would have to."

"So you stayed," Nicole said. "You made up names and were careful not to make an impression on people in town."

Adelai nodded. "We kept to ourselves."

"Then what happened?"

Adelai thought about that. Her teeth sawed at her bottom lip, her eyes straying to her baby, sleeping peacefully in his bassinet.

"We would have been married, but the paperwork was long and there was always one or two things more we needed to do with every answer we received."

"Because you were born in another country?"

"And I didn't have a copy of my birth certificate. We had to apply for that through the Syrian embassy. It took time. And then there were things we needed to do for our government here, for their approval."

They had tried going through the proper channels, a bureaucratic mess of paperwork and probably like scaling Everest.

"And now you fear, for your baby and yourself," Nicole said.

"There are plenty of reasons to fear," Adelai assured her.

Nicole nodded, because it was true. And she was just about to add to those reasons.

"You think Matthew is dead," she began.

"He would not leave us otherwise. He promised me only death would separate us."

"We found a dead man in an upstairs bedroom of your home, and we're missing two law enforcement agents," Nicole said. Neither surprise nor fear bloomed on Adelai's face, but then she had probably seen news of both on the TV. "I'd like to know if the two are connected. Can you help me with that?"

"I don't know how."

"Aren't you curious about the man we found?"

"I have accepted that Matthew is dead."

"I have a picture I'd like you to look at," Nicole said. Lars had taken the photo after MacAulay turned the body over for transport. The same photo Tandy had looked at, a head shot, with the bullet hole between the eyes clearly visible and some discoloration on the face where blood had pooled after death. She brought it up on her phone and turned it so Adelai could look at the screen. Nicole watched for her reaction. Her eyes flared with surprise and sorrow. There was recognition, and the young woman's tears flowed freely. Many emotions crossed her face, but Adelai said nothing.

"You know him," Nicole prompted.

"I do."

"Is it Matthew?"

"No, his brother," she said.

"How do you know?"

"Matthew kept pictures of his family. He has two brothers who mean a lot to him and parents who love him." Nicole heard a wistfulness in Adelai's voice that clearly said she did not.

"Was this man in the military?"

"No, but he was hoping to be. He wanted to follow in Matthew's footsteps."

"Matthew was a Marine?"

"Yes. For six years. He was a good soldier, and the military was good to him. He saw the world and took college classes." She nodded, thinking about the man Matthew had become, perhaps, with the support of the Marines. "He was injured in Afghanistan; that's why he left the Corps. They offered to reclassify him, but that's not what Matthew wanted."

"Was it an honorable discharge?"

"Of course."

"And his other brother?"

Adelai's eyes scanned Nicole's uniform, snagging on the gold star pinned at her left shoulder. "He is someone like you."

"A police officer?"

But Adelai shrugged.

"Local?"

"We moved here to be closer to his family."

Nicole nodded. She had gotten the bulk of what she had come for and wanted to leave something with this woman that she could count on.

"You gave birth to a child with an American father. Your son is a United States citizen. What this means," Nicole said, "is that your position has changed. You will be given priority citizenship. There's paperwork involved, but there are organizations that help with that." She caught and held the young woman's eyes. "It means you can stop running."

"Matthew told me that too," she said. "That's why I came with you last night. Why I asked you to take me to the hospital. My son needs an American birth certificate."

"I'm going to need names now," Nicole said. "You told Tandy, the midwife, that your name is Georgia Peach."

Adelai had the grace to color. "It isn't, of course."

"But is Adelai correct?"

She shook her head. "My first name at birth was Adila, so Adelai is close and easier to pronounce and, of course, more American sounding."

Nicole nodded and wrote down the spelling of the name. "And you're surname?" Adelai had given her surname as Franks to the hospital, and it was time to connect the dots.

The young woman cast her eyes down. "It should be Franks. It would have been."

Had she married the baby's father.

"We need your legal last name," Nicole said.

"Amari," she said. She had given that to the hospital as a middle name.

"And Matthew's full name is Matthew Franks?"

"Yes. Matthew Thomas Franks."

"And his brother, the man in the picture I showed you?"

"James Franks. He was just eighteen."

Nicole made note of the GSW's name and birth date. She thought about Matthew Franks, a decorated soldier, an honorable man with ties that bind—his loyalty to his younger brother and his love for a woman worth dying for.

"And the other brother?"

"Luke Franks. He's the oldest. In his thirties, I think."

Luke Franks, Border Patrol agent. Nicole had been expecting that, a loose thought tumbling through her mind from the moment Adelai had told her he was *someone like you.*

"Border Patrol," Nicole said softly, with understanding.

"Yes, it caused trouble," Adelai said, "but he would not turn me in."

But it put Luke Franks in a difficult position.

Nicole tucked her notebook in a pocket and settled her gaze on Adelai.

"The midwife, she followed you, and the men after you, into the woods. She noticed boats on the lake. Two of them. She heard voices. I know you heard and saw things too."

But Adelai shook her head. "I was focused on one thing only," she said, but Nicole pressed forward.

"You know something," Nicole insisted.

"I don't. These men have killed before and they will do it again, and you will not be able to stop them. And maybe that's what happened to

117

your agents. I saw the news this morning. All the busyness on the lake. Maybe they crossed paths in the night. Maybe your agents are the reason I am alive. These men were so close, right on my heels, and then they weren't." She looked up at Nicole. "They would not give up their mission for any small thing."

"How did you know they would kill you?"

"Matthew told me, and Luke told him."

"Were these men Border Patrol agents?"

If so, it was a piece that fit easily into the puzzle.

"I think so," she said.

Nicole took a moment to let that sink in.

"But you have no proof?" she asked.

"Of course not."

"And Matthew or Luke? Did they have proof?"

"Maybe. And maybe that's why Matthew is dead."

"We don't know that," Nicole said. "Not yet."

She moved Luke Franks to the top of her list. She would wait for Lars, and they would go back to the agent's home together.

"You didn't see the boats on the lake, Adelai?" she prompted. "Their running lights were on."

"I was running blind," she said. "Especially towards the end. I was in labor and feared for our lives. I wasn't thinking about the lake, about finding salvation there. I was so tired, and they were so close. I heard gunfire and the scrabbling of feet and thought for sure we would die out there."

"Gunfire?" Nicole asked.

"Several cracks. I was seven years old when we came here from Syria. The sound of gunfire is unmistakable. One of my earliest memories and one of the most enduring."

"How close?"

She lifted her shoulders in bewilderment. "With the lake and the mountains, sound is distorted. One thing is sure, I've had it closer."

Nicole considered Adelai's words, the vulnerability in her face. She was tired—emotionally exhausted and not much better physically.

"You're under guard here, until you're discharged." She pulled a card from her breast pocket. It had the office number on the front and Nicole's cell number on the back. She'd also written the number of an organization that assisted refugees. "Call me if you need anything, and don't go far. We may have more questions."

Adelai took the card, and Nicole said, "You may be right. Maybe you're not safe in Blue Mesa, not until we apprehend the men responsible for James Franks' death."

"The same men who broke into my home and want me dead too."

Nicole nodded. "You could be right about that as well." She walked toward the door, but turned and regarded Adelai before leaving. "Don't be too quick to discharge," she advised. "You're safe here, where we can keep an eye on you."

15

Nicole was back in the Yukon and pulling out of the hospital parking lot when her phone rang. It was Green. She pressed a button on her steering wheel and let Bluetooth pick up the call.

"The body of Melody Baker was recovered a few minutes ago," he said. "Along with a bag of cash and drugs with the BP evidence tags still on them."

"Where?" They had stopped dragging the lake the day before. It had been a frustrating process with so many downed trees tangling in the steel hooks.

"She washed up on the southeast shore of the lake. Just like you had thought."

Well, not exactly. She had spoken of the currents and natural drift and she had hoped the morning would turn up additional evidence, but they had all been thinking the same thing—bodies. There had been every chance the tide would push the bodies to shore. The sudden ice melt the night before, with the floes breaking away from the bottom of the lake, had probably helped their cause, pushing Baker's body toward land with greater propulsion. Anticipating that, Nicole had had deputies out at first light, walking the shoreline.

"No obvious cause of death, other than exposure and drowning," Green continued.

Meaning the agent could have fallen overboard or jumped to her death. Accident or suicide. But Nicole's money was on murder.

"And the evidence?"

"We found the satchel a short distance away. Not meant for water. It provided little protection for the contents."

"But the evidence tags, the BP print, it's still legible?"

"Clear as day. Those bags are watertight, and of course, they weren't in the lake long."

"You call out MacAulay?"

"He's en route. Your forensics team too."

He'd given up his king-of-the-mountain attitude, and she wondered why.

"No sign of Monte?"

"None," Green confirmed. "And at this point, I don't expect him to turn in with the tide. No, I think Monte will surprise us all and walk away from this and maybe right over the border."

The distance from the BP skiff to the nearest stretch of shore had been an eighth of a mile of frigid, limb-numbing water. It wasn't an easy shoreline to manage. Nicole had looked at the topographical maps yesterday. There were an undulating series of shallow pools and sudden drops of twelve to fifteen feet. The current pulled through these pockets and made the distance to safety deceiving. Once on land, the sandy beach was small, irregular, and strewn with rock and fallen trees. Then the geography changed once again, became thickly wooded and sloped upward. From there it was a climb of sixty or seventy yards to the road and possible help. Could Monte have done all that? Survived the swim and whatever preceded it, crossed the rugged terrain sopping wet and chilled to the bone? Even if he'd kept moving, his body would have begun shutting down. The impulses from his brain would have been sluggish.

"I'm on my way," she told Green, and signed off, then radioed Lars, who had stopped to interview the Embrys. "Meet me at site," she told him. "They've recovered the body of Melody Baker."

There was a pause, and when he spoke, she heard the regret in his voice. Officer down. It would impact the morale of all who were searching and those who'd been left on the line.

"I'm finishing up here," he said. "ETA fifteen minutes."

"A surprise package too," Nicole said. "Drugs and cash straight from the BP evidence locker, found in a satchel near the body."

"No shit?" he said. "Well, that's a tidy cleanup, isn't it?"

"Cash and drugs, still bagged and tagged," Nicole agreed. "Served cold." And she didn't like it. As Lars had said, it was too tidy. A present, gift wrapped and placed in her hands.

121

"It would take more than Baker and Monte to hold our GSW down and execute," Lars pointed out.

"And there are five unique boot prints at the house." She came to the only intersection in town and turned south, toward Lake Maria and the body of Agent Baker. "I spoke to Adelai," she said.

"You get the name of the baby daddy?"

"I did," she said. "And the circle tightens." In fact, she was beginning to think all the major players were already on their game board, Monte included. "Matthew Franks."

"Damn, isn't that something," Lars said. "Related to Luke Franks, obviously."

"Brother," Nicole confirmed. "And to James Franks, our GSW, also brother."

16

MacAulay was already on scene, crouched beside the victim and wrapping her hands in cellophane. He had a body bag beside him, and because it was clear plastic, Nicole could see that he had already collected pieces of human extract. She had never cared for the term, but it was textbook and it helped some of them keep an emotional distance from a tragic ending. In this case, when it was someone known, even by a single or double degree of separation, it seemed offensive. Nicole tried to shake that off and focused instead on MacAulay. He looked good. The color was back in his face, and he was moving fluidly and with energy.

She strode across the rolling grass, losing sight of MacAulay as she hit the troughs and recapturing the image of his rangy body bent over the victim as she crested the next hill.

The current had pulled the body more than a mile from where the BP skiff had idled, then floundered, and finally capsized and sunk, she would guess at an angle of 100 to 120 degrees. That would be measured later, but it seemed to fall in with expected parameters. Drift in the lake was legendary.

The wind lifted in cool bursts that tossed the ends of Nicole's hair and pitched under the collar of her department shirt. The weather was a paradox, but she loved it that way. Too warm for a jacket today but occasionally cool enough that she wished she'd had one. She turned, and her gaze fell again on MacAulay. He had one failed marriage behind him—one of those fiery passions of youth, as he described it. It had lasted less than two years, had produced no children, and he had returned home from his rotation in emergency medicine one evening to find that his wife had packed up and left.

"Those were lonely years," he'd said of it. "For the both of us. She was right about that. Medical school is twenty-four/seven and then some."

End of story, his tone had said, and Nicole hadn't pursued it further.

She stood on the crest of the hill and watched him a moment longer. His brown hair curled at his neck, and she could tell, even from a distance, that he had decided not to shave that morning. And not the morning before either. She liked when he kept a rough stubble. His whiskers were liberally salted and a contrast to his head of hair. It gave him an edge that belied his steady, thoughtful manner and was flat-out sexy.

"I'm glad one of us has something to smile about."

Lars had caught up with her and interrupted her musings. She felt her cheeks heat. She was glad the wind was cool enough that she could blame her color on it if needed.

She turned and regarded her second-in-command. The Nordic bull. He'd earned the nickname by build and temperament. He wasn't much taller than Nicole, but he was broad, with burly shoulders and a stubbornness that matched his smarts when in pursuit of leads and the solving of crimes. He had integrity and a similar career background as Nicole, with years rooted in big-city crime.

"Lois Embry admitted to knowing several members of BP. Two of interest, Monte and Luke Franks," Lars said.

"Yeah? How did you get that out of her?"

"I showed her pictures of both. Baker too. I told her we're missing two agents and it's beginning to look like they won't be coming home." He shrugged. "She melted a little. Enough to tap Monte's photo and say, 'He was a good one. A complete opposite to the other.' She meant Franks. Said he had a hard skin and flint for a heart."

"And Baker?"

But Lars shook his head. "She never saw her. Not even in passing."

"So they knew Adelai was a refugee?"

"Embry claimed they didn't talk about particulars, some truths being self-evident. When there's a knock at the door barely into sunrise and a young woman holding a baby covered in vernix on your doorstep, you know, she said. She's an attorney, by the way. Retired."

"I figured as much," Nicole said. "Immigration?"

"No. International law. Both her and the husband. Met in Cairo when they were working for the U.S. embassy." He nodded toward MacAulay. "He feeling any better?"

Nicole shrugged. "I haven't spoken to him. Looks it, though."

"He came by the hospital last night."

That surprised her. "Did he say why?"

"He had to collect fluids and tissue samples from the ice man and heard that we had brought Adelai in. He wanted to finish processing the placenta. Adelai was agreeable. She swabbed the inside of her mouth for comparison purposes but assured MacAulay that she had indeed given birth beside the lake. She couldn't give an exact time, but together they decided on two forty-five A.M."

Nicole nodded and began walking down the slope toward the center of activity. Lars fell into step beside her.

"And the GSW? Did Doc start on him?"

"Textbook," Lars confirmed. "Adelai wasn't open to blood comparison. She didn't want the baby pricked for a sample." To determine relation between the baby and the GSW. "But she did give a blood sample herself when MacAulay spoke of finding the ice man."

Her surprise deepened. "Why did he mention that?"

Lars shrugged. "I asked him that too. He said we're growing on him. Suspicions and connections. He said he doesn't like loose ends and the bodies are piling up in his morgue. And he pointed out that both Adelai and the ice man are Syrian."

"But not the only two in the world."

"Probably not the only two passing through Blue Mesa either. But at one point they were within a mile of each other."

Proximity. She saw it. And MacAulay was doing his job. Exceeding expectations again.

"He's living up to the mantle," Lars said.

She agreed, then changed the subject.

"Why do you suppose Monte isn't wearing his parka?" she asked.

"And Baker is?"

"Yes."

"Could be a number of reasons," he said. "But I think you have a theory."

"I'm working on one," she agreed. "Sounds farfetched."

"So try it on me."

"Maybe he knew he was going into the lake and discarded it," she said. "Or he was wearing it when he went in and quickly took it off."

"Because it was dead weight and useless besides."

"Exactly."

"You're thinking maybe he made it to shore?"

"It's a possibility."

"Slim," he agreed. "But you know those polar swimmers? The ones who dive into icy waters, swim a mile, then break for shore? They wear next to nothing."

"And survive the experience."

He pulled his phone out and started a search. "Sixteen minutes," he said. "That's how long a human can swim in water at freezing temperatures before they give in to exhaustion. Did anyone take water temperature last night?"

"I'm sure Arthur did." Nicole used her radio, clipped at her shoulder, to call in for the stat. While they waited for dispatch to contact the crime lab and a tech to come up with the answer, she had another question for Lars. "So he could have made it, then? I figure it's an eighth of a mile from the skiff to shore. That wouldn't take sixteen minutes, would it?"

"How fit is Monte?"

"He runs the trail at Latham. I've seen him there several times since I started back running."

"Doable for sure," Lars said, "unless he was being shot at, or pursued by a vessel."

"Adelai heard shots," Nicole revealed. "And Tandy saw a boat searching the water as it headed toward shore."

"Damn. Well, that trims Monte's odds for making it alive."

Nicole nodded. She expected another body to wash up, probably sometime today.

"Adelai said she neither heard nor saw anything else," she said.

"Do you believe her?"

"She knows more. Maybe not about Monte, but something."

The radio crackled to life, and Nicole paused long enough to get her answer—thirty-one degrees.

"So he had a little under sixteen minutes before his body began to shut down," Lars said. "The average man can swim an eighth of a mile in nine minutes. Let's say Monte made it to shore, then what did he do?"

"Whatever it was, he had to do it quickly. Hypothermia was already at work in his body and it was cold that night. Twenty-seven degrees. Monte told me that himself."

"So, running and the charge of warmth it gave the body, maybe he had twenty minutes, give or take, to make something happen for himself."

"Maybe he didn't have to go far for that," she said. "Remember those life packs BP placed along the shore after recovering the bodies of the women and children in January?"

Lars's face brightened. "Yeah. And he would know exactly where to find them."

"We need to check with BP. Get the coordinates for each. See if they've been disturbed," she said. Not just along the shore, but into the woods and north to the border. "One missing wouldn't be definitive that Monte had made it to shore, that he was the one who'd made use of it, but it would give us another direction to explore."

She shifted her gaze, seeking and finding Green several yards away, crouched with a handful of other agents beside a rotted tree that had fallen at the point where shore became woods. He lifted his hand and called over one of Nicole's forensics techs. She and Lars followed as well.

"You have an alternate light source?" Green asked the tech. "Could be nothing. Could be the break we're looking for." He rose as he watched Nicole approach the group.

"Sheriff." He nodded in greeting and included Lars in the gesture. "Thanks for coming out."

The sarcasm was like a slap in the face. Nicole felt her skin pucker in response. Lars rolled his shoulders and his lips flattened; he would have spoken, but Nicole beat him to it.

"We're sorry for your loss," she said. "Everyone here knows how hard it is. For some of us, it's a weight that makes us stumble." Even a good leader took a knee, however briefly, while leading the fight, and she allowed that to temper her tone. She watched Green take a deep breath as her words hit home. "We've been on the job since before sunrise," she continued, "chasing leads. I'm doling out overtime like its confetti, running thin around the edges, and in some quadrants the time between calls and response has doubled." She had moved men around the board so that those areas that were lacking patrol were sparsely populated and the least troublesome. She had put in calls and received promises that as soon as the need here at the scene lessened, she would have interagency support to fill her gaps. "All to have more officers here, where they're needed."

It took a moment, but he nodded. "I know that," he said. "I do, and I appreciate it. I apologize."

"Accepted," she said. "Now, why the ALS?"

"Possible blood. There's a trail up from the water. Not heavy, but enough. It's worth bagging some of these rocks, taking a piece of this bark. If it is blood and it's human, I can see a man staggering up the beach, sitting down on the log for a moment to get his bearings."

Lars nodded. "We're exploring the possibility," he began. "We figure Monte could survive a swim to shore but would quickly yield to hypothermia if help wasn't pretty much immediate."

"The life packs," Nicole said, and Green was nodding.

"We thought of that too, not an hour ago, and we're checking on it. We placed seven around the lake, then some deeper into the woods but further apart. One every half mile all the way up to the border." He turned north and contemplated the distance and the possibilities. "There's no way of knowing if Monte used any of them. It could be a wild-goose chase." Nicole heard the first threads of defeat enter Green's voice. Finding Baker dead was beginning its whittling of morale. He turned back to Nicole and connected with her gaze. "Two of the packs have been used. Your guys are dusting for prints and brushing for epithelial cells. I have one of our agents leading one of your techs north, to the first three beyond the lake. I cleared it with your head of forensics, Sleeping Bear. If Monte touched any of them and didn't have reason to wipe his prints, we'll know."

"Because he wouldn't have gloves." Those would have been the first thing he'd shed, before the parka, in order to make the swim.

Green pushed a hand through his hair and then anchored both on his hips. "We need fresh eyes and ears."

"Have you called in the feds?"

His gaze became heavy. "I like cleaning up my own messes. Bad enough I have my boss and his boss calling in for updates, poking and prodding me as if I need motivation to get to the bottom of all this. Those same fingers will starting pointing soon, and someone will need to take the rap."

Green was fighting to keep his job.

"It doesn't look good," Nicole agreed.

"It'll look better if I can solve this on my own. With your help, of course. I asked Highway Patrol to increase its visibility, not just in and around Blue Mesa but further afield. Jax Town and Shelby too. Those are your highest call areas, right?"

Nicole nodded. She looked beyond Green to the shoreline and the scattering of officers and agents. "We have to reopen the lake today," she said. "We don't get a lot of activity this time of year, but a few complaints have come in. I can maybe push it out until noon before the mayor is on my ass."

"And here?" he asked.

"This is new and will take hours to process, so closed to any and all civilian activity. But the boats aren't coming back." Not today and not at all unless they uncovered evidence to indicate it was worth the time and effort. "It's a mess out there. The lake bottom is filled with sheared trees and other detritus, and deputies have spent just as much time untangling their lines as searching."

"Understood."

"We have a press conference scheduled for noon," she told him. "The sheriff's department will make it official, claiming the lead in the investigation and making the shift in focus to recovery."

"They'll ask why," Green said.

"They will." Nicole held his gaze. "We'll make a statement about internal issues and volley any questions to your agency."

"So I should prepare myself," Green said.

"Yes, be ready."

"And the rest of us?" He looked out over his men. "We're already down to a skeleton crew. Surely we can stay?"

But Nicole shook her head. "It's our investigation, Green. Take your men and go home. By noon."

"You know I can't do that," he said. "It would be career suicide."

"I'm not asking," she said. "We'll keep you informed, and we'll need some cooperation in terms of personnel files and interviews if necessary."

Green snorted. "Interviews? That's not going to happen."

She'd expected pushback. So maybe she would ask the feds, if they came, to take care of the interviews. A middle, distant party carrying a bigger club was always the better choice in a matter such as this.

"It'll happen," Lars said, then changed the course of the discussion, his abrupt tone and manner making it clear he understood that their requests would be met. "I hear the dogs didn't work."

Border Patrol had the best-trained dogs in the region. Nicole had borrowed them herself on a few occasions, mostly missing-persons cases.

Green shook his head, and a quizzical expression screwed up his face. "I don't get it. I had scent dogs out here for live and cadaver. They sniffed off Monte's jacket, scampered up shore and into the woods, and came to a dead stop. I had an agent bring a scarf from Monte's desk. I saw the man wearing it myself a few days ago. They sniffed, ran into the woods, and began whining and prancing around. We took them north and south, different entries, but they got nothing off that. I had the handlers take them into the woods and backtrack to the last viable scenting, and they were stumped. Confused. It's rare something like that happens."

"So that's a dead end?" Lars pressed.

"The deadest I've ever seen." Green shook his head in disgust. "We've had eighty-seven men and women out here since four yesterday morning, and nothing gives. I mean, we literally have nothing."

But Nicole disagreed. "We have a lot of leads and more than one way in." She was hopeful.

"I want Monte back here, alive," he said. "I want that more than anything. And if I can keep my job too, all the better."

Corruption in the ranks never went over well, and Nicole had never known Green to become too involved in any particular case. He was strictly sidelines, managing people and paper. But in cases like this, when there were internal problems, the blame always pointed up. Maybe Green had been too distant. Maybe he hadn't kept his fingers on the pulse of his team. She hadn't heard that, or even the shadow of a bad comment, from

Monte or any of the other BP agents. But he seemed to be a boss none of them knew too well.

"How do checks and balances work in the BP?" Nicole asked.

"It's gradient, like it is in most agencies," Green said. "Agents report to supervisors, who report to shift commanders, who report to satellite chiefs—someone like myself."

"And who do you report to?" Lars asked.

"Augustus Woods. He's the director of the northwest region."

"And have you reported?"

"Morning, noon, and night," he assured them. "But he'll come, if not today, tomorrow," he said. "And I hope to have this wrapped up by then."

They all hoped for that, and more. Whether Monte was good or bad, she wanted him back among the living too.

17

The sun was well into the sky, but it was lukewarm at best. Nicole left Lars and Green talking logistics and turned toward shore. The breeze pulled a few curls from her hairline, and she pushed them back as she walked. There were fewer men on the water and far more beside it today than yesterday; there were more clues to uncover on land than at the bottom of the lake.

She had an ME to talk to and needed an update from her forensics team. She walked toward MacAulay and could hear him talking into his recorder. He turned his digital notes in to the forensics clerk for transcription, which freed up his time for autopsy and running tests.

She was careful to stop outside the halo and waited for a break in his dictation to speak.

"First impressions indicate Agent Melody Baker suffered from post-mortem abrasions within the parameters of a drowning victim in open water . . ."

He finished with the note and placed the mike down atop a slip of glassine.

"You look a lot better," she said.

"Feel tons better." He looked up and smiled, and it reached his eyes. "You got some sleep," he said, and his smile deepened and became intimate. It surprised Nicole, because they kept a professional distance from each other during working hours and this was the first time he'd made even a gentle volley over that line.

"I did." And damn if her voice wasn't a throaty whisper. MacAulay noticed. He rocked back onto his heels and his gaze became thoughtful.

"It's getting harder to pretend," he said, "and I'm not sorry about that."

Two solid days together. Every meal, long talks, longer walks. They had gotten layers deeper into what was undeniably a long-term, committed relationship. And in a decidedly professional moment, Nicole felt herself sink a little deeper into the personal warmth MacAulay extended.

"Yes," she agreed, but then gave herself a mental shake and changed the course of the conversation. She nodded toward the body of Agent Baker. "You have a preliminary cause of death?"

"Drowning."

"So she was alive going in," she said.

"Yes, but not necessarily conscious." He reached forward, his hands covered in latex, and turned the victim's head. "See that?" He pushed back a heavy lock of red hair, exposing the victim's temple. Bruising and swelling from the eyebrow to the cheekbone. "Definitely occurred prior to submersion."

"How do you know?"

"This contusion"—he held up the agent's arm—"happened after drowning. See how the edges are swollen around the wound, pulling open the skin? That's bloating. It happens to the body after drowning." He indicated the head injury. "Not so here. This wound had at least a minute or two to swell up on its own before the water could do its damage."

"Any idea what caused the blow?"

"I'll make impressions, use photo comparison, but my first thought? The grip of a gun." He ran his finger through the air above the affected skin. "See how the eruption is at the center, with bruising developing around it in a spiral fashion? That's standard results from such an injury."

"Can you tell me what kind of gun from the injury?"

"I will after I take impressions, but first off, the material was wood. You see that, if the grip of the gun was metal or plastic, the edges would be serrated." And there was no such pattern here, just a torn flap of skin. "And the bone beneath?" he continued. "I pressed my finger to it—it's in pieces. Not a break but a complete shattering."

"And wood would do that?" she asked. Handguns with metal grips made up the majority of gun purchases.

"A hard wood. Walnut is my bet."

"So someone carrying a piece with a wooden grip." That narrowed the search. Unless, of course, the agent's gun had been taken from her and used to impart the injury. Agents and officers alike were allowed to choose between department issue and preference, so long as their firearm fit reasonable parameters. She would follow through with Green on that.

"Definitely," MacAulay said. He shifted, leaving the victim's head and turning toward her feet. She was missing both shoes and a sock. A tattoo was on display on her right ankle.

Nicole couldn't step closer for a better look without breaking through the halo.

"Snap a picture of that and text it to me, please."

"Will do. You'll find it interesting and one of a kind," he promised.

It looked common enough to Nicole from where she stood. A braided leather chain, somewhat fraying, with a charm dangling from it.

"Why do you think so?" she asked.

MacAulay had his cell phone out and was lining up a shot. He took several, from different angles and distances, then opened up his contacts and sent some to her.

"You'll see," he said. "And just so you know, I wouldn't be opposed if you wanted to get a similar tat, only with my name written across your heart."

That piqued her interest. She felt her eyebrows rise in question, but he made her wait it out. She pulled her cell from her pocket just as it dinged.

"How old is the tattoo, would you say?"

"I'll have to examine a sample under a microscope to give you a better idea," he said. Nicole knew ink deposits in the skin were a great help in determining the age of tattoos, so long as they were less than a year old.

"Best guess?" she prodded, as she opened her messages and tapped a photo.

"Two or three months," he said.

The charm was indeed a heart. It was outlined in red ink, and the name written in a fancy script inside the shape was Monte.

"Monte." She spoke the word in a hushed voice. She had no doubt that Monte and Agent Baker had tried to keep their relationship a secret, but as she'd just found with MacAulay, as the heart became deeper entwined with another, it was harder to keep that under cover. There had already been whispers of involvement in the BP office. And now they knew Green's suspicions were valid.

"This opens other possibilities," she said. A lover's quarrel or suicide pact among them.

She turned and radioed Lars. He was still talking to Green, observing the collection of blood evidence.

"Tell Green I want a list of all handguns licensed to both agents. I want to know department issue and private stock."

"Will do."

She watched across the distance as Lars disengaged from Green and sought privacy by placing several yards between them. "Sounds like you have a theory," he said.

But she shook her head. "Pieces that might fit together," she said. "Process of elimination and fumbling in the dark." That about summed it up. "I want you to see something. Come down here when you're finished. And let Ty know I want to talk to him sometime today."

When she turned back to MacAulay, he was pulling debris from the agent's hair with a pair of long tweezers.

She gazed again upon the dead agent. In a town as small as Blue Mesa, Nicole knew most people and had at least a passing recognition of others. Not this woman, though. Which meant Baker had probably driven the seventy-five plus miles to the trendy shopping malls, restaurants, and movie theaters in Pleasant Falls. She lay in the sand, parallel to the lake, and her eyes seemed to look out over the water. She had muscle on her, long legs and wide shoulders. If all hope was lost, wouldn't she have fought back? She had training, darkness on her side, but had been surrounded by lake and frigid temperatures.

"Defensive injuries?" Nicole asked.

"One, maybe," MacAulay said. He reached across Baker's body and opened her hand, gently unfurling her fingers so that her palm faced up. A laceration about an inch and a half long stretched from the center of her palm to the fleshy padding near her wrist. "There could be transfer DNA in that cut."

"What do you think made it?"

He thought about that, pursing his lips. "It's superficial," he said. "A glancing blow. The angle tells me she had her arm up, above her head, and brought it down in a swinging motion that crossed her body. Arthur will need to confirm that, of course." But he liked his theory, and Nicole could tell the time he'd spent in Injuries Resulting From Mortal Combat training two months ago was paying off. "So maybe she had her arms up, at gunpoint, and she had an opportunity to try for the weapon."

She nodded. It was a reasonable action taken by a trained law enforcement officer, if it had happened that way.

"I've taken a primitive measurement here in the field. It could have been made by the front sight of a handgun."

"That's impressive," Nicole said. There was a time when she had worried if MacAulay would ever embrace his role as ME. He hadn't come looking for the job. Nicole had approached him because they were in desperate need. Coming from big-city policing, it was outside her comfort zone to stand in a crime scene, guarding a body passing through the natural decomposition stages following death, while the ME drove in from Billings—often more than a two-hour drive, during which evidence was forever lost. She had made funding the ME position her number-one cause when she took office. Into her second year, she was given budgetary approval. As it was a part-time position, she knew there was no hope of luring an ME from out of town, and with less than a handful of local doctors to choose from, MacAulay became the clear choice. He was a family practitioner who'd had rotations through Chicago's Lower East Side. He had seen his share of wounds from bullets and baseball bats, fists and knives and more. He turned her down without consideration the first time she asked. "I left all that behind," he told her. "I'm not suited to that kind of work, and I don't want to be."

Of the four local doctors, two were older and semiretired; the third, Nicole suspected, would have trouble meeting the demands of the job, which sometimes required battling the elements over rough terrain. MacAulay was fit. He had experience with violent injuries. He was their only choice.

Nicole tried again, two additional meetings. She laid out the importance of speaking for the victim. Emphasized that evidence collection was the only way to do that once a suspicious death had occurred.

"So it's not an entirely hopeless situation?" MacAulay asked.

"I prefer to look at our work as the only hope they have left."

He took that away with him and gave the offer serious consideration. Later, he told her he'd gotten on the web and searched, spoken to old medical school acquaintances, even interviewed a few standing MEs from the state medical boards. And he'd said yes, with conditions. He expected the department to pay for trainings but would pay for the additional certification himself. He'd gone back to school, online when possible and traveling to San Francisco one weekend a month plus a month in the summer to complete the requirements.

MacAulay drew her attention back to the present by wiggling his eyebrows in a ridiculous manner. "Give me a few hours and I'll raise that impressive to a stunning," he promised.

He was smiling, and Nicole got caught up in it. For a man who didn't believe in wild cards and grand gestures, his smile was like the rushing wind. It had lift and velocity.

"Sheriff Cobain?"

The interruption was jolting simply because it was unexpected. Because Nicole had been caught in a vacuum, floating on helium.

She turned, her knees and elbows making sharp, awkward cuts rather than moving fluidly.

Arthur Sleeping Bear, her chief forensics officer. He was tall and wide and followed some of the cultural norms of his Native heritage, today wearing a single feather fastened with a copper pin in his hair, which was beginning to turn gray.

A quizzical expression fanned out from his eyes, and he took a step back. "Sorry for intruding," he said, which only made Nicole more uncomfortable.

"Of course not," she said. She strived for an even tone and asked, "What's up?"

"A few things, actually," he said. "I spent some time in the lab last night. I wanted to run some preliminary checks. You know there's no way to add ballast to theory if the science doesn't add up," he said, and Nicole could tell he was troubled. He usually spoke in a sure manner, but today he was choosing his words carefully. "And sometimes the science builds momentum and completely changes the direction of an investigation. Both tracks are easy to follow. They rarely test the parameters of expectation."

"What's different here?" she asked.

"The reason they don't test parameters is because each stop has expected outcomes. Tried and tested and tested again."

"And that's not the case here?"

"No. I came back this morning, looking for obvious reasons for the outliers that are cropping up in the lab."

"What are the outliers?" Nicole asked.

But he wanted to take a step backward, begin with the tangible and connect some dots.

"Essentially we have five separate crime scenes, now that the body of Agent Baker was recovered. Our initial investigation centered around the ice floe, the sunken BP skiff, and a quarter mile of shoreline directly due east of the ice floe. Then we have the placenta and the surrounding area—remains to be seen if we classify that as a crime scene. We have the GSW in the house"—he turned and pointed northwest—"and we have this stretch of beach." He opened his arms to include Baker's body and the marshy grasslands that extended toward the Lake Road, less than a quarter mile south from where they stood. "Two homicides, one possible, the other a bread crumb, if you will, marking a desperate trail of escape."

Nicole nodded.

"But escape from what?" Arthur questioned. "Test results are coming in, Sheriff, and there's enough to move beyond speculation—the woman chased from the house, who gave birth next to the lake, was chased by law enforcement."

Green had insisted the GSW and that crime scene had nothing to do with their missing agents. He had fought the removal of officers to aid in locating Adelai and baby. But Nicole had had some suspicion BP was involved, as had Adelai. That suspicion was why Nicole had refused to give Green the young woman's name.

"I have castings and fibers that match a specific boot," Arthur continued, "supplied only to federal officers of the following agencies—FBI, Department of Treasury, and Border Patrol."

Nicole felt her breath bottle in her throat. "Only those?" she asked. "Are you sure?"

"One hundred percent," he assured her. "If I'd had one or the other—castings or tread—I would be far less certain. But the ability to cross-reference makes it absolute."

Nicole let that sink in. They had proof. This was more than one or two bad seeds. It was a handful, minimum. And how far up did it reach? Certainly Green had to be aware that he had a pocketful of bad pennies. Why hadn't he told her? Was he part of it as well? And those above him? Were they involved? She pulled her cell phone from her pocket and dialed Lars. He was presently standing within three feet of Green and several of his agents, and she didn't want to tip their hand by using the radio.

He had his cell in hand and raised it to check the caller ID. Then he turned on his heel, seeking visual contact even while he connected the call.

"Get down here," she said, and that was enough. The urgency in her voice, perhaps even the tension rolling off their little stretch of beach as they digested the ominous overtones of the evidence, alerted him to the importance of the matter at hand.

Lars disengaged and walked smoothly over the marsh, not hurriedly but in even strides. Nicole, MacAulay, and Arthur Sleeping Bear watched his progress without speaking a word.

But Nicole's thoughts were reeling. Were Monte and Baker among the crooked? Or victims of them? It seemed to Nicole that once this question was answered the rest would fall into place, like markers in the snow. An easy trail that would lead directly to the killers. One of whom could be BP agent Luke Franks. She had trouble sliding him into place anywhere on the board. He seemed to know too much and not enough at the same time. Adelai had spoken of him with hesitation, almost fear. And Lars suspected the agent was holding back. Luke Franks was a person of interest and possibly a suspect.

As Lars drew near, Nicole turned to Arthur and asked, "Have you recovered her boots?"

"She was wearing only one, and it was the first thing I bagged and tagged."

"From the same source as the others?"

"On visual inspection?" Arthur nodded. "I'd say yes."

"What's going on?" Lars asked.

Nicole let Arthur fill him in. She let her focus drift, first to Green and his agents, who were standing around one of her forensics techs while he meticulously cut a piece of bark from a fallen tree.

"Probably worthless," Nicole murmured.

"Worthless?" Lars followed her gaze.

"The bark. That and everything else they handed over to us."

"We have little gathered that BP didn't first discover," Arthur said.

"But there's something else," Nicole said. "When you approached me, you said outliers. Plural."

Arthur nodded. "Yes, there is one more thing. This came from the drifting party boat. Strands of long dark hair, the root attached. We have a preliminary match to the sample the doctor took from the pregnant woman late last night."

"Adelai was on the party boat?"

"Preliminary, but yes, I believe so. It will take up to a week for absolute confirmation."

"Who is Adelai Amari to the United States Border Patrol?" Nicole wondered. It had to go deeper than her relation to Luke and James Franks. What did the young woman have or know that made her a target?

"And how is Monte wrapped up in this?" Lars asked. "He made the call," he pointed out. "He brought you out to the lake. If he were involved in whatever corruption went down that night, he wouldn't have risked exposure."

"Not at face value," Nicole agreed. "MacAulay discovered a tattoo on Baker's ankle." She pulled her phone out and brought up the picture. "Take a look."

Lars did. "That's on her ankle?"

Nicole nodded. "Fairly new."

"There's more to be discovered," Arthur said.

"What can I do to help?" Nicole asked.

He looked at the shoreline, his eyes traveling up into the woods. "If you don't mind me saying so, we need them out of here."

"I gave them orders to vacate by noon," Nicole said, glancing at her watch. "They have less than an hour to make that happen before we assist.

I think we should keep to the timeline. I don't want them to suspect that they've become our target."

"I'm heading back to the lab," Arthur said. "Come when you are ready. I hope to have something to show you." He looked back at MacAulay. "I would like some time to speak with you."

MacAulay stood and faced them both. He nodded toward Sleeping Bear. "I'm encountering some conflicting data as well. A few things that don't add up."

"Such as what?" Nicole asked.

"For one thing, I'm not so sure Agent Baker washed in with the tide," he said.

18

When noon came, Green, as expected, dug in his heels. He postured, hands on hips and his face a florid shade of tomato. He encroached on her personal space, kicked at the damp soil with the toe of his boot, pulled in lungfuls of cool air and blew out tepid breaths that stirred the hair on her head, he was so close, and only capitulated when Nicole warned him, "My next call is the FBI."

She wasn't sure who would take jurisdiction over the investigation of the Border Patrol. The agency as a whole had many internal difficulties, but most of those along the Mexican border. Nicole had heard of both the FBI and the Department of Homeland Security delving into the corruption. But her words gave him pause, and that was the reaction she'd been hoping for.

"You wouldn't." Because law enforcement agencies didn't do that to each other. Green was many things, including a complete buy-in on solidarity among the ranks. It was an important piece of the anatomy of a fully functioning, high-achieving force. But not at the cost of integrity. Not at the forfeit of justice.

"I would," she assured him. "I'm required to. I should have done so already, and so should have you," she pointed out. "The moment you suspected corruption in your office."

Green's eyes turned hard and brittle.

"It's time you clean house, Green. Focus on that," she advised.

Lars came up then and stood beside Nicole. He had a way of appearing when the time was right, allowing her to charge forward in the lead, relying solely on the magnitude of her position, and then presenting a united front when the gauntlet was thrown.

He was sensitive to her role as a female sheriff—there weren't that many of them across the country—and the need for her to maintain the respect of the position. He was also one of the best detectives she'd ever worked with, and she would hate to lose him, or to lose to him, if it ever came to that.

"You going to round up your agents?" Lars asked. "Or would you like us to do that for you?"

As a reply, Green unclipped his radio and brought it to his lips. "We're pulling back," he said. "All of us. Meet at center. Five minutes."

When he was done with the announcement, he found and held Nicole's gaze. "I did, by the way. I want you to know that. When you're wading hip-deep through the sewage, you remember that I was the one who brought Internal Affairs in. And on their heels, Homeland Security."

"You called the dogs in?" Lars asked.

Green turned toward Lars. "It's like you said. Once I suspected, it didn't matter I didn't like it, I had to make the call. And I did."

Nicole nodded. "Noted," she said, but she wondered about the timing. "When was that, Green? Did you make the call before or after evidence went missing?"

"After."

"How long after?" Lars pressed.

"Months," he admitted. "December." And he turned his attention back to Nicole. "It wasn't an easy call. You understand that, Cobain."

Too little too late? Probably. The best of them sometimes had trouble measuring up.

"We'll need a point person," she said. "We have a growing list of needs that can only be fulfilled by someone inside your office."

"What kind of needs?"

"Evidentiary."

"Well, I'm not gone yet, am I?" he challenged. "You can run all your needs through me."

"Great. Let's start with that list of all firearms used by Monte and Baker," she suggested, and then thought better of it. "Actually, it might be a good idea to send over a comprehensive list of all firearms in use at BP."

"Why?" he challenged. "Why guns? I haven't heard word one that shots had been fired."

"Well, then, you haven't heard it all," Lars said. A snarl was building in his voice, and Nicole stepped in before their first request for cooperation turned into a confrontation.

"We have evidence of an injury consistent with a firearm. We'll need to run tests."

"It would help if you could narrow down type."

"Produce the list, and we'll let you know the weapons we want brought to our forensics facility."

She walked away from him then, feeling equal parts sympathy and disdain. Before this was over, Green would lose his job. There was no way he could survive the deterioration of his office. He led a far bigger team than Nicole, with nearly forty agents to her twelve officers. But months of knowing his agency was crawling with vipers and making halfhearted attempts at fixing it, that seemed negligent. In fact, it seemed incriminating.

Nicole stood atop the first rise and looked out over the beach. MacAulay had bagged the body of Agent Baker and transported it back to the morgue. BP agents were in various stages of packing equipment and moving out. The day before, the boats had broken up the floes, and beyond the shoreline the ice drifted now in smaller pieces that bobbed on the current.

In all likelihood, she had a polluted crime scene. What she was going to do about that depended a lot on what she learned from Arthur when she got to the lab, what she learned after she took another pass at Adelai Amari, and what was revealed along with the identity of their ice man.

Lars walked up beside her. He had his phone in hand and was scrolling through notes he'd taken using a stylus that looked like a toothpick in his hand.

"What do we know about Green?" he asked.

"Fifty-five, never married, no kids." That was the preliminary information she'd managed to dig up by simply working her phone earlier that morning. "He drives a fancy car—"

"A Cadillac Escalade," Lars said. "I've seen it. Brand-new or almost."

"—and has a house on the lake with a private dock."

"A lot of cash going out on a government paycheck."

Nicole agreed. "Deputy Casper is going over bank statements today."

"If you had to call it, one way or the other, what would you say about Monte?"

She knew what he was asking, and she was reluctant to go there. But time—it was everything, with the possibility of solving the case dwindling the further out from ground zero they got.

"We aren't going to find Monte." She hated saying it, but the odds weren't in the man's favor. "He never made it out of the lake."

"With Monte and Baker dead and evidence washed up in our crime scene, we've been handed a silver platter."

"Yeah, a lot of loose ends neatly tied," she said, her tone curling with distaste. "Is Green a pawn, or is he a player? The sooner we figure that out, the closer we'll be to solving this case."

19

The trail was a gradual uphill climb, wide and running parallel to a fork of the Astum River. Jordan and his troop would be grading patches in the footpath that winter weather had torn apart and spreading new seed from several indigenous plants that were threatened in the area. It was all good, except that it was too close to Nicole's crime scene on Lake Maria. A mile as the crow flies to the trailhead from where she stood amid the gathering of evidence, and she couldn't shake the uneasiness that seemed to be tapping her on the shoulder.

"Sheriff?"

Nicole turned. Ty Watts had emerged from the woods and was walking down the small stretch of sand toward her. An evidence bag dangling from one hand and a wide smile on his face were her first clues that he'd made an important discovery.

"What do you have, Ty?"

He stopped beside her and held up the bag. "I saw something in the grass. It's pretty thick in there and the sun doesn't always make it through, but it did this time."

"What is it?" Nicole caught the bottom edge of the bag and lifted it closer. "Not a button, exactly."

"No. It's a bronze pin. Monte wore one. It commemorates the tragedy at Royale. Monte served there, was right in the thick of it, and almost single-handedly brought it to an end."

The Isle of Royale tragedy. BP had lost seven agents in that ambush. An island and national park in the northwestern corner of Lake Superior, the Isle of Royale had been the setting of a deadly gun battle involving several boats loaded with immigrants, both undocumented and papered, and an unsuspecting handful of border agents. Reinforcements had wasted no time moving in but were met with a barrage of shoulder-fired missiles. It had happened eleven or twelve years ago, when Nicole was still a detective with the Denver PD. She turned the pin over in her hand, still wrapped in its glassine evidence bag. Etched into the metal was a five-point star, in the center of which was the torch carried by the Statue of Liberty.

"I didn't know Monte had been involved in it," she said.

"He was a hero," Ty said. "And that's why finding this is so important."

"Tell me why, exactly."

"It's bronze. Monte and one other agent—Monte's partner at the time—were pinned with bronze. The others—four of them—are brass."

"How do you know all this?"

"I asked him once, when I noticed the pin."

She caught Ty's gaze.

"So Monte passed through," she said. "He made it to shore and got at least as far as the woods. Or that's what we're supposed to believe."

"You doubt it?" he asked.

"Where exactly did you find this?"

He turned toward the woods and pointed. "About a third of a mile in, northeast trajectory."

How convenient, she thought. On parallel with the worn path up and over the Canadian border.

Nicole gazed again at the image in the metal. The torch, lighting the way to freedom. The irony wasn't lost on her.

"We'll see what Arthur can get from it," she said, though she felt little enthusiasm about it. Any of the BP agents on site could have planted the pin. It could have come off Monte's jacket that was found washed up close by.

"I'm on my way," he said.

But Nicole stopped him. "You and Monte run that water safety class together, right?"

"Yes, ma'am. We work on the trails too."

"So you know him a little better than I do," she said. "How long has Monte been stationed in Blue Mesa?"

Ty shook his head. "He never said. Not to me, anyway. We didn't hang out outside of work, and he was pretty quiet when we volunteered together."

"There's speculation Monte and Agent Baker were romantically involved. Did you ever have reason to suspect that?"

Ty gave it some consideration. "He never said. We were out at the creeks a few weeks ago—there was overflow wiping out the beaver dams—and he was more talkative than usual. Happier."

"What did he talk about?"

"The red-winged starling. It's making a comeback. The clean air. He said he didn't think he'd ever leave it, this part of the country. Promotion opportunities had come and gone and he let them pass without regret, solid with the decision until recently."

"He said that?"

Ty nodded. "Not like it was a serious consideration, leaving. More like he knew there was more out there, but he wasn't interested except—" Ty paused, considering his next words. "Well, yeah, maybe he is involved with someone. Someone who isn't local or a woman who was moving on." He nodded. "Was Agent Baker scheduled for promotion?"

Green had spoken about the necessity of moving one of the agents if a relationship had developed. But she really couldn't trust the head of BP North to come across with any credible information, even if she asked him directly, even while looking him in the face. So that was a dead end.

"What do you think happened out here, Ty?"

"I think Monte made it to shore and Baker didn't," he allowed. "I think they were approached on the water by someone they knew. As comfortable and sympathetic as Monte is with immigrants, he wouldn't let down his guard. Especially given the recent trouble out here and their find in the ice." He thought quietly. "Whoever motored out did it dark, or Monte would have called in the activity before contact was made."

In the party boat. Nicole could see that. Lights out and drifting on the currents. Powering up as they left the shadows at eight yards out and bearing down on the skiff. Maybe deliberately charging the BP vessel.

She thought about the timeline and the possibilities within it. She moved away from Ty, saying over her shoulder, "Check that in with chain of evidence." She nodded toward a deputy who stood near the lapping surf, a large box on all-terrain wheels beside him and a clipboard under his arm. Ty took off in that direction, and Nicole continued to pick apart the timeline. They were thirty-six hours since point of contact with the BP skiff. They had a window of eighty-two minutes, give or take, when all hell had broken loose on and around the lake. In a town as small as Blue Mesa, it all had to be connected.

"What are you thinking?"

Lars had come up beside her.

"Pieces of the same puzzle," she said, "and some of them are connecting. We have the edges in place. Center mass is the middle of this lake. We have Monte and the ice man." She nodded north. "James Franks is executed and Adelai is on the run, heading this way. Deliberately. Why?"

"She was running toward help. She knew that."

"Agreed. What else?"

"How did she know about the Embrys?"

"Luke Franks told them," Nicole said. "Yeah, he's a hard-ass BP agent, but she's a pregnant woman and his brother's girl."

"I like that." Lars considered the timeline, the pieces Nicole was placing in the gaping holes. "And Luke Franks sent his brother James to the house. Not to place him in danger but to get Adelai out of it."

"But how does he know she needs help?"

"He knows his brother, the baby's father, is dead," Lars said. "And he knows who's behind it."

"We have at least a handful of BP agents working against us."

They were quiet as that sank in. Then Nicole continued. "Say they got ahead of us," she posed. "They had the time. And they removed the pieces they could but had to leave something on the table because Ty and MacAulay and I had arrived on scene. Or maybe it's Adelai. She has something incriminating, maybe she's holding the prize, whatever that is, and she eluded them. What's their missing piece?"

"Drugs or money," Lars said.

"Or evidence that could identify and put them away."

"Greed. Freedom. Life. All good motivators," he agreed.

"I want to talk to Adelai again." Nicole worried she'd been blinded by her own vulnerability, by memories of similar circumstances, and hadn't gotten deeper into the young woman and her motivations because of it. "I missed something." Something big. Especially if Adelai had been aboard the party boat.

"Was she evasive?"

"Hard for me to tell," Nicole admitted, and watched just the smallest flicker of surprise spread across his broad features. "Could be new motherhood. Could be the fear of an undocumented alien when questioned by the police."

Lars understood that. They'd both questioned their share of immigrants across their careers.

"She was cooperative but skittish too." Nicole turned her back on the lake and the activity there. "Tell Ty he's up. Go over the particulars of leaving him in charge. Touch base with MacAulay too. See how far he's gotten with the ice man." They were a full day into the thaw. MacAulay had to have something to share. "Then meet me at forensics."

She started for the Yukon, but Lars stopped her.

"Hold up." He fell into step with her and set a brisk pace. "For the record," he said, "I expect the dominoes to fall."

"A complete collapse inside BP North," she agreed. Even the innocent would be painted with the same brush. The cast of suspicion would remain over them for the remainder of their careers, if they still had one to pull out of the ashes. "I called the attorney general's office early this morning," she said. It seemed so long ago that she'd been sitting at the breakfast table, with the sunrise scorching the sky and her son sitting close by, stealing the berries from her piece of pie. Those soft, sweet moments punctuated her life. Anchored her. "I left a message they still haven't returned."

"About BP, there'll be few survivors," Lars said. "And the guilty will be clawing their way out." His tone was somber, weighted. "We need to be careful," he advised. "You especially." Because she was the leader, and any harm to her would cause distraction and chaos inside the sheriff's department.

She nodded. "Comes with the paycheck," she said, because under such stress, flippant was the best she could do.

*　*　*

MacAulay held the sleeping bag in his hands, testing the weight. He had one, of course, but it was standard. Purchased when four pounds was the lightest they came and forty degrees challenged its capability. This one was queen-size, so not practical for a Scout trip, but he liked thinking about the hikes he and Nicole could take together and the nights they might spend snuggled in the tent in this shared bag. She was starting to think along the same lines—he could tell simply by the weight of her gaze, the ponderous quality in her eyes when she regarded him. It was about time. They had been seeing each other for more than a year, all clandestine, and he was more than ready to go public and permanent.

"That is not at all practical," Jordan observed, jarring MacAulay from his thoughts. Practical was the last thing he was thinking about, but of course he didn't say that.

"I'm a big guy," he said.

"That bag weighs almost nine pounds. You want to carry that on your back?"

Of course not. MacAulay nodded and returned the bag to the shelf.

"What's wrong with the one you have?" Jordan asked.

"It's a relic," MacAulay said. "Too heavy and doesn't hold up to the weather."

Jordan moved down the aisle, reading the specs on the bags as he went. MacAulay watched him. The boy was small for his age but resilient. He had a soft center but was building a thick skin and was emotionally tough. That fiasco at Christmas had given him grit, and MacAulay was glad to see it. He pulled a bag off the shelf. It was blue with gray lining.

" 'Waterproof and weather-resistant,' " Jordan read as he carried the bag back to MacAulay. "This is what you need. It only weighs two-point-eight pounds and comes with a compression sack." Both of which would make it easy to carry. "How tall are you?"

"Six two."

Jordan nodded. "This has you covered." He handed the bag to MacAulay.

" 'A comfortable sleep in below-freezing temperatures,' " he read. Cushioning at the shoulder and zipper kept out drafts. "I'll take it," he said.

They moved from sleeping bags to lanterns.

"No more oil and wick," he said.

"Wow, that's so yesterday," Jordan said, and pointed out a few cons. "They're too heavy, blow out easily, oil doesn't last as long as battery."

"Not to mention a fire hazard," MacAulay said.

"I think your equipment might need a complete overhaul."

MacAulay agreed. "I've replaced very few things."

Jordan considered that. "Is that loyalty or laziness?"

"If it works, no need to replace it."

"Actually, there is. Some things today are made better, lighter, more efficient."

MacAulay chose a lantern that had four lighting modes, including a dimmer, had a sturdy hook for hanging inside a tent or from a tree branch, and was at least a pound or two lighter than the antique he had at home.

"You planning a camping trip?" Jordan wanted to know.

"Nothing solid, but summer is coming and the high country is calling."

Jordan smiled. "Yeah, me too." He walked toward fishing equipment, and MacAulay followed. "We're headed up Sunburst, the Astum River Trail. Just one night. Eight miles up, plant seed along the way—this part of Montana is running low on golden currant and bitterroot—pitch the tents and bunk down, and then make our way out the next morning."

"Beautiful trail," MacAulay said. He'd taken it a time or two. It sloped gently uphill so it wasn't too rigorous, but it gave stunning glimpses of Lake Maria and the Astum River. Astum meaning *come here*. The river made beautiful music and lured people to its banks, which were lush with tamarix and yellow flag iris.

"You want to come with us?" Jordan threw a quick glance over his shoulder at MacAulay. "We need another chaperone."

"You do?"

Jordan nodded. "So far, only the leader is available. Sometimes it happens like that. Dads have to work the weekends, and some of us don't have a dad who can step up."

He shrugged, and MacAulay noticed a stiffness in the gesture.

"Well, count me in," MacAulay said.

"Yeah?" Jordan's face lit up.

"Absolutely."

"Great." He held MacAulay's gaze for a moment, his eyes revealing both vulnerability and no small amount of scrutiny, and then he turned around and resumed walking. MacAulay hoped he'd passed the test. "You'll need a decent backpack," Jordan said, cutting through poles and tackle and arriving at packs. "One that will balance the weight and not weigh a ton itself. You have one of those?"

"I think I bought the one I have off an old gold-rush prospector," he said, and Jordan's face froze at the horror of it.

"Not really," MacAulay said. He walked slowly down the aisle, looking at the possibilities. "But it weighs as much as a car, with about the same flexibility. I definitely need an upgrade." He pulled an Osprey off the shelf and tried it on for size, checked out some of the bells and whistles on it. "Not quite right."

"Try this one," Jordan suggested. "Same brand as mine, about as light as a feather, and has lumbar padding."

It would set him back about $250, but it was worth it. He was building up his equipment and, more importantly, his relationship with Jordan.

He tried it on, had Jordan add some weight to it, they listened to a salesperson talk up its good points and its very small list of shortcomings, and then he bought it, along with the sleeping bag, the lantern, some freeze-dried food packets, a rain tarp, warming crystals for his hands and feet, and a new water bottle complete with a cleaning filter. He had a relatively new, flyweight, two-person tent that rolled up like an umbrella and could be stashed in the pack no problem.

"I think I'm ready," he said.

They checked out and headed for the car.

"It'll take a couple trips to break even with all you spent today," Jordan said. He juggled his own purchases while opening the door for MacAulay. "But then it'll be sweet."

"It'll pay for itself by end of summer," MacAulay promised. And he hoped both Nicole and Jordan would help him with that. Long camping weekends and bigger trips into the national parks, the three of them learning to fit together as a family.

20

Adelai was gone. Nicole received the radio transmission from dispatch as she turned into the hospital parking lot. It was a busy day and a small facility, and she didn't expect to stay long under the circumstances, so she parked the Yukon in the red and climbed out to meet her deputy, who was pacing the sidewalk in front of the ER.

"I called it in as soon as I realized what she was up to," her deputy explained. "She had a visitor, but no problem with that, right? Everyone in the hospital gets visitors. So I didn't notice right away, not until a nurse walked in announcing 'discharge papers.' I took a peek in and noticed Ms. Amari was all packed up and ready to go." He let out a long, anxious breath that Nicole found concerning, given the mild circumstances and his response to them. He was a rookie, with six months on the job, but he should have had more stamina than this. "The doctor said she was ready for release and she wasn't under arrest, so what could I do?" he finished.

Follow her. Her life was probably in danger. And she was a material witness if not more. Nicole had received a call from forensics late the night before. They had tested her hands and clothing for gunshot residue, all of which had come back negative. Adelai hadn't even been in the room when the gun was fired, killing James Franks. Residue sprayed, and in a room that small, a spattering would have landed somewhere on her clothes, skin, hair. Adelai was not a person of interest in the death of the GSW in her upstairs bedroom, the baby's uncle. But she was a person of interest because evidence placed her on that party boat at some point.

"Where is she now?" Nicole asked.

"She wanted nothing to do with me," the deputy continued. "She said she didn't need protection and didn't want me following her. She was closing the door on this part of her life and starting new. She wanted that for her son."

"Where did she go?" Nicole tried again.

"I persisted," he said. "I know how to take an order," he assured her, "but that visitor, she's got to be an attorney."

"So Adelai left with the visitor?"

He nodded. "I heard the nurse call the woman Mrs. Embry. She was tall and sturdy. Older, with silver hair." He shrugged somewhat help-lessly. "She looked like a grandma, but she let me have it when I followed them down the hall."

"What did she say?"

" 'Step back, young man. You won't be getting into this elevator.' "

Sounded about right.

"Then she told me following Ms. Amari after they had asked me not to was a matter they would take up in the courts." His skin flushed from collarbone to hairline. "She accused me of stalking and promised she'd reduce me to department store security."

Nicole took pity on the deputy. He was, after all, a young man, fairly new with the department, and had followed protocol.

She smiled and said, "I've had a run-in with Mrs. Embry myself. I think she spent the long months of winter sharpening her claws."

"Yeah," he said. "Exactly." And Nicole watched as his breathing returned to normal, his skin tone too.

"There will be more like her," she said.

"I know it. And I stuck to my training—calm and cool and persistent."

And the rest would come with experience.

He pulled his cell phone from his pocket and began working it. "I took a picture anyway. I didn't know you knew Embry or how hard it would be to find her." He offered Nicole his phone. The picture showed the back of a blue Camry, license plate number clearly visible. "That's what they drove away in."

"Good work," she said, and forwarded the photo to her cell number.

"Yeah?"

"Yeah," she said. "Why don't you come with me," she invited. "I'm going to pay them a visit, and you can ride shotgun." It was an impulsive decision but one that felt right. An opportunity to educate by example.

"Let me do the talking," she advised. "You observe—facial expressions, gestures, surroundings—and we'll talk after."

They climbed into Nicole's Yukon and quickly returned to the Lake Road, lights rolling but siren silent. Lois Embry. She certainly possessed an overbearing confidence and the softness of a porcupine. Honestly, Nicole would want the woman in her corner if she ever needed an attorney. As she drove, she decided on her approach, which would be to speak directly to Adelai, with whom Nicole had at least a small rapport, and to take the bull by the horns if necessary.

As far as Nicole was concerned, there were two possible destinations. The first, the Embry household, which offered a safe but stifling hospitality. Adelai had told Nicole she hadn't felt comfortable there. So Nicole tossed that in favor of the house overlooking the lake, where they had recovered the body of James Franks.

*   *   *

There was yellow tape tied to the porch railings and over the front door. A screen was out and leaning against the siding. That's where they'd come in, Adelai decided. When she was upstairs, pacing the small rooms. Their bedroom, the nursery, and back again. She'd known the moment was at hand—she'd lived like that for days, poised for flight. And before that, for months, with the possibility. Because Matthew had warned her.

"You don't have to stay here," Lois said. She'd finished her call and come from the car to stand beside Adelai.

"I'm not staying," she said. "Not for long."

"They could come back," Lois said. "The police are right about that, and I don't feel good leaving you here."

"I'm packing our things."

What she needed. She had money, for careful purchases. She and Matthew had done well saving for what was supposed to be their future. When she'd run, she'd done it with a small envelope containing two documents—her Montana driver's license and the ATM card—and her cell phone that had been deafeningly quiet in the hours since her baby was born. *That's not the way it's supposed to be*, she thought. No one had celebrated her son. Well, except the sheriff. She had come to the hospital with bags loaded with clothes and toiletries. She had showered Adelai and her son with gifts. She had cared about them and been more than decent to them.

Even Lois hadn't done that. Adelai was part of a mission. A piece Lois would move around on a game board as she tried to thwart immigration laws. Of course, some of that was no longer necessary. Adelai had given birth and she had more potential than most to gain citizenship. Lois might be able to help her with that.

"I'll stay a day." Or maybe two. How long did it take to make plans that completely changed your life? She would need a job again, but that was nothing new. She would leave Montana, but where would she go?

"So I should pick you up tomorrow? And what? Drive you to a bus station?"

"I'll call you," she promised.

"This isn't safe," Lois said again.

But Adelai disagreed. The police had been here. They were probably keeping an eye on the place. The men who had come were smart. They were trained. They would wait until the margin for error was so small a dime turned sideways couldn't squeak through before they made their next move.

"The sheriff said I can get citizenship now," Adelai said. "Because I gave birth, my chances are good."

"Good but not guaranteed," Lois said.

"Will you make it happen?"

"I'm not a miracle worker." Lois breathed heavily, stirring the tendrils of hair that had escaped Adelai's ponytail. Adelai understood her frustration—she was not playing the game right. She was no longer a high-stakes player. She was, in fact, the ace up the sleeve. And Lois Embry liked an underdog.

"But you'll try?"

"I will," she agreed, though it took a moment of careful consideration.

They heard the tread of tires and the pinging of gravel and together turned toward the sound. There was a curve in the road, and the trees that lined it were dense with spring foliage. It took a moment, but then she saw it. The bar light flashing and the hood of the sheriff's SUV, and Adelai felt good about it.

Lois did not.

"Don't say a word," she ordered, raising her hands to her hips and growing tight in the shoulders.

* * *

Nicole smiled.

"You were right," Deputy Sisk said. "I didn't think she'd come back here."

To the place where she'd nearly lost her life. Where a man had been executed in her bedroom. But her options were limited.

"She's faced worse fears than this," Nicole said. She cut the lights and the engine and climbed from the vehicle. "Come on."

Nicole didn't get two feet from the Yukon before Lois Embry pounced. She went straight for her deputy's jugular.

"I told you if you followed us, we would consider it stalking," she began. "Harassment at the very least—"

"We know the law at least as well as you, Counselor," Nicole said. "This is police business, and I hope you won't be obstructing justice."

A faint burst of color played on Embry's cheeks, but it didn't slow her down. "There's a fine line between the two, isn't there," she challenged. "You can expect that I'll be dancing on it."

"Fair enough." She turned her attention to Adelai. The young woman looked better, stronger, rested, and Nicole was glad for that. Her son was wrapped in a flannel blanket and snuggled against her chest. "You look good," Nicole said.

Adelai smiled. "I am much better," she assured her. "I needed sleep and got plenty of it in the hospital. It was the right move, for me and for my son."

"Yes."

"I'll be going over to Shelby tomorrow," Nicole announced, and watched Adelai's face. Liquid pooled in her eyes, and she blinked several times. "I need to tell his parents."

"Yes, of course you do."

"Whose parents?" Embry demanded. She placed a hand on Adelai's shoulder as a warning to remain quiet as she addressed Nicole. But the young lady had a mind of her own.

"James Franks. Matthew's brother," Adelai said.

"The man executed inside this house," Nicole further clarified. She looked up at the second floor, where a light burned in what Nicole remembered was one of two small bedrooms.

"Say not another word," Embry advised. Not trusting Adelai to listen, she turned to Nicole and her deputy and announced, "Anything she does say will be tossed out in court. She is clearly under enormous distress, given the circumstances leading up to the delivery of her child, which took place while she was running for her life."

"She was not involved in his murder. Her hands were swabbed and her clothing tested," Nicole assured Embry, then turned to Adelai. "You weren't even in the room when it happened, were you?"

Adelai shook her head.

"But you know more, or suspect more, than you told me this morning."

"James came to warn me and they followed. That's what I want to think, anyway, that James died a hero."

"Did you speak to him, Adelai? Ask him about Matthew? You must have."

"There wasn't much time," Adelai said. "They were so close behind him."

"But you spoke."

"Of course I asked him about Matthew. 'Where is he?' I said. I needed to know, was he really dead?"

"And what did James say?"

"He said, 'He's alive, Adelai. Or he was.' " Fear made her eyes flare as she reached back into that night for more details. "He hustled me up the stairs and told me to pack, quickly. He told me the last thing Matthew said was, 'I love her.' He meant me." She smiled tremulously. "But James thought maybe Luke and Matthew were already dead, because the men knew where to find me and we kept that a secret. We were so careful." She stopped and took a deep breath, pressed back tears. "By then they were already climbing through the window. We heard them take out the screen, their boots on the wood floor, their footsteps up the stairs. James helped me out the window, and that was the last I saw of him."

"And he didn't say anything else?"

"He said, 'Run, Adelai. And don't stop.' "

Nicole thought about all of this.

"He's a hero. He saved me and my son."

"You came back today because you believe Matthew is still alive."

"I hope he is, and this is the only place he'll know to find me."

Nicole was impressed by the young woman's strength. "Nearly three miles, in labor—I don't know how you did it."

"I knew my followers would not stop," Adelai said. "And so I ran. Until the boats on the lake. I heard their motors, but at first I wasn't sure. I was thinking, wouldn't it be a miracle if a helicopter flew by, if they were on my side and help was at hand. But I realized it was the boats on the water and the sound of their engines that I heard. One had stopped and the other was pulling away from it."

"And that's all you saw?"

"The men must have seen too," she said. "The woods have a feel to them. I knew the stillness meant the men were there, close. Too close. But when I stopped and looked over the water at the boats, I realized the night was alive with sound. With the hooting of an owl, the croaking of frogs. Before, it had been as quiet as the dead."

"Who are the men?"

Adelai shook her head. "I promise you I don't know."

"Why didn't you tell me about James?"

"I answered your questions about him."

"And no more."

"I'd hoped he'd made it out too." She paused to get hold of her quivering voice. "Until you showed me the picture."

"Do you have reason to believe Matthew is alive?"

"I have hope, but only that."

"Tell me more about the lake, about the boats," Nicole said, putting a clamp on a welling sympathy she felt for the young woman. "You know about the missing agents."

Adelai shook her head. She took a step backward, brushing against Lois Embry, who decided that was signal enough to jump back into the fray.

"That's enough, Sheriff. Adelai has answered your questions. In fact, she's been too generous with her cooperation."

Nicole ignored the retired attorney. "I won't stop asking you about it, Adelai," Nicole said. "I can't, because we're still missing a man and we don't know if he's dead or alive. We can't bring peace to his family or give him aid. We can't leave a man fallen."

The words, and Nicole's sincere tone, moved Adelai. Her composure began to erode.

"I had help," she said. "When I could run no more, when the baby was coming, it was a horrible pain and I called out." She sobbed. "I tried not to."

"And someone came to you?"

"Yes. I opened my eyes and he was standing over me. And I knew right away that we'd make it."

"Why? How did you know?"

Adelai gathered the baby closer and over his head said, "I'd seen him before."

"Adelai," Lois Embry interrupted, her voice full of warning. "That's enough. Let us speak first, you and I alone, before you talk to the sheriff about this."

But Adelai shook her head. "I did nothing wrong," she said.

"You withheld information," Nicole said.

"Because he asked me to!" Adelai retorted. "He said it would save his life and I had to listen. He had stopped to help me, and I recognized him. I knew him to be good. I knew he would fight for us."

Nicole brought out her cell phone and called up a photo. It was an agency picture of Kyle Monte. "Is this the man who helped you?"

"Yes."

"How did you know he was good?" Nicole asked.

Adelai took a steadying breath. She turned her face so she could breathe in the scent of her baby. "I've been watching him for months."

"You've been watching the lake?"

"Every night. At first, we were afraid of the men finding us. But I watched for more than that." She paused to consider her words. "I left my family a long time ago. More than three years now. Do you know girls are sold for dowries in Syria? My father had these intentions. The money would help my family, and my father felt it was certainly worth the sacrifice. My mother was no help in this. I don't miss them. But I have a brother and a younger sister. I have a favorite aunt. And sometimes, watching the lake, I see them, in the faces of the people seeking freedom. And that's why I watch."

"Your sister," Embry interrupted. "We can go back for her."

"My father is dead. In a moment of weakness, I called my aunt. It was heaven to hear her voice, and I was not sad when she reported that my father had passed. My mother and my sister have moved in with her, and my brother is away at college."

Nicole recaptured Adelai's attention. "What did you see on the lake?"

"Your agent is different from the others," Adelai said. "For weeks we watched and wondered at what we saw. But never with the man who helped me."

"What did you wonder about?"

"The agents, sometimes once or twice a week, they had refugees in their boat, but they were not arresting them, they were setting them free. They cut across the lake, as far north as we could follow with the binoculars, and they gave them backpacks and showed them guns, and they spoke angry words—we could tell because their faces were twisted and fierce. And then they pushed them off the boat and onto the dock and the refugees ran, never looking back. That is what we saw, time and again."

"Once or twice a week?"

"Sometimes. And sometimes long weeks without seeing them."

"For how long?"

"We started watching in October."

"How was Monte different?"

"His boat was always empty when he motored in from the south. If he found a refugee, he brought them aboard, gave them a blanket and an energy bar. But he always took them back the way he had come."

"He arrested them."

Adelai nodded. "But he did it without guns, without anger."

"And he helped you."

"He delivered my baby. And he promised not to arrest me."

"If you promised not to tell about him."

Adelai nodded.

"Where did he go?"

"I don't know. He was not in good shape. He had bruising around his face and he favored his side. I asked him if he was all right, and he said, 'For now.' I didn't ask any more questions."

"He brought you by boat to the Embrys?"

"Yes. Not the usual boat, but something bigger with plenty of seating."

The party barge.

Nicole turned her attention to Lois Embry. "Did you know about this?"

The woman pursed her lips but did not think long about it. "We knew only that she had arrived."

Nicole turned back to Adelai. "What happened then?"

"He left," Adelai said. "He did not even get out of the boat but set me on my feet, with my baby, and told me to walk up the path. That I would be safe."

"And he asked you to not speak of seeing him?"

"Yes. We made promises, and I have just broken mine."

"Did he say why?"

"He did not need to. He is good and the others are not."

That simple. Adelai was growing tired. Nicole could see it in the circles under her eyes, which were deepening, and in the slant of her shoulders. Lois Embry saw it too.

"We're done, Sheriff. You have more questions, you need to call us in for a formal interview."

Nicole ignored her. "And there's nothing else you should be telling me, Adelai? Nothing else you saw or heard?"

She shook her head slowly, still mired, it seemed, in memories of that night. "There's nothing else."

Nicole nodded. She looked over Adelai's shoulder to the house. The yellow tape fluttered in the breeze, and the wind lifted a corner of the screen propped against the house so that it clattered against the siding.

"You shouldn't stay here," Nicole said.

"I'm not. Not for long, anyway."

"This is no longer an active crime scene, but nothing has been cleaned up."

"I will keep that door closed," Adelai said. "And put the screens back in. I just need a day or two."

Waiting for a man who might or might not show up.

Nicole thought a moment about numbers—budget and hours and her thinning pool of manpower. "I'll send a deputy back tonight so that you can sleep."

"Thank you," Adelai said. "One more night in what should have been our family home. It will have to be enough."

Nicole extended her hand. It didn't seem to be enough, because she felt drawn to this young woman, a sister connection sealed in mutual motherhood under dire straits. "Keep my card," she said. "And don't hesitate to call."

"I will," Adelai promised, then asked, "Is Luke Franks still alive?"

Nicole saw hope flare in her eyes. If Luke had made it, then maybe Matthew had too.

"Yes," she said. "But I've heard nothing about Matthew."

Adelai nodded, and Nicole turned and walked back to the Yukon, her deputy in step beside her.

"I wouldn't mind coming back here tonight," Sisk offered.

"Good, because those were my intentions." Her budget had been pushed through the shredder on this one, and she thought about ways to recoup some of the losses. She wondered if she could bill BP for the cost of the investigation. Or maybe apply to the Department of Homeland Security for some kind of reimbursement? "I'll drop you at your car. Go home and get a nap, pack a lunch or two and a thermos of coffee. The nights can get long."

21

Forensics was located in a new building less than a mile from the sheriff's station. It was three stories tall and currently under construction to put a bay in back that would serve MacAulay in terms of receiving bodies for autopsy. It was in the plans to move the ME out of his small cave in the basement of the hospital, freeing up space for them to expand, and into spacious accommodations exactly where he should be, among the forensics crew. MacAulay would share his domain with the MEs from neighboring Glacier and Liberty counties—all three counties had put money into the pot to make it happen. Nicole parked and made her way across the lot, gazing at the sky. The sun was overhead, but the cool breeze diffused the heat. It was four fifteen.

Lars was waiting for her, leaning against the hood of his Yukon and paging through the notes on his smartphone. He pocketed it when she approached.

"I spoke to MacAulay," he said. "He's off the grid for a while but finished up with Baker before leaving and won't need to check in with the ice man until ten PM. He has cause and TOD. The agent was knocked unconscious with not one but two taps to the head. One at the temple—the blow which would have rendered her unconscious—the other from behind, just below the cerebellum—this one got her attention and she turned toward her attacker. Cause of death is drowning, and given temperature readings from the lake and the atmosphere, he says she died between two and two thirty AM."

"Two thirty?" Her voice rose sharply. Nicole had spoken to Monte at 2:37.

"Exactly. Baker was dead before Monte placed that call to you."

And he'd made no mention of it. He had appeared calm, steady over the phone. He'd made small talk about the weather that hadn't, even in hindsight, seemed forced. Either Monte hadn't known about Agent Baker's murder or he'd had ice coursing through his veins.

"MacAulay also said that the body was moved. She was pulled from the lake, laid flat on her back long enough that her blood settled and coagulated, and sometime later placed either back in the lake or on the shoreline, facedown."

Nicole pulled her cell phone from her pocket and connected with Green's number. He answered after a single ring.

"Did you lie about everything?" she asked.

"What are you talking about? I've lied about nothing."

Nicole snorted. "Who was assigned to Monte that night?"

"Baker."

"MacAulay finished his autopsy on Baker. She was dead before Monte called me. So try again. Who was assigned to Monte?"

"Baker is on the duty roster," Green insisted.

She felt like she was banging her head against a brick wall.

"Is your entire department corrupt?" she said. *You included?* She didn't say it but implied it and severed the connection, refusing to listen to anything more the man had to say.

"Everything he's told us, we'll have to confirm," she said, and let out a breath of frustration.

Lars nodded. "He's been leading us around by the nose."

And like any piercing, it stung.

"Pisses me off," Lars continued. "We're supposed to have each other's backs out here."

The betrayal within the agency had a long reach. It put her men at risk, and that angered Nicole.

"Time to storm the fortress," she said.

"You get a call back from the attorney general?"

She nodded. "They're sending out a single agent. He should have been here by now, but we're not waiting around for a meet and greet."

"What do you have planned?"

"We need to get back to Luke Franks," she said. "We need to find Monte." She'd called Lars after her conversation with Adelai and given him the update. Neither she nor Lars was surprised the agent had survived the ambush on the lake or the swim to shore. "Anything come back on our call to border crossing?" Lars had checked to see if Monte's vehicle had passed over the border.

"They said within the hour." He checked his watch. "They have twenty minutes left."

"We need names, interviews, arrests, and Franks is a good place to start."

"Who's going to wait on the AG?" Lars asked. "You want me to call in Ty?"

She thought about that. The AG had taken its time in sending help and thrown them a bone with just one agent. She had no one to spare for a meet and greet and possible babysitting, and they couldn't put off seeing Franks. "We'll leave him in the wind," she decided.

They entered the building and rode the elevator to the third floor. The building had been intended as a modest suite of offices but had faltered in gaining the interest of Blue Mesa's thin crop of professionals, which meant that the county had secured it cheap. It also meant that the corridor was lined with windows into the lab. Three techs were at work. With two in the field, they were working at an all-hands.

They stopped at the door to the lab. Nicole's ID would get them past the security monitor, but Arthur liked to meet them at the door, so she rang the buzzer. Lars, whose ID would also gain them access, didn't grouse about it this time.

"Franks was uncooperative," Lars began, "but I didn't get a stink off him. He was wary but almost transparent when he was asking about the GSW. He was invested in my answer. I think he knew his brother was in Adelai's house."

Nicole nodded. "Deidre Franks was Jordan's fifth-grade teacher. She's solid, no-nonsense. I'd like to hear what she has to say." About family dynamics and about her husband, particularly in regard to his job. Tapping into a husband or wife was always enlightening.

"Okay, so we'll head over to Franks' place as soon as we're finished here."

"I'd love to hear what Franks has to say about Monte and Baker."

"If he'll talk."

"We have more leverage now. Confirmation on Franks' dead brother, and he's an uncle now."

Lars nodded. "That might get us something." Then he changed the subject. "Doc said he'll start the autopsy on the ice man between ten and midnight—there's a science to it, a preferred window of time in terms of determining TOD and cause. I'd like to attend that."

"Go for it," Nicole said. She had other threads to follow. A call to make to BP Isle of Royale to check out the pin. She wanted a list of all agents who had been decorated for valor over the incident. She needed to touch base with the boating company who had reported the party barge stolen—if that was really the case. She wanted to check in with Jane Casper before going home. And she'd like a few minutes with her son before he left for the Scout hike bright and early the next day.

"Uncle of Adelai's baby," Lars mused aloud. "That puts another spoke in the wheel."

"Adelai's an undocumented alien."

"A conflict of interest in terms of Luke Franks' sworn duty."

"The men chasing Adelai were BP agents." She believed that more than ever now. "And Franks wasn't involved in the chase," she said, thinking aloud. "He'd called in sick, but he was left out of the loop."

"That was real clear. He was pumping me for information," Lars said. "But why were they after Adelai in particular?"

"She has something. Did Mac get the results of the blood work—is Adelai related to the ice man?"

But Lars shook his head. "Another day for prelim on that test."

"Tandy thought Adelai ran because the men wanted the baby. And I think she's right. I think they would do anything to get what Adelai had, even use her son as leverage. She has evidence, maybe," she posed. "Or product."

"Either would make her a target," he said.

"And where is Matthew Franks in all this?" Nicole wondered.

"Dead or alive, Luke Franks knows," Lars said.

"Yeah, he does," Nicole agreed.

"You know what this all comes back to?" Lars said.

"The man in the ice," Nicole said.

"That needle in a haystack."

"The trigger. Monte calls it in and all hell breaks loose."

"We still have the tip about several possible UDAs crossing the lake," Lars said.

"They're long gone," Nicole said. "And given what Adelai told us about the agents and the refugees, I think evidence and drugs went with them."

"Along with a boatload of money."

"But not all of it," she said. The satchel found near Baker's body stuffed with cash and drugs, still bearing the BP evidence seal. "That bothers me. What a stroke of luck."

"Yeah, but pennies compared to what's already lost."

"But a direct link." In court, it would be a stepping stone down the path of conviction.

"We stumbled on a pipeline. I think Monte did the same."

"Monte and Baker," she agreed. "I'm checking in with Casper later. Hopefully by then she's cracked the code in Monte's notebook."

She pressed the buzzer again, leaving her finger on the button a little longer than necessary, which earned her a raised eyebrow from Lars.

"Let's get back to MacAulay," she suggested.

"Yes, let's." He was too agreeable, and she thought she detected a trace of amusement on his face but chose to ignore it.

"You're going to the autopsy tonight." She was happy to take a pass there. Next to budget, autopsies were her least favorite part of the job. "So after this, why don't you go home? Nap or see the kids. Spend some time with Ellie. Have dinner around the family table. It's April-you have the pool open yet? Take a swim, or—what is it you guys do? Cannonball rallies? Do that."

"I might do all of it," he said, and smiled.

She turned on him. "What?"

And he grinned like the damn Cheshire cat. "Pissed looks good on you," he said.

Nicole took a moment to collect herself. Anger was good only when it was harnessed, not when it was nipping at her heels. The corruption of law enforcement had a way of spreading out, tainting others, and she would make a point of separating her department from BP at the next press conference. It was the first time she was looking forward to one of those.

"We need to do next of kin on the GSW," Lars said. "I told MacAulay I'd like to do it."

"You're going to tell Luke Franks," Nicole said. Not the parents. "We can do it this afternoon."

"I want to see his reaction."

Arthur came to the door and punched his code into the keypad. The door released with a metallic click and a suction of air as it slid open.

"Welcome," Arthur said. He turned and walked deeper into the lab, and Nicole and Lars followed. "We're very busy, as you can see," Arthur continued, raising his arms to indicate the number of techs and the different stations and testing being conducted. "Three DOAs and the placenta in less than twenty-four hours, and we are scrambling to keep up."

Nicole knew where the conversation was heading and agreed. "I requested another full-time technician from the budgetary committee. It will be entry level," Nicole cautioned, but it was something, and Arthur seemed happy about it.

"A meaty bone thrown to the dogs." He cast a smile over his shoulder.

"I also included a request for funds to cover additional trainings and conferences." But she wasn't as hopeful that this request would be met with approval.

They stopped outside Arthur's tiny glass office at the back of the lab. He turned and looked over the stations and began his report.

"Here"—he raised a hand, indicating a long table with infrared lighting, luminol, and a scanning electron microscope—"a single drop of blood that doesn't match the victim was found on the sleeve of Agent Monte's parka. I love Gore-Tex," he said. "What it doesn't repel, it allows to seep deep within the woven fibers. Blood is one of those things. The lake water is low salinity, and it wasn't able to wash away the stain completely. And the drop was new enough that little breakdown had happened prior to submersion."

"What's the story on it?" Lars asked.

"Female." The surprise was clear in Arthur's voice. "Type AB negative, so rare. Less than one percent of our population has it. Elevated white cells."

"What does that mean?" Nicole asked. She'd heard of high white blood cells in relation to infection. "Was she sick?"

"That's only one possibility," Arthur said. "Infection, and that can be anything from an ingrown toenail to lupus. Leukemia and other blood cancers. Poor nutrition, extreme pressures placed on the body for an extended period of time—this would be a common find in a long-distance runner, for example."

"What about pregnancy?" Nicole asked. "Would that raise the white blood cell count?"

"Certainly," Arthur said. "It could be indicative of many things. Pre-eclampsia, for instance. Leukocytosis, which is the body's natural inflammatory response to a normal pregnancy. Or a bacterial infection, which is more common than you think during pregnancy. The female body is under a great deal of stress, particularly toward the end of her pregnancy, and this almost always has a direct impact on cell count."

"You're thinking Adelai?" Lars asked.

"I'm thinking of possibilities," she said. "We're running out of them." She turned to Sleeping Bear. "What is Adelai Amari's blood type?"

"AB negative," Sleeping Bear confirmed. "I have thought along the same lines as you. This will support the theory that Agent Monte assisted Adelai with the birth of her baby. However, he discarded his coat after, not before."

"He swam to shore wearing the parka?" Clearly, Lars doubted it.

"It's possible he didn't swim to shore at all," Arthur said.

"Then he boarded the party barge from the BP skiff," Nicole said.

"That is my guess, given what evidence we do have."

"We assumed, on finding his jacket, that he'd swum for it," Lars said.

"That and Tandy's description of the party boat sweeping the water. But maybe that was Monte and he was looking for someone," Nicole said. "Agent Baker, I think."

"I have more for you," Arthur said. "Come this way."

He advanced through the lab, past specialized equipment that Nicole regarded as their friends and worth every considerable penny.

"MacAulay was able to remove the coat and shoes from our ice man a few hours ago," Arthur said, stopping beside a table where several clear plastic bags lay sealed and identified. Nicole read the tags: JOHN DOE and the corresponding number, FLANNEL SHIRT—really just a small piece of fabric, as though torn from the shirt; the next held a shearling-lined denim coat; then a pair of hiking boots that still looked new and none the worse for wear after months encased in ice. "He also took samples of blood, hair, and nail clippings, along with scrapings."

"And what did you find?"

"AB negative," Arthur revealed.

"Really?" Lars said. "I like that."

"Me too."

If Adelai and the ice man were related, it would tip the case sideways. And as Nicole pondered that, out fell a number of tantalizing possibilities, along with the feeling that a web was beginning to reveal itself, with dots to connect and a shape materializing from the darkness. That shape, Nicole hoped, would fill out into the identity of their killer.

"We still have to wait another day for blood relation to be determined?" Lars asked.

"Yes, and that will be prelim. It's enough for us in the field, for now. But for a definitive answer, that's upwards of three weeks," he reminded them.

But the same blood type gave Nicole hope of a connection. It made sense that Adelai would have looked for more out on the lake *every night*. Especially if that something more was her brother. And if there was a relation there, then it was only a small step to identifying what Adelai had that the BP wanted so badly that they'd chased her into the night.

"Next up," Arthur continued, "the money." He turned and walked them to a computer terminal. "One hundred thousand." Found in the satchel recovered near Baker's body. "It's locked up, of course, but we have a plethora of fingerprints off the bills—all hundreds, by the way. One set of the prints are of interest." He turned and faced Nicole and Lars. "Care to place your bets?"

"I know a losing hand when I see one," Lars said.

"Green or Monte," Nicole said.

"Neither," Arthur said. "The money was meticulously counted, with the thumb and index finger appearing on nearly every bill." He pressed a button on the keyboard, and the screen saver faded and was replaced by a photo and identifying information. "Agent Melody Baker, BP."

"Could be that was her cut," Lars posed.

"The satchel belonged to Baker. She purchased it at the outlet mall in Pleasant Falls two months ago." He turned and regarded them both. "Jane is looking at bank statements, yes? What does she have to say about the money?"

"I'll find out as soon as we're done here," Nicole said.

Arthur nodded. "Then let's move along." They followed him and stopped at a small glass case. "The pin Officer Watts found. It's bronze and belonged to Monte. I did a little investigation there and discovered there were a total of six agents decorated with the pins. Helped that Isle of Royale and the year were inscribed on the back."

He handed Nicole a computer-generated list. Green's name was at the top, circled with a highlighter. The other names she didn't recognize. She passed the list to Lars.

"They served together at Royale," she said. "I didn't know that, but I should have. Early on Green said he's known Monte for sixteen years, but neither has been in Blue Mesa that long."

"And now for the finale," Arthur said. "The boot tread Molly pulled out of the windowsill. It came from Agent Baker's boot."

"You're sure?"

"Absolutely."

"She was at the scene of the GSW. Did we recover her side arm?"

"Yes, but it's still in ballistics." He grimaced. "Untouched, I'm afraid. Ballistics don't decompose, and we have a lot of evidence that does."

"I want to know if she fired the shot that killed James Franks."

"You'll know by morning," Arthur promised.

"What time did Adelai say she ran from the house?" Lars asked.

"Two AM," Nicole said. And it fit. Agent Baker could have been one of the five agents chasing Adelai. She'd had time to make it back to the lake, encounter trouble, and die within the time frame given by the ME, but just barely.

22

The AG was waiting for her when she returned to the station. He was sitting in one of the uncomfortable plastic chairs in reception with his feet up on the coffee table, cooling his heels. He was holding a used paper cupcake wrapper, pleating it over and over, and wasn't quick to unfold his body and stand.

The man was bored to the point of frustration.

"Sheriff Cobain?" he asked. His hair was cut close, with some kind of design buzzed above his ear. "Yep, I recognize you from your picture." He nodded as he considered her, then gazed toward the rows of photographs on the wall of all the sheriffs of Toole County, Montana, who had ever been. "That's a little dated. I like the one on the department website better."

His words were packed with powder, and she wondered if he was the type to explode or implode.

She followed his gaze. The picture on the wall wasn't more than three years old, and Nicole doubted she'd changed much since it had been taken. She didn't rise to the bait.

"Sorry you've been waiting so long," she said.

"People both love me and hate me," he returned, and stood. He was a solid six feet tall, with long arms and legs. "They have a schizophrenic approach to my arrival, a wish-you-weren't-here/glad-to-see-me kind of reception. But they do, usually, receive me."

Yeah, he was pissed. Nicole glanced at her watch.

"Two hours forty-seven minutes," he said. "That's how long I've been waiting. Save you on the math."

"I've been working while you were"—she hesitated but said it anyway, knowing it would nudge him a little closer to the edge—"sitting."

"On my ass." He gave her that. "I think you left that part out."

"Perhaps you don't realize that we're a very small department. I don't do a whole lot of meet and greet. I wear several different hats around here."

"I wouldn't have been sitting on my ass if you'd met me on arrival. I would have been working alongside you." He straightened his tie and rocked forward on his toes, which, she noticed, were shod in expensive leather. "That's my job."

Nicole had to choke that down. He was right, of course. And the description of his reception was equally on target—she wanted his help but didn't want him. And it was impossible to separate the two. She was as territorial as the best of them and schooled herself on reining that in.

"You're plugging a hole in an investigation that's wallowing in deep waters," he continued, summing up her current circumstances.

"Don't flatter me," she returned, falling back on humor to ease the situation. "But you're only half right. As happy as I am to see you, I can't wait for you to leave. True. But the slight wasn't a complete deliberation. I haven't had a moment to slow down." And that was the closest she would get to an apology.

"I can talk while I walk and chew gum at the same time."

She expelled a breath and didn't care if he realized she was running short on patience. "How long are you going to be upset about this?"

"Men don't get upset. We get pissed."

She smiled, because the AG was too tight to be anything more masculine than peeved, but kept that thought to herself.

"Well, let's try not to let that get in the way of good work." She headed for the back offices. The desk sergeant hit the buzzer that released the door, and Nicole pushed through it. She looked over her shoulder. "What's your name, anyway?"

His nose flared. "Devon Gates, special agent."

This time, Nicole managed to keep a straight face even while she was rolling film through her head—*Austin Powers, International Man of Mystery*. She hoped Devon Gates was at least a tad more competent. And that was a sobering thought.

"Are you coming, Agent Gates?"

She held the door for him, then led him through an arrangement of desks and past dispatch to her office.

"Have a seat," she offered as she walked around her desk and took one herself. He was still standing. "Or not." She sat back and regarded him. "Is this where we rock-paper-scissors for who goes first?"

"This isn't a game, Sheriff."

"No, it's not, so stop acting like you weren't chosen for sides and start cooperating."

That about blew his whistle, but Nicole stopped any outburst— unfair or not—by raising her hand. "I'll go first. This is what we know." She told him about the call from Monte in the middle of the night, about the dead and the missing, about the evidence at BP that was lost or stolen—but the AG already knew all about that, and in far greater detail than she did.

"Over thirty million dollars in missing fentanyl," he said. "A drop in the bucket in terms of supply, but someone's making a pretty penny off of it."

"And someone else got off easy."

Gates nodded. "That's right. Cases were thrown out and drug dealers walked right back into life as usual."

"A small price to pay," Nicole said.

"Right? Next up, cash. Best count places it at three million dollars. And that's not from sales; that's confiscated cash in the wind."

Nicole's eyebrows lifted. "We recovered a hundred thousand of it."

He waved that off. "Chump change," he said. "You know what's more precious than drugs or money to these people?"

That was easy. It came down to their inalienable rights. To the human condition. To the greatest common denominator. "Life and liberty?" she said.

"You got it. Blue Mesa BP made the arrest of the century. Marius Bernard. And he disappeared. We don't think he was in custody more than forty-eight hours."

She remembered hearing about the arrest right before Christmas. She'd had her hands full then, with the murder of a fourteen-year-old girl and with her son's life in peril. Still, if she had heard he'd disappeared, she'd have remembered. She questioned Gates about it.

"We're not advertising," he said. "We've tried to keep it hush-hush, and the Canadian authorities are cooperating."

"Canadian?"

"Bernard is a citizen of Quebec and a major drug dealer. He doesn't play nice and keeps his circle small, but we think he's involved in our little problem." Gates paused and considered his next words. "We think BP is pipelining the drugs, the money, the men up over the border."

"We do too."

"What kind of evidence do you have?"

"Witness testimony." She told him about Adelai and her surveillance of the lake.

"We have better than that," he said. "We have a man on the inside and enough physical evidence to turn that place inside out."

"Then why aren't you?"

"We were waiting on the big payout. One that stretched over the border and involved multiagency cooperation, including the support of Canada's Mounted Police."

"And when is that happening?"

"That was two nights ago," he said, and waited for that to settle in. "Yeah. That same night."

"You didn't get your man," she said. All hell broke loose instead.

"If we had, I wouldn't be sitting here and you wouldn't be knee-deep in carcass and cat shit."

"How long have you been investigating BP North?"

"From afar, a few years. But once Bernard disappeared, I swooped in."

"You've been here since December?"

"Christmas Eve," he confirmed.

"I haven't seen you." Nor had his office given any kind of courtesy call to let them know he was in town.

"That's the *special* part of special agent," he said. "We're supposed to be unseen."

"You didn't help much," she said, giving him no quarter. "What happened to Monte?"

Gates shook his head, disgusted. "Things started falling apart early. Monte's partner didn't show, but he put out anyway. His lights were spotted, or the sound of his engines, and they turned on him—men from his own department. That's the best we can do figuring out what happened to Agent Monte."

"Where were *your* agents?" Monte's backup. The net that would catch him when he plummeted.

"We had a seven-man team in the field. It should have been enough."

"Where?" she pressed. "We've been over every square inch of the lake and its surrounds, and there has been no sign of your guys."

"Hail of gunfire," Gates said. "An ambush from the inside—maybe Baker, we're not sure. Two of our men were hit. Another tangled with their men on the ground. It was short and not so sweet. We took a beating. Meanwhile, there was movement on the lake, and that drew our attention. One boat, possibly loaded with fifty pounds of fentanyl—that's a street value of thirty million dollars—was headed north. We knew from diligent surveillance that they would put in at one of three docks and move the drugs on the backs of refugees, up and over the border."

"Thanks for the heads-up," Nicole said. A multiagency effort, involving the AG and almost certainly the DEA and possibly the feds too, and no one had thought to clue in the locals.

"BP is infected, and we didn't know how far it spread."

Nicole felt a wave of heated anger sweep through her. "There has never been even the smallest indication of corruption within my department."

"No," he agreed, "and so we hoped, if needed, we could fall back and rely on your help."

Enlightenment dawned on her. "That's what you're doing now." The only reason the man was in her office, spilling his guts. "Did you draw the short stick, Special Agent Devon Gates? Or did the DEA and the FBI and all the other acronyms simply bully you into crawling into my office, tail between your legs and hands open?"

"Oooh, you get mad like a man," he said, sitting back in his chair and folding his hands over his midsection.

"And that's supposed to make me warm up to you?"

"No, not at all, but this kind of mad I can deal with. You're not throwing things and you're not crying, and in the end, you'll have to work with us anyway—that's your job, and you're even lower on the chain of command than I am."

That was bitter going down, and Nicole nearly choked on it.

"If it makes you feel any better, we were pretty impressed with your performance. You're a good cop and you do what's right."

"You've been watching from the beginning."

"We were out on the water when you approached the BP skiff," he admitted.

"I felt you."

"We thought so. Your defensive movements, blocking for your men when they were on the ice, coming around when the skiff went under." He nodded. "Risking your own life to pull them in. We knew then we could trust you, but we had to know you'd do us good."

"You waited until we had something you wanted," she charged. "I'm no fool, Gates."

"No, you're not. And you have a few things we'd like to get our hands on. But there are more important pieces still missing, and we'd like your help with those too."

"The fentanyl and Monte."

"The fentanyl," he corrected. "The shipment never made it to the border. It's out there, somewhere, in that vast wilderness. We figure you know the region as well as BP. We're hoping better. We counted three refugees and four BP agents on board when the shipment made land at the northern rim of the lake."

"And Monte wasn't one of them?"

"Monte's clean," he said. "He's a good agent probably laying low."

"Or dead."

Gates didn't even think about that. "We believe he's alive and off the board."

"And why do you believe that?"

"When the smoke cleared, he was gone. We looked," he assured her. "That and Isle of Royale."

Monte was good and he was courageous. He was the kind of agent who found a way.

"What happened to Baker?"

"She was ours to begin with. With BP cooperation at the highest level, we moved her to Blue Mesa after the first evidence went missing."

"She and Monte became close."

"He was suspicious. He kept notes and poked into a few things, and Baker noticed."

"And brought him on board?"

"We believe that."

Two against the world. No wonder they became lovers.

"We recovered her body this morning, but of course you know that."

He nodded. "She was aboard the boat with the fentanyl."

They'd lost Monte and Baker. And the drugs. "So far, the AG doesn't inspire a lot of confidence in me," she said.

"We're hoping to rebound."

"Baker died from drowning."

"Yes, that seems to be the MO," Gates said.

"Whose?"

"We're working on that."

"Surely you have some suspects," Nicole pushed.

Gates nodded. "Green and a handful of his agents. And maybe Baker."

"You think she double-crossed you?"

"We're entertaining it as a possibility."

"Based on what?"

"Erratic behavior—big pieces became bread crumbs and the time between communications came to a trickle."

"But you don't suspect Monte?"

"Not at all. He doesn't fit the psychological profile. You know, that single act of heroism followed by a life of integrity. Guys like that fall, but less than one percent of the time, and more often than not take themselves out of the game."

Suicide and sometimes murder-suicide. She knew the predictability and the numbers.

"You profiled Monte?"

"The FBI did."

And that was as good as gold as far as Nicole was concerned. Profiling at the federal level stood on years of training and experience. The wait list for outside agencies sending in personnel for training was years long.

"Who do you think has the fentanyl?" Thirty million dollars' worth.

"Green. He's our number-one pick. Possibly Franks."

"Luke Franks?" Nicole asked.

Gates nodded. "What do you know about him?"

But it was her turn to ask questions. "What do you know about Adelai Amari?"

He hesitated, debating what to say and what to keep squirreled away in a dark corner. The problem with that was that sometimes squirrels went rabid and bit you in the ass. She pointed that out.

"Full disclosure," Nicole said. "I won't walk into anything blindfolded, and neither will my men."

He nodded. "There's a shaded connection there," he admitted.

"Because she's involved with Luke Franks' brother."

"Yes. Maybe more important, there's a connection between the girl and the vic your people cut out of the ice."

"What do you know about the ice man?"

"His last name is Amari," he revealed, and that raised Nicole's eyebrows.

"You know that for sure?"

"Faris Amari didn't end up in Blue Mesa by accident. He followed his sister here."

"The ice man is her brother?"

He nodded. "People are complicated, aren't they? You think you're holding a puppy in your hand and what you actually have is a jackal."

"What the hell is that supposed to mean?"

"Adelai caused trouble. Luke Franks didn't like that his brother was dating an undocumented alien. They came to blows over it. But blood is thicker than water, isn't it?"

"Franks accepted it?"

"He chose life over death," Gates corrected. "Matthew Franks came to town. Brought his girl with him—"

"Adelai?"

"Yes, real name Adila Amari. And that was a mistake, bringing her. Coming at all."

"Why?"

"Because her brother, Faris Amari, followed and was rounded up by the wrong cops and put to work scaling the border. No easy feat in this backcountry. But Amari was in good physical shape, and young. He was promised many things, including that he could keep his life and that of his family. And they provided a signing bonus—twenty-five thousand dollars in cash.

"Amari kept the money. He completed his first run and came back for more, but he was a man with a conscious and he kept thinking there had to be a way out. He wanted to return to college, he wanted citizenship. He thought he could get both those things from us."

"He approached you?"

Gates nodded. "He walked right into our office in Helena. Put it all on the table. Green and Luke Franks included. And he had the presence of mind to keep a copy for himself. We think we'll find it on his body, or, more likely, he passed it off to his sister before what would have been his next border crossing. And we'd like access to both."

"Both Faris and Adelai?" Nicole felt unease shift through her. Adelai was quite popular, but with the wrong people.

"What Faris gathered, it's enough to put the whole ring behind bars."

"How do you know this?"

"He fed me a few pieces of the evidence he'd collected."

"And you think Adelai has this evidence?" Nicole asked. It made sense.

"BP thinks so. Either way, they'll want to cover their bases."

"They want the ice man and Adelai."

"Exactly, which is why we need to get to both of them first. And, as luck would have it, you have both tucked away right here in Blue Mesa."

"Our ME isn't finished with Faris Amari," Nicole said, stalling as she scrambled to identify why she felt a strong need to protect Adelai Amari. Why she wasn't about to serve her to Special Agent Devon Gates. "There's a science to defrosting a frozen corpse."

"I know. So what I'd really like right now is to move your ME along a little faster."

"You've talked to him?"

"I met with your ME when I first rode into town. He wasn't eager to please, and he Googled chain of authority before he'd even speak to me." Gates laughed. "He new to the job?"

"He's a good man and running to catch up."

Gates nodded. "Well, he's thorough. I don't think he missed a thing." Nicole heard respect in Gates's voice. "Maybe you could talk to him about his bedside manner, though. The man needs to learn how to share."

Nicole met his gaze and kept hers deliberately reflective. Rocks could have bounced off of them.

"Or not," Gates conceded.

"What are we looking for?" Nicole asked. "A USB? An encrypted link? A key?" And would any of that have survived months on ice?

But Gates shrugged. "Any of it. All of it. That's why I talked to your ME. I wanted to go through Amari's personal effects, but he refused. He hadn't gotten much off the vic yet and he wouldn't take an x-ray. Not until the time is right."

"Damaged evidence doesn't hold up in court," Nicole pointed out.

"True."

"How long has Faris Amari been working for you?"

"He came to us on October twelfth."

That was a long time—six months—for a secret operation to be conducted right under her nose, and she didn't like it.

"Get over it," he suggested. "We're playing nice now and it's getting us somewhere."

He was right. She could apply Band-Aids to her wounded pride later.

"Green and Monte go back a long way," she said. "All the way to Isle of Royale."

Gates nodded. "True. That was before Green ascended to region chief. And not long after that, he got Monte to join him here."

Two men decorated for heroism in the same battle.

A bond forged from horrific loss.

Monte was working for Green but with Baker. He was gathering evidence that could incriminate his boss, or simply end his career. He was the man in the middle, and it must have been a tight squeeze. She said as much.

"Not when your only allegiance is to justice," Gates said.

But that was about as black and white as could be, and most people functioned inside the gray, in the mire of human emotions, loyalty included.

"How did you lose Monte?"

"We underestimated the BP and the terrain. We were occupied across the lake. We already suspected that Baker was dead, but we still had fifty pounds of fentanyl on the loose."

"You had to stay with the drugs."

"You understand it's lethal? Not *if* but *when* it will kill? And I can tell you when, just minutes after it hits the streets. And not just one or two vics, but thousands. Possibly tens of thousands just from that fifty pounds."

"You cut him loose."

"And hoped that Monte could help himself." He held her gaze, his holding regret but not a speck of doubt about the decision. "We didn't like it either."

"Did he call over the radio? Did he ask for help?"

He shook his head. "One transmission," he said. "Short and sweet. 'An approaching vessel. No running lights.' "

"And that transmission went directly to BP dispatch?"

Gates nodded. "We had tapped into their transmissions, of course, and that was the only message from Monte that gave us concern."

Green had kept that from her. She was not surprised. Not even disappointed. No, she was furious.

"My forensics people found a hair on the party boat that belongs to Adelai Amari," Nicole said.

"Really?"

He tried to hide his hand, but the man was hopeless.

"Poker isn't your best game, is it?" she challenged.

"I can't put all my cards on the table."

"You'll have to if you want our cooperation."

Gates sat back and propped an ankle over his knee, considering her. Eventually he nodded. "We know Monte's alive because we saw him later. He'd somehow taken control of the party boat, and he had Adelai Amari with him."

"Where?"

"He was motoring north. He stopped at a private dock, and the girl got off."

"Adelai and her baby."

"Yes."

"And then what did Monte do?"

"We were pulling out. We were down to two hands, and that was suicide."

"You left him out there," she said. "You left him in the cross hairs."

23

When Nicole pulled into her designated parking spot at the station, it was ten after seven. She'd returned with Gates to the forensics lab, and together, with Arthur leading them, they had gone through the evidence so far accumulated—including the reports on the BP skiff and the party boat—and she had answered his questions. When that wasn't enough, they had all taken the elevator to the garage on the first floor and she and Arthur had given Gates a visual inspection of both boats. Arthur was about as welcoming as MacAulay had been, based on Gates's comments on the warm reception he'd been receiving.

"Definitely a chill in the air here too."

"The door won't hit you in the ass on your way out," Arthur invited.

Which Gates took in stride. "Well, you're nothing if not consistent."

"We're a hell of a lot more than that," Arthur said.

"You don't have to convince me," Gates said, and meant it. "It's the reason I'm here."

"Should have shown up sooner," Arthur groused.

"We did; we just didn't announce ourselves."

"Some would perceive that as trespassing."

Arthur was being nice. Nicole had been working on a mental list of formidable complaints. Her favorite—skulking.

"Not some," Gates returned. "All. It's a damned-if-you-do kind of situation."

Arthur nodded. "I can see how that would be the case." He softened a little. "Both hulls are abraded. Let me show you."

And Gates had slipped on a pair of latex gloves and taken a close look at the damage on the skiff and the party boat. He looked inside the

186

compartment where the drugs had been stored and asked if Arthur had taken samples from either boat and tested for the presence of fentanyl.

"Wiped clean, as far as we can tell," Arthur said.

Gates thanked Arthur for following through on that, and seeing as the AG was playing nice, Nicole left the men alone to finish up with the evidence she and Lars had already learned all about that afternoon. She had a lot on her plate and little time to tackle it.

Now she punched her code into the back door—her private office entrance—and slipped into the station unannounced.

Paperwork awaited her. Evidentiary reports, invitations for personal appearances and conferences, duty reports, vacation requests. She sat down at her desk and decided to split the chore down the middle—tackle the most pressing first and save the rest for tomorrow. A good plan, except she was distracted by phone calls.

She'd spoken to both Jordan and MacAulay by cell phone. They were seated at a table at the Artemis Grill, awaiting their meals, and had made it out of Outdoor Adventures with no shortage of treasures. MacAulay promised to have Jordan home by nine thirty and himself at the morgue and elbow-deep into the autopsy of the ice man not long after that. He confirmed the visit by Devon Gates, just before he'd left with Jordan—so the special agent hadn't been sitting on his ass the whole two plus hours he'd been in town. MacAulay had given Gates a list of the contents recovered and mentioned that Gates had been keen on having the x-rays completed first thing.

Nicole didn't tell MacAulay what the AG was looking for—that the real prize was big evidence contained in a small package. She figured the ME would call her on such a find.

Nicole's fast-fresh Cobb salad from the local drive-up had wilted beyond appetizing, but she took a few bites anyway. She sipped the coffee she'd ordered, which was room temperature. She picked up the next piece of paper from the stack—a complaint from the Silverton area. Wild horses were encroaching upon a ranch there, spooking the livestock and taking down fences. She made a note on the bottom of the page to have her assistant contact the Bureau of Land Management, which was in charge of protecting their small pod of wild horses. Then she set that aside and found her mind drifting again.

They hadn't gotten back to Luke Franks. Gates had taken up a chunk of her time, and Lars was catching a few winks so he could attend the autopsy that evening. She had yet to tell him about Gates's suspicions of the BP agent.

She took another poke at her salad, then dropped the remains in the trash and stood.

Jane Casper had promised to stay put until Nicole had the chance to speak to her in person. She made her way to the conference room and found the deputy peering at the screen of one of the two laptops that were up and running. A printer was churning out paper dense with type and a small map. The remains of fast-food wrappers and Diet Coke cans littered one end of the long table.

"Tell me you have something that will make my day," Nicole said, and dropped into the chair next to her deputy.

"Today and tomorrow too," Jane promised, and Nicole felt her heartbeat kick into gear. She sat forward in her seat. "Really?"

"I've earned every hour of overtime." She looked at her watch. "That would be sixteen of them, just so you know I'm counting." She smiled, and the freckles over her nose spread like a pattern of stars.

"So let me have it," Nicole said.

"Numbers are my thing," Jane said. "Lots of people see piles. I see patterns. I can pick out anomalies as easily as most people pick out socks, so some of this was easy-peasy." She stood and walked around the table to a pile of papers. She shuffled through them and brought back several sheaves, which she spread out in front of Nicole. "I found money. Lots of it. Some explained. Others not."

"Who has it?" Nicole asked. She felt her breath flutter in her throat. Her time in Denver, white-collar crimes, had taught her that following money almost always led to the culprit.

"All of them. Green. Baker. And Monte."

"Who has a reasonable explanation for it?"

"They all do," Jane said. "And then they all don't."

Nicole groaned. "Stop talking in riddles, Deputy."

"Look at this." She pointed to a list of deposits on a bank statement she had managed to procure after presenting the financial institutions with a signed warrant—easier to get one when the people in question were sworn officers. "They came in this morning by email, and I've been tracking them all day."

Nicole looked for the name at the top of the form. "This one belongs to Monte."

"Yes, and they go back a year. That's all the judge would give me," she explained. "If there's cause for a deeper probe, he invited me to resubmit. I did that midafternoon."

"Because you established cause."

"For each one," Jane confirmed.

Nicole scanned the statements. Monte didn't seem to spend a lot of money. There were the automatic deposits of his paycheck and debits for the usual—utilities, groceries, gas, and a gym membership. There was a large deposit of the same amount made—she went back and counted— four times a year. He had a savings that dwarfed Nicole's, and there had been no withdrawals from it in the past year.

"He has no consumer debt," Jane said. "His SUV—it's a 2015—is paid off, and he has a Mastercard he doesn't use." Jane pointed out the card number at the bottom of the statement and its corresponding zero balance. "I included a credit check on the warrant." She pulled that paper to the top.

"A credit score of eight-fifty," Nicole noticed.

Jane nodded. "He paid off his mortgage early, with two additional payments towards the principal yearly."

"He had a car loan that ran its course," Nicole added.

"Yes, and that bolstered his credit score. What I want to know is purchase history. Did he ever use that Mastercard? If so, for what? That will show us his discipline, and his extravagances. I also want to know how far back those large deposits go."

"And where they're coming from," Nicole said. A routing number was included with the deposit as well as the acronym of a bank or business, neither of which gave Nicole a clue about origin on the surface.

"Well, I did some sleuthing on that," Jane said. "I have confirmation and conjecture."

"Tell me what you know first," Nicole suggested.

"The deposits are made quarterly and issued through an attorney's office located in Austin, Texas. Each amount is twelve thousand five hundred dollars. Together, that amounts to fifty grand a year. So that's what I know. A lot of estates are disbursed in this fashion, so that was my first checkpoint, and they're pretty easy to confirm, but not here. I called the attorney's office; turns out they're big business. That's with an exclamation point. They do nothing else. Their clients are big-chain grocery and clothing stores—I'm talking Macy's Fifth Avenue, Saks, et cetera—a skateboard manufacturer, outdoor equipment suppliers. I put it all into the pot and started thinking about it and Monte and any possible connection."

"Did you find one?"

"Yes." Jane gathered up the statements on Monte and straightened them into a neat pile. "On February twenty-fourth, 2017, Monte's wife was killed in an auto accident." She shook her head, and a heaviness settled on her features. "Actually, she survived the crash but was pinned inside her crumpled car. Passersby stopped, talked with her, and administered what aid they could while they waited for first responders. One man tried using a crowbar to peel back the metal. It was of little use. Flames erupted from the engine area, pushing back the witnesses. The car exploded in flame."

"Damn," Nicole breathed.

"Yeah." Jane nodded and let the silence intrude a moment longer. "The truck that hit her? It was an eighteen-wheeler, a company truck loaded with sundries. The company is a client of this attorney's office."

"You think Monte sued them?"

"I do. The truck driver had had less than eight hours of sleep in three days."

"Gross negligence."

"Yes. Standard payout on something like this is a million dollars, spread out over twenty years."

Nicole worked the numbers. "An exact fit."

"Yes. And even if it doesn't play out this way, the attorney is legit and in good standing with the Texas Bar Association and the American Bar Association."

"So the money's good, no matter where it's coming from."

"Yes." She turned over the stack of papers, revealing what looked like an email communication with a rundown of numbers. She tapped a figure at the top. "This figure, however, is an anomaly. A hundred thousand dollars, dropped out of the blue, into Monte's checking account. It doesn't appear on his statement because the deposit was made two days ago, at eleven sixteen AM, the old-fashioned way."

"What's that?"

"Someone walked into the bank's branch in Kalispell with a cashier's check, filled out a generic deposit slip, and handed that and the check over to the teller. I called. The deposit was made by a female not matching Baker's description. In fact, the teller remembers it so well because the amount was large, the woman making the deposit was not listed on the account, and she seemed strung out and crashing fast. I requested the video of the transaction, so that's on its way. In the meantime, we can speculate."

Not a full day before Monte's call to her in the middle of the night.

"Did you request video from outside the bank during the same time period?"

"No." A frown settled on Jane's face as she thought that through. "Damn. My mistake."

"Call and make the request," Nicole said. "It's likely, from the description, that someone sent that woman in with the deposit. Maybe they waited outside. A cashier's is like a blank check. It would take a lot of trust not to watch it go down. Let's see who that was. And get a copy of the deposit slip for handwriting analysis."

"I did think of that," Jane said. "And it's on its way."

"You've done great work here," Nicole returned. "Now tell me about the others."

"Let's talk about Baker," Jane said. "She's the easiest of the three. No random big-dollar deposits. She has a good-sized savings, which I traced back to the sale of her home in San Diego. She withdrew from that for the down payment on her townhouse on the Lake Road. She also receives a small amount quarterly, which comes directly from her mother's estate. Her mother passed six years ago. Baker's older sister is the executor. She's also the next of kin, when you're ready to reach out. Baker has four credit cards, though only one with a balance. Her most recent purchases on it include a plane ticket, Billings to Toronto, round trip, departing tomorrow at four PM; a hotel deposit—Wyndham on Saint Charles Avenue; assorted tours in and around Toronto."

"She had a vacation planned."

"Looks like."

"Green hadn't mentioned that."

"A vacation is not unusual. But the timing and destination are suspect, I think."

"Me too. Anything else on Baker?"

Jane shook her head and pushed a separate stack of papers toward Nicole.

"What do you have on Green?"

"Complete chaos," Jane said. "The man can spend, and a lot of it isn't smart buying."

"Which would look like what?"

"A home, for example. Green is renting. It's a four-bedroom with private access to the lake. He's not married, has no known children, so I don't know why he's knocking around in such a large place. He's leasing his car—current-year Caddie Escalade. No investment there. His grocery bills read like a mortgage payment, and some of it comes from as far as a courier in Paris."

"For truffles?"

"Exactly."

"Really?" Nicole's sarcasm morphed into surprise.

"That and a case of wine ordered most recently on or around the first of the month." She pointed the transaction out to Nicole on the statement. "It appears only twice more on previous statements. But he buys his beef from Nebraska and had cases of oranges shipped from Florida around Christmas—probably gifts. But the guy lives large."

"Does he have any savings?" Nicole asked.

"Standard savings with a balance of two hundred twelve thousand dollars. A CD worth slightly more. He has an IRA approaching half a mil. And I get the feeling this is just chump change."

"What do you mean?"

"He has crazy deposits. No two ever the same amount, no month with the same amount of deposits. The money passing through his accounts this past year totals more than a million dollars."

"He isn't making that at BP."

"Hell no," Jane agreed. "His salary last year was a hundred sixty-eight."

"So what accounts for the remaining eight hundred thousand or so?"

"Some were cash deposits. None less than three thousand, none over five. Some were electronic transfers, but there were few of those and they totaled, oddly enough, the same amount as his salary."

"A hundred sixty-eight grand?"

"Yes."

"And the other deposits?"

"Seven of them. No rhyme or reason for their regularity. A cluster in October and then not again until January, for example. A few came in at fifty-five thousand. The rest were close to a quarter million dollars. All of them checks."

"What the hell?" Nicole said.

"Exactly."

"Can you trace those?"

"Working on it, but it'll be difficult. I asked for a copy of the checks, which the bank scans on deposit. But it will be up to the judge whether or not he adds that to the warrant. I put a tracer on those electronic deposits and hope to have a hit before I head home tonight." She turned in her chair and sat back with a satisfied grin. "So how did I do?"

"Fantastic," Nicole said.

"I'll send for the video."

"Make it the last thing you do tonight," Nicole said, and stood. "Still nothing from Monte's digital files?"

"I can tell you what you gave me isn't complete," Jane said.

"Explain."

"There have been deletions. They show up as black holes between text. Very similar to letters the government censored during WWII, only the digital version."

"Is there any way to recover what was deleted?"

"Not a chance. The deletions occurred before the text was added to the USB."

"So only if we have the original source?"

"That's right. I can tell you some of those deletions occurred around the following names: Green, Gates, and Franks."

"What were they trying to hide?"

"I don't know. What remains is mostly nonsense. Half thoughts. Like watching an R-rated movie with your mom holding the remote—she presses mute every time a bad word or sexy talk comes up."

"Any words that might interest me?"

"Money and drugs, but nothing, so far, that ties them together. Get me the original source and I'll get you a bedtime story too good to put down."

Nicole smiled. "I might be able to do that." She'd ordered the collection of Monte's desktop, laptop, iPad, and any other electronics still at BP. Problem was, if he'd recorded on his smartphone, he probably still had that with him. "Go home"—she nodded toward the wrappers and cans at the end of the table—"eat something healthy, and get a good night's sleep. You'll be working hard and nonstop again tomorrow."

"We're close," Casper said.

"Very."

They were standing in his draft. So close, in fact, that Nicole could feel his breath. Tomorrow, before the day ended, they would have their man.

24

It was almost eight o'clock. There was enough time that she could make it home before MacAulay dropped off Jordan. She stared at the stack of remaining paperwork, which she had moved to the credenza. Usually her assistant separated it all into a twisting pattern of varicolored file folders so that, on a good day, it looked like a pinwheel. Today wasn't good. Today it looked like a spur on the heel of Achilles. There were still duty rosters and overtime tallies to sign off on, all of which Lars had found the time to put together. There was correspondence still needing a reply, and a stack of message slips she hadn't even glanced at. She stuffed it all into her messenger's bag and exited the building through the back door.

Night had fallen. Inky darkness had gathered in the trees, but overhead the sky was a clear indigo. Stars were scattered in a random trail, as though they had fallen out of someone's pocket. Under this same sky, not forty-eight hours before, a woman had died while another ran for her life, and a man Nicole had known well enough to call a friend had been on the run. Or not.

Was the hundred grand his take or part of an elaborate scheme to frame Monte?

The more Nicole dissected the possibility that Monte had turned bad, the more a stubborn refusal to believe it rooted itself. Even with the evidence building against him, there just didn't seem to be enough cause. She knew the human spirit was in a constant state of response. Had he wearied from personal and professional tragedy? An affair and a large, random deposit were enough to damn the average suspect. And she had timed it. Monte could have driven to Kalispell, waited in the bank parking lot, and seen that the money was deposited, then made it back on time for his shift. Was she blinded by loyalty? Was she too heavily invested in an FBI profile that, as a matter of rule, held a margin for error?

Tension knotted in her brow, just above the bridge of her nose. She expelled a heavy breath and headed across the parking lot for her Yukon.

There were two other vehicles parked in the lot—dispatch and the deputy monitoring the lockup were the only remaining night personnel. They were a small department in need of growth, as the population in the county continued to climb. Transplants from both the East and West Coasts, and some states scattered in between, were making a steady influx into Toole County. The draw of the rugged mountains and open spaces was hard to ignore.

Nicole needed more deputies; Lars needed a raise. The numbers easily supported another full-time forensics tech and an assistant for MacAulay. And though the ME either didn't see it looming or was in denial, his position was on a trajectory to grow as well. In the beginning, Mac had called it moonlighting. Two years in, he had opened his family practice to a partial partnership, sharing the patient load with a vested physician's assistant. For more than a year now, MacAulay had spoken of either offering a full partnership into his practice or wooing an intern into the morgue from any number of medical schools. He saw patients three and a half days a week and worked autopsies around that. It all balanced until the county was hit by wrongful death, and then he worked around the clock. He managed conferences and the occasional vacation by utilizing the backup ME from Glacier County and hiring per diem doctors to fill in in his absence.

She was thinking about strong wording to place in her report—the meeting of the county board of supervisors was coming up next week, and she would submit her budgetary needs then—when a shadow separated from the driver's side of her Yukon and took a stance. Tall, broad shouldered, clearly male, and backlit by the lampposts, rendering the person completely unrecognizable.

Nicole stopped, her hand clenched around the handle of her bag. She moved her right hand to her holster and popped the snap.

"It's Green," he called over. He spread his arms wide and made a show of his hands, which were empty.

Yes, she recognized the voice, but she didn't feel any better about the situation.

"Why didn't you come inside?"

"I should have," he said. "But news of that would have made fast work across town and between agencies."

"And you want to keep this visit quiet?"

He brought his hands down and rested them on his hips. She kept her palm in touch with the grip of her Glock.

He took several steps closer, and Nicole stood her ground. He stopped when there was six feet between them. Just two law enforcement officers having a conversation.

"What do you want, Green?"

"For all of this to be as if it never was."

"I don't have a magic wand."

"Neither do I. And failing that—just another failure in a list of many—how about an update? Have you heard anything about Monte?"

"No, have you?"

But he shook his head. "Talk is one of your deputies found his bronze medallion."

Nicole nodded. "True. Forensics is processing it."

"We wore those, you know, every day. To remember. Not just the fallen, but that we were tried and true." He laughed without humor. A dry, scratchy sound that irritated her nerves. "Eight of us survived, and Monte's act of heroism"—he shook his head in disbelief—"he gave it all up for the rest of us. Sacrificed himself so we could scuttle to cover. There was no way he was walking out alive. He cut across the line of fire, drawing aim. But damn if he isn't the luckiest SOB alive."

Nicole nodded. She felt her throat go dry, and her fingers curled around the grip of her Glock.

"Monte saved my ass once. I thought he could do it again."

"Isle of Royale, and what else?"

He raised his arms, indicating everything that had gone down in the past forty-two hours. Still somewhat in shadow, he looked like a giant bird of prey. "When I was promoted, I asked Monte to come too. A man like that, a man who would die for you, I knew to hold on to him."

"Is that what Monte's doing right now? Dying for you?"

Green nodded. "Looks like."

"Like Baker did?"

"Exactly like that. I didn't kill her, but make no mistake about it, there's blood on my hands anyway."

"Explain that to me," Nicole demanded. "Tell me what I don't know."

But that only stirred him up. "You know more than I do," he said. "A day leading the investigation and I bet you have a list of suspects and maybe even a few confessions."

"Are you afraid they've given you up?"

"If they did, it's a lie." He shifted on his feet, and Nicole heard the scraping of his hard-soled shoes on the cement. "So how bad is it?"

"At least a handful of men," she said. "But don't you already know that? The AG has been inside since December."

"He tells me nothing," Green said.

Because Gates suspected he was at the center of the ring.

"Ah, the wheels are turning," Green said. "It doesn't say a lot for my character, does it?"

"You've been under suspicion from the beginning," Nicole said.

"I'm going to lose my command."

"You have a lot of money coming in," Nicole said, remembering his bank statements and lavish lifestyle.

"My bank accounts have been thoroughly investigated. Internal Affairs followed every deposit to origin."

"So ease my mind," Nicole said.

His reluctance was palpable. She watched him roll his shoulders back to try to ease the tension. "Nothing ever stays private," he complained. "So don't bother with platitudes."

"You won't get any from me."

"Real estate holdings," he said, and tried to leave it at that.

"This is starting to stink," Nicole warned.

"Gambling is an addiction. We pretend to know how big it is, but the general public sees just the tip of the iceberg. I'm about mid-tier, not a player but a predator," he said. "I have interest in a casino is Las Vegas. And business is so good, we're branching out. We're opening doors in June in Tahoe. Something for everyone there. The wife and kids can enjoy the lake while the man of the house gambles it away at our tables. Or vice versa. There are plenty of female players, and we're happy to indulge both."

"The deposits are from a casino interest?"

"Yes. For the first half of the year, we weren't pulling any profits because we were building the new place. Then we had an insurgence of income from summer play in Vegas, and we split that up in rounds until all of that was depleted," he explained. "Gambling is big business. As a rule, profits are split quarterly, January, April, July, and October, giving the money a chance to compound while it's in reserve."

"How did you get involved in this?"

"It's a legitimate business," he said. "Even if it's morally reprehensible."

"But you don't play?"

"Not even the slot machines."

"So again, how did you get involved in this as a business?"

"My brother. He started out working the tables, made it to assistant manager. Squirreled money away and then came to me with the proposition. We're not alone, of course. There are a dozen of us, all equal stakeholders. But you can ask the AG. I walked him down this lane back at Christmas, when he first arrived."

"I think I should talk to Internal Affairs," she told him. "It's really about time."

"I knew you'd be wanting this. A natural step after talking to the AG."

He reached into his pocket, but with the shadow and play of light, he could just as easily be reaching for his weapon. Nicole moved her hand, drawing her Glock from its holster just enough that she could fit her finger into the trigger guard.

"I don't have my side arm," he said, picking up on her thoughts or feeling the press of night as much as she was. "I left it locked in my car. I have a smaller piece in an ankle holster."

He pulled a swatch of white paper out of his pocket. It was creased, and she could see there was some print but also a logo on the card. He handed it across to her. Nicole had to make a decision—either set her bag down or remove her hand from her pistol. She chose caution. An action not lost on Green.

"And I thought we were building trust," he said.

"A dark, deserted parking lot and a desperate colleague," she pointed out, but took the paper and stuffed it into her pocket without looking at it.

"Now let's talk about the satchel," she said.

"Too easy, huh?"

"Where did it really come from?"

But he shook his head. "I wasn't the one who recovered it."

"And we're supposed to believe it washed up with the body."

"A stroke of luck." His tone wasn't light on the sarcasm.

"The AG said more than thirty million dollars in fentanyl is missing."

"My guess, it's up and over the border."

"No. He says they stopped the flow, but not for long. He thinks there's something else at play. Evidence so good it'll make the courtroom a formality."

Green's gaze caught the light from the window, and he squinted. "Have you found it?" he asked.

It. Singular. One piece that, when pulled, would bring down the whole house of cards. She tried to ignore the skittering of nerves over her scalp. That first wave of primitive awareness, trembling between the fight-or-flight mechanism in her brain.

"Not yet."

"It all comes back to the girl, doesn't it?" he said.

"You didn't think so," she offered.

"It's starting to make sense now," he said. "If the UDA on ice doesn't have it, then maybe he gave it to his sister."

"I never told you that," Nicole said.

"Maybe the AG did."

But she was shaking her head. "He wouldn't."

Nicole pulled her Glock, but Green was already moving, ducking into a crouch as he pulled a gun from the small of his back, where he'd tucked it into his waistband.

She threw herself into the shadows. The crack from Green's handgun bounced off the walls of the office buildings and set off the car alarms down the street. The bullet missed, striking the blacktop at her feet. Nicole felt the shower of gravel spray her legs as she ran for cover. She scrambled behind a dumpster positioned at the back of the sheriff's office, and when she peered around its metal side, Green was gone.

25

She'd had new gravel poured and graded on her driveway the week before, after what she'd hoped was the last serious snowfall before the winter season began in late September. The tires of the Yukon turned evenly and she crested the hill, planning to slide easily into the detached garage, but a car was blocking her way. And it wasn't MacAulay's, who she expected at any moment. He and Jordan had finished dinner in Pleasant Falls and were long into their drive home, their treasures tucked safely in the cargo area of MacAulay's Highlander.

Nicole stopped the Yukon and hit the strobe light, illuminating the interior of the low-slung sports car. It was empty. She cut the light, all the better to see the surrounding area. The car was familiar, but she couldn't place it. She doused the headlights and the yard settled into darkness, including, oddly, the security light, which was run off a solar panel.

Green passed through her mind. She saw him again, crouched and firing, but then banished the image. She had an all-points bulletin out on him with an order of arrest attached to it. She didn't think he'd come to her home. He wouldn't want to risk capture.

She'd pulled the paper he'd given her out of her pocket shortly after he'd taken a shot at her. It was a business card, his own, and the act had been a ruse. He had wanted her to release her gun. To step closer and reach for the paper, rendering her vulnerable. He had arrived planning to kill her. And all the talk before that was an attempt to get information from her. He'd wanted to know where he stood amid the investigation, and, it turned out, he wasn't happy between a rock and a hard place.

She reached now for the radio mike clipped to her shoulder. "Dispatch, this is Sheriff Cobain."

"Go 'head, Sheriff."

"Checking in," she reported. "I've arrived home. I have a vehicle parked in my driveway. No obvious occupants." She gave the plate number and waited for dispatch to look it up.

"A 2018 Ford Mustang, license plate number"—Lodi repeated it—"belonging to Deputy Tyler Watts."

An uneasiness shifted through Nicole. She couldn't pin it down. She liked Ty. He was a good worker, sharp and on his toes, full effort always. So maybe it was the absolute stillness. Not even the dog was barking from within the house. That had only happened once before, four months ago, when Nicole had returned home to find that Benjamin had kidnapped their son and locked Mrs. Neal in the woodshed.

"Call his cell," Nicole ordered. "If you connect, patch him through." Better that way, as there would be a recording of the conversation over open air.

While she waited, she reversed the Yukon and turned it so that the nose pointed down the driveway. She thought about calling in backup, Lars in particular. She had plenty to tell him, revelations made during her conversation with Gates and then Green's attempt to shoot her, but that could wait another hour, when they headed over to Luke Franks's place. She chose instead to hit speed dial on her cell. MacAulay picked up on the second ring.

"Where are you?" she asked.

"On the Lake Road," he said.

Ten minutes, no more than that, and he and Jordan would be spinning gravel on their way up the driveway.

"Stay there," she said. "Until I call you back."

"What's wrong?"

"Maybe nothing," she admitted.

It was something.

Nicole's property wasn't big—three and a half acres, most of it wooded. Nestled into a hill, the backyard was big enough for entertaining, with a concrete slab patio and a western view that framed the setting sun. In deference to Mrs. Neal's sensibilities, after the old trestle woodshed had been processed as a crime scene, Nicole had torn it down and purchased a prefab shed to replace it. It was made from a sturdy, resin-coated plastic-rubber mix, and from where she sat in the idling Yukon, she heard the door to the shed bang against the jamb. It was a flat, jarring sound that repeated itself within the motion of the rustling wind.

The door shouldn't be open. It had a perfectly good latch.

She felt her pulse pick up its beat, pinging against the walls of her heart with every slam of the shed door.

She talked herself down from adrenaline overload, knowing that when it was harnessed, it provided a keen edge.

Dispatch got back to her. Ty wasn't answering his phone. And that decided it. She hoped Lars had gotten at least the chance of an uninter-rupted dinner with his family. He picked up on the second ring.

"What's up?"

"I wish I knew," she said. "I'm at home. Haven't gotten out of the car yet. The dog isn't barking. Ty Watts' Ford Mustang is parked in my drive-way, but he's nowhere to be seen and isn't answering his cell. And the door to the shed is ajar and beating in the wind."

"I'm on my way."

"That's probably a good idea," she agreed. "And Lars, Green took a shot at me earlier."

That was met with a moment's silence. "No shit?"

"No, and I have a lot more to tell you—all from the AG—but we'll do that later. Be careful," she said, and hung up.

There was a thin line between foolishness and bravado. She worried, though, that she was being controlled more at the moment by events that had played too close to home. She was determined that Benjamin wouldn't reach out from the grave and continue to torment her. And that Green wouldn't put her in a mental choke hold.

She released the snap on her holster for the second time that night. She liked the feel of the textured grip against the palm of her hand. There was safety in that. A level of comfort few people outside law enforcement understood. She drew her weapon, slipped her index finger into the trig-ger notch, and then allowed the Glock to rest against her thigh as she scanned the front yard, the side of the house, craned her neck to glimpse the backyard and the peaked roof of the shed. The department Yukons were special order, as was standard among policing agencies. The siding was reinforced by steel that slowed the progress of bullets through the metal. The windows were shatterproof, half an inch thick, and centered with bullet-repelling mesh.

The first bullet hit at the same time she heard the discharge. The glass in her driver's side window fractured, beaded, all but caved in and rained on her head. Instinctively, she had ducked, and it was from that crouched position behind the steering wheel that she released the emergency brake, shifted into drive, and pressed on the gas. She sat up as the Yukon shot forward, in time to see Ty step into the beam of her headlights. He wasn't in uniform and had pulled his weapon. Nicole wavered. The shot had come from the northeast, directly opposite Ty's position. He could not have fired it. And then the squirreling thought, *What if Ty isn't acting alone?* She stepped on the brake, the back end shuddering and fishtailing to a stop.

She hit her radio mike. "Ten seventy-one. Shots fired," she reported.

Dispatch responded immediately, "Location, please, Sheriff Cobain."

She gave her address. "Deputy Watts is present. No injuries." Yet.

Ty scrambled the fifteen yards to the side of her vehicle, and Nicole sought and captured his gaze. The eyes were the windows to the soul. She believed that. She also believed that the best of them could camouflage the most evil of intents. That it took a deliberate and close scrutiny to see through the cracks in the plaster. She didn't have that kind of time.

"Units on the way," dispatch reported.

Ty pulled on the door handle. Another shot rang out. This one punctured the rear driver's side tire. She knew she could get as much as fifty miles on the damage before the tire flattened, shredded, and the metal rim drew sparks off the asphalt. That wasn't her immediate concern.

She held Ty's gaze—he was alert, pumped, confused—and sought and released the automatic door lock with her left hand.

Ty lifted himself into the passenger's seat and pulled the door shut. "Go," he said. He dropped his gun in his lap as he wrestled with the seat belt.

"Leave your gun there," Nicole said. She moved her foot to the accelerator and spun out of the driveway. Her Glock was in hand, and she had no intention of changing that.

"What?"

"Better yet, move it to the floor," she ordered. She took her eyes from the road for a moment and connected again with Ty's gaze.

Surprise flared in his eyes. "I have no idea why you were at my home, who was shooting at me, or what's going to happen next. We'll play that by ear, beginning with you following my direct order in regards to your weapon and finishing with some answers I know are going to be incredible."

Ty took a deep breath and let it out slowly. He probably did it for both of them, training 101. Stabilize the situation. But he followed through. He picked his gun up with finger and thumb, bent over, and laid it on the floor by his feet.

When he was sitting upright and back against his seat, Nicole began.

"You were at my house for what reason?"

"I figured it out," he said. "It's after nine, and I thought you'd be home by now."

"Why didn't you call me? Or meet me at the station?" she wanted to know.

"I did call the station. They said you were on your way home." She cast a glance his way. Color was high on his cheeks, a by-product of adrenaline rush, but his breathing was level. "Monte isn't dead," he said. "He's alive, and someone's helping him stay that way. I think that someone is Luke Franks."

"Explain," she ordered. "Beginning to end, flushed out with details."

"Monte never went into the woods. We're supposed to believe he did. The medallion I found, the life pack rummaged—we were meant to believe he survived whatever happened on that boat and then made for the border, but I just don't see that happening."

"Why?"

"For the same reason you don't—instinct, reputation, the stink of a frame." His voice grew in intensity. "And the dogs. No way they didn't pick up Monte's scent if he made land."

She didn't like that either. Green's reasoning, his play to sound as confused as the rest of them, was cunning. And she'd fallen for it. The heat of that error scalded her skin.

Nicole nodded.

"I'm not saying Monte is innocent. I don't think any of us can say that yet. But I do think he's alive and right under our noses."

"How do you figure Luke Franks fits into this?"

"He called in sick that night, along with several other agents. But he stands out among them, and you know why? Luke Franks is a good agent with the track record to prove it."

"You've been through the personnel files?"

"Only a handful. They didn't come in until a few hours ago," he said. "But Franks was on top. It was given priority because he didn't always agree with Green and didn't mind telling him so."

And Green was their one sure thing—rotten at the core.

"So you went into Franks' file looking for someone outside Green's circle."

"And that's what I found. Both Franks and Monte. Two good agents. Never a hint of impropriety. Evaluation remarks filled with all the right buzz words—'integrity,' 'moral fortitude,' 'exceeding standards,' et cetera. It makes sense they would team up," he concluded.

"So we'll go to Franks' house," she said. "But first we have a crime scene to secure."

That scene being her home. It disturbed her. She had installed a top-shelf security system, including floodlights around the house, and they had a dog that alerted them of company, and none of that had stopped another incident in what should be her safe place.

"I drove by Franks's house earlier. There was a light on in the kitchen. I might have seen shadows moving around in there. I didn't stay," he explained. "I thought I should have a little backup."

And so he'd come to Nicole's home looking for her. That made sense. She felt the tension loosen its grip on her muscles.

"Definitely some backup." She spared him a more thoughtful glance. "Where is your vest?"

"In the trunk of my car."

"That's a good place for it to be."

"I'm off duty," he pointed out.

"But you're not acting like it."

He was poised to argue but then thought better of it and closed his mouth, sat back in his seat, and accepted the criticism.

"It's a requirement, not a preference," she said.

"Understood," he said.

"Who do you think was shooting at us?"

"I think they were shooting at *you*," he said. "I'd been waiting close to fifteen minutes. A sitting duck inside the car, but then I got out when I heard noise behind the house."

"The shed door?"

He nodded. "Wind had been blowing a while and the door was just fine. Then it started up. I think now it was meant to draw me out of the car."

"But they didn't fire?"

"Not until you showed up."

"How long after you got out of the car was that?"

"Three or four minutes."

"Did you get a look at the shed?"

"Yeah, someone had to open that latch. The door was flung wide open."

"Did you touch anything?"

"Hell no." He sounded offended. "I know better than that. Besides"—and he rolled his shoulders up over his ears—"I started getting that prickly feeling on the back of my neck. I trust that—always—and scooted into the tree line. Just about then, you came up the driveway."

"You took your time showing yourself."

He shook his head. "I didn't know it was you, and with that all-points out on Green, I didn't want to take any chances. I worked my way around to the front of the house, and then all hell broke loose."

"You didn't answer your cell phone."

"It's in the car."

A lot of plausible reasons, but none of them felt good.

"I don't like impromptu meetings under the cover of darkness," she said.

"I'll remember that."

A burst of static came over the radio then, and dispatch provided an update on response. Lars and Jane were closest, just a few minutes out.

"Stop units on visual with me," she said. "I have Deputy Watts with me. We are off the property, shouldered at Spruce and State. Pull two more units and have them routed here."

"Already done. Those units are coming in from Sunburst and Emmerson. ETAs are looking in excess of fifteen and twenty minutes."

The wide-open spaces of the North Country, Nicole thought. Some responses, though immediate, were not fast.

But dispatch had done its job, was following protocol with an officer-involved shooting seamlessly. The trainings, both in-house and afield, were paying off.

At the bottom of Spruce, where it formed a T with the state road, Nicole slowed and performed a U-turn. She brought the Yukon onto the shoulder of the road and idled there. Her cell rang again. MacAulay. Nicole opened the call.

"Are you still on the Lake Road?"

"Yes, pulled over at the boat ramp east side. What's going on?"

"Shots fired at the house," she explained. "It'll be hours before we clear it." And even then she wouldn't sleep easy. "Can you take Jordan for the night?"

"Of course," he said. "Are you all right?"

She nodded, but of course he couldn't see that. "No injuries," she reported. No return fire.

"Will you come by later?"

It would take at least an hour to secure the scene, employ a strategy, get forensics on the ground. And then there was Monte. They would run by Franks's house and see what they could shake out of the eaves. "Yes, but it won't be soon."

She heard the bark of a dog. It was gruff and halfhearted, an attention-getter and nothing more, and every bit Cooper.

"You have the dog?" she said. Relief flooded her voice.

"Yes. He wanted to go. Climbed into the car before we could stop him."

Cooper loved to take a ride, his blond head out the window, nose lifted into the air.

"Okay," she said. "Good."

"You were worried," he said. "Sorry about that. I guess we forgot to mention it."

"It's all good." And it was. "I'll see you later, then," she said, and would have disconnected, but MacAulay stopped her.

"I have the ice man," he reminded her.

The autopsy. She checked her watch. MacAulay wanted to start that at ten.

"I'll call Mrs. Neal." The woman had never been to MacAulay's home, but she'd had the opportunity to meet him on more than one occasion.

She heard the first approaching sirens. Not one, but two, slightly off beat.

"I'll call when I get a chance," she said, and signed off.

Nicole turned back to Ty.

"Can I pick up my gun?" he asked.

"Did you discharge it?" If he had, it would have to be cleared by forensics.

"No."

"Holster it," she said, and did the same herself. It was an act of trust that should have come easily, but reluctance made her movements slow and heavy.

26

An hour and forty minutes later, with shell casings collected and plaster castings made of fresh footprints found in and around the garden beds, shed, and garage and comparison castings made of Deputy Watts's shoes, Nicole was ready to call it a night. She let herself back into the house. It hadn't been breached by an intruder. Nicole had scrolled though the activity log on the alarm system, which reflected a calm evening inside the home. She pulled a uniform from the closet, collected a few additional essentials, including her toothbrush and Jordan's, and stuffed them all into a small duffel she found in the hall closet. After their trip to Luke Franks's house, Nicole planned to go directly to MacAulay's. She hoped to get there before midnight.

She had to get Jordan to the trailhead at seven AM, which meant they would be up by five thirty. She had to bring him back to the house for his hiking equipment, most of which, a quick peek into his bedroom revealed, looked to be packed. She had taken her messenger's bag, stuffed with a day's paperwork, from the Yukon. It was waiting for her by the front door. She would grab that on her way out but with little intention of getting to it that night.

She brooded over her decision to release Lars for the autopsy. It meant she would go to Franks's house with Ty as her backup, and that made her slightly uncomfortable. She knew it was a matter of association, so quickly on the heels of Green's betrayal, and Ty's unannounced arrival amid gunfire. She had checked—Ty had called the station looking for her. Still, the discomfort had settled on her like razor burn. It would take time to heal.

Lars had been reluctant to leave. He'd wanted contact with Luke Franks, to bear witness as the man was interviewed a second time and the murder of his brother was confirmed. But an officer was needed during the autopsy on the ice man, at least for the initial stages as clothing and other paraphernalia were collected into evidence. Arthur would also attend, as lead CSI. But Lars would be her pipeline to instant information she would otherwise have to gain from a report dense with medical terminology and slow to get to her desk. Information as seen through the eyes of a homicide detective, which could lead to the direction and apprehension of the killer they were seeking.

She called Mrs. Neal, needing the lift of her son's voice, which was like bottled sunshine to her.

"Jordan's already sleeping," Mrs. Neal said. "He has that big hike tomorrow he's very excited about and turned in just as soon as he finished a snack."

Mrs. Neal was big on food and board games.

"He borrowed a pair of the doctor's pajama pants, which fit about as well as a tent on a tadpole, but while he was eating I did a little hemming."

"Thank you, Mrs. Neal."

"You know I love to do it," she said. "Now, how are things at the house?"

Nicole stood at the kitchen sink, looking out the window. She and Ty had driven her Yukon back to the house, leading Lars, the patrol cars, and a forensics team that had responded to the call. It had been processed, the back tire removed and bagged as evidence, and was, at that moment, hooked up to a tow bar and shuttling down the driveway. Losing the window meant she'd have to borrow an older vehicle from their very small motor pool. Specialty glass meant at least a week's wait while it was ordered and shipped and a mobile glass company came out to replace it. But there had been no other damage, to vehicle, house, or surrounding buildings.

"Better than expected," Nicole said.

"You were shot at," Mrs. Neal said. "I suppose it can only get better from there."

"I'm alive," Nicole agreed. And undeterred.

"And unharmed?"

"Not so much as a hair on my head out of place," Nicole assured her.

"Well, then, if you or the doctor returns by midnight, I'm planning on going home. I figure you won't need me tomorrow, so I'm going into Pleasant Falls and want an early start. I have some shopping to do before I leave next week."

Mrs. Neal was traveling to Florida for two weeks with her daughter and three grandchildren. Nicole glanced at the clock on the stove. That gave her two hours tops. And MacAulay would be in autopsy at least that long.

"I'm sorry, Mrs. Neal," Nicole said. Jordan insisted he was old enough to stay by himself, but Nicole wasn't ready for that. "I don't know that either one of us will make it back by midnight."

"Not a worry," the older woman said. "Do you think I could take the small bedroom off the kitchen?"

"I'm sure that would be fine."

She disconnected the call and pressed speed dial for Lars.

"Has the party started?" Nicole asked when he picked up.

"He's up to his elbows in leads," Lars confirmed.

"Yeah?"

"We have something," Lars said. "Fentanyl is my guess. Mac was able to peel away the guy's T-shirt and jeans, skin still intact." That had been MacAulay's biggest concern—preserving the vic's body as best he could. "Get this, the ice man was wearing a watertight bag strapped to his torso. It was stuffed with about seven pounds of the drug and ten thousand dollars in cash."

"So the AG was telling the truth," Nicole said. And she wondered about her own words. Did she doubt the agent's facts or his veracity? He had tried to withhold information, but that didn't make him a liar or a suspect.

"There's more. A few defensive wounds, hands in particular, and MacAulay was able to get some scrapings from under the fingernails. There's blood evidence on the vic's shirt, so that was packed and is ready for the lab in Billings, but preliminary shows a blood type not matching the vic. Got that straight from Sleeping Bear before he packed it himself and sent it with a night courier." She heard the score in Lars's voice. When the man grinned, he looked more grizzly than cop. "He thought, this being a high-profile case, the extra cost was a necessity."

Trace evidence and blood. That was better than ID through a formal lineup. Better, even, than a high-resolution video capture.

"That's good work," Nicole said. It would be days before they got something more definitive.

"It's a damn lucky break, but there's more. Inside the bag was a scrap of paper with a list of phone numbers. No names. One number is Canadian; the other two are cell phones I traced back to carriers here in the U.S. Neither number is working, but we're within the six-month stasis before reregistering the numbers for use. I've put a request through for most recent owner, which we'll get as soon as the judge signs the warrant."

The vic was a treasure chest of evidence to them and a land mine to whoever had killed him.

"And we've only just started," Lars promised. "MacAulay found two electronic pieces sewn into the vic's shirt. We're not sure what they are yet, but Sleeping Bear will take those back to his lab and work some magic. They could be trackers, but two is overkill. And one seems to have a receiver."

"A recording device?" she asked.

"We hope."

"Are they working?"

"That's for Sleeping Bear to figure out."

She wondered if this was the evidence Gates had referred to, the bag from which Faris Amari had fed bread crumbs to the AG. But why hadn't Green and company searched the vic before dumping him?

"We're leaving for Franks' place," Nicole said. "Update me when you can."

"You do the same."

They drove over in Ty's Mustang. He was a little heavy on the gas pedal and took the curves in the road fast enough that Nicole felt the pull of the seat belt. He had taken his Kevlar vest out of the trunk and shrugged into it. Nicole had been wearing hers since six that morning. Sixteen hours later, the heaviness and bulk of the vest were beginning to chafe.

"We're going in drawn," Nicole said. "If Monte wanted to be found, he'd have called us."

"Right," Ty said. "Could be he is wrapped up in this at some level."

Agreed. Love sometimes pulled a person into a swill of other, less honorable emotions.

And Luke Franks, with one brother murdered and the other missing, could be as deep into the misconduct as Green.

Franks's house was small, square, and sat on an acre of prime property. He and his wife had lake access, and the natural geography included close-knit tree lines and a rolling field that would soon look like a drop cloth sprinkled with the bright colors of spring as the sun drew out the wildflowers. The windows were dark. As Nicole and Ty drew closer, security lights snapped on. They parked in front of the garage, under a basketball backboard and net that had weathered over the years.

They were at a definite disadvantage.

Nicole didn't like rolling onto the scene of possible conflict without everything her Yukon had to offer. Her Colt Commando, backup ammo, a first-aid kit.

She turned to Ty. "If he's here, I'm doing the talking. Most of it, anyway. Jump in if you think I'm missing something."

"Got it," he said.

They climbed from the Mustang and stood under the halo of the security lights. Ducks in a crap shoot. The house windows remained impassively opaque, mirrors of a night sky blotted with clouds.

Was Monte hiding behind them?

"Don't hesitate to use your weapon," she said. "Are we clear on that?"

He nodded. "Clear."

She moved toward the front door, then thought better of it when she realized that climbing those steps and standing on the small, squared porch would put them on a pedestal and make them an easy shot from anyone hiding in the trees. She turned and tucked herself against the siding, motioning Ty to do the same. This had been a night of uncomfortable confrontations, first with Green lying in wait for her in the department parking lot and then with the shooting in her own driveway. It warranted a cautious response to the current situation. She followed the house around back, where she tapped on the glass insert of the back door. A small light was on in what she assumed was the kitchen. Perhaps over the sink, just as Ty had reported. And something about that snagged on the sharp teeth of her mind. Hadn't Ty said he'd driven by the house? He hadn't gotten out of the car. Yet the kitchen was located in the back of the house, the light not visible from the road. Nicole felt the fine hairs on her neck stir. Was she remembering correctly?

She knocked again, this time on the wood, louder and more insistent. She listened, but there wasn't so much as the creaking of the house as it settled in for the night. She let her eyes wander the backyard, which was groomed and spread evenly some thirty or forty yards to the tree line. An owl hooted and the cicadas were singing, but neither did anything to ease the tightness in her chest.

She flattened her shoulders to the house and gazed over at Ty. He stood three feet distant, his gun grasped in both hands and pointed directly at Nicole. He had his finger on the trigger, but his hand shook.

"They pay better," he said.

Who? she thought, as acid bloomed at the back of her tongue and thought became action. Nicole pushed away from the house as the first shot exploded from the end of Ty's gun. The bullet passed so close, she felt the heat of it and the stirring of the air.

She turned, zigzagged, dipped and shuttled across the patio. She was too far from the tree line to make that a possibility, so she used the furniture as cover, the adobe stove as something solid to crouch behind as she thought of next moves. She was speaking into her shoulder mike when the next bullet discharged. *Officer needs assistance . . . Shots fired . . .* It hit the clay stove, and fragments flew into the air and showered down on her head and shoulders.

She had to move, but there was nowhere to go.

Better to run than to wait for it.

She sprinted. Shots fired. Multiple. From the house, where Ty had remained, standing tall, feet planted apart, gun extended. As she watched, a tongue of fire burst from the muzzle and lapped at the air. Bullets from behind her too. A rustling in the trees. And then a figure emerged, dark head to toe, masked. A semiautomatic held waist-high. He was running toward her, followed by a second and then a third figure.

Ambush.

She didn't wait to fire. With no backup, she was facing the end, and she would not go down without a fight. She ran toward the edge of the patio, jumped over a planter, crouched and got off a round.

Target hit. Not center mass but above the kneecap. She watched the leg kick back at an unnatural angle and then the man pitch forward. With any luck, the bullet had severed the femoral artery and the guy would bleed out in less than a minute.

A barrage of bullets cut through the branches of the saskatoon bush over her head, and she pushed away from the planter. She heard a shot behind her and turned as Ty buckled and fell to the ground. Behind him, Monte lowered his gun, lowered himself into a crouch, and left the shadowed back door, scrambling toward the limited safety of the barbecue grill.

"There are two more," he called out. "At least. Stay low and try to circle around the house."

He was helping her. He'd left cover behind, had taken out Ty, her closest threat, and was just then rising to a stance and firing toward the two remaining men from the trees.

And then another man emerged from the house, a handgun steepled between his hands. He was wearing a BP uniform.

"Behind you," she yelled to Monte.

"He's good, Nicole," Monte said. "He's with us."

Us? Who were *us?* And how many of *us* were there? How far out was help she could trust?

She left her crouch at the edge of the patio and put distance between her and the BP agents. Both of them, agents in a polluted department. Distance and obstacles increased her chances of survival. She circled around a table and chairs.

Monte had come out of hiding to help her, she reminded herself. He could have dug a deeper hole, or scurried out the front door and into the wind. Actions of the guilty. But he hadn't. He seemed to sense her conflict, or notice her retreat.

"I'm on your side, Nicole," he said. He fired three shots in rapid succession as he tracked the run of their assailants across the expanse of green. No hits. "You'll have to take my word for now," he continued. He dove behind a potted sapling. Fired again. One of the men dropped to the ground. The third pulled up short, and Nicole wondered if he thought of cutting his losses, but then he raised his weapon, a Ruger, and took aim at Nicole. Before she could squeeze the trigger, a shot rang out from behind her. The assailant was hit, dropped his weapon, and sank to his knees. Nicole turned and watched the uniformed BP agent rise from his stance at the kitchen door.

Luke Franks. It had to be. Both he and Monte had come to her aid.

The acrid scent of gunfire was thick in the air, and it was smoky— enough that she felt her eyes burn. An unnatural silence descended with a heavy-handedness that seemed to press against her shoulders. Neither she nor Monte moved.

"If there are others, they've turned back," he said.

"You were sure there would be," Nicole returned.

"I know of seven, suspect there has to be nine or more. Maybe not all showed up for the party." He stood, but lowered his shooting hand so that his gun rested at his thigh. "Come inside. We'll be safer there, and I have some explaining to do."

Nicole stood, canted so that she had sight of the tree line and of Monte. And behind him, Franks.

She raised a hand and spoke into her radio. "ETA on response?" Less than ten minutes. She gave the order to approach with caution. She asked for EMTs. She reported at least four injured. She heard Lars's voice over the waves. He was en route but no closer than patrol.

Sweat gathered in the palm of her hand holding her Glock. She had it pointed toward the ground, as did Monte. The other agent was more cautious. His left hand was wrapped under his right, which cradled his Sig Sauer, pointed downward, and he peered over their heads, watching the perimeter.

She regarded Monte with indecision.

"Between a rock and a hard place," Monte agreed.

She nodded, a simple, economical act, as she continued to consider Kyle Monte, standing across the patio from her. Ten, maybe twelve feet between them.

"If you wanted to kill me, you would have done it."

"So come inside," he said again. "Out here, we're an open invitation."

27

Monte turned, crossed the patio, and slipped inside the back door, which he left ajar for Nicole. She thought about what could be waiting for her just inside. No worse than what was out here. It was true: Monte had had plenty of time to kill her or let their assailants take her out. And her people were on the way. She paused long enough to call the stats in to dispatch, reading Agent Luke Franks's name off his pocket tag. He stood now at the far side of the door, still on point. Tension rolled off his shoulders in waves. There were others. Monte had said so, and Franks believed it.

Ty had walked her into an ambush. A chill settled at the base of her skull. He would have watched her die tonight and more. He'd have killed her himself. She wondered if he'd sabotaged their original crime scene, had somehow hastened the BP skiff's sinking. He had lain in wait for her at her home, a weak spot following the disruption there four months before, and the call he'd made to dispatch, seeking her location, had been made to assist him in her downfall.

She made an effort to know her people. She had been happy with Ty's performance on the job, his involvement in the community as a recent newcomer to Blue Mesa. He'd been easy company off the clock, at department barbecues and their monthly beef and brew. His betrayal had side-swiped her, put serious cracks in her confidence.

The evidence Ty had collected was all suspect now. The whole investigation was a wash. Except the science. They still had plenty of that. And she had never been more grateful than at that moment for an ME who was conscientious and meticulous and a CSI as talented and persistent as Arthur Sleeping Bear.

"Don't brood over it," Franks said. "Wasted time, and we have little of it."

She tore her eyes away from her fallen deputy and caught Luke Franks's gaze.

"You knew Monte was alive," she said. "You knew it all along."

Franks nodded. "He was outnumbered, outgunned, and damn if he didn't turn them on their tail."

"You didn't tell Lars when he interviewed you."

"No."

"You're a sworn officer," she pointed out. He had an obligation to convey all that he knew about the commission of a crime. "You risked prosecution with your silence."

"Hard to know who to trust when your boss is the ringleader."

She would give him that. She wondered for how long Franks had gone in to work, always looking over his shoulder. How often his calls for assistance had gone unanswered.

"Were you out there, with Monte?" she asked. "On the boat?"

He shook his head. "Monte called me right before he called you. I already knew they were on the move. I didn't know it was planned as their last hurrah, not until they killed Baker. There was no coming back from that. Too much had happened already, and everything since then has been cleanup, just trying to stay one step ahead of you."

"And they used Ty for that, didn't they?"

Franks nodded, his look somber.

"Why didn't you say something before now?"

"We did," he said, "but to the wrong people."

Monte appeared in the door. "Please, Nicole, let's talk."

The only reason she was still standing were these two men who had no allegiance to her but stood high on moral ground.

She looked past Franks, her eyes sweeping the grass, the trees beyond. The unnatural silence continued to hold. She turned away, briefly, and walked toward the fallen body of her deputy. She had watched him go down and known he was dead before he hit the ground. Still, she felt for his carotid artery, pressed her fingers against already cooling skin. Gone. She looked over her shoulder, toward the tree line. There were others. Three lying in the grass just beyond the full blast of the security lights.

None seemed to be moving. All too far out to risk her life if there were others in the trees.

It was hard to do, but she turned her back to Franks and followed Monte into the house, using her elbow to nudge the door a few more inches until she could look around it. Monte sat in the breakfast nook, his gun on the table in front of him.

Next to him sat a young man. Fair, a buzz cut, and a scar at his temple, irregular in shape and rigid. She wondered if it was shrapnel that had ended his military career—she'd seen similar in other soldiers featured in the nightly news following tours in Afghanistan. He had a broken nose, recent, with racoon bruising under his eyes. He'd been hit, probably hard enough that he was rendered unconscious.

"Matthew Franks?"

He stood. "Yes, ma'am."

Nicole nodded. "Congratulations. You're a father, did you know that?"

"Thank you, Sheriff. I just fed him dinner and tucked him in for the night."

"Here?" The thought was alarming, with armed men rushing the house just moments before.

"No. I brought them to the Embrys. They'll be okay there, for now."

And Nicole felt a slim smile soften her lips. "Yes. I've met Lois."

But she had a deputy guarding an empty house and possibly a material witness sheltered with a pair of plucky senior citizens. She called in and had dispatch send Sisk over to the Embrys.

"I was in the house when you arrived this afternoon. I should have made myself known then. But there was too much I didn't understand, and I needed first to keep Adelai and the baby safe."

"Where have you been?"

"Hospital, ma'am."

"Glacier Community?"

Luke stepped into the conversation then. "He was admitted Tuesday late morning."

"And was still there when we brought Adelai and the baby in?"

"Yes," Luke said. "He wasn't yet conscious. Not for more than a few minutes at a time, anyway."

"A concussion?"

"Yes, ma'am," Matthew Franks said, "but I have my wits about me again."

She turned to Luke Franks. "And you've been standing guard over him ever since."

"They came after my family," Luke Franks said. "I sent my wife and girls to San Diego a month ago. We have family there. Matthew and James, they were stubborn. They wouldn't leave town."

"We have a life here," Matthew said. "Family. That's important to Adelai, and to me."

Nicole studied Matthew's face. She saw a stubbornness there, strength of conviction, and an earnestness that seemed pure. He hid nothing, including a small wince as he shifted on his feet. He was favoring his right side. "What happened to you?"

"Green happened to him," Luke Franks said.

"They jumped me," Matthew said. "They followed me out of town. I service electrical lines, and some of that is really rural, but they didn't have the patience to wait too long before they had their lights and sirens going. I called Luke right away, before I even pulled over."

"I'd warned Matthew there were problems."

"Did they say anything to you?" Nicole asked.

"That it was a shame the only way to teach Luke a lesson was to kill me."

She turned to Luke. "You've been trying to stop them?"

"I was working with Gates. Or thought I was. Same as Monte and Melody."

She let that settle. Agent Devon Gates. He'd been working the case for months with little progress. And the people he'd been moving around on the board were dead or lucky to be alive.

"You have doubts about Gates?"

"Nothing seemed to happen," Luke said. "No matter what information we gave Gates, it was never enough."

No arrests made. No transfers of personnel. Nicole's investigation had revealed that much.

Nicole turned to Monte. "So, let's start talking," she said. "What are you doing here?"

"Waiting," he said. "For you to get the upper hand in the case. I think you're almost there."

"What am I missing?"

"Evidence," he said. "You're going to find some of it on Faris Amari. I think you already know that. But the key to unlock it all is here."

He reached into his pocket and withdrew a USB flash drive. It was slim, black, plastic, and perhaps worth the thirty million dollars loose on the mesa.

"Are those your notes?" Nicole asked.

"Notes, maps, recordings, video surveillance."

"We have a copy," Nicole said. "Abridged, of course." Their copy of Monte's digital notes contained no recordings, no video, and a lot fewer words.

"You mean Green cleaned it up before he handed it over."

"That's what I mean. Will yours be any different?" she asked.

He leaned forward and withdrew his cell phone from his back pocket. He laid it on the table next to the flash drive and his Smith & Wesson. "I took all my notes on this. You'll be able to verify that."

"I believe you're a good man and probably a better agent," she began.

"Aren't we all," he agreed. "But I'm not squeaky clean. Is that what you're getting at?"

"What happened out there, Monte?" she asked. "From the top."

Nicole took a seat at the table. She kept her Glock in hand, resting it on her thigh. Across from her, Matthew Franks resumed his seat. Luke kept his vigil at the door. In the distance she heard the first peals of sirens as her units responded.

"Melody was working with the attorney general's office," Monte began.

"They moved her here, to Blue Mesa," she said.

"Yes. Eleven months ago. Soon after the first piece of evidence disappeared. The first we know of, anyway. It's possible, probable, that some arrests, and the evidence with it, never made the books."

"Okay," she said. "Let's move forward from the moment Agent Baker arrived."

"I didn't know, at first, that she was working with the AG," he said. "I mentored her."

"And you slept with her," Nicole said.

Monte held her gaze even as color bloomed in his cheeks. He nodded. "I did," he confirmed. "We had a romantic relationship, but it didn't last long."

"Why?"

"Some things weren't adding up. She started getting cozy with Green, long meetings and some of those over dinner or lunch. I thought maybe we were like one of those nebulas—burned bright and fast and then burned out. I understood that—there are a lot of years between us."

"You thought she had moved on to Green?"

"Yes."

"But it wasn't that?"

"She insisted not. That sidling up to Green was what the AG wanted her to do. It was the order coming down from BP as well. They were onto Green, and they needed Melody to get the proof."

"Did she?"

"She was aboard the boat when Faris Amari threw himself overboard."

"He threw himself?"

"Yes. He said he'd sooner throw himself on his own sword than allow this to continue. He felt dishonored and had lost hope in finding an end to it. It's on the recording." He nodded at the flash drive. "Green is on there too, along with a few other agents. Most of them identified as they talked amongst themselves."

"Talked about what?"

"The pipeline and what they expected Amari to do for them—there's more than one conversation covering that. From Melody's recordings, we have Green ordering the killing of several refugees when they refused to be used or Green felt they had become a risk."

"Why didn't she show up for work that night?"

"She was with Green and company. A total of seven men. Two—Green and one of his minions—were on the party boat, securing their lake passage. Five were to roust Adelai Amari."

"Agent Baker was there," Nicole said. "We have castings and tread to prove it."

Monte nodded. "What we don't know is, was she there undercover? Or was she one of the gang?"

Nicole turned and connected with Luke. He stood close to the window, occasionally lifting an edge of the curtain to peer out at the backyard. She adjusted her gaze to include Matthew. "I'm sorry," she said. "I don't have good news for you." She paused and allowed her first words to prepare the way for her next. "Your brother James is dead."

"They killed him?" Luke said. "I thought so."

Matthew's lips thinned and trembled. He blinked rapidly as tears rushed his lashes. Luke grew still and somber.

"Did you send him?" she asked.

"Yes. To get Adelai. I stayed with Matthew."

"Because you couldn't help a UDA," Nicole said. She kept her voice neutral, stating a fact, but Luke took exception.

"Yes, that was part of it. But I stayed to protect my brother. I knew Green wasn't done. He wanted what we had. He'd killed for it already— we have that on wire." He nodded at the USB. "And he wanted what was buried in the ice with Faris Amari."

"Evidence that will lock him up," Monte insisted.

"It's so much harder to enjoy life when you're on the run," Luke said.

"But Green gave that up tonight," she said. When he'd shot at her. Not only did they have her testimony on that, but they had surveillance footage from cameras outside the sheriff's office as well as the bank and several other businesses along Main Street.

"The man has no patience," Monte said.

"It's not a matter of patience," Matthew Franks said. "Your boss, he has a king-of-the-mountain perspective. By nature, that means people will die."

Nicole liked Matthew Franks's take. It was clear to her that his military training was an asset. Here only on the fringe, he had been able to sum up Green's character and put it into words that rang true with her. King of the mountain. Not only in the criminal deeds he was executing but also as leader of BP North. It was why few of his men knew him well. And why none of the related agencies knew him at all.

"I want them more now than I did a moment ago," Luke said.

"We'll get them," Monte promised.

"Include me, Luke," Matthew said. He stood, tall and sure. "I want in, for James and for Adelai. For all the refugees he used and terrorized. For the lives he's taken while in a position of authority."

Nicole stood. She faced Matthew Franks. "I'm leading the investigation," she said. "And you are a civilian." Maybe one day he'd like to change that, she thought, ignoring the taunting voice that reminded her she had believed in Ty Watts too. "You need to stand down."

"I can do some good," he protested.

"I believe it," Nicole returned. She felt herself loosening. "So we'll keep you close," was the best she could give him. "Now back to Amari." She turned to Monte. "He gave this evidence to Gates." Gates had told her so himself.

But Monte was shaking his head. "Not all of it. Faris Amari was smart. He trusted no one. He gave them teasers. Sound bites. But the bulk of it he'd hidden." Intensity built in his voice. "Tell me, Nicole, did the ME find anything on Faris Amari?"

But she would tell him nothing. She believed the story he'd woven but felt the need to keep what she knew to herself.

"I've spent the night being shot at. Three times," she told him. "So I've been scrambling. I'll be in touch with the ME in the morning. You're not done telling me about that night."

"Green came in dark," Monte said. "And too fast. He hit the skiff after I'd called you, nearly knocking me overboard. Which turned out to be a good thing. I took to the floe, and they followed."

"On foot?"

"That's the only way," Monte said. "But I doubled around and got into their party boat—the skiff was taking in water and not worth the risk. I pulled out the same way they arrived—dark. That was the last I saw of them, up close, anyway. Later, I watched a boat pull up to the floe and Green and company board."

"And Agent Baker wasn't with them?"

"No."

"Who killed her?" she asked.

"I think she was aboard the party boat with Green and Shepherd— one of his minions—before they came after me. Green had said as much. And he said he killed her. That they had just dumped her body. I thought he was taunting me. He knew Melody and I had an affair."

"That's who you were looking for when you motored away from the BP skiff?"

"Yes, but it was useless. Too much time had passed, if he'd truly tossed her overboard." He winced, and it wasn't the bruising on his face causing it. She heard the urgency, the regret, in his voice. "But I had to do something."

A desperate search as Monte made his escape.

"What happened to your face, Monte?"

"I fell into the console when the party boat made contact." His fingers probed the welting on his cheek and the discoloration that reached into his hairline. "I felt their approach, the change in the current, and turned in time to catch sight of the bow emerge from the dark. I reached for the radio but too late."

She considered his words. They fit but blanched beneath the pall of impropriety. Monte had made a mistake. He'd had an affair with a fellow agent. An agent later murdered. Nicole didn't see how he would ever walk out from beneath the shade of that decision.

"Tell me about finding Adelai," she prompted.

"She was close to shore, and I heard her call out," he confirmed. "She was having the baby."

"And you helped her."

"Yes. And after the baby was born, I got them onto the boat and took them to the Embrys."

Because their sympathies were well known. "And after that?"

"By then I knew Luke was waiting for me, at the southern edge of the lake. I motored back, cut the engine, and jumped ship as I got close to the shoreline. I met up with him on the Lake Road."

"You left your parka to wash up on shore."

"I took it off because it would sink me," he said. "But then I realized it would buy me some time, and I was glad for it. If BP thought I was dead, they wouldn't go looking for me."

But neither would the sheriff's department. The back-and-forth between innocence and guilt was wearing on her. She left Monte square in the middle and decided to let time and evidence bear that out.

"Where are the drugs? The thirty million in fentanyl?"

Monte leaned to his side and picked up a waterproof pouch off the floor. It was tagged as evidence, and both he and Franks had signed for it. He placed the bag on the table, next to his gun and the USB. "Right here."

He'd taken it off the party boat.

226

28

"**D**id you know about Ty?" Lars asked.

"No," Monte said. "I'd have gone down swearing he was one of the good guys."

Lars would have done the same.

Sleeping Bear walked into the kitchen, bringing with him the cool night air.

"Your side arm, Sheriff."

He held out a box, top off and an evidence sticker already fixed to the cardboard. Lars noted Nicole's natural reluctance, but she surrendered her gun. Sleeping Bear collected side arms from both Monte and Luke Franks in the same manner. A deputy came in and began a search of Matthew Franks, who raised his arms and turned as requested. He wasn't carrying.

Nicole had already given Lars the details she'd received from Monte and Luke, but he would have to interview them again, separately. Matthew Franks too. He watched her walk to the window and gaze out at the backyard. CSIs were setting up halogen lamps. EMTs had already transported two of the men to the hospital. He had taken their IDs. Both were BP agents, men he recognized in passing. The ME from Glacier County had yet to arrive.

Lars approached her.

"MacAulay's not coming," she said.

"No. That was a good call," he said. MacAulay had run for his life alongside Ty Watts. They didn't need to cast shade on that connection, especially when it reached the courtroom.

She nodded. "Agreed."

"Make sure you interview Matthew Franks," she said. "If I'm any tell of character, he's a good guy."

"We all thought Ty was good," Lars said.

She turned and held his gaze. "I need to do better," she said. She rolled her shoulders and let out a deep breath. "So let's get this over with, okay?"

He had to interview her. She had discharged her weapon, striking a man. And one of her deputies lay dead on the patio, just ten or twelve feet from where he stood with her in the kitchen.

"We'll take the living room," he said. She turned, and he followed her out of the kitchen and into a small room with a single sofa, two side chairs, and a map keeper that doubled as a coffee table. They sat, and Lars set the recorder on the table, opened his phone, and began to take notes. He asked her to detail the drive from her home to Luke Franks's house on the lake, to break down the details following her and Ty's arrival but before the shooting began. What had been her first indication that Deputy Watts was a danger to her?

"He said he noticed the kitchen light was on when he drove by Luke Franks' house," she said. "He told me that when we were still at my place."

"But the kitchen is at the back of the house." Lars understood. "Then what?"

"I thought maybe I heard him wrong. I hoped I had. I turned toward him. His gun was drawn. He was three feet away."

"And he fired?"

She shook her head. "He said, 'They pay better.' And I watched his finger on the trigger. He was shaking. I threw myself to the ground, rolled out of it to my feet, and found shelter. By then he had fired twice. The second bullet hit the adobe stove, just above my head."

"Had you fired your side arm yet?"

"No. I fired only once. The assailant running in from the trees. I hit him in the leg, above the knee."

"Why did you fire only once?"

"It was chaos," she said. "One of my men was trying to kill me. Someone I suspected might be involved in the death of Agent Baker had come from the house and was, well, my backup suddenly."

"And Luke Franks?"

"He was the last man out of the house. He took position in front of the back door. He covered me as well."

"He fired his gun?"

"He shot one of the assailants. The one lying furthest from the house."

"Who shot Deputy Watts?"

She hesitated. This was where loyalty was split like kindling. Where a natural allegiance to the men who stood with you made betrayal an impossible thought.

"Ty tried to kill you," Lars said. "He fired at you twice. You told me that. Monte told me that. The video from his security system will bear it out. But I need you to say it. Who shot Deputy Watts?"

"Monte," she said, but her composure was fractured, and Lars had to fight with himself to stay the course, to keep the recording rolling, to capture the truth, and that included her tears. "He saved my life."

29

MacAulay's house had been built in 1954. It sat on a full acre of prime lakefront property, with a private dock and a detached, single-car garage he'd turned into a workshop while he went about upgrading and remodeling the existing structure. He'd been at it four years now, and Nicole had noticed, over time, the sometimes intricate details that went into his work. He'd driven as far as West Virginia to select and transport home the iron inlays in the porch railings, which had been forged by a modern-day blacksmith, and had sent away to the Netherlands for a forked footbridge that now spanned the lake runoff that appeared every spring. The plumbing and electric he'd dealt with prior to moving in. From there, he'd worked with a draftsman and carpenter to extend the kitchen and master bath and add on a third bedroom and office. He had plans of framing out the upstairs attic into a second master suite and a sun-room. But Nicole's favorite feature was the wraparound porch.

Mrs. Neal's Subaru was gone. Nicole parked next to MacAulay's Highlander, pulled the duffel bag from the back seat of her borrowed cruiser—a late-model Ford Explorer where the only thing automatic was the engine—but didn't bother with the cache of paperwork she'd brought home. As she moved past his vehicle, she placed her hand on the hood. Still warm.

She stood there a moment, caught in the warm light from the windows. It felt like home. It'd been a long day, and she was glad to be here. The cleanup at Luke Franks's house was still under way. She had turned the scene over to Lars as soon as he'd arrived, as was protocol in an officer-involved shooting. He and three other officers had completed a perimeter check before she'd left, discovering fresh boot prints representing perhaps five men. Nicole had a contact in the FBI who had a friend in the DEA, and Nicole had let it be known that she was dealing with drugs and money and betrayal several layers deeps, involving multiple agencies, including her own. And that had hurt.

She had trusted Ty, with her life. With MacAulay's life. And thinking about that, about leaving MacAulay out on the ice with Ty, made her gut twist and bile crawl up her throat. That she had been so wrong about one man shook her confidence. But now wasn't the time to dive into that. Right now and until first light, all she really wanted was MacAulay.

He was waiting for her in the kitchen.

"Jordan's sleeping," he said.

She dropped the duffel on the floor and stepped into his arms. He was strong and steady.

"Tell me about the ice man," she said, her voice muffled against his shirt. "Lars said you recovered some electronics."

"We did," MacAulay confirmed. "But first, tell me about the deputy parked outside my morgue."

"We think the ice man might draw some attention."

"Well, he should," MacAulay returned. "He's one of a kind."

"Yes, but does he have the goods?" she asked.

"He had fentanyl. About ten million dollars' worth."

"How many packets total?"

"Three one-kilogram bags. They were evidence bags, all bearing the seal of the Border Patrol on them."

"Nice touch," Nicole said. "Where are the drugs now?"

"Your deputy took them with her, en route to your evidence locker."

She hadn't caught that transmission, but she had spent an hour with Lars. And during interviews, all forms of communication were turned off.

"I'm going to call in. Make sure she made it in okay and we're locked down tight for the night."

"First, you might want to hear about the Enduro black box recorder." MacAulay was beaming with pride, almost as if he'd delivered a baby rather than a standard listening device. "And the Flash Drive Recorder Pro," he added.

"Two listening devices?"

"He was a determined man," MacAulay said.

And Amari had probably realized, early on, that Gates was no help to him. Having been stonewalled and sent over the border time and again, the man had decided to gather what he could in terms of evidence.

"Do we have his last moments on audio?"

MacAulay nodded. "Not just moments. We charged up the devices and downloaded their data. Jane thought it was prudent to make a backup before she left, and I agreed. Seems you might have more than a night's conversation."

"Did you check the quality of sound?" she asked.

"That's for Arthur to do. But Faris Amari was a careful man. He had the devices sealed in dry bags. One was sewn into the waistband of his slacks, into the hollow of his hip, the other under the shirt collar."

She had enough acquaintance with the devices to know that they were voice activated, extending battery life, and carried a recording capacity of almost three hundred hours. But five months submerged in Lake Maria, most of that time frozen—she worried that what they really had was nothing.

She hoped Arthur would have good news for her in the morning and added him to the list of calls she would make.

"Anything else?" she asked.

"That's not enough?"

"It is," she insisted, smiling. "Maybe more than enough." She stepped out of his arms. "So now I'm going to call in."

MacAulay waited as she spoke, first to her dispatcher, then to Jane. The evidence was under lock and key. A deputy was stationed outside, and Casper had plans to work another three or four hours in the back conference room, with Nicole's permission. She gave it, knowing they were going to need a lottery win to pull them out of the budget shortfall.

Nicole pocketed her cell phone and said, "I'm going to check on Jordan." She made her way to the back of the house. The door to the guest room was ajar, and Nicole nudged it with her fingers. She stepped over the threshold, her hand braced on the frame. Her son slept easily, the rise and fall of his chest, the slight snarl of breath in his nose, familiar and calming.

Though Benjamin was dead and no longer a threat to them, tonight's shooter had trespassed onto her property. A place of fortitude. Of safety. And had knocked a few bricks out. No, there had been no threat made toward Jordan, but Nicole felt the burn of a close call. There were degrees of separation, some thinner than others.

She stayed a moment longer, leaning against the door frame. Jordan had saved her in a way few would ever understand.

MacAulay came up behind her. She felt his body absorb the space between them and then his heat wrap around her.

"We had a great afternoon," he told her. "Thank you for that."

She wanted to thank him because he had filled in for her. Because she knew Jordan had loved every minute of it. But she recognized a need fulfilled in the tone of MacAulay's voice.

"You're welcome," she whispered.

"I'm going with him tomorrow, did you know?" he said. "I mean, if it's okay with you."

"He asked you?"

"He did." And she heard the smile in MacAulay's voice.

"I'm glad." It wasn't lost on her, Jordan's gravitational pull toward MacAulay. It felt good and right. And tomorrow, when her son left on the Scout trip, within scant miles of the crime scene at Lake Maria, on a route that ran north and paralleled the flight of refugees and the criminal pipeline, Nicole wouldn't worry so much, knowing that MacAulay stood beside her son.

"I've done all I can in the morgue for now," he said.

"And anything that comes up can wait until you come back Sunday afternoon."

"Calabasas will start the autopsies tomorrow morning," MacAulay said. "It's better that way."

"Agreed," she said.

She turned and allowed her lips just the briefest touch along his jaw. And then she left the doorway and the comforting sound of her son's breathing and returned to the kitchen.

MacAulay followed. There was a long trough of silence, easy, lulling, through which tension snapped like an angry dog. For once, she ignored the need to fill it and listened to MacAulay clear his throat.

"You want to talk about it?" he asked.

Ty Watts. No, she didn't want to talk about him. Nor Green and his attempt to end her life. Not the shootout, Monte and Franks, where this was all leading. Not any of it.

She stood her ground, in the middle of the newly remodeled kitchen, and looked up at MacAulay. He had a steady gaze and smile lines around his lips; a face that reflected integrity and welcome. Damn, he was a rare form of pure and becoming as addictive as an opiate.

Lars knew more about Benjamin than MacAulay did. How did you tell the man you loved about your severe lack of judgment? She'd fallen for a street dealer, hoodwinked and happy about it at first.

Nicole had hired Ty Watts. Believed in him. She had let Green slip through her fingers.

How had she missed the bad in each of them?

She needed sleep. Food. The touch of another human being. The solace of this man's arms. But it was easier to ask that her physical needs be met than her emotional needs.

"Any chance you and Jordan brought home leftovers?"

"You're in luck." He moved to the refrigerator and brought out a white paper sack and a carton of 1 percent milk. "Buffalo strips," he offered. Not her favorite, but she could drown them in bleu cheese and be happy. He pulled the Styrofoam container out of the bag, followed by two others. "Chicken pot pie and curly fries."

Carb overload, but she needed it.

He arranged it all on a plate, covered it with plastic wrap, and nuked it. Then he poured her a glass of milk, sliced a tomato and salted it, and set a place up on the island.

"Come and sit," he invited.

She wanted to. But her body strummed with a vibration she knew could blow wide open, like the shifting of tectonic plates at the start of an earthquake. It wasn't often that she pushed herself this far. Exhaustion. Emotional overload. She was rooted to the spot, wavered on her feet, convinced it was the air around her that shifted and certainly not her, and watched as MacAulay came around the island and gathered her into his arms.

He was soft that way. He noticed the smallest flicker of emotion that she chased across her face. Why did she always feel like she had to hide it? Weakness was what made people the most human. Nicole let her forehead fall against his chest. The soft press of his arms pulled her close and kept her there. The touch of his lips in her hair. And the vibration in her body grew to a quaking.

"I haven't eaten since lunch," she said, offering it as an excuse for her present state.

"And slept little last night," he agreed, allowing her the distance from her emotions.

If she'd kept up with self-care, she would not be on the threshold of emotional meltdown.

"A few hours," she said. She lifted her hand and brushed her fingers over her cheek. As she suspected, they were wet with tears. "Stupid," she said.

"Big girls don't cry?" he said.

Tears did little to change a bad situation. Except that with them came release. She felt its slow unwinding. The tension in her shoulders eased, the clamp on her lungs loosened so that each breath came easier, the fog in her brain cleared. It was like a washing of the windows—she could see better.

"I'm thinking about changing that rule," she returned.

"It was meant to be broken," he agreed.

And anything else was nonsense—his tone made that clear, and it was what she needed to hear. MacAulay balanced her, and he was a safe place to land. His touch was equal parts comfort and need. She had hit the jackpot with him.

"Thank you, MacAulay," she said. "I need exactly who you are."

He let that rest for a moment. Sometimes he tiptoed around what was building between them, but he decided on, "We've been doing this for more than a year now."

"What's this?" she asked, though she knew, of course. But she wanted to hear how he defined their relationship.

"Sneaking around in the dark. Hiding in the shadows."

"Are we going to step into the light?" she asked.

"I'd like to."

"Me too."

"I want more than that," he said. "I've wanted it almost from the beginning."

"I know," she admitted. It had scared her, and not just the first weeks. Months into their relationship she had worried about where they were going and if they could sustain it. And if she wanted to. Some moments she had been breathless with fear. Others she had drifted on that warm current, flush with the knowledge that someone on this planet cared more for her than he did his own existence. "So ask me," she said. He was traditional that way, and she wanted him to have that.

"Here in the kitchen?"

"Would you prefer the bedroom?"

"No."

"Do we have to have dinner first, with a linen tablecloth and candles?"

He thought about that, and she could feel that the conflict was real.

"I didn't think it would happen in my kitchen, at midnight, with you fresh from a crime scene," he said.

"Then wait and ask me at the right time," she said. "Just so you know, I'm a sure thing."

"Yeah?" His mouth curled into a slow, satisfied smile. He took hold of her left hand and raised it between them. "You're not much for jewelry," he said.

"I wear a watch."

"That doubles as a compass and keeps time on sprints."

"But I clean up good." They had never had an occasion where she could prove it. Never a dinner out at a nice restaurant. "You'll just have to trust me on that."

"So, when it comes to engagement rings, are you fancy or a minimalist?"

"Somewhere in between."

"You're no help," he complained.

"Square or round but not marquis. One carat but no more than three. Platinum rather than gold. How's that for help?"

"It gives me a place to start."

* * *

She slept with him, though she probably shouldn't have. Not with her son two doors away. But she set the alarm on her watch and a backup on her cell phone and lay both of them on the nightstand. And when she woke, rested, her muscles full of the languid pleasure of a good night, MacAulay was already up. She threw back the covers, realized she'd never made it into her nightgown, and pulled the sheet with her as she made her way to the en suite bathroom.

She turned on the taps but stood a moment longer with his scent on her skin.

Showered, in a clean uniform, Nicole still made it to the breakfast table before Jordan shuffled in, fresh from sleep.

"I'm sorry I missed you last night," she said.

"I tried to stay awake," he said. "But the hike today is a long one, with all the repairing we have to do along the way."

"I'm glad you slept. Just wish work hadn't kept me busy."

"Who was shooting at our house?"

"We don't know yet."

"MacAulay's coming with me today," Jordan said, changing the subject and his face lighting with excitement. "We put a serious dent in his savings account yesterday."

"Yeah?" She looked over Jordan's head at MacAulay, who shrugged.

"A lot of my stuff was ancient."

"Ancient and clunky and way too heavy to carry on his back."

"You'll have to put it to use this summer," Nicole said.

"We were thinking about Banff."

"Cold, even in summer," Nicole said.

"We're not afraid of a few goose bumps," Jordan said. "And we think you'll do fine too."

"Yeah? You talked about that, did you?"

Jordan nodded. "With all the running you've been doing, hiking and camping in Banff will be easy-peasy for you."

"Well, thanks for that vote of encouragement." She didn't have to work hard to keep the enthusiasm out of her voice, and both Jordan and MacAulay chuckled. Nicole was fifty-fifty on the camping experience. She loved nature, mostly from afar. She enjoyed her runs along the Latham trail, being outside on blustery days, drinking her coffee on the deck as the sun rose, and kayaking the currents and shallows of lake and river. She did not like waking up, stiff and cold, and rolling out of a sleeping bag into frigid morning temperatures. Outdoor plumbing by flashlight, days without a shower, and freeze-dried food were beyond uncivilized; they were unpleasant inconveniences that bordered on torture. But by her second cup of coffee and all the way into sunset, she was a happy camper.

"We bought you a little something yesterday," MacAulay said. "It will completely change your mind about sleeping in the great wide open."

"A blow-up Sealy Beautyrest?"

"Close," Jordan said, as he tucked into his pancakes. "Better, because it's lighter to carry and rolls up so you can fit it inside your pack. It's water-resistant and has thermal crystal technology." He gazed at her over his forkful. "A guaranteed cozy sleep."

"Sounds like you read that off the packaging."

"Has more than eight hundred reviews, four and a half stars." He was luring her.

"And self-inflates," MacAulay added, wiggling his eyebrows at her.

Nicole burst out laughing. "Okay," she said. "You guys win."

"You'll go?" Jordan asked.

"At least as far as the backyard."

"Mom," Jordan protested. "Dig a little deeper. Adventure awaits."

"Well, I do have three weeks' vacation time waiting on the books," she said. She had been planning a week at Disney, now that Star Wars had opened at the Park. A surprise for Jordan. "I suppose we could spend ten of those days in the wild."

Jordan whooped, and she caught MacAulay's gaze over her son's head. He smiled broadly. And all of this felt good and right.

She rose from the table. It was already six AM. She was meeting Lars at eight and had a mountain of paperwork to get through before that.

"I'll get you a thermos," MacAulay said.

"You're going to drive to the trailhead, then?" she asked.

"Yeah. We'll stop by your place first, load up Jordan's things."

"Be careful out there."

"Always."

"Especially now," she stressed, but it wasn't necessary. He nodded once, but the ponderous look in his eyes was telling.

She ran her hand over Jordan's head and said, "Stand up and give your mom a hug good-bye."

"It's only one night," Jordan said, but he complied.

His head came to just below her chin, and his arms and shoulders were starting to fill out. He was steadfastly marching toward his teen years, and time seemed to be escaping her.

"You're into that growth spurt," she said. He'd taken longer than his peers to move up the growth chart and had been somewhat preoccupied about it lately.

He pulled back and smiled big. "I know, right?"

When she pulled out of MacAulay's driveway, she left her two men, happy and safe, behind. The two most important people in her world.

30

Nicole arrived at the office when it was still dark. She checked the clock on the dash. She had ninety minutes to get paperwork done before Lars arrived. It would be like scaling Everest without O₂. Crushing. Impossible. She would have to be happy with making a dent in a pile that threatened avalanche. She pulled out her baton before she exited the vehicle, having had enough of surprise meetings in the shadows of night. She had a replacement Glock holstered at her hip. She'd pulled her Colt from the blasted Yukon the night before and took that along with her briefcase and walked across the parking lot.

She let herself in through her private entrance at the back of the station. It opened directly into her office. Usually she would check in with the desk clerk, stop by dispatch for a hello. This morning she sat down, cradling the to-go cup of coffee MacAulay had prepared for her, and made neat stacks of the paperwork she needed to get through. She approved pay first, then set MacAulay's autopsy reports and Sleeping Bear's forensic conclusions side by side.

She went with the more pleasant of the two. Arthur Sleeping Bear had been busy. There were detailed entries on the evidence he'd already shared with her when she'd stopped by his lab. Those she skimmed for any developments. She stopped when she hit the report on Green's handgun. Arthur had pulled a single strand of hair that had been tangled in the sight. Seven and a quarter inches long, cuticle intact. He was able to cull DNA. In a prelim test, he had used hair taken from Agent Baker, along with skin samples, and determined it was a match. The hair in Green's gun had come from Agent Baker. Further, the measurements, indentations—"cratering," as Sleeping Bear noted—indicated that the gun had been the one used to strike Agent Baker in the head. Margin for error on analysis was less than 2 percent. Green had killed Melody Baker.

He's in the wind. The thought taunted her. He'd probably left late last night. Been one of the shooters in the trees and then, cutting his loses, made directly for the border. It made sense. With all the movement along the drug and money pipeline, certainly Green had enough to live happily ever after, so why wait around for more? Why risk losing life and liberty?

Sleeping Bear hadn't gotten to the sound recorders—they hadn't been recovered until after midnight.

There was a knock at her door then, and Nicole closed the folders in front of her, stacking one on top of the other, before calling for him to enter. It was Lars. He looked somewhat refreshed. At least, he had on a clean shirt and had taken time to shave.

"You got some sleep," she said.

"You too." He sat down across her desk, grinning suddenly, which softened his face. "But not at your place. I stopped by last night after finishing up at Luke Franks' place."

"Did you?" she said. She tried not to squirm. She would not be a worm dangling at the end of his hook.

Recognizing her discomfort, he burst out laughing. "I'm going to let this go, I promise."

"But not anytime soon."

"In another minute or two."

Nicole felt her skin warm but refused to pull at the collar of her uniform to let in a little cool air.

"You see, I had this thought. Wasn't sure if I was at the heels of our killers or barking up a tree. Wanted to run it past you before I lost it."

"So try me."

"I called your cell phone. Did you get my message?"

"No." She reached for her cell, but he stopped her.

"I didn't leave it on voice mail. I gave it to the ME."

That stunned Nicole.

"Don't worry," Lars said. "Your secret is safe with me. Just wanted you to know that I know." And then he smiled again, and it was packed with satisfaction and guile. "Really," he said, but it wasn't reassuring. "I'm going to get some mileage out of this. But nothing too over-the-top."

"Well, gee, thanks for that," she said. "MacAulay didn't give me the message."

Lars nodded. "He was half-asleep, thought he was answering his own phone. I confused him. Told him I'd see you in the morning."

And then Lars sat back and stared at her with a shit-eating grin on his face.

"Thirty seconds," she said. "That's how long you have to get comfortable with this and never bring it up again."

"Oh, I'm comfortable with it."

"Really? Why? We work together, MacAulay, me, and you. You don't think there'll be some awkward moments?"

"Oh, I'm hoping there'll be some. In the beginning, anyway." He tried to keep his tone even, but she heard the anticipation in it. And then he gave it up and laughed aloud. "I think we have a week or two before this becomes old news between the three of us."

"And work will be as it always has been?"

"Of course. I figure you and Doc have been at it for a while. You're comfortable with each other at work, never even tiptoed across the professional line that I've noticed. Why would you start now?"

"We wouldn't," she said, then raised her eyebrows in question. "Your theory?" she prompted.

"Yeah." He leaned forward, and Nicole could feel the energy behind his idea radiate off of him in waves. "If Ty was still with us, Green would use him to steal the drugs out of our evidence locker and then they'd all hustle up over the border, probably at Shoe Horn."

"Why there?"

The Shoe Horn was a well-worn path through an outcropping of rocks east of Lake Maria and above the Astum River Trail. It wouldn't be the quickest route to the border and probably not even the safest. It was a steep climb that opened on the Canadian side above a deep canyon and swiftly moving river. Neither an easy pass.

"It would be hard to follow them," Lars said.

"They'd be counting on that," she agreed. "If they could get down the canyon wall, they'd have the river to float them."

"Only as far as the nest. Then they'd take to foot. But with the ground cover—" Lars shrugged. "Maybe they'd have a chance." The nest was a small satellite station of specially trained Canadian Mounted Police. They were a handful of rock climbers and river divers who knew the terrain, who could read it like the blind could read Braille.

"Or think they would."

"With that much money in hand, they'd risk it," Lars said.

"But Ty is dead, so how will they get the drugs?"

"I thought they might try to take the station, like in the Wild West. Charge through with guns blazing. But then we took out half their crew last night. So what does that leave them with? A burning greed but not enough manpower to make things happen."

"So what then?"

"So they wait for the transport," Lars said. "That's been their MO all along—steal it in transport."

"Hell yes." Nicole shifted through her pile of folders, located the one she was looking for, and flipped it open. "Ten thirty AM," she said. "The drugs are due to leave our evidence locker and transport to Billings in three hours."

That didn't give them a lot of time.

"Ty wouldn't have known the drugs were scheduled to go today," she said. MacAulay hadn't even discovered them until after Ty was dead. And Monte hadn't turned over the stash from the party boat until hours ago. "But he would have known there was a transport scheduled."

"And there's one more thing," Lars said.

"The USB," she said. She'd known Lars had listened to it by now. "Was it as good as Monte said?"

Lars nodded. "It's enough to lock Green away for life. And a few other agents too."

She heard hesitancy in his voice. "But?"

"There's someone else. Someone as big as Green, maybe bigger."

"And we don't know who?"

"They never mention him by name. Well, a nickname that's less than flattering. Cupcake."

"It's a woman?"

Lars shook his head and said, "They refer to him with the masculine pronoun."

*　*　*

The transport vehicle was an armored van, had puncture-resistant tires, and was usually driven by a single deputy who pulled roster duty. Nicole made a few changes, using Sisk to drive while she and Lars tucked themselves in back with an empty cargo bin. Not willing to risk the contamination of evidence, they had never moved it from the station. Jane Casper had buried herself behind digital doors in the back conference room, and Nicole had given her a heads-up before they pulled out. There was a possibility that Green and company had caught wind of the switch and, as Lars had suggested, would try to rush the station for the now forty million in fentanyl. Casper had made her way to weapons and checked out a Colt she promised to keep at hand in addition to her service revolver. Nicole had prepped the desk clerk and called in an additional deputy before leaving.

"You get ahold of Franks?" Lars asked, interrupting her thoughts.

Nicole nodded. They sat on the cargo floor with their backs against the sideboard, Commandos across their laps, Colts and Sigs and Glocks strapped to various body parts. Forty million. The big heist. Worth hanging around for. Worth the trouble, the danger, and the possible arrest in trying to get it back. People had died for less.

Greed was a powerful motivator.

She liked lining her nest, just not as much as some. She liked what money could do for her—let her keep a comfortable home, spend time with Jordan, go adventuring, pay for a dress and a DJ. The thought of marrying MacAulay no longer left her breathless. Now that she'd decided, she hoped he wouldn't take his time asking. She'd fallen in love with a man who needed tradition. A man who was slow and methodical, which certainly had its benefits, but it also pulled at the threads of her patience.

"Luke Franks thinks you're right," Nicole said. "That Green won't leave without the fentanyl."

"And our greatest vulnerability?"

"It could go either way," she said. "Either they'll think we're transporting it, with a cargo of deputies, or they'll think we're the decoy."

"They'll have to pick their battle."

"And it'll be transport. They won't risk the drugs getting away from them." She agreed with Franks. She expected trouble, and she didn't like being pinned inside a tin can, no matter how thick the skin. "Left at the station, they can go back for it, make an attempt there later. If they have a later."

They had reinforcements. Nicole had ordered a charge of four deputies, coming in from a variety of geographical points and at intervals of time. None too close. Green and his small army of agents were trained in surveillance. Nicole had ordered a wide window—maybe too wide?—at six minutes.

"So maybe they're lying in wait along the route, with just one scout following from town," Lars said.

"My thought too." One man to make sure the transport was in motion. So far, Sisk hadn't noticed even a distant tail. "Does Ellie still worry about you?"

Lars raised an eyebrow. She watched as the corner of his mouth twitched, and then to hide it, he pursed his lips in a pretense of consideration. But the struggle was real. His eyes gleamed with a wicked humor.

"Forget I asked," she said.

"No. It was a good question."

"Shut up."

He laughed. It was low, amused, and blessedly short. "Yeah, she worries. We don't talk about it a lot." He shifted. Sisk turned a corner, and they both swayed with the movement. "The Esparza case a few months ago, with the murdered girl. That got to her." Because the victim had been very close in age to their daughter, Amber. "When the bodies started piling up, I could tell she was struggling with it."

"And what do you do about that?"

He shrugged. "Make sure I'm home for dinner more than not. The kids are old enough now they head straight into their rooms after we eat, and then Ellie and I sit on the deck and talk. Not always about the job. Almost never about that. Sometimes about how we met, the early days, where we'll go on our next vacation. We'll start a fire, drink some coffee, wrap up in blankets."

"She likes to snuggle."

"She's not the only one."

Nicole let her gaze fall on him, full of skepticism.

"Hey, from a guy's perspective, what's not to love about holding a soft woman and making plans about the future?"

Nicole noted that his tone was a shade defensive and decided to believe him.

"It's just that you're so"—she scrambled for a word— "reserved, I guess."

"We're different away from the job," he said.

Nicole was just beginning to realize this.

"Are you worried about MacAulay's reaction to the danger of your job? If that's the case, he already knows all about it. Doesn't mean it won't make him uncomfortable from time to time," Lars warned.

"Yeah." She changed the subject, but since they were talking about worries, it seemed to fit right in. "I called the Scout leader," Nicole admitted. "I thought maybe canceling the trip altogether would be a good idea."

"Hmm," Lars said. The van slowed and bumped across a cattle guard. They bounced off each other's shoulders, but she heard the tone in his voice.

"I don't think it was unreasonable."

"We have no tangible basis for the request," Lars said.

"It wasn't a request. I just suggested maybe next week was a better time."

"Based on a hunch. We might end things here and now. Or Green and company might skirt the lake and cut into the trees there. It's the usual route."

"It's a hunch," she agreed. "But a good one."

"With nothing to back it up."

"Yeah. That."

"What did the Scout leader say?"

Nicole grimaced. "That he appreciated my call but there's nothing to worry about. The Scouts aren't heading for the Shoe Horn. They're only covering sixteen miles of trail, round trip. How sure am I? he wanted to know."

"He treated you like a worried mom?"

"Exactly."

"Well, we don't know what to expect. If the wind shifts, we can call the Scouts in then."

Nicole nodded, but she didn't feel good about it. She'd emailed an advisory to the local news outlets about the possibility of increased traffic over the border, about the need for caution in the burled stretch of Toole County's highest points north.

The sudden lurching of the vehicle broke through her thoughts. There was a screeching of metal, the burn of rubber. The back of the van lifted and shuddered. The sway bars, the heavy armor, kept the van on the road, but barely. Nicole and Lars were thrown across the cargo area. Caught off guard, Lars let his Commando skitter toward the back doors, and he crabbed after it.

"Sisk?" Nicole called.

"Hell if I know," her deputy returned. "Maybe a spike strip?"

His adrenaline was pumping, but his voice was steady.

"Have to be spikes with the cut of a machete," Lars said.

They were both crouched behind the front seats.

"I think one tire blew," Sisk said. "Back left. The others are holding on."

Nicole figured the same, judging from the violent swaying and pull of the vehicle.

"What do you see?" she asked.

From her position, she watched Sisk scan the geography in front of him, take a quick look in the rearview mirror. He returned to it twice.

"Nothing in front of us. We're closing in on the exit ramp for Route 9," he said. "But behind us—" He shot another look through the rearview mirror. His hands tightened on the steering wheel. "Plumes of dust, coming in from several points. Fast."

"How many?" she asked. "Count the plumes."

"I see five. There could be more." The uncertainty wavered in his voice.

"Five is a good place to start," she said. She turned to Lars. "Green and some of his agents."

"Looks like."

"Call it in."

She turned back to Sisk. "Pull over," she ordered. "Get into the turn-out there on the right, and position us so the passenger side of the van is facing incoming."

Nicole heard Lars on his cell, sending out the alert. He glanced at the GPS and provided their coordinates. There would be no radio use, because even when the message was scrambled, some people were able to break through and make use of information that would leave them vulnerable.

"It's like we discussed," she said. "You listening, Sisk?"

"Yes, ma'am."

"You're out first. Throw it into park and stay in the protection of your door."

"I remember."

They had gone through scenarios and likely outcomes before starting out.

"The van is armored, but it doesn't make you invincible." Bullets could still penetrate the metal, especially if they were high caliber and shot at close range. Same thing to blow out a window. All these precautions really did was slow down the inevitable.

"You hear me, Sisk?" she asked, as his door swung open and he scrambled onto the gravel roadside. She watched as he positioned a Colt Commando in the crook between window and door.

"Loud and clear. I'm set up northeast as ordered."

And he was a damn good shot. She'd double-checked that before making the switch in drivers that morning.

Lars hit a button, and the driver's side back door opened. They both jumped out and took position, Lars at the rear of the vehicle. Nicole sidled past Sisk and took a stance at the hood, directly in front of the passenger's seat. She cast a glance behind her at her deputy.

"You didn't see the strip?"

Sisk shook his head. "There were a couple of dusty patches. Been seeing them here and there the whole drive. Some clodded pretty thick."

"Left by cattle and horse crossings." Nothing irregular about that.

"Must have been hidden in one," he said.

She nodded and turned back to the road, a two-lane state highway framed by open fields. It was in these fields that their adversaries were approaching, on what Nicole thought might be dirt bikes or ATVs.

"Coming on fast," she said.

"Looks like they're on Yamahas, one-seaters," Lars said.

"Steady at five," she returned. And they were a measured distance apart. Green and company could easily surround them, overtake them. Nicole knew they were outmanned and possibly outpowered. She leaned against the hood of the van, propped the stock of the Commando against her shoulder, and looked through the sight. She tried to get a bead on each of the men, make a quick study of visible weaponry.

Her breath clutched in her throat. Each man had an ammunition belt wrapped bandolier-style around his torso and the muzzle of a rifle peeking over his shoulder. Thirty or fifty caliber. Enough firepower that a single bullet could blow her and her officers off their feet.

"They're armed with machine guns. Every one of them," she said.

"Yeah, looks like each of them has a Deuce," Lars said.

Nicole spared Sisk a glance. The deputy held his rifle steady. They were positioned so that Nicole was three feet clear of his trajectory and a good foot under the fire line. Still a pretty tight margin for error. Though his hands were still, she noticed that some of the color had left his face.

"How do you stand, Sisk?" she asked.

"Solid, ma'am," he said.

She nodded once, turned back to her Commando, and peered through the sight.

She trained on the figure farthest north and staked her claim.

"I'll take the guy furthest south," Lars said.

That left the three in the middle, from which Sisk could take his pick.

"Whichever is the sure thing," she told him.

"Easy," Sisk said. "Like lunch at the buffet."

The Commando was midrange. She counted under her breath. One thousand, two thousand . . . at the current rate of approach, she calculated engagement at forty-five, maybe fifty seconds.

Strike line.

The wait seemed protracted, minutes rather than seconds. Green pulled up in center and the four additional agents fanned out around him, forming a half circle around Nicole and her men. Standard agency procedure when attempting to apprehend an armed suspect. They wore helmets and BP-issued ballistic vests. Nice touch, and Nicole felt her mouth twist with derision. In addition to machine guns, they carried pistols in shoulder harnesses and possibly more than that concealed in the barrel seating of their Yamahas.

They climbed out of their ATVs and stood beside them, engines idling and their machine guns raised but crossed over their shoulders rather than aimed at center mass. There was a distance of twenty-five yards between each man, and the only hide-behinds were the Yamahas they rode in on.

Green raised the visor on his helmet. "You know what we came for, Sheriff," he said.

"Of course I do," she returned. "You could have saved yourself the trouble and called ahead."

"Now's not the time for banter," he advised.

"Yes, you're running out of time," she agreed. "The net is tightening."

She knew she'd scored a hit as she watched his lips thin. He brought his Deuce down and set his aim on Nicole.

"Feels like a noose, doesn't it, Green?"

"You can give us what we came for," he said. "Not a shot fired."

"Or we'll take it," one of his agents said. "After we walk over your dead bodies."

"You're no fool, Green," Nicole said. "You know we lured you out here, that we have men closing in. So why don't you lay down your weapons and raise your hands in the air?"

"I'm not that evolved, Nicole. The drugs," he demanded.

He lifted a hand, and Nicole watched as his men responded. All guns lowered, all trained on Nicole. She said a small prayer that her vest would hold out against a blast the size of a fist.

"We don't have them, Green," Lars said, drawing their attention. "You must have realized by now that what you got instead are three top guns and incoming calvary."

"I wouldn't risk contaminating evidence that will put you behind bars for the rest of your life," Nicole added.

"What!" An agent stepped out of formation, swinging his gun wide as he approached Green, nearly prancing in his anger. "What the fuck! I told you she would do that. We needed to divide and conquer. We needed to take the station and the transport."

"Divide?" Green snarled. "There's not enough of us left to split the deck. And that was your fuckup."

She knew his voice, his build, and even his swagger. "Gates?" she called. "What a surprise."

He swung toward her, sliding his finger through the trigger guard. "Shut the fuck up!" He opened fire. And the others followed. All except Green, who seemed to stand unnaturally still while rage consumed his face.

Bullets kicked up dirt and gravel that pinged against the undercarriage of the van. Windows were shattered, the glass pebbling but not falling from the frames. Bullets plugged the armored siding. Nicole and her men returned fire. Their singular pops lost under the barrage of automatic weaponry. And above that came the distinctive chop of an approaching helicopter.

"This keeps up and the gas tank on this thing is gonna blow," Lars warned.

Sisk got a piece of one of the agents, a shoulder shot that caused the man to spin like a top and fall to the ground. It created a pause in the shooting as Green and Gates assessed the situation, and into it Nicole shouted, "You hear that, Green?"

Gates did, and he looked up. The chopper was still off in the distance, just a pinhole against the blue, cloudless sky. He dove into his ATV and gunned the engine. The other agents followed, even the injured man clambering aboard his Yamaha, fishtailing as he spun it around.

It shook Green from his stupor, but instead of making a hasty getaway, he bore down on them. He pulled the trigger, the bullets feeding from his bolero. He swung the rifle back and forth, driving Nicole and her crew back from the van as he advanced. Overhead, she heard the crackling static of the chopper PA system. Demands were issued: *Drop your weapon . . . lie facedown on the ground . . .* The message was broken, scattered, but it reached Green; it sank deep enough to mean something.

It aborted his anger and triggered the survival mechanism inside his brain. He stopped, finger resting on the trigger, then canted and took aim at the back of the van. At nearly one hundred rounds per second, they were already out of time. He was going to blow the gas tank. It would turn the sky into a hailstorm of shrapnel.

Nicole, Lars, and Sisk turned and ran, stumbling over brush and uneven terrain. And the van blew, followed by a rush of heated wind that singed their heels and knocked them to the ground.

"Cover your heads," Nicole yelled.

By the time the last of the metal fell to earth, Nicole could see only a distant plume from Green's ATV.

"He wanted to make sure we couldn't follow him," Sisk said, getting to his feet.

He wanted them dead. *King of the mountain.* Matthew Franks could not have called it better.

"The chopper will do that," she said. It would give direction to her men on the ground as well.

She brushed dirt and debris from her uniform, walked the short distance to where she had dropped her Commando, and picked it up.

Lars stood, his hands propped on his hips, his gaze locked on the horizon. Each of them was covered in pinpricks of blood drawn from shrapnel that had penetrated their uniforms. No serious injuries.

"His mistake was to leave us standing," Lars said.

31

It was afternoon by the time Nicole and Lars were back at the station, bent over maps and reports on the desk in her office. Her team had lost Green and Gates and another man when the fields merged with the wooded vales. They had been able to skinny through the trees, where the Sheriff cruisers could not; ATVs had given them the edge, the ability to take to back passes and beyond. The two men they had arrested had been cut off from the others by the deputy closest to the scene. The man Sisk had hit was nearly faint from blood loss by then. Neither man was talking. They had lawyered up and shut up.

Nicole couldn't waste her time on them. It was conceivable that Green and company could make it over the border by nightfall. She wanted to stop them before that.

"I say they'll go by way of Shoe Horn," Lars said, tapping a spot north of Sunburst. "Green and Gates won't risk being spotted by law enforcement. They'll know we put out their photos on every available outlet, that we won't be the only ones looking." He shook his head. "They won't go anywhere near Lake Maria."

Nicole was inclined to agree. Lake Maria was closer. It was an easier way across the border, but it was also a popular place with boaters and hikers, picnickers and fishermen. The area was a magnet for day-trippers, especially on the weekend.

"Then let's do it," she said. "We direct all our resources towards the Shoe Horn."

Nicole studied the map, circled the spot Lars had indicated, and traced with her eyes the distance from that point to the small curve in the Astum River Trail where the Scouts would hit the midway mark in their round-trip hike. There wasn't a lot of geography between the two. The area was heavily wooded and the Scouts would raise their overnight tents just off the trail, tucked between the thick trunks of white pine and lodgepole. It was a 7.2-mile climb from this highest point of the trail to the border at Shoe Horn, with the elevation increasing sharply. Sheer walls created channels through which a person could slip through but required careful navigation, as many were bedded with shale. It was a damn obstacle course for those who didn't know the area well.

She was sure Green had at least a passing acquaintance with the Shoe Horn, being the man in charge at BP North. Gates too, since they had so clearly hooked up and had probably investigated the area as a possible rabbit hole. She didn't know that she and her men would fare so well tracking them into this wilderness. She hoped it wouldn't come to that.

Lars's cell phone rang, and he looked at the screen before answering. "Radio transmission from the chopper," he reported.

They had sent a pass over to warn not only the Scouts but also members of the public at large who were currently using the trail or fishing from the river. They'd kept the message vague: *Be aware . . . possible criminal activity in the area . . . for your safety, return to your cars . . . Be aware . . . possible criminal . . .*

She waited for him to finish the call.

"Well?"

"Visual contact was made. Pilot reports the Scout leader confirmed receipt of message with a salute."

They'd gotten the message. They would turn around and head toward safety. Nicole breathed a little easier.

"It'll take some time, though," Lars said. "Pilot noticed that several tents had already been pitched and the group was divided by about a mile or so, with some Scouts at the river's edge and the others at camp."

Nicole nodded. Nothing they could do about that. They'd gotten the message. They would make their way down the mountain, and Nicole and her men would make their way up, aboard ATVs. Were Green and Gates and the third man the last of the dirty crew, or were there others? Franks and Monte weren't sure. They'd given a guesstimate based on observation, and so Nicole would move with caution.

She picked her vest up off the desk. It was made to sustain heavier artillery, and each of her men moving uphill would wear one. Including Matthew Franks, who would accompany them as a deputized observer. As a Marine, he had trained over challenging terrain and performed while under fire. But it was his perception of Green and company that would benefit them most.

Green had a voracious greed that rendered human life insignificant.

She shrugged into her vest. It was heavier than her usual Kevlar, bigger, the gaps at the arms and neck narrow. It covered the hips and pelvis and had a notch that fell neatly into place just under her throat. It wouldn't be comfortable to wear, but dead would be a lot worse.

"Let's go," she said.

The trail was a steady climb. It meandered in places, and there were washboards from the winter snows that were in need of repair. They bumped over those and caught air, and a few times their engines coughed and torqued down but didn't quit. By ATV, taking the trail from the east end, they'd reach the farthest point, where the Scouts had pitched camp, in twenty minutes.

She rounded the final curve. Lars had his own ATV as well, but the others—Sisk, Casper, and the Frankses—rode in side-by-sides behind her. Each fanned out as much as the width of the trail allowed. Nicole spotted several things at once—the pitched roof of a red tent just south of the trail, under a canopy of thick pine, and Green and Gates in the center of the trail, dressed as they had been earlier, complete with boleros and Deuces. But that wasn't the most alarming part of the scene. They were waiting for her. Gates had the Scout leader on his knees, placed so that the man partially shielded his body. As Nicole came to a sputtering stop, Green raised his rifle until he had a bead on her.

Behind her, her men came to a stop. Nicole rose from her Yamaha, pulling her Commando, positioning it so that she had it aimed between Gates's eyes. Her men followed suit. She felt them form a half circle behind her, listened to the crunch of dirt and rock and branches beneath their feet.

She scanned the small clearing, her gaze falling on the gathering of boys, among them Jordan and MacAulay. All lined up like toy soldiers. The wind picked up and pulled through the tents, snapping the nylon.

She turned back to Gates.

"So you're the big man now," she said.

"I should have been in charge from the beginning. This whole thing has been a fuckup."

"You bring the drugs, Nicole?" Green wanted to know. "We're open for a trade."

Nicole pretended to think about that. Beside her, Lars shifted on his feet, seeking a window through which he could safely fire. She hoped the same was true for Sisk. Their sharpshooter. They had outfitted him with a Remington 700P, expecting a shot at longer range.

She nodded at the Scouts. They stood close enough that their shoulders rubbed as they wavered on their feet.

"Let them start walking down the trail," she said, "and then we'll talk about a trade."

Green laughed. "You're not very good at poker, are you, Cobain?"

"Let me ante up," she returned, "and then you can decide."

She spread her arms wide, holding the Commando in her left hand, and then bent at the waist, reaching into the barrel of her seat. They had planned for this, with the Scouts so close to the trail. With the possibility of random day-trippers crossing their paths and Green and Gate's desperation. She pulled out a bag of fentanyl and stood up. She raised it into the air and waited.

It was an evidence bag, clear and tagged. Inside were ten one-kilogram bags of the drug. Nearly ten million dollars street value—a quarter of what they had lost. Gates and Green paused. Their facial expressions opened in surprise—they hadn't expected this of her, and she had counted on that. And then she waited more. Longer than she should have. Long enough to know there was a problem. Sisk didn't have a clean shot. Or his nerves had spiked a fever. She shifted. She was turning to get a visual when she heard the crack of his rifle, felt the rush of the bullet as it burrowed through the air, smelled the singe, heard Gates yelp.

She had been in the way. Sisk had waited for her to move.

And then everything canted off-center.

She heard MacAulay ordering the boys into the brush. She watched the Scout leader scramble to his feet even as Gates staggered backward. He ran off after the boys, and Jordan was with them, retreating into the thickly wooded mountainside.

She swung her gaze back in time to see Green and a third man dive into the trees north of the trail. Luke Franks followed. She brought her gaze back to center. Gates was raising his rifle.

The shadow of a bird passed over the landscape. The rustling of the boys as they scattered through the brush grew impossibly loud. She prayed Jordan had gotten deep into the trees, outside the scope of Gates's assault rifle. That they had all reached a place of safety.

"Sisk tapped a wing," Lars said. "Gates won't be worth much."

The bullet had ripped through the man's bicep, shredding muscle and sinew, particularly the ligaments that connected to the elbow joint. That arm was useless.

And yet he was positioning the rifle with his right hand, snugging it up against his shoulder. It wasn't possible to control a Deuce single-handedly.

Nicole shook her head. "You have nowhere to go, Gates. And no way you're going to shoot your way out of here in a blaze of glory."

And the world slowed down. She caught a blur of motion from the corner of her eye. A mix of colors, green and orange. She'd seen it before. His jacket. MacAulay was closing in from her right, entering the zone, between her and Gates. Flame burst from the muzzle of Gates's automatic rifle, the metal cartridges popped into the air, and MacAulay's body jerked and shuddered with the impact. Three times. He'd taken three bullets. As he fell, clearing the strike zone, Nicole squeezed the trigger. The crack of the gun broke the spell terror had cast over her. She heard more shots, watched, even as she advanced toward MacAulay, Gates's body absorb the bullets from her men.

"What did you do?" she demanded, as she knelt beside him. "MacAulay, what did you do?"

Blood oozed at three separate points on his jacket. One beneath his collarbone, another two inches lower and toward his side, the last above his rib cage.

"Saved your life," he said.

"That's my job."

"Not this time," he said. His breath came rapidly. He was going into shock.

"Lars!"

"Right beside you."

His voice was close, and Nicole turned and found Lars on his knees, an open medic box on the ground in front of him. It wasn't a complete case, like the ones they stored in the trunk of their cruisers. It was the portable version, packed with bandages and, what they needed most, QuikClot. She grabbed the case from him.

"Call in a chopper for transport. Check on the Scouts. On Jordan."

She rummaged through the case and brought out a sleeve of the powder. Half a dozen. Twice what they needed. She hoped.

And then she heard a barrage of shooting, the kind that could only come from a fully automatic machine gun. The rounds seemed to overlap, so possibly Green and his man were firing together. A hundred rounds or more spent in less than half a minute. There was return fire. Franks had gotten off several rounds before he was either silenced or had changed strategy.

Lars returned, jogging up from the encampment.

"They're fine. All of them. Scout leader is holding it together too."

Nicole followed Lars's nod. Jordan stood amid a group of boys. His face was pale and he was on the edge of tears, but she couldn't muster even a reassuring smile for him. She scanned the area and found Sisk and Casper. They had secured Gates's body. He was clearly dead, no longer a threat, but they had removed the Deuce and any other weapons he might have had on his person and formed a clear zone around the body.

"Sisk," she called across the trail. "Luke Franks went in pursuit of Green. Assist."

She watched Sisk. He opened the magazine on his Remington, counted bullets, added a few more, and snapped the piece back into place. And then he faded into the woods.

Another pair of hands appeared on MacAulay's chest.

"How are you, sir?" It was Matthew Franks.

"Been better," MacAulay gasped.

"We're going to get you off this mountain," Franks said. He worked the buttons down MacAulay's jacket, then took hold of the collar of his T-shirt and began to tear it.

"What are you doing?" Nicole demanded.

"I have medic training," Franks said, and caught Nicole's gaze. His was steady, confident. "In the field."

"Because you were a Marine."

"Yes, ma'am." He turned back to MacAulay. "You're a doctor, sir?"

"MacAulay," he said. "No 'sir'."

Franks nodded. "Tell me where you've been shot."

Franks took the QuikClot from Nicole and began tearing open packets and pouring them directly into MacAulay's wounds.

MacAulay began a medical assessment of the damage the bullets had done. It was brief and punctuated by gasps as he struggled to catch his breath. "Collarbone not a worry . . . bullet tucked up against the pectoralis major. Second bullet all soft tissue . . . the third . . . not so lucky."

"Shattered a rib?" Franks guessed.

MacAulay nodded. "Let's hope . . . that's all it did."

"Pierced your lungs?"

"Possible."

Which was bad. They could stop the bleeding from the outside with the QuikClot but could do nothing for internal injuries until MacAulay was at the hospital.

"Nicole?" Lars caught her attention. "Chopper is on its way." But there was something more. She heard it in the heaviness of his tone.

"What?" she demanded.

"There's no way for them to land up here. No place clear enough."

She knew that. Had known it as she watched MacAulay's body absorb the bullets, as he came crashing down to earth.

"Where?"

"Two-point-two miles due south," he said. "An open meadow. They'll be waiting for us there."

They had the ATVs. That was the only way. They wouldn't be able to lay MacAulay flat, but they would get him to the medevac quickly.

"We don't know where Green is."

"Franks and Sisk are on him," Lars said. "He won't double back for a chance at us. Freedom calls."

Matt Franks caught her attention. "It's time, Sheriff."

She glanced at MacAulay. He was pale but conscious.

She stepped back, and Lars and Matthew Franks lifted MacAulay to standing. Each supporting him under an arm, they walked him the few feet to the waiting ATV, and Nicole followed. Once they had him seated, she took the seat belt and stretched it over his shoulder and chest, fastening it.

"Not too tight?"

"Lots of padding," MacAulay said.

Matthew Franks had done good work. There was no evidence of blood flow through the thick gauze bandages that she could see.

MacAulay grabbed her hand when she would have stood clear.

"Probably not the time," he said, and paused for a breath. "Will you marry me, Nicole Cobain?"

Nicole blinked back a rush of tears.

"Yes," she said. "Soon."

He smiled, slim and waning. "Glad that's out of the way."

"You knew I was a sure thing."

"No. You kept me guessing from the beginning."

"I'll be at the hospital," she said.

"I know you will."

She caught and held his gaze. "Don't die on me, MacAulay."

"Not a chance."

Franks leaned on the throttle, and Nicole stepped back from the Yamaha. She raised a hand and prayed it wasn't their last farewell.

They weren't quite out of sight, around the curve in the trail, when Luke Franks came stumbling out of the tree line. He had his Commando in one hand and he looked alert, but blood was streaming heavily from a head wound. Sisk came out of the woods behind him, back first and Remington raised and ready.

She and Lars rushed to meet them.

"You shot, Franks?" Lars called.

"Green's not that good, and that pissant he has with him couldn't shoot an elephant out of a tree." Franks swiped at the stream of blood. "Green got the trees around me, damn shower of wood chips. Probably just a splinter."

Lars looked at the wound. Made Franks sit while he pulled a bandage and antibiotic cream from the quickly emptying case.

"Did you get close to Green?" Nicole asked.

"Within fifty yards or so. Any more and you'd be cleaning gray matter off the tree trunks. He's headed for the Shoe Horn, though." He looked at Lars. "You were right about that."

"He funnel up through the channels?"

The fastest approach to the Shoe Horn was a series of narrow paths through the mountain, steep and covered in shale.

"Yeah. And he didn't have to look for them."

Nicole turned to Sisk. "Did you have a shot?"

He shook his head. "He kept to the trees like a damn bunny, hopping in and out of cover."

She had to send a team in after Green, but she wouldn't be on it. Sometimes the personal had to trump the job. It was possible Green had slipped through their fingers. That he would make it over the rough terrain and into Canada. But she didn't want to make it easy for him. The man was responsible for an untold amount of deaths, of theft so large that its magnitude was still being tallied, of corrupting justice and setting loose criminals who no doubt were continuing to wreak their havoc, victimizing the vulnerable. Green needed to be brought in, tried, and convicted.

"I'll call our Canadian counterparts," she said. "You're going to take lead on this, Lars."

"As it should be," he agreed.

"Pick your men. Take three."

"I want Luke Franks along."

Nicole nodded. "Good call." Franks knew Green better than any of them. He would be an asset to Lars.

"You'll need horses and packs." They could be gone for days. "Take the satellite phone. Answer it, Lars. Don't keep me guessing."

"Will do."

"Minimize risk."

"Always."

"I'll get started on arrangements." She would have turned away, found her son and her ATV, and made a start for town. For the hospital. For cell range so that she could put into motion all that needed to be done, but Lars stopped her.

"Hey," he called after her.

Nicole turned back to him.

"Don't rush to the altar," he said. "I'd like to be part of the show."

32

They borrowed the horses from a rancher who thought they were tracking illegals. Nicole did nothing to change his perception. They were keeping this as hushed as possible, moving in the early-evening light like shadows against the deeper gray of the mountains. Sunset, in its glorious array of oranges and pinks, had already closed its show and left the sky a shade of deep ore. She watched as Lars, two officers, and Agent Franks faded into the distance. They were to meet up with a Canadian mounted unit just over the border. RCMP knew the terrain better, which was at times treacherous. They would weave through trees and over land bridges and, when the woods grew thick, shimmy through fir and birch until even that was no longer possible. There was a point where they would have to dismount and walk their horses, fitted with blinders, across a footpath no more than three feet in width over a sheer drop of three hundred feet into the valley below. It was the way Green had gone. It was the way they must go.

Part of her hoped Green had lost his footing and lay at the bottom of the canyon. Better that than to lose any of her officers. But an aerial search, conducted just before dark, had all but dashed that hope.

Nicole looked over her shoulder. Darkness had already descended and was almost complete. The Astum River Trail behind her blended into the foliage. They had watched Lars and his crew head northwest, toward the border and Green, and had started their hike down the mountain. Matthew Franks flanked her left side. He knew how to ferret a man out of a rabbit hole. He had wanted to go, but she couldn't risk sending in a civilian.

"What are you going to do?" she asked him.

"About what?"

"Your life," she said. He knew that she sympathized with his situation. Silently, she was glad Lois Embry was on their side. The woman had the tenacity of a dog with a bone and would make sure Adelai got hold of her birth certificate and any other documents she needed to move on with her life. "You have Adelai and a child. You need permanence, a career, and a home."

"I have a brother and Faris Amari to bury first," he said. His voice was solemn, his words stirring the shadows.

"I'm sorry about that," she said.

"They both died heroes."

She agreed. "You're good people."

He nodded and lapsed into silence.

"When you're ready," she said, "come see me."

"About a job?"

"We'd be lucky to have a man with your skills on board."

They continued down the sloping, winding trail, using head lamps to light their way.

"I spoke to your brother before they left. He thinks Green knows the Shoe Horn well."

"Green's been sending undocumented aliens that way for more than a year now. That's what Luke thinks," Franks said. "There's a gap in sensors almost a quarter mile wide over the pass. Probably because you'd have to be desperate or crazy to go that way."

There was no fence, no wall denotating where one country ended and the other began. The border between the United States and Canada was the biggest in the world, and such was not feasible. Instead, there was a border vista, maintained by both countries. Forty feet of land cleared of brush and, where there were shared bodies of water, buoys marking the spot and measured and adjusted twice yearly to allow for drift. Sensors that detected movement were hidden in wooded areas, but they were few and far between, and who better to know where they were located than the members of Montana BP?

"You took a look up there." When Nicole had been at the hospital, checking on MacAulay, who was in surgery, and when she was rounding up the necessary resources to outfit a group of men taking off into the high country, Matthew Franks had gone ahead to track the escaped. "What do you think? Lars said you tracked Green through seven miles of switchbacks and scree, all the way to the border." And he'd been able to give them a starting point. "So, tell me something beyond the obvious."

He nodded, considering her request. "He's carrying something heavy," Franks said. "A loaded pack—the heels of his boots dug into the soil deeper. And he's got some kind of high-powered rifle slung over his shoulder."

She raised an eyebrow. "And how do you know that?"

"Because it's spring. New leaves, the thin branches of saplings. The stock of the gun is up—solid wood, steel pin. I know this because in a few places it tore through the saplings, stripping it of the leaves, and put a distinct nick in the branches."

"So he has more than the Deuce."

"Definitely. He was carrying that in his arms."

She was impressed and said so.

"But that was the good news."

Nicole didn't know how the possession of heavy artillery was good news and braced herself.

"He's not frantic. Not yet," he said. "He has a steady, measured walk. Fast but not fleeing. He's keeping his cool."

"Too bad for us."

He agreed. "Time will wear on him. He'll grow tired. He'll be look-ing over his shoulder," he said. "Tensions will rise, and maybe he or his buddy will lose their cool."

"He'll make a mistake."

"Yeah, that's the way it happens," he agreed. "But this man, Green, he knows something about the outdoors. Something about fading into the landscape. I picked up his track but lost it a few times too."

A heaviness settled on Nicole as she went through possible outcomes. The best, of course, was capture without incident. The worst, the loss of her men. And somewhere in between, that Green managed to escape.

She was glad Lars had chosen Dan Carly, their department tracker, as one of the three to accompany him. If he could keep them on Green's heels, that left Lars, Sisk, and Franks to apprehend him.

It was the best they could do.

A horned owl announced their arrival through the brush. The cicadas chirped. Still carrying the burden of her men, Nicole changed the subject.

"How old is Adelai?" she asked.

"Eighteen," he said. "Nineteen in June."

"Cutting it close," Nicole said.

He nodded and wasn't quick to pick up the conversation. She waited. She wanted to know more about Matthew Franks. Needed to know more about him. She didn't want to hire blindly—skills were one thing, integrity another. There couldn't be a giant leap between the two. And she couldn't make another mistake. She might not survive it.

"We started dating when she was seventeen. And I knew it. Wished like hell that wasn't the case." He thought over his next words before he spoke. "I tried to pretend it was just a friendship. She needed that, on her own so young. But it started becoming more even before I shipped out." He stopped and turned to her. "We didn't consummate. Not until I returned stateside, and she was already eighteen by then."

"In the state of Montana, the age of consent is sixteen."

"I know, but seventeen is young, even with all the responsibility she'd taken on. And I was twenty-four." He held her gaze. "So we waited."

He spoke openly, and that was good enough for her. It had to be. He trusted her, and she needed to trust the officers she hired.

"Adelai said you were honorably discharged," she began. "That you were wounded and wouldn't be able to return to your position."

He nodded. "I was a pilot. That's all I ever wanted to be. I flew an Osprey—an assault helicopter," he explained. "Shrapnel"—he tapped his head—"was superficial, all except one piece which lodge in my inner ear, right up against the auditory nerve."

"Does it affect your hearing?"

"No, but they worried it would affect my balance. It hasn't yet," he said, "but I get it."

She stopped and turned toward him, careful to keep her head lamp averted. "That's a tough break."

"There's worse," he assured her.

"You're right about that." She cleared her throat, which had thickened with emotion when she thought about the worse that could have fallen close to home. "Thank you," she said. "For your help with MacAulay."

"You're welcome." He shrugged. "It comes naturally."

"The training. But it's more than that."

"Yeah, I miss it," he admitted.

* * *

Nicole paced. Jordan sat in the chair that opened into a bed and munched on takeout from McDonald's. He was growing, for sure, but she thought it was more about maximizing this occasional treat that he'd ordered two quarter pounders with cheese, upgraded to a large fry, and gotten both a vanilla shake and a Coke. Or was this how teen boys ate all the time? Although they had time before that milestone happened. The trip to Disney and the Star Wars attraction to celebrate Jordan's twelfth birthday was still four months away. It would be a family trip. A mother, father, and son trip. For sure, she and MacAulay would be married by then.

He hadn't woken yet. It was late, close to ten PM. Three gunshot wounds from a fifty-caliber, and every one of them had managed to miss important anatomy. Relief made her feel weak in the joints. She sat down beside him, on the edge of his bed. He would need PT to recondition the pectoral muscles and he had a fractured rib. The rib had stopped the bullet, but a piece of that bone had punctured an air sac and deflated a lung. He would have respiratory therapy too. But the doctors expected a full recovery.

She felt his hand tighten around hers and brought her gaze back to his face. His eyes were open.

"Hey," she said, her voice soft, hushed. "You've been asleep a long time."

"Blood loss," MacAulay said. "And Demerol."

The ride down the mountain in the ATV had been bumpy, jostling MacAulay. Nicole knew Matthew Franks had done his best, but the QuikClot had begun degrading. By the time they'd reached the evac chopper, MacAulay had lost a pint of blood.

"You look good," she said. His color was back.

"My ability to recover quickly is legendary," he said, and managed, somehow, to waggle his eyebrows.

Nicole laughed, and it loosened up the tightness in her chest.

"How did it end up there?" MacAulay asked.

"It's not over," Nicole said. "Lars left earlier, on horseback. He has Luke Franks with him, and Sisk. They'll meet up with RCMP. Green's the only man left standing."

Lars had called in earlier and reported finding the body of the third man. He was a BP agent, fairly new to the agency, and had been shot in the head.

"Gates is dead," MacAulay said.

Nicole nodded, and the imagery flashed in front of her eyes. Gates lifting the Deuce, MacAulay throwing himself in front of her. The shots. The impact of the bullets on MacAulay's body. The blood.

"No more heroics," she said. Her voice was thick with emotion.

"No promises," he said.

"I was wearing a vest."

He shook his head. "It wouldn't have helped you."

"No," she agreed. Gates had aimed for her head and, with automatic delivery, was likely to have hit his target. She bent over MacAulay and brushed her lips against his. "Thank you."

"Anytime."

"Let's hope not."

Jordan abandoned his food on the tray and came up alongside MacAulay's bed.

"Hey," MacAulay said. "It's good to see you."

Jordan nodded. Nicole could tell he had something to say, but his lips trembled and his eyes became fluid. MacAulay gave him time, and he reached and lay a hand over Jordan's, which seemed to help.

"You gave it all up for my mom," Jordan said.

"I love her," MacAulay said.

"Me too."

"I asked her to marry me."

"I know." And Jordan smiled. "I was there. You showed some serious moves."

"Yeah? I thought I kept it rather simple."

They all laughed until MacAulay clutched his side, over the gauze wrap, and winced. "I guess I'm not ready for that." He grabbed the remote and raised the head of his bed slightly, and he sought Jordan's gaze. "But we should have told you before I made it public like that."

"You were in the clutch," Jordan said. "Some of the best plays are made that way."

"Well, maybe on the football field," MacAulay said. "I just knew I didn't want to miss my chance."

"I'm pretty sure Mom knows she's got a good thing going." Jordan looked past MacAulay and connected with Nicole's gaze.

She nodded. "I know I have the best men in the world right here in this room and I'm lucky enough to call them mine."

* * *

Lars felt the satellite phone vibrate against his side. They were nearly six hours into their search and he had little to report, but he pulled the cell from his pocket and kept his voice low. A few minutes before they had crossed a land bridge, the edges of which were crumbling and slippery with loose stones, and had entered the lip of a wooded area that was too quiet. Green had gone before them, on foot. They'd caught glimpses of him through the night-vision binoculars, borrowed from BP. And they were getting close.

"Nothing yet," he spoke into the receiver.

"Coordinates show you've made it across T-bone."

"The dark made it easier." Lars had a mild aversion to heights. "We're into Caspian." Rough terrain, mountain lion haven, thick with poison oak, and he wouldn't be surprised if an alligator bit him in the ass. "RCMP is closing in from the southeast. About a mile or two distant."

"You have Green closed in," she said. He heard relief in her tone.

"We hope so." Lars thought the man might have the speed and luck of a rabbit. Even with his head start, they should have overtaken him before now.

"Matthew tell you?"

"That Green is a cut above the rest in surviving the great wide open?" Lars returned. "Or that he's carrying heavy weaponry and has the heart to use it?"

"Both," she said. "Don't stand still too long."

"How's MacAulay?"

"The doctor says he expects a full recovery." She considered her next words. "Luke Franks is a crack shot," she said. "And Sisk passed with close to sniper status."

"Message received," he said. "I'm good at picking teams."

She smiled and heard it in her voice when she said, "That and a whole lot more."

She signed off, and Lars dropped the phone back into his pocket. His Commando was strapped over his back, and he had his Glock in hand. He was, by far, more accurate with a handgun than a rifle, but still an embarrassment. Center mass, he reminded himself. All he had to do was plug the guy just once, and Green was wide in the chest. That increased Lars's odds of success. Still, he was going to hit Sisk up for some range time when they got back to civilization.

They were on foot, reins in hand and leading the horses into the gloom. By starlight. They had all felt the stillness, the gathering menace, and had extinguished their head lamps a mile back. Lars had the lead now, with Carly dropping back. He had picked up exactly where Matthew Franks had indicated, and they had followed Green with only a few false starts. But they'd had visual several times over the past half mile. They were closing in, and for that they needed the guys with the target practice up front. Franks flanked his left and Sisk his right.

"He pulled up," Lars said. "He's positioned somewhere close." He felt it, in the silence but also in the energy in the air—a mounting tension that had no other explanation. He was under the trigger, and that made his ears ring and his skin pucker. He took long breaths, which slowed the adrenaline buzz and kept his head clear.

"He's taken to the trees," Franks agreed. "Height would give him an advantage and he'd take it."

They stopped and pulled the night-vision goggles out of their saddlebags. Lars and his deputies were still adjusting to the view, to the opaque, green landscape revealed through the lenses. Four sets of eyes scanned the treetops and the shadowed pockets between trunks, the dry scrub and the boulders, some of which stood as tall as they did.

"Nothing," Franks said.

"He's in there," Lars returned.

"My scalp is crawling," Sisk said. "I feel him bearing down on us."

Lars felt that too, the tingling at the base of his skull, an all-systems alert that was ancestral, that kept the quickest alive. It also made his breath thin and quick, and he made a conscious effort to slow that down.

A spray of gunfire rang out, off that bandolier belt Green had been wearing earlier that day. Impossible to tell how many shots were fired, they were so crowded together. A dozen or more. Lars felt the earth at his feet kick up. Dirt sprayed his legs and he stumbled backward, his shoulder falling against the breast of his horse, which neighed and reared its head.

"Easy, girl," Lars murmured. He stroked her flank, the length of her neck, and felt her quaking nerves subside. Then, his Glock tight in hand, he peered again through the night goggles. "Where the hell is he?"

A flash of movement from his periphery, belly to the ground, caught his attention. "What the hell was that?"

"Mountain lion," Franks said. "Flushed out by the gunfire."

The horses caught scent of it and began tapping at the ground with their hooves, rustling together. Lars lay a hand on the flank of his horse, a long calming stroke down her side. "Easy," he said.

There was an outcropping of rocks and scrub to scuttle behind, and they did that, using it as a shield as they made their way into the tree line and greater safety. They huddled there and took account of the situation.

"We were right about the treetops," Sisk said. "The bullets came in at an angle."

"Due west," Carly said. "Hard to follow trajectory in this murky sky, but I'd say twenty to thirty meters west to northwest."

Lars turned and faced the given direction, searching the foliage, damning the thick leaves of spring that offered concealment.

"Fluttering in the trees," Sisk murmured. Lars turned toward him and noticed that the deputy had his Remington snug against his shoulder and his eye at the sight. The nozzle was pointed at a sharp angle upward, at eleven o'clock.

"You have a shot?"

Sisk shook his head. "No visual. Branches swaying. Too heavy for an owl, an unlikely perch for a mountain lion." His head lifted slightly with the barrel of his gun as he seemed to follow the progress of motion in the treetops. "It'd be shooting blind," he said.

"You're not likely to hit an innocent bystander," Lars said.

That was all the push Sisk needed to pull the trigger. The bullet ripped through the foliage, stopping when it slammed into the bark of a fir tree. Through the night goggles, Lars watched a few leaves drift from the branches, and in the silence that followed, they heard pine-cones drop to the ground, the scraping of limbs against bark, the low grunt of a man.

They'd found Green. It could be no other.

"Missed the son of a bitch," Sisk said. His voice was thick with disappointment.

"Green," Lars called into the darkness. "Drop your weapons and come down from there, hands up when your feet touch ground."

There was no response.

Through his earpiece, Lars listened as RCMP hailed them. They were still a half mile out but had heard the shots and wanted confirmation on origin. They wanted their position, but Lars didn't have time to consult his GPS compass. He pressed the com button on his bi-way radio and said, "Stand by."

He turned to Sisk and nodded toward the grouping of trees in question, a mix of oak and fir crowding each other, with branches intermingled and a sure possibility of traversing between them.

"You get a fix on him?" Lars kept his voice low.

Sisk nodded. "He's moving, though. It's not going to be one and done."

"It'd be good enough to flush him out."

Sisk nodded, moved around his horse and Lars, and took up position close to Franks.

To Green, Lars shouted, "You're surrounded! RCMP has the northern rim locked down. You're not going anywhere."

"That includes jail, Solberg," Green shouted. "My only way out is on fire," he continued, panting between words. "And I want a little company."

Green preferred death to incarceration. A hero's fall as opposed to shame. Not uncommon with law enforcement turned bad. But it made Lars wince, from the inside out. Green was thirsty for bloodshed, and he would use every last bullet he had to get it.

"You sound tired, Green," Lars said. "And a little out of breath."

"Save your psychobabble bullshit, Solberg. I speak the language."

"Okay." Lars was agreeable. "How 'bout this: get your sorry ass down here before we shoot you out of the trees."

"That's what I'm hoping for."

Lars spoke into his radio then, updating RCMP. "Suspect engaged." He gave their coordinates and their plans to flush Green out of the trees, then turned to Sisk, who was locked and loaded. "Now," he said.

Sisk adjusted the stock of his gun, resting his cheek against cold metal. He bore down again on the scope but didn't have time to get a round off before Green was firing. Lars took position behind the trunk of a fir. The others scattered for cover. The horses took refuge in each other, huddling together.

"Pin him while I frame a shot," Sisk said.

Lars and Franks took the lead, stepping out from behind their cover to take aim at the canopy above them. The bushy arms of the firs absorbed their bullets with a low thumping, but they tore through the new leaves of the oaks. They heard a scrabbling, and Lars realized too late, that Green was sliding down the trunk of a fir not twenty feet forward. The strap of his Deuce hung from his neck, the stock jammed in his armpit. He hit the ground running.

He'd made them his own personal firing squad.

Green pulled the trigger, and the bolero jerked and fed the Deuce.

Lars, Sisk, and Franks stood their ground and returned fire.

The horses reared and scattered.

Green's shoulders and torso shuddered with the impact of what turned out to be seven bullets, one of which lodged in his aorta. He fell to the ground midrun. Lars stood in the billowing smoke of discharge and counted the heads of his people. All accounted for.

Epilogue

The night air arrived early, a chill in the cloudless sky. The sun was reduced to shards of gold. Only a few guests remained, mingling in small groups. Nicole had just said good-bye to Matthew and Adelai Franks. Lois Embry worked fast. She had a razor on the end of her whip and had not only received a portfolio of Adelai's life documents but pushed through their petition for marriage. Three days ago the couple, holding their infant son, had married quietly at the courthouse with Nicole and Luke Franks standing up for them. They were leaving tomorrow too, for a long weekend in Colorado Springs. That was all the time they could spare, as Matthew was due at the police training academy in Billings on Monday. He'd accepted her job offer.

The day she buried her brother, Faris Amari, Adelai handed Nicole a USB drive he'd given her. It was in the shape of a charm—a sleeping cat—and Adelai had worn it around her neck as a piece of jewelry for five long months. "He died a hero, and now the world will know."

Monte had sent a gift with his regrets. Though cleared by BP and the attorney general's office, he had decided it was time to retire. He had claimed his unused vacation and sick leave and taken off for some unknown part of the world. He wasn't looking for himself, he'd said, but for a soft landing. She hoped he found it.

The breeze picked up again, and Nicole rubbed her arms, left bare by a languidly flowing wedding dress that was surprisingly all her. Poor Jordan, he had trooped along beside her from shop to shop, shaking his head at most of her selections. Until this one. The hem fell at the knee, the strappy sleeves cupped her shoulders, and the silk was a creamy ivory that suited her. MacAulay had been surprised too. He had watched her walk up the path with Jordan, his eyes wide and fluid.

She turned and watched him now, moving with his usual grace. He was lighting the lanterns and the BTU warmers on the deck. Tomorrow she would wake up here, watching the sun from the master suite as it rose above the lake.

Lars approached her. "So how's married life?" he asked.

Nicole laughed and pretended to check her watch. "Well, the first four hours have been perfect."

"It'll get better," he promised.

"Ellie and the girls look lovely," Nicole said.

"Yes, they do," he agreed.

"Thanks for taking Jordan," she said. "I could still ask Mrs. Neal—"

"No," Lars said. "We want to have him. I thought I'd take him fishing."

"He'd love that."

"And you're to worry about nothing. The ten days will fly by, and sometimes it'll be all the fuel you have in your tank."

"Marriage is that bad?"

He shook his head. "No, it's everything else. The job, mostly. It'll put a lot of pressure on your relationship. That's really all the advice I can give you—be mindful of it, Nicole. Make sure you and MacAulay get time away from it. And time away from the kids too."

"Kids? That's plural," she said.

He smiled, and it was Cheshire. "I read tarot cards too," he said.

She snorted. "Don't reserve a table at the county fair just yet."

"We'll see," he said. "I told Jordan to grab his bag. It's time to say good night."

"We're serving after-dinner drinks." Capping it at one per guest so everyone had a safe drive home. And just to be sure, Jane Casper was doing sobriety checks at the door.

"None for us." He pushed away from the railing.

Lars would be acting sheriff while she was gone. He was more than fit for the job. She'd asked him why he hadn't challenged her at the last election, but he'd told her, "It didn't feel right." And she understood that. She was his boss, but he was her partner and friend as well.

"Call if you need me," she said.

"I won't, even if I do." He turned, waved over his shoulder, and made his way back to his girls.

Nicole and MacAulay were honeymooning on the Big Island, with luaus and a hike up Kilauea and long naps on floating lounge chairs. Nicole was determined to slow down enough that she had plenty of memories to pull out if the going ever got tough. And MacAulay was ready. He'd had six weeks of PT and RT and only felt a twinge every now and then from the rib that had shattered on impact with a bullet meant to end Nicole's life. A delicate shiver ran up her spine. She could have lost everything, her life included.

"Cold?"

MacAulay came up beside her. He had taken off his jacket and cuffed his sleeves. He'd chosen a soft beige tux with a silk vest and bow tie, and he'd looked both elegant and dreamy.

"No," she said. "Think we can rush the gin and tonics?"

"I told the servers to fill the glasses only halfway." He winked at her, a conspirator.

Behind him, Jordan approached. He had a duffel bag over his shoulder and had already changed from his tux to jeans and a T-shirt.

"You're bringing a hoodie?" she asked.

He almost rolled his eyes. "Two," he assured her. "And I'll do my own laundry, clear my place at the table, and even wrestle Ellie for the frying pan."

"You raised this boy right," MacAulay said.

And she had, despite the odds.

Jordan opened his arms, and Nicole stepped into them.

"Don't worry about me," he said.

"Never gonna happen," she said.

Nicole stepped back and looked at Jordan and MacAulay. Side by side, they were the gateway to her happiness.

Acknowledgments

I am incredibly grateful for my children who are, in every way, amazing. Madeleine, Ava and Lilah there is no greater beauty, no deeper strength than that found in each of you.

Thank you, Anne Tibbets, for your steadfast integrity, wisdom and passion.